THEY CHOSE
BY
NANCY ROBARDS THOMPSON

AND

PRIVATE PARTNERS
BY
GINA WILKINS

MILLS
BOON

Dear Reader,

Did you ever want something so badly you didn't know how you'd survive without it? How far would you go to get it? Those are the questions plaguing Olivia Armstrong Mallory, daughter of the founder of the Armstrong Fertility Institute.

On the outside, Olivia seems to have it all: she's young, beautiful and married to the man of her dreams, Jamison Mallory, the oldest son of a wealthy political dynasty. He's heralded as a future contender for the US presidency. Olivia plans to be right there by his side when he makes his bid for the White House. The only thing missing from their picture-perfect life is a baby.

As Olivia comes face-to-face with her worst nightmare, she realizes that all the money and power in the world can't buy the things that matter most: love and family. In the process, she discovers a capacity to love that she never knew she possessed.

I hope you enjoy Olivia and Jamison's journey. I love to hear from readers. So be sure to let me know what you think. You can reach me at nrobardsthompson@yahoo.com.

Until next time,

Nancy Robards Thompson

THE FAMILY THEY CHOSE

BY
NANCY ROBARDS THOMPSON

First published in Great Britain 2011
Harlequin Mills & Boon Limited,
Eton House, 18-24 Paradise Road, Richmond, Surrey TW9 1SR

THE FAMILY THEY CHOSE © Harlequin Books S.A. 2010

Special thanks and acknowledgment to Nancy Robards Thompson for her contribution to The Baby Chase mini-series.

ISBN: 978 0 263 88862 1

23-0211

Harlequin Mills & Boon policy is to use papers that are natural, renewable and recyclable products and made from wood grown in sustainable forests. The logging and manufacturing processes conform to the legal environmental regulations of the country of origin.

Printed and bound in Spain
by Litografia Rosés S.A., Barcelona

Award-winning author **Nancy Robards Thompson** is a sister, wife and mother who has lived the majority of her life south of the Mason-Dixon line. As the oldest sibling, she reveled in her ability to make her brother laugh at inappropriate moments and soon learned she could get away with it by proclaiming, "What? I wasn't doing anything." It's no wonder that upon graduating from college with a degree in journalism, she discovered that reporting "just the facts" bored her silly. Since hanging up her press pass to write novels full-time, critics have deemed her books "funny, smart and observant." She loves chocolate, champagne, cats and art (though not necessarily in that order). When she's not writing, she enjoys spending time with her family, reading, hiking and doing yoga.

This book is dedicated to Gail Chasan and Susan Litman. Ladies, thank you for your patience and commitment. Working with you makes me a better writer.

Chapter One

The chime of the house alarm alerted Olivia Armstrong Mallory that someone had opened the front door, rousing her out of her light sleep. The door squeaked open and then clicked shut, the sound echoing in the cavernous hallway.

As footsteps sounded on the parquet floor, she sat up on the couch, smoothed her brown hair and blinked at the Christmas tree—the sole light illuminating the expansive living room.

She'd only closed her eyes for a moment—or so she thought. However, a quick glance at the mantel clock begged to differ. It was after three in the morning.

Jamison.

Her husband had finally arrived home.

As a United States senator who was being groomed for the presidency, Jamison Mallory wielded a lot of power, but one thing beyond his control was the weather. It wasn't his fault that ice and snow had grounded all planes coming in and out of Washington, D.C.

It's a wonder he's home now, she reminded herself as he appeared, suitcase in hand, in the archway that divided the living room and the foyer hall.

"Liv, you're still awake?" His deep voice was flat. "You didn't have to wait up for me." Even in the low light, she could see that his handsome face looked drawn. His chiseled cheeks looked hollow, despite the day's growth of blond razor stubble. The dark circles under his pale blue eyes hinted that he suffered the kind of travel-weary exhaustion that comes from long flight delays and blisteringly cold weather.

"Of course, I waited up for you. It's Christmas Eve, Jamison—well, it was. Merry Christmas." Olivia stood and smoothed the wrinkles from her red silk dress. She made sure the clasp to the pearl necklace she always wore was in the right place. When her husband didn't move toward her, she swallowed her pride and crossed the room to him.

One of them had to extend the olive branch. In the spirit of Christmas, and for the sake of their marriage, she'd be the peacemaker tonight.

Two-and-a-half months apart—with only a brief Thanksgiving Day visit—was more than enough time to help her realize that her marriage was *that* important. In their seven years of matrimony, this trial separation was the longest they'd ever been apart.

She'd missed her husband so much it hurt—a deep, gnawing pain that only grew worse each day they were apart.

Jamison set down his bag and raked a hand through his short, wavy blond hair before opening his arms to her. Olivia slipped inside the circle of her husband's embrace and tried to find that place where she fit so well. She wanted nothing more than to bury her face in his chest, to lose herself in the feel of him. But his hug felt stiff, almost perfunctory. As she shifted to find *her spot,* he dropped his arms and pulled away ever so slightly.

She hesitated a moment, processing the conflicting emotions that swam to the surface as she stood face-to-face with this handsome familiar stranger. But, no, she wasn't going to make an issue of it. So she slammed the door on the irrational thoughts goading her to take his aloofness personally.

Spending Christmas Eve stuck in the airline's Executive Lounge surely wasn't his idea of a good time. He must be so tired and—

"You must be starving." She started toward the kitchen. "I kept dinner warm for you. Sit down and I'll fix you a drink and a plate."

She glanced over her shoulder in time to see his frown deepen as he shook his head.

"Olivia, I'm exhausted. I just want to go to bed."

His brusque tone made her wince. As was often the problem between them, it wasn't so much *what* he said, but *how* he said it that cut her to the quick.

Tonight, though, she was willing to overlook it.

"Yes, of course," she said. "I can see that you're worn-out."

He picked up his suitcase, walked over and kissed her on the forehead. Then, without another word, he turned and took his bag into the first-floor guest room, closing the door behind him.

Olivia stood alone in the living room. Confused, she crossed her arms over her chest, trying to ward off the numbing chill coursing through her. She could understand that Jamison was bone tired. She could even accept that he didn't want to eat a meal and go to bed on a full stomach. But choosing the guest room over *their* bed?

That hurt worse than his gruff tone.

Suddenly, the cold distance between them yawned like a vast canyon, full of all the reasons they'd decided to separate in the first place.

She'd had such high hopes for the evening. But nothing was turning out as she'd hoped.

Wasn't that par for the course these days?

It hadn't always been that way, though. Once upon a time, not so long ago, their love seemed invincible. There was nothing like it from the moment they'd set eyes on each other. She'd never forget the first time she saw him. In person, that is, because every red-blooded woman in America knew of Jamison Mallory, *Panorama Magazine*'s "Sexiest Bachelor in the Universe" for several years running. With his tall, bronzed, quarterback body and his All-American blond, blue-eyed good looks, the man simply needed to flash his lightning-strike smile and women fell under his spell.

As a Harvard Law graduate and the youngest elected U.S. senator, Jamison had come back to his alma mater to deliver a commencement address. They'd bumped into each other—literally—as Olivia rounded a corner, rushing from one of her classes to a rehearsal for a Harvard Ballet Company performance of *Sleeping Beauty.* She'd dropped her dance bag and books and he had helped her retrieve her ballet slippers from underneath a shrub. Somewhere between, "Excuse me," and "It was so nice to meet you, Olivia," he'd asked where she was going and she'd nervously rattled off information about the ballet performance, which was the next night. She had never dreamed he'd be in the audience—front and center.

Because he was *Jamison Mallory.* She was simply a shy, college freshman who'd barely had any experience with men. After all, up until meeting Jamison, her one true love had been dance.

Later, they'd both sworn it had been love at first sight.

He'd often said that from the moment he'd looked into her eyes as he handed her those slippers, he'd known he'd met the woman he would spend the rest of his life with.

"It was cosmic." He used to flash his devastating smile when he'd tell that to reporters. "The feeling was so much bigger than anything I'd ever felt before, I knew it was right."

Now it was the small things that stood between them and what was really important. The minutiae blurred the perspective so that they couldn't keep the big picture in focus anymore. If they couldn't get past the small stuff, how in the world were they going to reach the real issue that was keeping them apart?

Feeling as if she were dragging a heavy weight, she made her way into the kitchen to put away the uneaten dinner. She and Jamison had always spent Christmas Eve with her family and Christmas Day with the large Mallory clan at his mother's palatial compound in the Berkshires. This year, she'd opted out of Christmas Eve with her mother, father and three siblings—all of whom were married to their careers at the Armstrong Fertility Institute. Well, except for her brother Paul who, though he was still the consummate workaholic, had recently met his love match in Ramona Tate, at the institute. Olivia wanted to spend their first night back together alone. Just the two of them. Little had she known how alone she'd actually be.

Staying home had seemed like the right thing to do at the time, especially since none of the family knew about her and Jamison's current living arrangement—that Jamison hadn't come home on weekends during the congressional session. Or that he'd stayed in Washington after the session had adjourned. They'd told everyone he was busy with a particularly demanding committee, that he needed to focus so that he could wrap up work in time for Christmas. They'd played their roles so well that no one had a clue that their marriage was actually deeply in trouble.

Olivia hoped to God she'd find a Christmas miracle in her stocking, because it seemed as if nothing less than a miracle would save them now.

Jamison awoke to a slant of sunlight streaming in through the white plantation shutters, hitting him square in the face. He blinked, disoriented for a moment, and then it all flooded back to him. He was…home.

He glanced at the clock on the bedside table: seven-thirty. Although he could've told the time without the clock, thanks to his internal alarm. No matter how little sleep he'd gotten the night before—in this case only about four hours—his system awakened him at seven-thirty every morning. It was fail-safe, and there was no sense fighting it. He might as well get up, because he wouldn't be able to go back to sleep. Plus, he and Olivia needed to get on the road by noon to make the two-hour trek to his mother's for the Christmas Day festivities.

He stretched, and his arms slid over the cold, empty side of the queen-size feather bed. He wished he was waking up in his own bed, with Olivia in his arms, rather than realizing another morning alone—

especially Christmas morning in the guest room of his very own house.

He'd been so exhausted by the time he'd arrived home last night, he'd barely been able to string together a coherent sentence, much less have a discussion with her about sleeping arrangements. After being separated from Olivia for two-and-a-half months, he wanted to be fair to her. Even though sleeping apart from her wasn't what he wanted, he didn't want to seem presumptuous on their first night back together—and even more, he didn't want to fight.

He'd been beyond exhausted and, yes, a little cranky. He knew himself well enough to know that combination was a recipe for disaster. But now, in the bright light of morning, his head felt clearer, his purpose stronger. Eager to talk to his wife about their next step in their relationship before they joined his family for the annual Christmas Day festivities, he showered, shaved and dressed before making his way toward the kitchen in search of a good, strong cup of coffee…and Olivia.

The house was dark and quiet. Even before he flicked on the kitchen light, he could see that the room was pristine—everything in its place. The only evidence of the dinner Olivia had offered him last night was the ghost-aroma of something delicious mingling with the faint scent of dish soap and the slightly smoky traces of the fire that must have blazed in the fireplace.

He breathed in deeply, relishing the familiar, comforting scents of home. But as he did, guilt tugged at him. He knew his wife had not only prepared a delectable Christmas Eve feast that neither of them was able to enjoy, but she'd probably stayed up long after he went to bed putting everything away and cleaning up the mess of a dinner that never happened.

The least he could do was let her sleep a little while longer and then make her some coffee.

No, he'd go one better and surprise her with breakfast in bed.

Before their separation, the kitchen had been foreign territory to him. One thing he'd learned in the time they'd been apart was how to cook up a mean batch of scrambled eggs—the trick was to use low heat so that they cooked slowly and the outside didn't scorch. Hmm…the low-heat approach would also benefit their marriage. Because the other thing he'd learned during this time apart was that he loved his wife desperately. He missed her…he missed *them.* It was time to put all the ridiculous fighting and blaming behind them and move on.

Time to use the *low-heat* approach.

And to think the root of their problems started over

something that meant so much to both of them, the common ground on which they'd always met: family. Or, more specifically, the lack of a family of their own.

Cold, twisted confusion wrapped around him when he thought about it. He was so torn. On one hand, Olivia would make such a wonderful mother. On the other, how could they even bring children into the world when their marriage was so shaky?

When they weren't even living together?

They had to talk about their relationship. They had to get back on track. But before they could get into that, he had to break another bit of news to her—the news that he had to return to Washington earlier than expected. Earlier as in *tomorrow* morning, rather than January third as they'd planned.

That would go over about as well as telling her that the holidays had been canceled this year. With the way their plans had been preempted, that wasn't so far from the truth.

Jamison made his way toward the stainless steel refrigerator and tugged opened the double doors. The precise arrangement of the cartons, jars and stacked glass and plastic containers echoed the kitchen's tidiness.

One of the many things he admired about his wife was the pride she took in their home. He'd encouraged her to hire a cook and a full-time housekeeper so that she'd have more time for herself and time for the Children's Home, a non-profit orphanage where she sat on the board of directors. But she'd refused, because she loved cooking—and was darn good at it. She's said while it was just the two of them she could get by with someone coming in and doing the deep cleaning a couple of times a month. She claimed she enjoyed keeping their house, making a home for them. When it came to home and family, there was no one more dedicated than Olivia. That's why their fertility issues had been such a struggle. They desperately wanted children and had jumped through many hoops to get pregnant—all to no avail. Too much testing and too many treatments had set them on an emotional roller coaster and taken a serious toll on their marriage. How ironic, when marriage had to be the bedrock on which the family was built.

Liv wouldn't take well to the suggestion, but he'd been thinking about asking her to agree to put having children on hold until they could heal their marriage. It was the only thing that made sense.

But one thing at a time. First, he had to break the news about the change of holiday plans.

Jamison found the eggs, butter and cheddar cheese and was just turning around with his hands full when Olivia walked into the kitchen.

"Good morning," he said. "I thought you'd still be asleep."

She shook her head. "I thought you'd sleep in since you got home so late."

She didn't sound like herself, and she looked at him with a wariness that took him aback. But she did look beautiful standing there perfectly made-up and dressed, wearing the pearls that he'd given her as a wedding present, her dark hair twisted up in a way that accentuated her porcelain skin, fine cheekbones and gorgeous dark eyes—deep brown, like the coffee he craved almost as much as he thirsted for her.

"What are you doing?" Her voice was flat. She sounded tired.

He adjusted the goods in his hands, fidgeting as if he'd been caught trespassing. This was her territory after all. In the seven years they'd been married, he'd barely set foot in the kitchen, much less cooked a meal.

"I thought I'd fix you some breakfast." He grinned sheepishly, suddenly feeling out of his league.

"You don't have to do that." She gestured toward the items in his hands. "Just put those things down and I'll do it. I have a special breakfast planned."

Oh. Of course she would, it being Christmas.

"Well, I just thought—" Their gazes snagged for a brief moment before she looked away. With that, he knew beyond the shadow of a doubt that something was wrong. Of course something was wrong, but he'd been so bent on moving forward with the next steps they should take to fix things between them that he hadn't counted on having to delve backward into their problems before they could move on. Suddenly the clarity he'd felt moments before was replaced by a dread that riveted him to the wooden kitchen floor.

Olivia walked toward him and took the food from his hands. Then she set to work, returning the cheese to the dairy drawer and removing various other items from the refrigerator and pantry. Jamison stood and watched her for a moment, feeling superfluous.

Since she hadn't made any moves to start the coffee, he decided it would be a good task and began opening cabinet doors to locate the beans.

"What are you looking for?" Olivia asked.

"Coffee," he replied.

"It's in the freezer." She gestured to the drawer below the refrigerator. "I keep it there so it will stay fresh since I'm not drinking it these days."

"Really? So, no coffee for you?"

She shook her head.

"How come? You love coffee."

She turned and squinted at him, looking plenty annoyed. "Jamison, I haven't been drinking coffee for the past two years. Don't you remember the doctor suggested that I cut caffeine from my diet while we were trying to get pregnant?"

Well, it was an honest mistake since they hadn't had the opportunity to *try* during the past couple months. Even so, he thought as he rummaged through the freezer drawer, his not knowing felt like a failure. Funny how he felt perfectly at home on the senate floor, where he knew every nook and cranny of the issues he passionately presented, yet he'd forgotten that the doctor had nixed caffeine from his wife's diet.

Bad show, man.

When he pulled out the unopened bag of whole-bean French roast, Olivia was right there ready to pluck it from his hands.

This time, he held on tight.

"I can do it," he said.

"Since when do you know how to make coffee?" she asked, tugging every so slightly, but he refused to let go.

"Since I haven't had you to make it for me," he said, looking her square in the eye. For an instant, a look—surprise, hurt, disappointment…maybe a combination of the three—flashed on her face.

"I'll make it for you," she insisted. Once again her expression was flat and there was no warmth in her eyes where mere seconds ago there had been a pileup of emotion.

The distance between them was killing him. He had to do something.

He glanced down at their hands still holding on to the bag of coffee. They were so close, yet not touching. He stretched his finger until it touched hers. She flinched and snatched her hand away, leaving him holding the bag of French roast.

She looked startled for a moment then turned back toward the kitchen counter, busying herself with the breakfast preparation, taking eggs from the carton with shaky hands.

"Liv," he said. "We need to talk about this. It's not just going to go away."

She placed the eggs in a bowl and stilled but didn't respond.

"I don't know about you," he said, "but I've missed you so badly it's tearing me up."

He saw her grip tighten on the edge of the counter until her knuckles turned white.

"I'm sorry last night didn't work out the way we'd hoped. I wish you would've gone on to your parents when we realized my flight was delayed."

He saw her shoulders rise and fall, and dreaded delivering the news that he had to leave tomorrow.

"It wasn't your fault, Jamison. I know that."

She turned to face him. "But sleeping in the guest room last night—that was your choice."

"What?" As tightly wound as she appeared, he was expecting her to unleash what was bothering her, but he wasn't expecting this to be part of the problem.

"You heard me." She was clutching her hands in front of her, again gripping so tightly that her knuckles were turning white. She looked so small, so fine-boned and fragile standing there, it was a wonder her fingers didn't snap like twigs.

"Liv, I was exhausted." He ran a hand over his face. "I didn't know up from down. I couldn't even form the words to ask you where you wanted me to sleep."

He reached out and touched her hands, hoping the gesture would encourage her to relax. "But it's a new day and there are a few things we need to talk about before we head up to my mother's place."

Olivia's face shuttered, but he saw her throat work as she swallowed.

"Such as?" she asked.

"Such as whether or not we should tell the family we're separated. Despite how much I love you, I can't go on pretending. What are we going to do, Liv? What are we going to tell them?"

Chapter Two

The moment they turned onto Stanhope Manor's long, cobblestone driveway, Olivia could see that the Mallory mansion was bursting at the seams with family and festivity.

Lights, decorations and a blanket of new-fallen snow transformed the stately home into a winter wonderland. An army of children ran and played on the rolling lawn. Some made snow angels; others joined forces in a collaborative snowman building effort. The bittersweet sight of all those children brought tears to Olivia's eyes.

She wanted to believe that someday her kids

would play on that lawn, but she and Jamison seemed further away than ever from having a family of their own. That morning, the double whammy of a Christmas present he'd dropped into her lap was not only that he was returning to Washington early, but also that he wanted to put their baby plans on the back burner. It was the last thing she'd expected. The last thing she wanted. Because of that, the two-hour ride up to the Berkshires was mostly silent. What more was there to say? They were officially at a standoff. Jamison insisted they shouldn't have children until they were happy as a couple; Olivia couldn't see how they'd be happy until they had a baby. Or at least *she* couldn't be happy. Not with Jamison spending more and more time away from her.

They were supposed to spend Christmas week together, but he'd said something about an unexpected diplomatic visit. She'd always prided herself on being supportive of her husband's demanding career. But lately it seemed the more she gave, the more one-sided their life became. And balance didn't seem to be a part of Jamison's New Year's resolutions.

She tried to persuade him that this was the perfect example of how there was no *perfect* time to have children. It was simply another excuse to wait. Even worse, she didn't understand why he felt compelled to wait. She got the distinct feeling that he wasn't telling her the real reason behind his hesitation. But no matter how many times she told him having children was exactly what they needed to mend things, he'd come back around to "We need to fix *us* first."

So, what was she supposed to do?

Passively give in?

Just give up?

No way would she do that. Not when their future depended on it.

So they'd reached a standoff, except for agreeing to not saying anything to the family about their separation until they'd had a chance to talk more. That seemed code for "Let's continue this vicious cycle of pretending." She had a sinking feeling that they were set on a collision course with disaster.

As Jamison steered the car under the porte cochere, anxiousness threatened to pin Olivia to her seat. She really wasn't in a mood to put on a happy face for her mother-in-law and extended family. After the disastrous discussion with Jamison, this masquerade felt beyond her. But the alternative of announcing their marital problems to the bunch was worse. With one last wistful glance at the kids, she steeled herself to enter the lion's den.

The only consolation was that Jamison was a true

gentleman. No matter how bad things had gotten between Jamison and her, he still stood up for her when his mother started in with her power plays—such as her insensitive queries about why Olivia wasn't pregnant yet and her attempts to pressure them into selling the house in Boston.

For the past year—since it had become clear that Jamison had garnered enough support to be considered a viable candidate for his party's nomination for a future presidential race—Helen Mallory had been turning up the pressure for Jamison to claim his birthright and move up to the family home in the Berkshires. Olivia knew it was a posturing on Helen's part, a way of positioning herself as close to her influential son's inner circle as possible. If the future president of the United States lived with her, in *her* house—because if she and Jamison moved in it didn't mean Helen would move out—then she would have an even better chance at having his ear and an even stronger chance at asserting her considerable influence, much in the same way she'd done with her late husband.

Stanhope Manor had been in the Mallory family for seven generations. It had always been passed down to the oldest son. At thirty-nine, Jamison was still young, and would have plenty of time to enjoy the place with his own family, just as he and his five younger brothers had when they were growing up.

Despite how much Olivia wanted to uphold the Mallory legacy, she wasn't in a hurry to move out of the city into the rambling, eleven-bedroom, twenty-two-thousand-square-foot mansion until she could give her husband a son—or a daughter—who would carry on the tradition. What was the point without a family to fill the rambling house?

At least in Boston Olivia had her family and her volunteer work. One thing she did not need was further isolation.

Nor did she need—or want—to live with her mother-in-law. Especially with Jamison spending so much time in Washington. That living arrangement would surely prove to be a ticking time bomb ready to explode.

Residing in Boston meant Helen was a safe two hours away in the Berkshires. Long distance, it was more difficult for her to remind Olivia that she and Jamison had yet to gift the family with children. Except for the occasional obligatory phone call, Helen mostly ignored Olivia, saving the pregnancy barbs for personal delivery. For times such as this.

Olivia braced herself at the thought.

It hurt that she and Jamison had confided in her about their fertility struggles, yet Helen publicly persecuted them as if their childlessness were a choice. Sometimes Olivia had to summon every ounce of

strength to keep from tossing Helen's barbs and pa-
tronizing tone right back at her. But out of respect
for her husband, Olivia bit her tongue.

To Jamison's credit, he fully understood how
painful it would be to live with his mother. Despite
how he longed to move into the house in which he'd
grown up, he always sided with Olivia, refusing to
let Helen bully them into moving and demanding she
lay off when her pregnancy digs got out of hand.

The valet opened Olivia's door and helped her
step out of the Jaguar. Jamison walked around the car
and took her hand, expecting her to play along. To
put on a happy face and pretend they were the perfect
couple with the perfect marriage.

"Are you okay?" he asked as they climbed the
steps to the porch.

"Truthfully?" She slanted him a look. "No, I'm not."

His face fell, as if her words had knocked the
wind out of him, but before he could say anything,
the elaborately carved wooden front doors swung
open and a uniformed doorman greeted them.

"Merry Christmas, sir, madam."

Ever the politician, Jamison flashed his famous
smile. "Merry Christmas."

Olivia managed a polite nod. She didn't recognize
the man at the door. He wasn't part of the small band
of live-in staff employed by Jamison's mother. He

was obviously among the extra help she'd hired for the holidays. Like a steadfast queen clinging to her castle, she'd remained in the house after Jamison's father died and all six boys had moved out to begin their own lives.

"Mrs. Mallory is in the great room. Follow me, please."

"Thank you, but that's not necessary," said Jamison. "I grew up in this house. I know the way."

The doorman stood back and motioned Jamison and Olivia onward. "Very well, sir. Happy holidays."

Their footsteps sounded on the marble floor. The place had a museumlike air that inspired silence. As they made their way down the long, arched hallway toward the great room at the back of the house, neither said a word.

Instead, Olivia let her gaze stray over the elaborate paintings lining the walls. Generations of Mallorys dating as far back as the Revolutionary War hung in grand, gilded frames. Their eyes seemed to follow Olivia and Jamison as they passed. Though she'd experienced this sensation many times, today it was eerie and a little unnerving. She shifted her gaze straight ahead, focusing on the crown molding at the end of the passageway.

In the great room, a harpist strummed Christmas

carols from her post in the corner. Her angelic music was barely audible above the crowd that was at least seventy-five strong. A giant Christmas tree stood in front of the large picture windows on the west wall that looked out over the snow-covered back lawn with its beautifully frozen pond. In the distance, the mountains painted a breathtaking picture. A roaring fire blazed in the oversize fireplace. The room was a little stuffy with all the people milling about talking, laughing and filling plates with fancy hors d'oeuvres that had been laid out on an antique trestle table that stretched nearly the entire length of the wall opposite the windows.

In the center of the crowded room, Helen Mallory was holding court, talking to her loyal subjects who were dutifully gathered around her. Her platinum hair, as white as new-fallen snow, was teased into a meringuelike coiffure. Her white cashmere suit and plethora of diamonds brought to mind the term "Ice Queen." As if sensing their presence, she looked up as Jamison and Olivia approached.

"Darlings, there you are," she said. Her drink sloshed as she raised her glass toward them. "I was beginning to think you'd never arrive." It was barely noon and judging by the glass Helen held like a scepter, she'd bypassed the traditional Christmas

Day pomegranate mimosas and had dived headfirst into the martinis. Depending on how many she'd had, they could be in for a bumpy ride.

Jamison bent down and kissed Helen's cheek.

"Merry Christmas, Mother. You're looking… well. We would've been here sooner, but last night my flight in from D.C. was delayed, and I didn't get home until after three."

Helen held out a diamond-laden hand to her daughter-in-law.

"Merry Christmas, dear." She looked Olivia up and down with disapproving eyes. "You're looking beautiful, as always. But awfully thin. I was so hoping you would've plumped up by now."

Helen pulled her hand from Olivia's and patted her daughter-in-law's flat stomach.

Trying to ignore the uncomfortable stares from the others gathered around them, Olivia took special care to keep her smile firmly in place. Especially since she had a feeling of what was coming next— right in front of everyone.

Olivia did a mental countdown. *Three, two, one—*

"When on earth are you going to give me a grandchild?"

Right on schedule.

"You do know that Payton is pregnant again, don't you?" Helen slurred the words.

Olivia fought back a sudden rush of emotions that brought with them the stinging threat of tears.

Payton. The wife of Jamison's younger brother, Grant. The perfect, fertile daughter-in-law. One only need talk about pregnancy in the vicinity of Payton and she got knocked up.

"Mother, don't start." Jamison's voice was flat.

Helen sighed and dismissed him with a curt wave of martini, diamonds and bloodred nails. The gesture sent a wave of gin sloshing over the side of her glass, leaving a wet spot on her white suit. She seemed not to notice.

"I'm not *starting* anything," she slurred. "I'm simply finding it terribly ironic that Olivia's father is one of the nation's leading fertility experts— Gerald Armstrong, of the Armstrong Institute—yet they're still not pregnant. I just don't understand." Helen directed her words to the others, spouting off as if this weren't a deeply private issue, acting as if Olivia and Jamison weren't standing right there.

Every fiber in Olivia's body went numb and she had to inhale sharply and bite the insides of her cheeks to keep from defending herself. Because what was the point?

Helen was drunk. Again. Come to think of it, Helen always said what was on her mind and seemed to get more brazenly outspoken with each passing year. Her drinking was also out of control, and the family seemed to be in complete denial about it.

It wasn't Olivia's place to say anything about her mother-in-law's imbibing, but these barbs…they were inexcusable. Talking as if Olivia's father were a banker refusing to lend money rather than seeing it for the intensely painful, sensitive—and private— issue that it was.

"Mother, stop it," Jamison insisted.

Normally, when Helen started with her polite bullying, Olivia didn't let the woman's barbs get to her—but today Olivia felt vulnerable. Fragile, almost.

So, when Jamison put an arm around her and locked gazes with his mother, Olivia sank into him. Against her will, her body responded to her husband's offer of solidarity and protection.

Despite what had transpired earlier, she was glad that at least he was taking her side, as he always did.

At least that hadn't changed.

Before Helen could say anything else, the uncomfortable standoff was interrupted by a ringing voice.

"Merry Christmas, all!" Payton waddled over to them, her freckled cheeks rosy and her baby bump looking much more pronounced in the holly-green velvet maternity dress than it should for a woman five months' pregnant. Of course, it was her fourth pregnancy.

Fourth baby in four-and-a-half years. Olivia swallowed the lump of sad envy that had burned in her throat until it slid down, settling like a hot coal in the pit of her barren belly.

"Payton, darling." Helen stood and pulled her favorite daughter-in-law into a gentle embrace. "How are you feeling, love?"

Payton pushed an auburn curl off her forehead, then beamed and rested her hands on her swollen belly. "I've never felt better."

Helen held her at arm's length, taking in her entire being. "It shows. You are positively radiant."

Payton preened. "I always feel my best when I'm pregnant."

Of course she did.

Lucky for her since she was *always* pregnant. Resentment flared inside Olivia. It seemed like Payton and Grant produced a child to commemorate each wedding anniversary.

"Here, sit, sit. Next to me. Get off your feet." Helen returned to her seat on the sofa and patted the cushion beside her.

"Well, Mom, we have been in the car all morning." She braced her right hand on the small of her back, which made her stomach stick out all the more. "But I guess I could sit a while longer while we catch up."

"You know, if you keep giving me grandchildren at this rate, I'm going to have to move you up here to Stanhope Manor so that there's a place big enough to house all of you under one roof. Jamison doesn't seem to have any interest in the place."

Helen shot a pointed look at her son as Payton planted herself next to her mother-in-law.

"It would be wonderful to live with you up here. If you keep talking like that, we just might take you up on it."

Olivia glanced at Jamison, who was wearing an *over-my-dead-body* look on his face. She had a hunch that his sour expression wasn't simply a remnant of his mother's earlier indelicate blurting, but had more to do with the threat of his younger brother's status-hungry wife bumping him out of his birthright with her pregnant belly.

Maybe, for once, Payton's selfish antics could actually help Olivia by making Jamison change his mind about holding off on having children. Even so, it seemed unlikely that an army of children could keep Helen at bay if they moved in with her.

Payton must have sensed Olivia staring because she smiled up at Jamison and Olivia and said, "It's been a long time. How are the two of you?"

They made small talk for a few moments until Grant entered with an infant seat in one hand, a toddler on the opposite hip and their oldest boy trailing behind him. Grant flashed his trademark toothy, white Mallory smile, greeting everyone as he walked over to kiss his mother's cheek.

Grant had been a latecomer to politics, winning a New Hampshire congressional seat just last year. He and Jamison had always been competitive, but when it came to politics, there was an unwritten agreement that Jamison was the one who would make a bid for the White House. After he'd had his go, then, if Grant was game, it was all his.

Olivia wondered if the same accord applied to Stanhope Manor or if Helen would seriously offer the home to Grant and Payton—even as a strategic move to force Jamison and Olivia's hand. On top of everything else, the thought was more than Olivia could deal with. So she pushed it out of her mind, vowing only to worry about it if and when the crisis came up.

"Merry Christmas, son," Helen said to Grant. "And where's your nanny? Surely you didn't give her this week off? Now more than ever your wife needs the extra hands to help her."

Grant and Payton had imported a woman named Ingrid from Sweden to help with the kids. Payton took pride in flaunting her Swedish nanny, so it was a surprise when Grant said, "She went home for the holidays."

Helen shot Payton an alarmed glance. "Oh, you poor dear. However will you manage?"

Olivia was delighted to fall off of Helen's radar as Payton dutifully played the martyred mommy, regaling her audience with details of how it would indeed be a challenge, but that she would somehow get by.

Anger and shame rose in Olivia's throat like bile, as she moved as far away from Payton as possible.

As the day progressed, Helen wasn't the only one driving the baby train. Payton and her brood—and pregnant belly—drew inevitable comparisons and incessant questions from friends and relatives about why Jamison and Olivia weren't keeping up with his younger brothers.

If Olivia had been in a certain frame of mind, she would've taken offense at their questions. Asking a couple about when they were going to have a baby was not so far off from quizzing them about their sex life. It was a private matter. Didn't people understand that?

Obviously it took sex for pregnancy to happen.

Unless the couple went the in vitro route, as Jamison and Olivia well knew. They'd tried to conceive the usual way, and when that failed, they'd opted for in vitro.

The hormones to help Olivia produce more eggs for harvesting had wreaked havoc with her physical well-being, causing headaches and mood swings and overall malaise. She and Jamison had ended up fighting, so much so that they'd decided to separate.

The thought of how something as wonderful as having a baby could create such turmoil in a marriage was beyond Olivia.

She wished Jamison could understand it was the side effects of the hormones that had caused their problems. Not the possibility that their marriage was unstable. And certainly not the act of having a baby and building their family. Looking at it rationally, she could understand his hesitation. She just wished he could believe that it would be different when they tried again.

Because it would be.

This time she knew what to expect. This time she would be prepared.

A new doctor had recently joined the Armstrong Fertility Institute. Chance Demetrios was one of the leading fertility research specialists in the world. Her brother Paul had hired him away from a teaching hospital in San Francisco. Olivia had seen him once, just before she and Jamison decided on the trial separation, and she hadn't followed up when he'd said there was a slim chance she could get pregnant. Slim, but a chance nonetheless. Since the pain of their separation was so fresh, Olivia's mindset made her question the point of following up if her husband wasn't on board.

But now, especially as she watched Payton, Olivia was looking at things differently. Suddenly, there was an urgency. There was no time to waste. Maybe it was Jamison's sudden hesitation, but Olivia was feeling her full twenty-nine years. She certainly wasn't getting any younger. Maybe, if Jamison wasn't willing to cooperate, it was time to take maters into her own hands—even if it meant getting pregnant without her husband's blessing.

After all, once she was carrying his child, he'd come around.

Wouldn't he?

Jamison retreated into the library with his glass of wine. As a kid, he'd always enjoyed the solitude of the room—the built-in mahogany bookcases and never-ending stacks of books felt like comfortable old friends. When life overwhelmed him or he had a problem that needed sorting out, he'd come here, grab a book and sit in the window seat. Sometimes he'd lose himself in a classic. More often than not, he'd lose himself in his thoughts as he gazed at the panoramic view of the mountains that stretched like a grand painting framed by the horizon of the backyard.

Tonight, the moonless sky hid the mountains as

if nature had drawn a black velvet curtain. So he bypassed the window seat, placed another log on the dying fire and settled into one of the leather club chairs in front of the hearth.

It was late. He and Olivia really should head home soon, but he needed a few minutes alone to gather his thoughts before they climbed into the car and endured another long, silent journey.

He didn't blame her for being mad at him. It seemed that since he'd been home he'd committed one seemingly thoughtless blunder after another. He'd even managed to blow it with Olivia this evening after the friends had gone and the party shifted into a mode of opening Christmas presents and snapping family photos. Oh, she hadn't said it straight out—in fact she'd barely said more than, "Thank you," but the flash of confusion in her eyes had been unmistakable when she'd opened her gift from him and had seen the gaudy cocktail ring that was not in the least bit her style—and several sizes too big to boot.

Crunched for time, he'd asked his mother to pick up a gift for Olivia from him—jewelry, something nice, of course. "You know Olivia. Pick out something she'd like."

When his tiny, pearl-wearing wife had opened the jewelers box and pulled out the multi-colored boulder of a cocktail ring, he'd wanted to snatch it back and claim that there had been a mistake. On her delicate hand, it looked like a wild, golf-ball-size piece of stained glass; certainly nothing he would've ever picked out for her. And that had been obvious. He hadn't shopped for his wife. She'd been well aware of that since the ring had his mother's signature written all over it.

For someone who prided himself on intelligence, he felt pretty dumb for entrusting his mother, of all people, to shop for Olivia. That blunder, on top of the fact that it probably hadn't been the best time to tell Olivia he wanted to hold off on getting pregnant. Not on the heels of disappointing her with the change of plans for Christmas week. But thoughtlessly, he'd done it. It had slipped out as they'd talked earlier that morning. They'd digressed back into the dubious tug of war over commitment and priorities, which went from bad to worse when he'd broken the news that he had to leave because he had to play host to the visiting ambassador. She hadn't taken it well. No matter that a lot was riding on this meeting, and if he pulled it off it would be a major coup, a feather in his political cap.

The flames crackled in the fireplace.

The ridiculous ring felt like a third strike in a game he was already losing. He was between a rock and a hard place. Olivia knew their life would be this way and if he did make that run for the White House in 2016, not only did they need to find solidarity in their marriage, they had to be a solid twosome before they could add to their family.

Still, it didn't mean he loved her any less. As a matter of fact, he was standing firm on his position to hold off starting a family because he loved her. Children added a whole different dynamic to a marriage, and he wasn't so naive to believe that a child would fix something that was broken. He'd seen plenty of evidence to support that fact as he'd watched his parents' marriage come apart under the pressure of public office and the weight of lies and deception. The only reason his mother and father hadn't divorced was because of his father's untimely death.

Well-shrouded secrets and, of course, the soft focus of layers of decades had allowed his mother the privilege of playing the well-respected, grieving widow of a political hero—a senator who would've been president had his life not been tragically snuffed out. But as the oldest of six boys, Jamison had gotten a first-hand look at the real life behind the gossamer curtain that cloaked political power couple, Judson and Helen Mallory.

Jamison sipped his cabernet. He was nothing like his old man, aside from carrying on his father's political legacy. In fact, Jamison had consciously tried to stay clear of the womanizing and scandal that not only plagued the Mallory name, but had driven his mother to the bottle and kept his family life in constant upheaval. If he'd gleaned nothing else from observing his parents' destructive relationship, it was that he knew children could not fix a rocky marriage.

Children simply got caught in the cross fire.

Behind him, the library door creaked open. A slant of light yawned across the wall then disappeared as the door shut. Jamison turned around, hoping Olivia had decided to join him. Instead, his mother stood there, tall and proud and expressionless. Her angular features were rendered even sharper by the dim amber glow of the fire. She glided across the room and slid into the chair next to him.

He could feel her gaze on him, as palpable as the heat of the fire at his feet.

"I thought I'd find you here," she said. "Anytime you had something on your mind, you'd always hide in here."

"I'm not hiding, Mother. Simply enjoying the solitude."

"Don't try to fool me." She shifted in her seat, angling her knees toward him, crossing her legs at the ankles, folding her hands in her lap. "You of all people wouldn't leave a party unless you had something weighing on your mind."

Jamison took a slow sip of wine, buying time. Interesting that his mother had been drinking most of the day and she still had the uncanny ability to read him. Of course, his retreating into solitude had probably been a big tip-off. Rather than slipping off, he probably should've rallied Olivia and simply headed for home. But he'd wanted to think, wanted to find common ground on which they could meet as they drove home.

"I'm exhausted," he said. "Thanks to work and the weather, it hasn't exactly been a jolly holiday."

He set his wine on the end table next to his seat, got up and stoked the fire. It flared, spit and crackled as he turned the log.

"I can see that you're exhausted," she said to his back. "You haven't been yourself all day. I do wish you would stay the night and get a fresh start tomorrow. Grant, Payton and the kids are staying."

He returned the poker to its brass stand. "Thank you, but we can't stay. I have an early flight tomorrow. We really should head for home."

A chain of silent seconds stretched between them.

"You always did love this room," she said. "It's too bad you can't enjoy it more often."

He shrugged and glanced at her. "I don't even get to enjoy my own home as often as I'd like."

A flash as hot as the glint of a flame lit her eyes. "Why are you going back to Washington so soon?"

He disengaged her gaze and turned his attention back to the dancing fire. "An unexpected meeting came up."

"A meeting. During Christmas week." There was a goading, knowing tone to her voice, as if she'd caught him in a lie, but was willing to keep his secret.

Despite the pause in conversation, Jamison didn't elaborate.

"The one-size-fits-all excuse. That's the one your father used to use all the time. 'I have a meeting.' And how was I supposed to know differently?"

"Mom, don't."

He hadn't realized how badly she was slurring her words. He really didn't want his mother to string together all of his father's flaws and illuminate them like tawdry lights on a tainted family tree.

"The wife never knows until it's too late. When she finds out, all she can do to save face is go on pretending she's none the wiser. It's a miserable life, Jamison. Don't put Olivia through that. I hardly think she's strong enough to cope."

Was she implying that he was having an affair? It rankled him. Even so, he wasn't going to defend himself against something he had no intention of doing. Besides, she was drunk and probably wouldn't remember the conversation in the morning.

"This is your house, Jamison. I know Olivia doesn't want to live here, but she needs to understand that Mallory men…well, affairs just seem to be a way of life. If you move in here, I can help her cope. I can help her understand that it's just something Mallory men do."

He held up his hand. "Mother, stop. I am not having an affair. I have no intention of having an affair. I love my wife."

Helen threw back her head and guffawed a most unladylike sound. "Oh, Jamison, you can level with me. I'm not going to tell her."

She was talking utter nonsense. It was definitely time to go.

He stood and walked toward the door.

Helen's body swiveled as she followed him with her gaze.

"Where are you going?" she demanded.

"Home, Mother. It's late, but I thank you for a wonderful evening. Merry Christmas."

"Jamison, don't walk away from me. I need to ask you a question."

He stopped, his hand on the doorknob.

"Seven generations of Mallorys have lived here, son. How much longer are you planning on allowing that woman to deny you what's yours? You need to set your wife straight. Tell her it's time."

"It's not time, and it won't be until and unless Olivia is ready."

Helen made a clucking sound and stood up, wobbling as she did.

"You're just like your father, Jamison, always letting a pretty face cloud your judgment and sway your decision. Stand up and be a man, son."

Jamison shook his head. "Oh, Mother, what you don't understand is that the main difference between Dad and me is that I am being a man. The pretty face that influences me is my wife. I'm sorry he never showed you the same courtesy."

Chapter Three

Where do you go when you can't go home?

Back to the purgatory of Washington, D.C., Jamison thought. Even though it was the last place he wanted to be.

But duty called. Olivia should understand that.

Jamison stood in the dining room of his house, pouring himself a stiff glass of scotch.

It was nearly nine o'clock. The tense ride home from his mother's had mirrored the mostly silent drive up. Olivia was upset, and he understood why— on so many levels. The only problem was there was nothing he could do about it.

He carried his drink back into the living room where Olivia waited for him, perched on the edge of the white living room sofa, anxiously fidgeting with the too-big cocktail ring he'd given her for Christmas, twisting it around and around on her index finger.

He'd been so bogged down with work he'd hadn't had time to shop. His mom had offered to pick out something nice for Olivia, something tasteful, yet lavish. Why hadn't Helen opted for a bracelet or a necklace? No. Not a necklace because that would've paled in comparison to the diamond necklace Grant had had designed for Payton—one obscenely large diamond representing each child they'd had together. Payton, of course, had been very quick to notice and point out that the design provided plenty of room for endless additions. A sudden rush of guilt washed over Jamison as he remembered Olivia opening her gift that was noticeably too large and, really, more his mother's style than her own.

So maybe his wife was partially right. Maybe they needed to reevaluate, reprioritize. In fact, that's exactly what they would do right after this diplomatic visit was over. Then after they'd worked on themselves, they could revisit babies and parenthood.

"Are you sure I can't get you anything?" he asked

as he walked over to the fireplace. He set his glass on the mantel and picked up the poker to stir the fire he'd lit when they arrived.

"No, thank you," she said. "I'm fine."

But she wasn't *fine*. She was looked anything but *fine*, and he almost couldn't stand it. He plugged in the Christmas tree lights and dimmed the rheostat, hoping to gain a more romantic atmosphere that would lift her mood and turn the tide in their favor for once.

"I'm sorry the ring is too big. The jeweler can resize it."

"I guess your mother didn't know my size?" The corners of her mouth turned up, but the smile didn't reach her eyes.

"You know I didn't plan on having to go back to Washington so soon," Jamison said. "No more than I planned on spending Christmas Eve at the mercy of the weather."

Inhaling a weary breath, she said, "I thought that story was strictly reserved for the family's benefit." The words weren't sharp or nasty. More disappointed…or, worse yet, defeated.

For a moment, neither of them said a word.

"I'm just tired of begging for your time, Jamison," she said as if answering his thoughts.

"Honey, you knew when you married me that sometimes my job would preempt pleasure."

Even the pleasure of making love to his wife. What a pity that they were arguing rather than doing exactly that in the small amount of time they had together.

She simply shook her head.

"I don't want to fight, Jamison. Not tonight. It's just too exhausting." She stood.

"Where are you going?"

"I'm going to take a bath, and then I'm going to bed. What time is your flight tomorrow?"

"Nine o'clock. The ambassador arrives at one."

She nodded. "I'm sure the weather will cooperate for you."

As she brushed past him, he was enveloped in a light floral breeze—the scent of her. He longed to reach out and pull her back, pull her into his arms. Because it felt as if every time she walked away from him, she was that much closer to walking out the door.

Olivia turned the bathtub faucet on as hot as it could go, and went to lie down while the tub filled.

The bedroom was spacious enough to comfortably house a king-size bed, antique armoire and dresser. There was also a sitting area with a couch, two chintz-covered wingback chairs and a coffee table arranged around a good-size fireplace.

They'd moved into the massive three-story brick house about five years ago. At the time, even though they'd been married two years, they still acted as if they were on their honeymoon—so much in love, dreaming and planning for the future.

Olivia rolled over on her side and hugged a silk throw pillow to her middle.

She couldn't remember when their relationship had taken such a bad turn. Or maybe it wasn't a turn so much as they'd simply lost themselves somewhere along the way.

Funny how they were still fooling even those closest to them. Everyone looked at them in their fancy dream house and thought they had it all—the perfect American dream.

Yet, here she was on Christmas, feeling further away from her husband than she ever had, rather than putting back together the marriage they'd secretly taken apart. Her head throbbed and her heart ached and she closed her eyes for a moment, trying to block a pain that wasn't physical as much as emotional.

Obviously, there was no reasoning with Jamison once he'd made up his mind. But no matter what happened between them, she was bound and determined to have the baby she so desperately wanted.

Which meant since things were so uncertain

between them, she'd better get pregnant as soon as possible, while their friends, families—and Jamison's constituents—still believed they were the happy couple.

The ache of regret deepened as her heart bucked against the thought of her marriage ending. She wasn't trying to be negative, just the realist she'd become over the years she'd been married to Jamison. Another possibility niggled at her. If…no, *when* she got pregnant, it would be an insurance policy for her marriage. After all, when Jamison made his bid for the presidency, he certainly wouldn't win any votes if his constituents learned he'd divorced his wife when she was pregnant.

She sat up stock straight in her bed. She couldn't think that way. Nothing negative, only positive, good thoughts for the baby.

Across the room, a blinking light on the telephone caught her eye. Absently, she got to her feet, padded over to the phone and pressed the button to check the messages.

"Merry Christmas, Olivia and Jamison," a male and female voice rang out in unison. It was her brother, Paul, and his fiancée, Ramona. Hearing their voices brought an involuntary smile to Olivia's lips.

"We missed you last night at Mom and Dad's." Now it was only her big brother's voice on the message. "I just wanted to wish you well. Please call when you get back from the Berkshires."

Even though she and Paul were as different as night and day, they'd always been close. In fact, she was much closer to him than she was to her younger sister, Lisa, and Paul's twin Derek. Her three siblings were career-minded, following in their father's footsteps, running the institute, while Olivia had no interest in the family business. All she'd ever wanted to be was a supportive wife and good mother—to invest in a family of her own. She wasn't unambitious—making their home and supporting Jamison in his career made her happy.

Or at least that's what had made her happy once upon a time.

Now, the only way she could recapture that contentment was to have a baby. To accomplish that, she needed to talk to her doctor, Chance Demetrios, as soon as possible.

As the medical director at the Armstrong Institute, Paul would know Chance's schedule. Plus, hearing Paul's voice would be like an infusion of sunshine, and the voice of reason, to boot. While she couldn't confide in him about her marital woes—she couldn't risk trusting *anyone* with that personal information—she *could* trust him with the secret that she'd decided to move ahead with the artificial insemination.

She turned off the tub, then walked back into the bedroom, settled into one of the wingback chairs, and dialed his number with a nervous hand.

Chapter Four

Jamison climbed the stairs toward the master bedroom. It was Christmas, for God's sake. He couldn't let her go to bed mad. He hated that things had digressed to this point. Before he went to bed he had to try and apologize, because the last thing he wanted was to leave for Washington with things like this. They were supposed to be gaining ground in their relationship, not losing it.

As he raised his hand to knock on the door, he thought he heard a voice—Olivia's voice. Was she talking to someone?

Her tone was light and happy—a bit giddy, in

fact—though he couldn't make out what she was saying until he got to the door and heard her say, "I have to see him as soon as possible. If not, I think I'm going to die."

See who?

He resisted the urge to eavesdrop and rapped lightly on the door. It wasn't just the way Olivia flinched when she turned and saw him standing there, or the way she stiffened when he walked in, but it was the way her voice changed that gave him pause.

"I have to go," she said. "I'll talk to you soon." With that, she abruptly ended the call.

They looked at each other for a moment. When it became clear that she wasn't going to offer any information, he asked, "Who was that?"

"Nobody." She spit the word too fast, stood too quickly and crossed to the bed, aimlessly smoothing wrinkles from the comforter.

"Nobody?" His tone was a little sharper than he'd intended, but something was up. She wasn't talking to *nobody.* "It sounded like somebody to me."

She ducked her head, refusing to look him in the eye. He fought the urge to cross to her and take her face in his hands and force her to look at him. He'd never been a suspicious man, but then again, his wife had always been very open and sharing. They'd never harbored secrets. This definitely smelled like a secret.

He heaved an exasperated, full-body sigh that was laced with anger and resentment.

She must have sensed his mood.

"It was Paul." Her words were flat with a terse edge. "He called to wish us a Merry Christmas."

"He called? I didn't hear the phone ring."

She squinted at him, shooting poisonous darts with her eyes. "He and Ramona called earlier and left a message while we were at your mother's house. I returned their call. Any other questions?"

Yes, he had question, such as how she could be so light and giddy one moment and then turn so cold and guarded when he walked into the room. And who was this man she so desperately needed to see?

Jamison knew his wife well enough to sense that something wasn't quite right. Something that stretched beyond the baby issue. Something that she wasn't telling him. Even though he might not get it out of her tonight, he'd find out eventually...one way or another.

At seven o'clock the next morning, Olivia and Jamison sat at the dining room table eating poached eggs on whole wheat toast, which Olivia had prepared. A peace offering after the run-in last night. Actually, it was an olive branch after a reunion that had more closely resembled a train wreck than the rekindling of the relationship they'd both wanted.

She tried to keep her mood light. She shouldn't have been so defensive last night, but she wasn't sure how much he'd heard after surprising her while she was talking to Paul, who'd told her that Chance Demetrios was indeed in town this week. Jamison had walked in as Paul was explaining that Chance had planned to use the week while the institute was closed to catch up on some paperwork. Paul had promised to have Chance call her as soon as possible.

Jamison was quietly subdued this morning, and as each minute passed without him asking questions or flat out telling her what he'd heard, she relaxed a little more, allowing herself to believe that her plan was still securely in place.

She hated keeping secrets from him. Frankly, she wasn't used to doing so and obviously wasn't very good at it—as evidenced by her defensive display last night, when she was tired and emotionally drained.

Now that she was rested, it was sinking in that Jamison's having to return to Washington this morning might actually be a blessing in disguise. With her husband away, she wouldn't have to lie to him about her decision to pursue the in vitro fertilization on her own.

Rather than looking at it as a lie of omission, she chose to think of it in terms of asking for forgiveness later rather than asking for permission right now.

"Breakfast was delicious, as always," Jamison said after he swallowed the last bite. "I'll try to get home by New Year's Eve. I'll call you tonight and let you know how things are shaping up."

Olivia nodded and sipped her herbal tea. "That sounds like a plan."

He smiled at her and reached out and covered her free hand with his. "You do know how much I love you, don't you?"

The earnestness in his voice tugged at Olivia's heart, and when she looked at him, the depth of emotion in his blue eyes nearly took away her breath.

"Yes, Jamison, I do. And I love you, too."

He leaned in, and his lips brushed hers. A whisper of a kiss so unexpected, it made her stiffen and brace her hands against his chest. But then, like sweet ice cream melting in the heat of the sun, she softened and kissed him back, slowly at first.

His mouth tasted of grapefruit juice and coffee and that indefinable flavor that was uniquely him— something for which, she realized suddenly and desperately, she'd been hungering—no, starving—for far too long. She didn't want him to stop. So she slid her arms around his neck and opened her mouth, deepening the kiss, and fisting her hands into his shirt, pulling their bodies closer.

Maybe he'd changed his mind and would stay with her in Boston rather than going back to D.C. The thought made her heart pound. On one level, she relished the feeling of being alive again, having her husband touch her and respond to her touching him back. Yet on a deeper plane, she sought refuge in the shelter of his arms, their kisses healing the hurt they'd both suffered during their time apart.

At that moment, she knew that they would be okay. They had to be. Because there was no alternative. Plain and simple, she simply couldn't imagine life without him. She intended to tell him so by leading him up to the bedroom, but the ringing phone preempted her physical love note.

"That's probably the driver," Jamison whispered. "Wow, he's early." He kissed her again, trailing his lips down her neck, but even that didn't stop the incessant ringing. Finally, holding her, his forehead pressed against hers, he sighed. "I hate it that I have to go. I'm sorry. It's not what I planned." He gathered her hands in his. "Would you mind answering and telling him I'll be right out?"

Olivia answered the phone on the fourth ring, just before it switched over to the answering service.

"Hello?"

"Good morning," said a deep male voice. "May I speak to Olivia, please?"

"This is she."

"It's Chance Demetrios. Your brother, Paul, asked me to call you this morning about setting up another appointment."

Olivia's heart slammed against her breastbone.

She glanced toward the kitchen door for signs of Jamison, then lowered her voice and started walking toward the office where she could close the door and not risk her husband overhearing. "Thank you for calling, Dr. Demetrios, especially since the institute is closed for the holidays."

"It's not a problem. I'm working through the holiday. I noticed that your file indicates that we called and ultimately sent you a letter several months ago asking you to come in for further tests. Did you receive that letter?"

Olivia swallowed a twinge of guilt. "Yes, Dr. Demetrios, I did. For a while, we were thinking of delaying starting our family, but that's no longer the case. We're ready to move ahead."

"Wonderful," said Demetrios. "If you're available, I can see you tomorrow."

"That would be lovely. I must apologize for not following up sooner."

"Well, I was reviewing your file a moment ago and I think I may have some new insight to what is causing your problems."

Olivia's heart leaped. "Does that mean you know how to fix what's wrong with me?"

There was a pause on the other end of the line, and Olivia couldn't tell if that meant the doctor had good news or bad.

"We'll need to run some more tests, but we can do that and talk about it tomorrow when you come in."

After wheeling his bag into the living room, Jamison came back into the kitchen to kiss his wife goodbye. She wasn't there.

"Olivia," he called. "I have to go, the car's waiting."

No answer.

He fought back a surge of impatience. *Calm down.* Things had finally started getting back on track. He didn't want to ruin it now. But where had she disappeared to, knowing that he had to leave?

Rather than stew over it, Jamison decided to signal to the driver that he'd be out in a moment. Maybe by that time Olivia would reappear.

Yet when he opened the front door and looked out into the impossibly sunny cold morning to busy

Commonwealth Avenue, the car wasn't there. Perplexed, he stepped back inside and closed the door. Then, as if driven by a sixth sense, he followed his intuition down the hall to the study. He stopped outside the door when he heard Olivia talking in hushed tones.

"That sounds absolutely perfect," she said. "But may I call you back? I can't really talk right now."

At that moment, the doorbell rang. The car, no doubt. Jamison walked soundlessly down the hall so that Olivia wouldn't see him and ducked back into the living room.

When she finally joined him a moment later, he patted his pockets. "I think I forgot something. Would you tell the driver I'll be right out?"

"Sure."

Jamison went into the spare bedroom where he'd spent the past two nights, picked up the phone extension, and pressed the record for the caller ID log.

The name that appeared was Chance Demetrios. The doctor that she'd seen only once—or at least only one time that he was aware of.

All sorts of questions raced through his mind: Why was he calling her now? Was this the man who, last night, she'd sounded so anxious to see?

Feeling threatened on a number of levels, when he got to the front door, Jamison pulled Olivia into a tight embrace—and again he kissed her as if he really meant it.

So what if he was being territorial. He had good reason. He loved her and he couldn't stand the thought of her keeping secrets from him or worse yet, turning to another man when she should be confiding in him. He'd given her too much space. Been too busy. Too wrapped up in work, his thoughts focused firmly on the future presidential election. Even so, he still hoped she'd turn to him before she ran to someone else. Even if the man was her doctor.

It was a shame it took something like this to remind him that they belonged together.

His lips found her earlobe, her jaw, her neck and he trailed possessive kisses down to her collarbone. He knew he had to stop. The driver was waiting and if he didn't stop now, he'd sweep his wife up in his arms and take her upstairs to their bed and prove exactly how much he loved her, like he should've done the minute he got home on Christmas Eve.

"Jamison, you'd better go," she said breathlessly, breaking the contact.

She slid her hands from his shoulders down his arms and took his hands in hers.

There they stood, face-to-face, eye-to-eye—and the words just slipped out.

"Who was on the phone?"

Just like that, her face shuttered again, closing him out. Her eyes held the mysterious darkness of kept secrets.

"No one." She stepped away from him, opened the front door. The cold winter wind blew in, cutting him down to the core of his body.

"Well, I heard the phone ring and it wasn't the driver. Was it a wrong number? Your sister? The Salvation Army?"

She looked at him as if he was crazy. For a desperate, furious moment he felt he was stark, raving mad.

"None of the above," she insisted. "You're going to miss your flight if you don't go."

He looked at her closely. "You're keeping something from me."

"No, I'm not."

The protest came a little too quickly and fervently. The shuttered look on her face made it difficult for him to read her. That's why he was so taken aback when she reached up and cupped his jaw in her hand.

"I love you, Jamison. You just have to trust me, okay?"

Trust her? When she's obviously keeping something from me? Even so—

"I love you, too. Please don't ever forget it, okay?"

He gave her one last hug before he walked down the red brick steps and got into the car. As soon as the vehicle pulled away, he took out his BlackBerry and dialed Cameron McInerney, his aide.

"Good morning, Cameron. I need you to do a background check on a Dr. Chance Demetrios of Boston. Hire a P.I. if you need to. I want to know everything about this guy, every move he makes."

Jamison hung up the phone and slid it into the breast pocket of his coat. He stared out the window at the tall buildings of downtown Boston. It was his home, but this morning it felt so strange.

Soon enough he'd know if Dr. Demetrios was, indeed, *no one,* as Liv claimed…or if he was someone that Jamison needed to be concerned about.

Either way, he intended to discover exactly what his wife was keeping from him.

Chapter Five

The next day Olivia arrived at the institute early so that she could thank Paul for arranging her appointment with Chance Demetrios. True to form, he was back at work even though the institute was closed for the holidays for the rest of the week.

She rapped on his door. When he looked up, she wriggled her fingers at him.

"Hello, stranger," he said, rising from his desk and walking to meet her. He pulled her into a rib-crushing bear hug. When he let her go, he asked, "Where's Jamison?"

Olivia donned her best *happy wife* smile.

"He had to go back to D.C. yesterday." She shrugged. "I was disappointed, but I understand that duty calls. He hated to disrupt our plans. He's coming back next week, though."

When Paul started nodding, she realized she was babbling and stopped.

"So how are you?" he asked.

"I'm doing fine. I can't tell you how much I appreciate your help getting me an appointment with Dr. Demetrios today."

He waved it off. "Oh, it was nothing. Both Chance and I are here this week. So I figured it would be a good opportunity to get you in. Otherwise, he's pretty booked. Business is booming."

Paul smiled proudly as he motioned her to sit down. Her brother was the consummate workaholic. Even so, he used to be worse before his fiancée, Ramona Tate, came into his life. Before they met, he rarely took a day off. Ramona had been good for him in that respect, and it was wonderful to see him so happy. Not only that, her brother's love story was encouraging. His and Ramona's relationship had grown out of the worst sort of adversity when Paul's twin, Derek, had hired her without consulting either Paul or their sister, Lisa. Plus, Derek did not do a thorough background check. If he had, he would have discovered that Ramona was an investigative reporter intent on going undercover to write an unflattering exposé on the institute. Olivia was the only one of Gerald Armstrong's kids who had opted out of the family business. She just wasn't wired for business the way her brothers and sister were.

It was times like this that she was glad she'd followed her own path.

Olivia and her siblings had made their father proud by graduating from Harvard. But that's where the similarities ended. Instead of studying business and medicine, Olivia had majored in literature and minored in ballet. In fact, in her sophomore year she'd had the great honor of being tapped as one of Harvard Ballet's youngest assistant artistic directors. She'd spent her entire stint at Harvard performing with the company in which she'd taken such pride.

Even so, as her relationship with Jamison had become more serious, it had eventually eclipsed her love of dance and she'd given it up for marriage and a family of her own.

Despite her traditional values, she'd always danced to her own tune. Perhaps that was why she was having such a hard time letting Jamison dictate when they'd have children.

The situation with Ramona had caused a lot of family strain, and Olivia took heart in this perfect example of love conquering all. If her brother's relationship could come up against such strife and survive, surely Jamison could forgive her extreme measures of starting their family. Because despite her husband's belief otherwise, there was never a perfect time to have a baby. She was sure Jamison would understand that, once he held his child in his arms.

When Olivia got to Dr. Demetrios's office, she was surprised when he asked her to come in and sit down rather than having her change into a gown and wait for him in one of the examination rooms.

She sat in a leather-upholstered chair across from his desk, clenching her hands, nervous and giddy at the same time.

"I'm glad you decided to come in, Mrs. Mallory."

He was a handsome man, and Olivia was surprised that a woman hadn't snatched him up by now. Her mind did a quick inventory of single friends who might a good match for him. The single list grew shorter every year. Not surprising, since Olivia and most of her friends were now happily married.

Happily married.

The thought made Olivia shift in her seat as she ignored the nagging voice that asked what she was doing here alone if she was *happily married.*

"Please call me Olivia."

He smiled at her and pushed a wisp of dark hair off his forehead. "Certainly, Olivia."

He cleared his throat and for the flash of a second, she noticed a hint of something in his chocolate brown eyes that didn't bode well.

She tightened the grip on her hands, digging her fingernails into her palms.

"I don't quite know how to say this other than to come right out and say it, but your symptoms indicate that you might be having trouble conceiving because it's possible your body is going through early onset menopause."

His words rang in her ears.

"Menopause?" she heard herself utter. "But I'm only twenty-nine years old, Doctor. How can that be possible?"

He raked a hand across his handsome face as if this wasn't easy for him. "It's rare, but it does happen. The blood tests I did last time showed low levels of estradiol, which indicates your ovaries are starting to fail."

"You've known this for two months and you didn't tell me?" she asked as a burning salty sting in the back of her throat brought tears to her eyes and nearly choked her.

"I'm deeply sorry," he said. "I did try to contact you. My nurse even sent you a letter asking you to follow up with me, but you didn't respond. Because of patient confidentiality laws, I couldn't leave a more detailed message."

She'd received the vague letter that had asked her to set a follow-up appointment to discuss her test results. She'd thought it meant that he wanted to discuss which procedure they'd try next time and she hadn't followed through because of the trial separation.

How foolish she'd been thinking she had all the time in the world, that she could let nearly three months go by without making any effort to conceive. At least this further justified her being here today— her not mentioning to Jamison the meeting with Dr. Demetrios and making the decision to move ahead— all on her own.

"Do my brothers and sister know about this?" she asked. If they knew and hadn't told her she might never be able to forgive them.

"No, they don't know. Again, that's because of confidentiality laws."

Olivia swiped at a tear and Chance nudged a box of tissue toward her.

"But before, you said there was a slim chance that I could conceive."

"I'm sorry. That was before I received the test results."

Olivia swiped at the tears streaming down her face. It certainly wasn't the news she wanted to hear, especially with Jamison being so far away… She had to be strong and hear him out. One step at a time. She'd do everything he said she had to do to reverse this condition and then maybe that would be the answer to Jamison's and her fertility problems.

"As I'm sure you can understand, this comes as a total and complete shock, but I'm willing to do whatever needs to be done to reverse the situation. Please tell me, what's caused this and most importantly, what can we do to correct it?"

Chance shifted in his chair, his handsome face looking pained.

"It's hard to pin down the exact reason this has occurred, especially since there isn't a family history of it. But I do have to speculate that your low body weight may have been a contributor. Have you always been this thin, Olivia?"

Her weight had always been a sensitive subject. A war she'd battled in much the same way as some people battled excess weight. She'd always been naturally thin, but as a ballerina she was encouraged to be even thinner. *The thinner the better.* But even though ballet had been a big part of her life before she'd met Jamison, she would've given it up and gotten downright plump if she'd known her low weight was causing such harm.

Again, she choked back a rush of tears. "But my other question, Dr. Demetrios, is what do I have to do to reverse this condition?"

He looked stricken and Olivia knew what he was going to say before he said it. Even so, as the words, "I'm sorry, early onset menopause isn't reversible," spilled out of his mouth, Olivia's vision went white-hot and fuzzy around the edges. The walls were closing in—she had to get out of that office.

The next thing she knew, she found herself in the parking lot, huddled against the biting cold December wind, sobbing uncontrollably and fumbling in her purse for her keys.

As she pulled them out, Chance was standing beside her saying something about not letting her drive when she was so upset, but the words were so jumbled she couldn't quite be sure.

When he touched her arm, she nearly crumpled and fell into a heap of sobs and tears right there in the parking lot. Dr. Demetrios caught her in the nick of time and held her as she sobbed. But the feel of his strong arms around her made her long for Jamison. She jerked away from him, clicked the car door remote and tried to slide her slight frame into the driver's seat. Chance caught her arm and kept her from doing so.

"Olivia, you're too upset to drive." He'd chased after her without a jacket and he shivered against the cold. "Please come back inside until you can get a hold of yourself. It's cold out here and you really have no business driving right now."

Get a hold of myself?

She glared at him. He had just shattered her world with a single revelation. How was she supposed to *get a hold of herself* when she no longer had a foundation to stand on?

"I can't go back in there," she said through gritted teeth. "I'm not ready to tell my family about…" She took a deep breath. "About my condition. Not until I've had a chance to process it myself and discuss it with my husband."

Chance nodded.

"I understand. But I still can't let you drive right now. Let's walk over to the Coach House Diner just up the street. Then I'll take you home. We could get some coffee at the diner—"

"I don't drink coffee," she snapped, and immediately regretted it. Especially since he didn't bristle back at her. He remained calm, unfazed. His dark eyes were patient and kind.

"I'm sorry, Dr. Demetrios. It's just that…" Instinctively, almost protectively, she laced her hands over her belly.

He smiled his patient smile and nodded to let her know he understood.

"No apology necessary. You've received shattering news. What kind of a doctor would I be if I didn't cut you some slack? But as I said, I'd still like to discuss your options."

"I have options? The prognosis sounded pretty final."

"There are possibilities. I don't want to falsely raise your hopes, but this isn't the end of the line. If you'd prefer not to come back inside, let's go to the diner."

Olivia sucked in a breath. She was feeling markedly stronger now.

"I suppose I could go back to your office."

"Good, I'd put on a fresh pot of coffee just before you arrived and I'm dying for a cup. I'll steep you a cup of herbal tea and we'll talk."

Her options were slim.

Chance drew more blood and said he'd have to send it out to be analyzed to see if her ovaries were still producing eggs. If they were, he advised that they harvest as many as possible for future in vitro procedures because, according to the files, they'd used up the rest of her harvested eggs in the last procedure. There was still plenty of Jamison's frozen sperm—and more where that came from—but for a future procedure to be possible, they'd need more from her.

If not, their best chance at a family was adoption.

The thought made her feel queasy. Not so much the thought of giving someone else's child a home as much as the implications that it meant she would be barren.

Either way, Chance promised to put a rush on the lab and set an appointment for her at nine o'clock in the morning on December 31.

New Years Eve.

On the last night of the year she would learn her fate. The last night. Her last chance.

Olivia left Chance's office with a heavy heart, but a firm resolve to think positive. Chance had told her to discuss the options with Jamison—as if that was going to happen—at least not in the near future, and that made things all the worse.

As she started to tear up again, she reminded herself firmly that it wasn't over until it was over. Right now, she just had to believe the best would happen.

She didn't want to see anyone as she was leaving. When she left Chance's office, she'd mustered every ounce of calm self-control she possessed so that he wouldn't commit her to the psych ward or make her go to the Coach House Diner. Not that there was anything wrong with the diner. She'd been there on several occasions, but today it was the last place she wanted to be. Rather than sobbing her heart out in public, she wanted to be in her own house, surrounded by familiarity and the things she loved. Maybe she'd bake some bread today. She could take it to the Children's Home tomorrow. She was on the board of directors and was due for a visit.

Her shoes echoed loudly on the cold, barren hallway floors of the institute, and there was no hiding when she rounded the corner and came face-to-face with her brother Derek.

"Olivia? What are you doing here?" Derek was Paul's twin, but the two couldn't be more different if they came from different mothers. Where Paul was warm and personable, Derek was steely and calculating.

Olivia's shaking hand fluttered to her face and she swiped at her eyes. She must look a mess.

She opened her mouth to answer him, but instead, she choked on a sob.

"Livie, what's wrong?" Derek demanded. The change in him was instant. One second he was the cold professional sporting his "work face," the next he was big brother to the rescue. When he switched into that mode, Olivia automatically regressed into the role of little sister.

The next thing she new, Derek had whisked her down the hall and into his office. Behind closed doors, she found herself blubbering and confiding in him, sister to brother, divulging the bleak prognosis Chance had just leveled and confessing her marital woes.

Even though she wasn't particularly close to Derek, he always managed to get her to open up whether she wanted to or not. He had a way of getting her to confess things she didn't even share with her closest friends. Maybe it was because they were a bit removed from each other, therefore there was no risk of disappointing him or being judged.

"Jamison doesn't even know I'm here today."

Derek regarded her with a frown from across the desk, his eagle eyes sharp and piercing.

"Don't be so hard on yourself, Liv. Based on what you've told me, his not knowing might be the best thing. He wants you to wait to get pregnant, but obviously waiting might not be an option and if he won't even discuss it…well, that gives you free rein to take matters into your own hands. Who is he to dictate what you can and can't do with your body?"

Olivia felt sheepish. "Well, he is my husband."

Derek slapped the desk. "I know that, but he doesn't own you. If you want a kid, then you should have a kid. Especially you. If we were talking about Lisa, I'd be singing another tune, but you were born to be a mother."

Heat spread across Olivia's face and she felt every bit the old-fashioned, 1950s housewife. Their sister, Lisa, ran with the big boys. Even though she was the baby of the family, she had no trouble matching her brothers move for move.

"I mean if Demetrios is right—and I'd stake my own reputation on him—then you have no time to waste."

Olivia chewed on her French manicured index fingernail, hoping to stave off another wave of tears before she could speak. Once she'd composed herself, she said, "Going on what Dr. Demetrios said, if we're not able to harvest my eggs, this is all a moot point. So please don't hold it against Jamison, Derek."

Derek frowned. "I thought we'd stored your eggs?"

Olivia shook her head. "We used them up in the last in vitro attempt."

Derek squinted at her, a look that concerned her because when he pulled that expression he'd usually latched on to an idea that wasn't always conventional. Then he turned to his computer and started tap-tapping on the keys.

"What are you doing?"

He didn't answer her, but instead donned a pair of reading glasses and focused intently on his computer screen. A moment later, he said, "I've pulled up your file. I see we still have plenty of Jamison's tadpoles frozen away. Reports indicate that they're healthy and viable."

Olivia shifted in her seat. "Yes, but they're no good if I can't bring my half to the table."

"Not necessarily."

Derek pursed his lips and pinned her with his intense gaze. He had his work face on again and was firmly back in professional mode. But she recognized something else in his expression.

Olivia knew from experience that her brother's line between right and unethical was sometimes a little blurred. She had a feeling that what he was about to say next might be a little speculative.

Even so, she heard herself asking, "What do you mean?"

Derek didn't answer immediately. He paused as if giving her a chance to retract her question and get away. But she sat there as if bolted to the seat.

Derek folded his hands and rested them on his desk. Then he leaned in.

"How would you feel about using donor eggs?"

Olivia cocked her head to the side, "I couldn't do that."

Derek moistened his lips. His eyes darted from side to side. Then he pinned her with his steely gaze.

"Why not? Demetrios could fertilize a donor egg

with Jamison's sperm and the zygote could be implanted in you to carry it to term. Voilà! You'd have your baby. Problem solved."

Olivia pulled back as if her brother had offered her poison.

"Derek, it wouldn't be *my* baby."

"Olivia—" his tone mocked her "—no one outside this room has to know."

"Chance Demetrios would know. Do you remember me telling you that we were just talking about how my biological cupboard is bare?"

Derek rolled his eyes.

"Wonder boy doesn't know *everything* that goes on around this place. You have no idea the secrets we keep in here. There's a whole section of classified files to which only a select few have access."

His maniacal expression made her uncomfortable, and for a moment she wondered if he'd gone a little mad.

"If I tell Demetrios we have a special *emergency* stash of your eggs, he'll believe me."

Olivia was chewing on her fingernail again. "But why would you have a special emergency stash of my eggs? It doesn't make sense."

He looked at her as if she was insufferably dense. "Because, Olivia, you are likely going to be the first lady of our country, and that makes you pretty special. And if, perchance, there was an emergency—such as the one you find yourself in today—the eggs would be available to you. Understand?"

No, she didn't understand, because what he was suggesting sounded reprehensible. She looked at him as if in his face she could find the piece of the puzzle she was obviously missing—something to help her understand how this devious scheme could be okay.

"You're suggesting that I not include Jamison in this decision?"

Derek shrugged a single shoulder, as if he were too annoyed to expend the energy to raise and lower both.

"Go ahead and tell him if you think he'll go for it."

Of course Jamison would never go along with this plan. She felt dishonest enough even being here behind her husband's back. But even talking about getting impregnated with a child that wouldn't be fully, biologically, theirs and trying to pass it off as theirs… This…if she did *this*…well, she wouldn't be able to look her husband in the eye, much less live with herself.

She was just about ready to say *Thanks, but no thanks* when Derek said, "Livie, don't look at me like I'm a monster. The only reason I'm suggesting this is because you desperately want a child and it could very well save your troubled marriage."

His words hit like a painful punch to the gut.

"I know it's a lot to think about, but keep an open mind. I'm going to go ahead and relabel the eggs— they're all from the same woman and according to the file she even has your coloring—just in case your New Year's Eve test results don't come back the way you'd hoped."

As much as she hated to admit it, Derek had a point. What if the test results proved that she'd waited too long? What if using donor eggs was her only option?

Jamison would never agree to it.

But she'd already come this far.

What if what Jamison didn't know was the only thing that could save their marriage?

She certainly had a lot to think about before she dismissed this final option.

Chapter Six

Before heading off to dinner, Jamison excused himself from the delegation of Middle Eastern dignitaries and ducked inside his office to call Olivia.

After living apart for more than two months then seeing her for two days, he didn't think he could go four more days without her.

He missed her that much.

So when the group started making noises about staying in D.C. through the New Year, Jamison had promptly told them he'd be happy to leave them in the capable hands of his aide, Cameron McInerney, but he wouldn't be in town.

The dignitaries protested but Jamison simply joked that if he left his wife at home alone on New Year's Eve he'd have to spend the rest of the year making it up to her.

When the visiting sheikh shared his philosophy that women should never dictate a man's actions— especially when it interfered with business— Jamison retorted respectfully, "Obviously, you've never met my wife."

And he meant it as a sincere compliment.

It wasn't that Jamison was heading home out of obligation. Not this time. As he'd said goodbye to Olivia earlier in the week, something had shifted. Right now, he longed to see his wife. He longed to wipe the slate clean. Longed to start off the New Year right.

With Olivia in his arms.

Somewhere recently he'd heard the idiom "a happy wife makes for a happy life." It made so much sense. If she was happy, he wouldn't have to worry about her seeking comfort in another man's arms. With Olivia as his top priority all his plans would fall into place: his congressional work, his eventual bid for the White House (because what would it mean without Olivia by his side?) and their family.

He'd been thinking and, depending on how things were between them this next week, maybe they should start trying again.

That's why he needed to call her right now.

She answered on the second ring.

"Hello?"

"Hi, Liv, it's me."

She paused a few beats too long.

"Jamison. Is everything okay?"

"Yes. Everything's fine. I was thinking about you and wanted to call."

"Oh, I see. That's very sweet."

She sounded a little distant and formal. He wanted so badly to pull her into his arms and show her that everything was going to be okay.

"I'm also calling for another reason," he said.

"What?" She sounded wary. "You're not calling to tell me you can't make it home for New Year's Eve, are you?"

"Don't worry," he said, eager to put her mind at rest. "Actually, I'm calling to find out what your plans are on New Year's Eve."

She was silent on the other end of the line, and for a moment, he wondered if they'd lost their telephone connection.

"Olivia, are you there?"

"Yes. I'm here." She still sounded guarded and distant. "What do you mean?"

He sat down behind his desk and picked up a photo of her. The juxtaposition of seeing her beautiful face smiling at him from the frame and hearing her sound so remote on the line made his heart ache.

"I'm calling to ask you out on a date. This is my feeble attempt at being romantic." He chuckled, then his voice got serious. "After being apart for so long, I didn't want to be presumptuous and assume you'd be waiting for me."

"Thank you, Jamison. But of course, I wouldn't make plans without you."

Her saying that made him smile.

"I'll be home late afternoon and we can do whatever you want. We can go out and paint the town or we can order in and have a nice quiet evening alone together." He hesitated. "Maybe we could spend the whole night in bed and start talking about…babies?"

"Oh, Jamison." Her voice caught on his name. "As long as we're together. That's all that matters."

He let out a breath of relief. Now that the world had finally righted itself again, it almost felt as if it could start spinning in the right direction.

"Even though Christmas didn't go as planned, seeing you again after being apart for so long made me realize how much I love you. It also made me realize that even though I couldn't admit it to myself until now, I've been afraid to start our family. Growing up in a broken home—knowing how my father's leaving affected my mother and brothers, seeing what the hormones did to you, what the experience did to us, I guess I wasn't as prepared as I thought I was. But knowing how important having a baby is to you… Let's just not let it change *us,* okay?"

Olivia held the phone for a moment, although their call had ended, using it as a touchstone. In the span of mere seconds, she'd gone from being petrified that Jamison was calling to cancel their plans yet again to through-the-ceiling joy after hearing Jamison say he was ready to start trying for a baby again. That bipolar moment had finally evened out, settling somewhere in the middle, tempered by the guilty secret she was keeping from her husband. The only way she could fix this was to tell him that she'd already started seeing the doctor again without him.

But she couldn't tell him just yet.

Not when he'd just come around. After fearing a baby would change their relationship, he'd need more time for the baby idea to gel before she told him the truth—that she'd moved forward without him.

Not to mention that, first, she needed to hear her final prognosis.

The next day, Jamison didn't pick up the call from Cameron. He let it go to voice mail along with the other two-dozen voice mails McInerney had left that day. It was their routine, of sorts. Anything that could wait went to voice mail to be checked at designated times during the day. But when something needed urgent attention, Cameron followed up with a 911 text.

The 911 came in at 2:22, the afternoon after he'd talked to Olivia to make plans for New Year's Eve. The text read: Have received the background check on Dr. Chance Demetrios. Results require your immediate attention.

Chance Demetrios?

He'd been so busy, he'd put Demetrios out of his mind. Besides, it was just a momentary lapse of reasoning. He trusted his wife. So the message sent a jolt of anxiety through him. Jamison excused himself from the meeting, citing urgent business.

What McInerney had waiting for him when he got back to the office made the anxiety he'd felt earlier seem like a warm bath: photos shot outside the Armstrong Institute. Photos of Olivia in the arms of Chance Demetrios.

Jamison wanted to punch a wall. He wanted to hop on a plane and punch Demetrios. He wanted to look his wife in the eyes and ask, *"Why?"*

He would ask her, all right. When he saw her in three days. In the meantime, though, he couldn't talk to her. He needed to keep his distance, keep his cool, so that he didn't do something he'd regret. Also, if he heard her voice there would be no way he'd be able to keep this to himself. And he needed to see her eyes when he asked her about it.

How the hell was he going to hold this inside for three days?

He ran through the options in his mind. He could cancel his meetings, saying he had a family emergency to attend to.

No, if in fact Olivia was carrying on with Demetrios…though his heart still couldn't reconcile her betraying him like that—not his Olivia. No, if he left it might draw attention to the situation, and he had to do everything he could to keep this under wraps.

As anger simmered, he felt like a ticking time bomb that he hoped wouldn't explode before he gave Olivia a chance to explain.

Chapter Seven

Dressed in a cobalt-blue suit and pearls, Olivia drove across the Salt-and-Pepper Bridge, which stretched over the Charles River, connecting Boston with Cambridge.

The formal name of the bridge was actually the Longfellow, but locals had dubbed it "Salt-and-Pepper" because the structure's central towers resembled salt-and-pepper shakers.

The Children's Home was located just across the river, not too far from the Massachusetts Institute of Technology. Olivia had served on the Children's Home board since the year she and Jamison had married. Before she'd been appointed to the Children's Home board of directors, she'd volunteered there when she was in college and knew it was such a worthy organization that it deserved as much support as it could get.

In the nearly ten years that she'd been involved, Olivia had been instrumental in helping Pam Wilson, the executive director of The Children's Home, write grants, raise funds and secure other means of political and community support for the Home.

Other times, she filled in where they needed her. Whether it was answering the phone, taking the kids shopping for school supplies, or rolling up her sleeves and scrubbing toilets when the janitorial service didn't show, she did what she could. Her favorite task was baking dozens of delicious cookies for the kids to take to school for birthday celebrations or bake sales, or sometimes the cookies were simply for them to enjoy as a special treat.

Olivia's goal as president of the board was to give the children—many of whom were here because of abuse, neglect or tragedy—as good a childhood as possible. Sometimes that meant singing songs and reading stories. Other times it meant getting her hands dirty. But she was game for whatever the kids needed, because she was passionate about the Children's Home and the kids they served.

It was never easy, though, when a new resident arrived. Usually the child was scared and skittish, oftentimes suffering emotional trauma after being displaced. Today, Pam needed all hands on deck because not one, but two little boys were arriving.

Danny and Kevin Kelso had lost both of their parents in a nightmarish accident on the day after Christmas. The parents were coming home from a party and were hit head-on by a drunk driver. The boys had been home asleep in their beds, in the care of a babysitter.

Since the boys had no living relatives, Boston's Department of Children and Families had prevailed upon Pam to take the boys so that they could stay together. The home really didn't have room, but when Pam called Olivia for special dispensation, Olivia had agreed that the boys should stay together at all costs—even if she had to bring them to her house until the Home could make a place for them.

Keeping them together seemed extra important since three-year-old Danny had recently been diagnosed with autism.

Little had she known when she'd decided to distract herself with baking bread and cookies, that the home would be in need of fare to welcome the new charges.

There was nothing like good, homemade sugar and

chocolate chunk cookies to make a child feel welcome.

Olivia had promised Pam that she'd be there to help, because even under the best circumstances, welcoming a new resident wasn't easy. Given the younger Kelso boy's situation, today was sure to be doubly challenging.

Shortly after nine o'clock, Olivia arrived at the Georgian-style mansion that housed the Children's Home. The old home once belonged to the charity's founder, who left it to the organization in trust to be used for kids left homeless or orphaned by abuse, neglect or tragedy. Olivia parked around back by the carriage house, which served as the nonprofit's offices, and let herself in the kitchen door. She set the bread and cookies on the counter and went in search of Pam, whom she found in the great room.

"Olivia, thank you so much for coming in today," Pam said. "It seems like a lot to ask during the holidays."

Olivia shook her head. "I'm happy to do it. Besides, Jamison had to go back to D.C. and he won't be back until New Year's Eve."

"Big plans?" Pam asked.

Olivia blushed. "We're staying in and having a nice romantic evening—alone, for a change."

Over the years, Pam had become a friend—and

someone to whom in the beginning, Olivia had confided in when she and Jamison had decided to start trying to get pregnant. But after it became clear that pregnancy wouldn't come easily—and then with the ensuing bumps in their marriage—Olivia had become a bit more guarded.

"Really?" Pam arched a brow, her blue eyes shining. "Anything you'd care to share?"

For a moment, Olivia was tempted to tell her everything—well, almost everything—not about Derek's bizarre suggestion that Olivia try to pass off another woman's child as her own. Because essentially that's what it would amount to if she allowed Chance to implant another woman's egg in her body.

The thought made her shudder, and that brought her to her senses. Despite how good it would feel to confide in a friend right now, until she heard the New Year's Eve prognosis, she needed to keep everything to herself.

"Oh, nothing exciting, but you know I'll tell you as soon as there's news."

Just then the door opened and two of the saddest little boys Olivia had ever seen walked in hand in hand. Both had mops of glossy dark hair and large, haunted brown eyes.

The larger of the two stood slightly in front of his younger brother, in a protective stance.

Karen Cunningham from DCF stood behind them. "Good morning, I have a very special delivery for you. This is Kevin." She gestured to the older brother. "And this little guy is Danny."

"Hello, boys. I'm Pam, and this is Mrs. Mallory. We want you to know you are very welcome here."

The boys gaped at her but remained silent.

"You make yourselves right at home," Pam said. "Mrs. Mallory is here for you while Mrs. Cunningham and I go take care of some paperwork."

Olivia knelt in front of the boys.

"Hi, guys. Now, tell me again, which one of you is Kevin and which one is Danny?"

"I'm Kevin," said the older brother. "I'm seven years old."

Olivia offered her hand to the boy. "Hi, Kevin. You can call me Olivia, if you'd like."

Kevin shook her hand like a little man, much too grown up for his age.

"He's Danny, he doesn't talk because he's special."

"Hi, Danny." She offered her hand to the smaller boy just as she'd done for the older brother, but he didn't take it. Instead, he started rocking back and forth, paying no attention to Olivia.

"He's sad because our mommy and daddy got killed in a real bad car wreck."

Kevin's lower lip quivered and for a moment Olivia

thought he might cry. She was surprised when he didn't.

She took his hand in hers again. "Kevin, it's okay to cry. I know you must be very sad, too. Just like Danny is."

Still holding Olivia's hand, Kevin focused on a spot somewhere over her shoulder and didn't let down his guard.

Olivia squeezed his hand. "Well, I want you to know I think you're very brave, but even the bravest men in the world cry sometimes. And that's okay."

Suddenly, Danny stepped forward, reached and touched Olivia's pearl necklace.

"Duck!" said Danny.

Kevin grabbed his brother's hand and held it.

"Don't touch, Danny."

"Duck!" Danny repeated.

Olivia gazed down into his little upturned face and smiled. She pointed at her necklace. "These are pearls, Danny."

Kevin shook his head. "It doesn't matter how many times you tell him. He's still going to call it a duck, because that's what he thinks it is. I told you, he's *special* and he doesn't know any better."

Olivia nodded and gave Kevin a conspiratorial wink. "That's good to know. If he wants to call it a duck, then this can be my…duck. Say, Kevin, do you and Danny like cookies? I just made some. They're in the kitchen. Why don't we go get some?"

Kevin's face shuttered again.

"My mommy doesn't let us eat cookies between meals."

His little bottom lip trembled again, but he raised his chin a notch and refocused on his spot over Olivia's shoulder.

Her heart was breaking for these two sweet boys. She was about to tell Kevin that she was sure his mother wouldn't mind just this once, and praise him for following her rules, when Danny's hand snaked out again and grabbed a hold of Olivia's necklace.

"Duck!" he yelled, and gave them a firm yank.

His grasp was far stronger than she might have imagined because the necklace broke. If not for the individual knots between each pearl, the necklace might have scattered all over the floor. Instead, the broken strand held together in a limp line trailing down Danny's arm.

"Danny! No!" reprimanded Kevin.

He turned to Olivia. "I'm sorry. I'm really, really sorry. Please don't be mad at him. Please—"

With that, his voice broke and he dissolved into a heap of full-body sobs.

Reflexively, Olivia gathered him in her arms and held him while he cried on the shoulder of her blue suit.

Rubbing his back, she said, "I'm not mad. It was just a silly old duck anyway. I can get it fixed later."

Pam and Karen rushed in to see what all the commotion was about, but Olivia waved them away. She was no expert, but instincts told her that now that Kevin was finally letting down his guard, now that he was finally allowing himself to feel his loss, the last thing he needed was an audience gawking at him.

As he continued to sob on her shoulder, she mouthed to them, *It's okay. He'll be fine.* Hesitant, they retreated to Pam's office, throwing concerned glances Olivia's way as she rubbed the boy's back in slow, circular motions.

Of all people, she understood the loss he was grappling with—only in reverse. She'd had a hard time processing the sense of loss she felt, not being able to get pregnant. The loss—or empty spot—in her life that Jamison's and her child was supposed to occupy. It felt like a gaping hole in the place where her heart beat. Some days she wanted to sob on someone's shoulder, too, but instead, like Kevin, she'd chosen the stoic path.

She pulled the weeping boy closer. Holding him, for the first time ever, she felt that gaping hole begin to close.

"Duck?" Danny murmured.

"Duck," she whispered, smiling at him through her own unshed tears.

Once the boys were settled in the dining room at the table enjoying milk and cookies with the other Children's Home residents, Olivia and Pam retreated into Pam's office.

Pam slid in behind her desk and Olivia claimed the chair facing it.

"Here's the report from Danny's doctor." She nudged a slim stack of papers across her desk toward Olivia. "Karen filled me in on Danny's condition. Apparently, he was recently diagnosed with Autism Spectrum Disorder, and he had just started speech and behavior therapy before the holidays."

Olivia skimmed the report. "So, he's not enrolled in school yet?"

Pam shook her head. "He just turned three in November and I believe they were waiting until after the first of the year to enroll him in a public school exceptional educational program. But with all that's happened, we're going to have to talk to his doctor and see what he suggests is the best course of action. The little guy has had so much to digest, losing his parents and all, that I'm not certain starting him in a new program right away will be the best thing."

The fifteen other kids who lived at the Children's Home were all in school. That meant Danny would need someone to look after him during the day. Pam would have to bring in one of the part-time employees to help out. It would further tax the organization's already stretched budget.

"I can come in a couple of days a week to help out," Olivia offered. She wished she could offer more—for one quick, insane moment, she was about ready to offer for Danny and Kevin to come live with her. But it was an irrational thought. Completely emotional and off the cuff. With her steady lineup of doctor's appointments, she'd be lucky to be able to give Pam two solid days of help per week.

Her heart was breaking for the boys. She wanted to ease their grief and give them…a home. But what would happen once her baby arrived? Reflexively, she slid a hand over her stomach.

She couldn't adopt them. No, it was best to let the boys get settled into their new home. That was the right thing to do.

Even so, why did leaving them here feel completely wrong?

Chapter Eight

Three days later, Olivia awoke early and placed yet another call to Jamison. It was New Year's Eve and she'd been trying to reach him for the past two days. All the calls went to voice mail, and he had yet to return a single call.

As she'd done at least a dozen times already, she left yet another message.

"Jamison, it's *me*. I don't understand why you're not calling me back. I'm worried."

What she didn't say, despite the urge, was that it was six o'clock in the morning and she couldn't reach him at home, the office or on his cell.

What was with this sudden change in him? Just a few days ago, everything seemed so good. Now here she was, wondering not only if her husband was letting business preempt their plans, but also if maybe he was going to stand her up altogether.

No. He wouldn't do that. Would he?

In the months that they'd been separated, he'd never gone more than a day without calling her. And he'd certainly never let her calls go unanswered. She didn't understand the sudden change in him, which sent her into another spiral of panic that maybe something was wrong.

She had no choice but to call McInerney to make sure Jamison was okay. She got his voice mail, too.

"Cameron, hello, this is Olivia. I'm trying to reach my husband. When you talk to him, will you please ask him to call me? Thank you."

She hung up the phone in disbelief. All the worry and anxiety on top of this being the day that Dr. Demetrios would have her test results.

Nervous, she brewed herself a cup of cinnamon apple tea and took the delicate china cup upstairs to the window seat in the master bedroom.

The cold December air seeped in through the windowpanes. From her perch on the third floor, she could see across Commonwealth Avenue, over the tops of the stately trees that lined the street where she lived, straight into Public Garden. The garden and adjacent Boston Common were an oasis in the heart of densely populated downtown Boston. A sanctuary laced with gorgeous statues, it was a haven even in the dead of winter.

Olivia pressed her hand to the glass and the cold bit her palm, as if it were taunting her. When she and Jamison had purchased the house, proximity to the lovely park was one of the things that completed their dream house. Since the day they'd moved in, Olivia had fantasized about arranging long playdates at the park for their children, and spending leisurely Sunday afternoons on a picnic blanket while Jamison tossed the football with their kids.

The ringing phone startled her from her reverie and she spilled hot tea on herself as she stumbled for the phone.

Finally, she thought as she grabbed up the receiver.

"Jamison?"

There was a long pause on the other end of the line before a male voice—not Jamison's—said, "Good morning, Mrs. Mallory. This is Cameron McInerney. I hope I'm not calling too early, but I see on my call log that you called a few moments ago."

"Yes, I did. Is Jamison okay?"

Another pause. "Yes, ma'am, he's fine. In fact, he

asked me to call you and let you know that his flight gets in at six this afternoon. He will be home shortly thereafter."

Confused as to why Cameron was calling her rather than her husband taking the time to do so, Olivia paced as she listened.

"Cameron, I appreciate your call, but why isn't Jamison calling me himself? I have been leaving messages for days."

Again, Cameron paused a few beats too long. Finally, he said, "I don't know, ma'am. I'm simply relaying the message he asked me to deliver."

When they hung up, a chill seemed to permeate the air. Something wasn't right. Despite how she tried to blame her uneasiness on nerves over her appointment with Dr. Demetrios, Olivia knew she was justified being upset with Jamison.

Couldn't he even spare five minutes to call her himself?

At least he still planned to be home this evening, and she had a doctor's appointment to get ready for. Right now she needed to use every ounce of energy to prepare herself for the news Chance Demetrios had waiting for her.

News that was going to change her life…one way or another.

* * *

Olivia paused in the threshold of Paul's office and knocked lightly on the door frame. Her brother scowled up at her from the open magazine on his desk, *Northeastern Journal of Medicine*. When he saw her, he closed the magazine and changed his expression in a flash.

"Well, hello! Look who it is." His voice rang with cheer, and if she hadn't seen the annoyance on his face a moment ago, she might have believed nothing was wrong.

"I'm a little early for my follow-up with Chance, and I thought I'd stop by and say hi," she said. "I don't mean to disturb you."

He drummed his fingers on his desk.

"Of course you're not disturbing me. Come in. Please." He gestured toward the chair in front of his desk.

"What are you reading?" she asked.

"Nothing."

"It sure looked like something judging by the way you were scowling. Is everything okay?"

He breathed an exasperated sigh and raked a hand through his curly, dark hair. In that moment of letdown, she could see the dark circles under his brown eyes. He looked exhausted.

Olivia reached out across the desk and touched his arm. "What is it, Paul?"

He shook his head. "I might as well tell you now, because it's likely to come out in the near future."

Paul hesitated and held up the issue of the medical journal he'd been reading when she walked in.

"The institute is teetering on the brink of a public relations disaster. It's a nightmare, Liv. A ticking time bomb that could explode in our faces if we don't act fast and smart."

She'd never seen her brother look so distressed, not in all the years since he'd picked up the Armstrong reins and started running the fertility institute that his father had dedicated his life to building.

"What's going on?"

Paul cleared his throat. "This periodical ran a story saying that the institute used donor eggs and sperm to impregnate many wealthy couples."

"Right, there's nothing wrong with that. That's what you do here."

Paul frowned. "They alleged that some of the couples were unaware of the substitutions. That they thought they were impregnated with their own sperm and eggs."

A cold wave of shock slapped her, and Olivia's blood turned to ice. That sounded exactly like what Derek had suggested she do. Except he'd told her. He hadn't tried to do the substitution behind her back. Though he'd urged her to lie to her husband in exactly that same way.

Oh, my God. "Paul, forgive me, but I have to ask. Is the allegation true?"

Her brother pulled a face. "Of course it's not true. I can't believe you'd think for even one second that it would be."

She felt queasy watching her brother in such distress. His identity was so closely tied to the institute that if one questioned the business practices, they were essentially questioning his personal integrity.

Paul took pride in his scrupulously clean record. Derek, however, was altogether another animal. It was amazing how twin brothers could be such polar opposites.

Slow simmering anger roiled in the pit of her stomach as Derek's suggestion rang her ears. There was no way she could tell Paul that Derek had essentially offered her the same arrangement.

No, if she told him, World War Three would erupt.

Even so, the longer she thought about it, the more she wondered if there was, perhaps, some truth to the allegation…brought on by Derek's doings.

Somehow, she managed to ask, "What are you going to do about it?"

Paul sighed. "It's tricky. Right now, only two

minor medical journals have run the story. None of the mainstream news outlets have picked up on it—yet. Our attorneys have threatened to slap the publishers with libel suits, because they presented no hard proof."

But *she* had proof. *Right from Derek's mouth.*

"The problem is," he continued, "if we file, it's likely to let the cat out of the bag. Reporters are always trolling the court dockets. They could easily get wind of the case that way."

Olivia scooted forward in her seat. "They're going to print a retraction, aren't they? They have to, since they have no proof."

Uncertainty clouded his expression. "That's another dangerous catch twenty-two. On one hand, it would be vindicating to have them admit in the pages of their own journals they were wrong. However, they'd probably bury the retractions in a places where they would go unnoticed. Besides, rehashing only gives new life to the story. Every day that the story goes unnoticed by the mass media means there's less of a possibility that it'll be discovered and broadcast to the world. So, a retraction could do more harm than good in the long run."

Olivia's mind swirled with doubt over whether she was doing the right thing by keeping the secret from Paul. But no, no, she had to talk to Derek first. As she stood to go, she asked, "So, you're not going to do anything except hope it'll die a quick, silent death?"

Paul nodded.

"Unless the story explodes in the mass media. Heaven forbid, but if that happens we'll slap libel suits on both journals faster than they can say shoddy reporting. In the meantime, we're putting together a crisis PR plan that we hope we won't have to use."

"I'm with you on that," she said as she edged toward the door. "I hope you don't have to use it. Listen, I'm sorry this has happened. Please keep me posted, okay? But I have to go."

Olivia glanced at her watch as she made her way through the institute's empty halls. She had ten minutes until her appointment. Just enough time to have a chat with Derek.

So the institute had come under fire for egg swapping? And Paul was claiming it wasn't true?

Paul, she knew, was as ethical and squeaky clean as they came. She couldn't say that much for her other brother, though. If he smelled money or a way to feather the nest, the ethics line blurred.

Had he gone too far this time? From what Paul said it sounded as if this could set the institute up for a legal mess. It wouldn't only tarnish the family name, it would destroy her father's life's work.

A thought struck her and she stopped in her tracks.

The scandal might even be big enough to affect Jamison's career. Because in politics, every skeleton and scandal was fair game and fodder for mudslinging.

A scandal of this magnitude could seriously set back Jamison's shot for the presidency. The realization nearly knocked the wind out of Olivia.

Strike one: Jamison's mother had never been very fond of Olivia.

Strike two: Olivia hadn't been able to give him children.

Even if he didn't want them now, he would eventually. That's what the Mallory family was all about. They were one big, boisterous, the-more-the-merrier kind of clan, and once Jamison worked through these fears, he'd realize the importance of a family.

If, heaven forbid, there was a strike three—an Armstrong family scandal—it could spell the end of their marriage.

She flung open Derek's office door, walked in and closed it behind her.

He glanced up from his computer, peering at her over the top of his reading glasses, looking plenty annoyed.

"Well, come in, Olivia." His voice was dark with indignity. "Make yourself right at home."

She walked toward him.

"Have you been switching donor sperm and eggs, Derek?" Her voice held all the fury that had been bottling up over the months that she and Jamison had been apart.

Derek reared back in his chair, looking utterly confused. "Excuse me?"

She leaned in over his desk. "You heard me. Have you been switching donor sperm and eggs to keep wealthy clients at the institute?"

He blew out a breath between his pursed lips. "Are you talking about that ridiculous story that ran in that hack medical journal?"

He laughed, and something about the hollow sound convinced Olivia he was covering up something.

"I'm talking about the story that ran in those journals. A story with allegations alarmingly similar to the solution you offered me the last time I was here."

He smirked. "Oh, don't be ridiculous. There's no similarities there whatsoever. Who told you about this, anyway?"

"Paul told me," Olivia spat. "And he's pretty upset over it. Have you been engaging in unethical practices? This could ruin the institute, Derek!"

"Olivia, I simply offered you a means of saving your troubled marriage. That's all. There are no similarities between what that rag asserted and what I offered you. If I'd done what the journal suggested, then I wouldn't have told you. I would've just relabeled the viable eggs with your name. Good grief, Olivia. What kind of monster do you take me for?"

She hated it when he talked down to her. But she wouldn't let him intimidate her.

"Would you please explain where the eggs you offered me came from? Whose eggs are they?"

He looked at her as if she had two heads. As if this was painfully simple and she should understand. "They're donor eggs. Ovum we paid for so we could help women like you who can't produce eggs of their own. Pardon me for trying to help you."

His words were a low blow even if they were true. He must've seen it in her face because he softened his tone.

"The ones I offered you are from our 'egg bank' and are absolutely free and clear. They do not 'belong' to anyone but the future recipient."

He regarded her for a moment with piercing brown eyes. The longer he stared at her, the smaller Olivia felt.

"I'm sorry," she whispered. "I didn't mean to accuse you of anything. But I still don't understand why you implied there should be so much secrecy around giving me the eggs? Changing the files so that everyone thought they were mine rather than donor eggs? I mean, Derek, come on, you have to admit the allegations in the exposé mirror your offer."

Derek sighed and rolled his eyes.

"There is no similarity whatsoever. The secrecy was simply for your and Jamison's benefit—for privacy. As I said, I was just offering you a way to save your marriage and a means of keeping up appearances. Now, if you don't mind, I have to get back to work."

He got up, walked to the door and opened it.

Olivia exited his office. When the door clicked behind her, she was in greater turmoil than when she'd entered.

She dialed Jamison's cell, but got his voice mail. *Again.*

She was tired of pretending their marriage was solid. Would having a baby actually save their troubled relationship? For the first time ever, she wasn't so sure.

She heard footsteps down at the end of the hall and looked up. It was Chance Demetrios. The man with the results. The answer that was key to the rest of her life.

"There you are." His voice was maddeningly neutral. Neither happy nor sad. "I got your test results back. Why don't we go to my office and discuss them."

They walked in silence. Olivia was glad he didn't try to make conversation, because she was still suffering aftershock from the conversation with her brothers.

"I have news," he said. "And I have *better* news. Where would you like me to start?"

Olivia sighed. "Give me the *better* news first. I think I need to start in a good place."

When Chance nodded, Olivia noticed that he looked solemn. Her gut clenched and she laced her hands protectively over her belly.

"When I was reviewing your file, I saw something I'd overlooked. Apparently, the doctor you saw before I arrived at the Armstrong Institute harvested and flash-froze a couple of emergency stashes of your eggs."

Olivia tensed. So Derek had gone through with the egg transfer after all, even though he hadn't mentioned it earlier. She hadn't really given him a chance to get a word in.

"I'm guessing that despite his not indicating it in your file, the doctor must have suspected there was a problem with egg production since he had the foresight to freeze thirty eggs. That gives us enough for three more in vitro procedures."

Three more.

Suddenly, with a breath-stealing blow, it dawned on her where this conversation was going.

"What's the other news you mentioned?"

She braced herself, knowing what he was going to say and feeling queasy because of it.

"I'm sorry, Olivia. Your tests prove that your ovaries

have stopped producing eggs. I hate to be so blunt, but if you want to have a baby, I suggest that we start the procedure as soon as possible since you'll need to be on the hormones for about three weeks before we can fertilize your eggs and implant the embryos. Would you like to start the hormones today?"

Tongue-tied and shaken, she stared at him. She hadn't been prepared to act this quickly since she thought they'd simply be discussing the test results.

"So, you're saying I don't have any time to waste?"

Dr. Demetrios rubbed his chin with one hand as he regarded her.

"I suggest you not let too much time pass. But if you need to think about it, or perhaps discuss it with your husband, we can start the hormones on your next visit. It's up to you."

Why was she hesitating?

Why was she so conflicted?

The need to have a child had driven her here today—without her husband. Was it her conscience, or simply self-doubt making her waver? She wanted a baby more than anything. Yet a little voice deep inside her was whispering that if she walked out that door without setting the process in motion today, it might be hard to come back.

Dr. Demetrios smiled at her. "What would you like to do, Olivia?"

Chapter Nine

Jamison used the flight to Boston's Logan Airport and the subsequent ride home to mentally prepare himself for seeing Olivia.

He'd had the days since seeing the photos to weigh all the options, to look at the situation from all angles and to think about what he would do when he saw her.

It had opened up childhood wounds he'd thought had healed over the years, brought back memories of his distraught mother crying over the telephone, desperately trying to track down her husband. In those days of no cell phones or pagers, when a person wanted to get lost, it was a lot easier than it was today.

Judson Mallory would sometimes *get lost* for days. His staff would cover for him, inventing meetings that Helen had no way of confirming or disproving.

Of course, Jamison had been too young to know what was really going on when his father would disappear. All he knew is that there would be long stretches of absence during which the household staff would care for him and his brothers because his mother "had taken ill."

As Jamison got older, it didn't take long to realize his mother wasn't really sick at all. She was either too drunk to function or too hung over from the benders brought on by her husband's going MIA.

It wasn't until years later, long after his father had died, that once-faithful friends and confidants crawled out of the woodwork offering tell-all books detailing that all wasn't as rosy as it seemed behind the manicured Mallory hedges.

Piece by painful piece, Jamison learned about a much darker side of the man he and an adoring public had idolized. The havoc that his father's womanizing had wreaked on their family and the subsequent betrayal by friends was enough to convince Jamison that he would never live his personal life the way his father had—fathering six boys he'd never wanted and leaving all responsibility for them to a mother who was unable to cope.

Jamison did want a family…someday. But he didn't want to repeat his father's mistakes. He wanted to wait until he was ready. Obviously with the way he was waffling back and forth—one minute ready to do it because it would make his wife happy, but the next minute feeling so unsure about his marriage, which in turn made him feel uncertain about having kids—meant that he wasn't.

In the same way that he'd committed to marriage once he'd pledged his life to Olivia, he felt that strongly about waiting until his marriage was on firmer ground before having children. Especially now that there was the possibility that his wife had strayed.

On the car ride home from the airport, he thought about the photos and what might have driven Olivia into another man's arms. He knew he'd been a little selfish over the past couple of years, a little insensitive to her needs. The purely rational side of him that could separate facts and emotion—the attorney in him—had leveled the verdict that maybe this had driven her to another man. But that was about as far as the rational side went. The thought of her in another man's arms nearly drove him over the edge.

So he clung to the last shred of hope he had. That even though the photos showed Olivia in Demetrios's arms—in an embrace that looked intimate—there wasn't a single shot of them kissing…or worse.

The fact that there was no kiss left a huge gray area open to interpretation. That's when common sense dictated that he had to give Olivia the benefit of the doubt. And he still needed to see her face—her eyes—when he presented the photos. That would be key.

He knew her, and he'd be able to recognize if she was lying about something. But at least he'd had time to figure out that he was willing to fight for his marriage if Olivia was willing to meet him halfway.

Of course, they'd be back at awkward square one. Another thought that remained constant in his mind as he sorted out everything was that he was glad there were no children involved.

So, despite his earlier, impulsive change of heart, essentially they were back at the starting line. He'd have to insist that they mend their marriage before they brought a child into their world. He'd grown up in a broken home and, above all else, he'd vowed to never put a child of his own through that hell.

His father had strayed and his mother had put him out. Had Olivia been talking about having his child one minute and then turning to another man the next? *No!*

He wouldn't jump to conclusions. He wouldn't trip down that slippery path, he reminded himself.

The car turned onto his street and stopped in front of his house—their house.

He'd go inside, hear Olivia out and then they'd decide together if their house was still a home.

Olivia felt bare without her pearls. They'd been a gift from Jamison and in some ways they were like a link to him when he was away. Wearing them made her feel connected to him. They made her feel safe. She'd taken them to the jeweler to be restrung as soon as she'd left the Children's Home, but because of the holidays, they wouldn't be ready until next week.

She put her hand up to her naked throat. She'd tried other necklaces, but none felt right. Even though she felt bare without them, and she wanted to look her best for Jamison, she felt better with nothing at her neck than something that was not her pearls.

Maybe she'd opt for a brooch instead. She pulled a white-gold snowflake pin out of her jewelry box and was just about ready to pin it to her emerald-green cashmere sweater when she heard the alarm signal that someone had just opened the front door.

Jamison?

Her heart raced. She was as nervous as a high school girl awaiting her first date—and not being one hundred percent sure the guy of her dreams would actually show to pick her up.

She breathed a sigh of relief that he was finally home. But that relief was soon pinched by the ugly reminder that for days Jamison hadn't even had the time or desire to call her.

She considered pretending nothing was wrong, so as not to spoil their time together. Really, the last thing she wanted was another fight. But she knew herself well enough to realize that it would be best to get it off her mind first thing, stating her case plainly and without drama rather than letting it come out explosively at a random moment.

She wasn't being a nag. She had a valid reason to be upset. First, work had preempted their holiday— and she'd been understanding. But then, he had taken her compliance for granted and decided he didn't even need to talk to her.

Enough was enough.

Her hand was shaking too badly to pin on the brooch. So she returned it to her jewelry box and headed downstairs to say her piece.

She found him sitting in the living room. He hadn't fixed himself a drink as she'd imagined he would. He was simply sitting there in the overstuffed burgundy chair with his elbows braced on the arms and his chin in his hand. A large manila envelope lay in his lap.

He didn't smile when she walked into the room. He just sat there watching her with a neutral expression.

"Well, welcome home, stranger." Her tone was a touch more sarcastic than she'd intended, but he didn't seem to notice. He just sat there with a deadpan expression that was starting to annoy her.

She walked over and sat on the edge of the chintz sofa that was closest to him. His chin didn't move from his hand, but his gaze followed her.

"Jamison, look, I don't want to fight with you, but I think we need to have a little chat and clear up a few things before we do anything else tonight."

"You're right." Jamison reached over and set the manila envelope on the coffee table in front of her.

"What's this?" she asked.

He glowered at her "Why don't you open it and tell me, Olivia?"

Olivia eyed him speculatively, wondering for a moment if she should tell him his envelope would have to wait until after she'd said what she needed to say. But curiosity got the better of her and, a moment later, she found herself holding a stack of five-by-seven photos.

She did a double take when she realized they were photos of herself—in the arms of Dr. Chance Demetrios.

"What is this?" she asked as numbness engulfed her.

"Why don't you tell me, Olivia? I think you're the one who needs to explain."

She blinked at Jamison, confused. Then as her gaze skittered from him to the photos, and back to him, an ugly realization set in.

"You had me followed? Why, Jamison? Why would you do that?"

He gestured toward the photos. "For obvious reasons that are self-explanatory."

Her heart drummed a furious cadence, and she stared at the photos again, this time taking a longer look.

"I don't understand," she said. "Tell me exactly what it is you think you see."

He scooted to the edge of his chair and braced his arms on his knees. "I see my wife in another man's arms. The very man who called my house on the morning I left for D.C."

What? Olivia squinted at him. "How do you know he called?"

His brows shot up. "I checked the caller ID when I went back into the bedroom. Chance Demetrios's number came up. Do you deny that you talked to him?"

Jamison sounded like a lawyer prosecuting his case. She hated it when he took that superior tone with her.

"Stop talking down to me." She flung the photos onto the coffee table. "I am not on trial."

Jamison flinched and his face softened to a heart-breaking look of anguish.

"No, you're not. But…" He gestured to the photos. Then, as he reached down and picked up one, Olivia saw that he had tears in his eyes.

Oh, my God. This is why he wouldn't return my calls.

"Jamison, listen to me. This is *wrong* on so many levels that I don't even know where to begin. Except to say it's not what it looks like. I am not having an affair with Chance Demetrios."

His throat worked in a hard swallow, and he looked her square in the eyes. She held his gaze. "Why don't you start at the beginning?"

The beginning? Where did the story begin? Their relationship had been deteriorating for so long, she really didn't know where to start. Even so, she knew she had to tell him the truth.

"Chance Demetrios is my doctor."

Jamison nodded. "I'm aware of that. Until the photos, I was aware that you'd seen him once a few months ago. For professional reasons."

"He called the morning you left because I told Paul I'd like to schedule another appointment with him."

Jamison's brows knit together. "An appointment? Why?"

Olivia sucked in a deep breath. This was it. She had to fess up. Level with him. "After Christmas with your mom and seeing Payton the baby-making machine, I just…I *needed* to try and have a baby, Jamison. For *both* of us. I decided to go ahead with another in vitro procedure on my own."

Jamison's confused expression deepened. "Exactly what are you saying?"

"It's pretty simple. Except, actually, it's not. When I went in for the appointment—on that day right there—" she pointed to the photos and grimaced at him, making it clear that they'd revisit the issue of the P.I. photos "—Dr. Demetrios delivered news I didn't want to hear. He told me that tests proved that my body is going through early menopause, and most likely, that's why we're having trouble conceiving. He said that there was a very limited opportunity left for me to get pregnant. So, as you can imagine, I was quite upset. When I ran out of his office, he came after me in the parking lot because he didn't want me to drive. Sure, he hugged me— that's what you're seeing there. He was comforting me—as my brothers might have comforted me. There certainly wasn't anything illicit going on. Believe me."

Jamison stared at the photo for a moment.

"Why didn't you tell me, Liv?" His voice was so soft it was almost a whisper.

"I tried, but you didn't return my calls."

"Oh, my God." He raked a hand over his anguished face and sighed a miserable sigh. "I am so sorry."

"Jamison, look at me."

He did. Square in the eyes. With their gazes locked, she said, "There has never been another man for me. Never has, never will be. I love *you.*"

He got up and went over to her, sat next to her and pulled her close.

As he kissed her tenderly, first her lips, then her neck and her collarbones, she decided that there was no need to rake him over the coals over having her followed. She had nothing to hide. She'd told him everything…and now she wanted to give him everything.

He'd never felt such overwhelming relief in his entire life. Deep inside he'd known Olivia was true to their marriage, to *him,* but he hadn't realized just how afraid he was to lose her.

He felt as if he'd been given a second chance, a new lease on life, on their marriage, and he was so overwhelmingly happy that they'd wiped the slate clean, that they were starting over.

He wanted to show her how much he'd ached for her, how much he'd missed her and longed for this reunion. He wanted to show her with his lips and hands and body why he was the only man for her.

Right there in the living room, on the chintz couch, she responded as he held her and touched her and tasted her. In response his own body swelled and hardened. He loved the feel of her slight body, so fragile to his touch. When he moved his hands to her hips, cupping her body and pulling her closer, she arched against him, firing the hardness of his desire.

"I've missed you so much," she murmured breathlessly.

He raised his hands to her small breasts, cupping them through her thin sweater, savoring their slight curves before teasing her hard nipples. She gasped. Her head fell back and she seemed to lose herself in his touch.

But only for a moment when she slid her hand down the front of his trousers and claimed his erection. Over and over she teased him, rubbing and stroking his desire through the layers of his wool pants and briefs. It had been so long and the sensation was almost too much to bear.

He wanted to savor this moment. So, he took her hands in his and eased her down on the couch, kissing her throat and playfully biting down on her earlobe as he did.

The thought of making love to her sent a hungry shudder racking his whole body. Suddenly he needed her naked so that he could bury himself inside of her. *Now.*

When he pushed up her skirt up around her waist, he saw that she was wearing a garter belt and stockings. The sexy sight of her almost undid him.

She must have sensed as much, because she reached up and unbuttoned his pants. She slid down the zipper and he moved so that she could push his pants down so that he was free.

It felt like the first time again. Wanting to savor the moment, he slowed down and undid each button on his shirt, shrugging it aside so that it dropped to the floor. In one swift, gentle motion, he lifted her so that he could remove her buttery soft sweater.

She lay beneath him in her bra and stockings looking like a slice of heaven. He must have been crazy to have thought they needed time apart.

Slowly, he unhooked the front clasp on her bra. As he freed her breasts, he lowered his head and, in turn, took each one into his mouth, suckling until she cried out in pleasure. As they lay together naked, despite the need driving him to the edge of madness, again, he purposely slowed down, taking a moment to drink in the way her beautiful body looked and to bask in how much he loved her.

And then they were reaching for each other and kissing each other deeply, body to body, skin to skin, tongues thrusting, hands exploring, teeth nipping—hungrily devouring each other. As he buried himself inside her, he knew without a doubt that this was where he wanted to be, where he needed to be. Because their time apart had proved that life was nothing without her.

Chapter Ten

A few hours later, Jamison awoke with Olivia in his arms. It was so good to be lying here next to her, back in his own bed, making love to his wife.

Somehow, they'd found their way up to the bedroom, stopping to make love on the staircase, in the hall and finally on the bed.

Then they did it again.

Olivia shifted, stretched and snuggled closer to him. He buried his nose in her hair, breathing in the floral fragrance of her shampoo and the notes that were uniquely her mingling with the scent of their lovemaking. It was enough to make him crazy. He wanted her so much, he got hard simply thinking about it.

He kissed her neck and, when she stirred and kissed him back, he tried to shift her on top of him, but she resisted.

"What time is it?" Her voice was husky with sleep.

"Ten-fifteen." He breathed the words into her ear and again she moved so that her body spooned perfectly with his, her tight little rump teasing his erection.

"Aren't you hungry?" she asked.

"I'm ravenous." He nudged her, wanting to part her legs and slip inside her warmth, but she turned and faced him, just out of reach.

He moaned and she ran her finger along his jawline.

"I ordered us a feast from Juan Carlo's. Endive salad with blue cheese, walnuts and honey, stuffed dates, salmon with crème fraîche and caviar, beef skewers, and cream of artichoke soup, with chocolate fondue for dessert. Plus, we need to open that bottle of champagne that's been waiting for us since Christmas Eve."

She started to get out of bed, but he pulled her back down on top of him.

"I'm starving, but not for food." He trailed kisses down her neck and chest to her breasts. Then he gently took her nipple between his teeth.

Her soft moan stoked the fire, and he sucked her

breast into his mouth. She felt so small and fragile in his arms, which, in turn spawned a protectiveness that he hadn't felt in a very long time. But when he looked up, the resolve in her eyes reinforced the strength of her determined spirit, which she demonstrated as she smiled, pushed away from him and got out of bed.

"Come help me," she said. "We can put the food in a picnic basket and bring it up here. We can have a feast in bed. Who knows what we might do with that chocolate fondue…for dessert."

She crooked her finger and beckoned him to follow. He was trailing after her in a flash.

Before too long, they were back upstairs, with their gourmet picnic spread out around them on the bed.

Jamison popped the cork on the champagne, and Olivia held out two flutes.

"Are you drinking?" he asked.

"Well, yes. Why?"

"You were always so adamant about staying away from alcohol in the weeks before you had the in vitro procedure. We are going to try again, aren't we? Because since you went to see the doctor, I'm guessing you've already started the hormones, right? If I learned one thing—no, two things—while we were apart it's that I love you very much and that I'm ready to start our family. Olivia, I think we need this to complete us. And with your condition, it sounds like we don't have any time to waste. I love you, and I want you to have my baby."

Olivia's gaze searched her husband's face as the implication of his words sank in.

I love you, and I want you to have my baby.

Finally, he was ready.

But this was just as she'd learned that her only option for getting pregnant was the donor eggs. And she hadn't told him that part. Mainly because she didn't know how to.

It was never so apparent that they needed a child to keep them together. If she couldn't give him that, it might spell the end of their marriage.

She would do anything to keep them together.

Technically, even with a donor egg, she would be having *his* baby. His sperm would fertilize the donor egg. And as Derek said, no one need be the wiser.

Even so, her conscience niggled at her. She tried to stave off black clouds of doubt by reminding herself that in a roundabout way, their situation was similar to Paul and Ramona's ordeal. Not literally, of course, but loosely, in the same way that Ramona had deceived Paul, but he'd forgiven her.

Ramona's mother had needed a bone marrow transplant, and Ramona had been desperate to find someone who was a match. She'd learned that years ago, her mom had donated eggs to the Armstrong Institute. Going on a hunch, Ramona had taken a job as a PR specialist at the institute to gain access to the files to see if she could find out if anyone had delivered a baby using her mother's eggs. A child with her mother's own DNA, who might be the answer to her prayers.

Unbeknownst to anyone, she was also on assignment for *Keeping Up With Medicine.* The journal had hired her to write an exposé on the institute as she searched the files for the identity of the recipient of her mother's eggs. Sure she'd written the damning story, but she'd tried to pull it before it went to press. Her editor had acted against Ramona's wishes, publishing the story anyway.

Ramona had initially deceived Paul for the greater good of her family, and once the truth—and why she'd done it—was out in the open, their relationship had not only survived, it thrived. Not immediately, of course. They'd had to mend and heal their trust. But love had triumphed.

If there was one thing Olivia still believed in, it was the power of her and Jamison's love.

As he toasted her and their family-to-be, she resolved to do whatever it took to give her husband the family they both so desperately wanted. She'd come this far, she couldn't give up now. Because what else would she have left if she lost him? She'd given up ballet and a career of her own to foster *his* career and nurture their family. If she didn't deliver her end of the bargain and give Jamison that family, she'd lose him. She couldn't afford to let any options slip by untried.

Three weeks later Jamison held her hand at the institute as Dr. Chance Demetrios implanted three fertilized embryos into Olivia's body.

Now, they simply had to sit back and wait to see if the procedure took.

After the procedure, she encouraged him to go back to D.C. He couldn't spend the entire nine months holding her hand—or even the agonizing two weeks she had to wait before she could get the pregnancy blood tests. Olivia might have felt desperate, but she never, ever wanted to be perceived that way.

So she insisted that he go back to work while she busied herself at the Children's Home. Staying busy would keep both their minds off whether the procedure had taken hold.

Dr. Demetrios had told her not to even bother with over-the-counter home pregnancy tests because, this early in the game, more often than not, they gave false negative results. So, her only recourse was to get lost in her work at the home.

Pam needed plenty of help with the Kelso boys. Not that they were difficult, although the little one, because of his autism, did need extra help—which he didn't always want. Danny often insisted that only his brother could help him, which posed a problem now that the holidays were over and Kevin had returned to school.

Pam and Olivia had established with Kevin's school that he could finish out the year even though the Children's Home was out of the district. The routine and familiarity would be good for him, considering all the drastic changes in his life. The only drawback was that the county could not provide school bus transportation for him. Someone had to drive him, and Olivia had decided that someone would be her.

This morning when she walked into the Children's Home, the mansion's spacious living room had been restored to rights, the Christmas decorations put back in storage. The first thing she saw was Danny sitting in a corner alone, rolling something between his thumb and his first two fingers.

When Olivia went over to see what he had, she realized that the small, white object was one of the pearls that had fallen to the ground the day the necklace broke.

When she'd picked up the repaired necklace from the jewelers, it had felt a bit snug. Olivia had had no idea how many pearls were on the strand, so maybe the necklace felt shorter because there was a pearl missing?

She knelt down in front of the small boy. "Hi, Danny. What do you have there? May I see it?"

"Duck," he quacked. "Duck. Duck. Duck!"

Olivia had done some research on autism and discovered that often a child afflicted with the condition would fixate on a certain object and assign it a name that had nothing to do with it. Just as Danny called her pearl a duck.

It was unfortunate that Danny had fixated on her pearl. He was only three years old and if he put it in his mouth, he might choke on it.

"Sweetie, could I please have that?" Olivia tried to take it from his little hand. Not only did he refuse to let go, but he started screaming at the top of his lungs.

Kevin was at his side in a flash.

"What are you doing to him?" Kevin demanded.

"I'm trying to take that bead away from him," she said over the screams. "I'm afraid he might swallow it."

Olivia noticed that Kevin didn't touch Danny or even try to comfort him. Instead, he'd assumed a protective stance between Danny and Olivia, and verbally took up his younger brother's battle.

"He won't put it in his mouth," Kevin said. "He

never does that, but he won't stop screaming if you keep trying to take it from him."

Kevin seemed totally unfazed by his little brother's ruckus, but it was all Olivia could do to keep from covering her ears with her hands.

Pam rushed into the room, her eyes bright with alarm. "What's wrong?"

"Danny has a bead and I tried to take from him because I don't want him to put it in his mouth. He didn't like it."

"Yeah," Kevin chimed in. "I told you he'll pretty much scream until he thinks he's safe and that you're not going to take it away from him."

Pam shot Olivia a frazzled, worried, what-are-we-going-to-do look as the other Children's Home residents started to gather around to see what all the fuss was about.

"Well, he has to learn that he won't get his way just because he screams. Everyone has to abide by certain rules."

Kevin shrugged, as if he couldn't understand what all the fuss was about.

"It's not like he's going to try and eat it or anything. He just likes it because it makes him feel safe."

Kevin's sage insight made Olivia catch her breath. The little guy was wise beyond his years.

Pam took a step forward and frowned. "Is that one of your pearls?"

Olivia shrugged. "All I'm concerned about is his safety. I don't want him to put it in his mouth and swallow it."

Pam frowned. "Danny, give me the bead, please. It doesn't belong to you."

The boy screamed louder. Pam and Olivia offered him a succession of toys, to no avail. Danny held tight to the pearl, continuing to scream when they tried unsuccessfully to pry it from his grip.

Pam turned to Olivia. "What in the world am I going to do?"

Olivia understood Pam's dilemma, but at the same time, her heart was breaking for this poor little guy who was barely out of the toddler phase of his life and for his brave, older brother, who was also much too young to be all alone in the world at the tender age of seven.

All Danny wanted was to feel safe. Olivia wished there was some way she could comfort him. But she knew that sometimes all the pearls in the world—all the things that money could buy—could never take the place of a family.

Something Kevin said kept going through her head. *"He just likes it because it makes him feel safe."*

As she racked her brain for a solution and came

up short, suddenly she saw Kevin standing next to Pam holding a large toy dump truck. He started spinning the shiny wheels around and around.

"Look, Danny," he said. "Truck! *Vroom! Vroom vroom! Vroom vroom vroom! Truck!*"

The little boy stopped screaming. His gaze fixed on the spinning wheels. He didn't say anything, but he stared at the truck for a long moment before reaching for it. When Kevin handed it to him, the single pearl Danny had been holding fell to the floor, bouncing as it did.

Pam caught it on the up-bounce, closing her hand around it before stashing it out of sight in her pocket.

"I'll give it back to you later," she whispered to Olivia.

Olivia smiled. "No worries. I know where you live." Danny plopped down in the center of the living room and spun the truck wheels. The only evidence of his earlier outburst was his tearstained face. Satisfied that the boy the was fine, Olivia said, "Come on, Kevin. Let's get you to school."

When they were in the car, they rode in silence for a few moments. When they reached a stoplight, Olivia said, "Kevin, that was a wonderful thing you did, figuring out how to help your little brother."

The boy stared straight ahead and shrugged, a quick, it-was-nothing hitch of the shoulders.

"I mean it," Olivia said. "Pam and I didn't know what to do. We didn't know how to help him, but you did."

The boy looked up at her, his expression very matter of fact. "He likes shiny things. Not all shiny things, but I thought he'd like the truck because he likes shiny things that spin around."

Olivia nodded. "He's so lucky to have a big brother like you."

Kevin's face clouded and he turned away and looked out the window. "Are you really going to make me and Danny go live in separate houses with different families?"

The question knocked the air out of Olivia. "What makes you ask that, Kevin?"

Another quick rise and fall of the shoulders.

The light turned green and Olivia drove through the intersection with a death grip on the steering wheel.

"The kids said you're gonna send me and Danny far away from each other and we wouldn't be brothers anymore."

This time, his sad words forced a gasp from Olivia.

"Oh, sweetie, have they really been saying that?"

She slanted a glance at him in time to catch his quick nod. In turn, she steered the car into the first parking lot she came to—a doughnut shop. As she put the car in park, she weighed her words. The sad truth of the matter was that she couldn't guarantee that the boys wouldn't be adopted out to different families. She didn't want to lie to him, but when she looked into his haunted brown eyes, she knew she couldn't tell him that the chances of them going to the same family were very slim.

"Kevin, you and Danny will always be brothers. And I want you to know that Pam will do everything in her power to keep the two of you together. Okay?"

He didn't say a word. He simply sat stock still, staring out the side window. The sight of him broke her heart.

Say something to make him feel better, she chided herself. She glared at the neon sign of the doughnut shop. She couldn't just blow sunshine at him, because if her thin promises ended up falling through, they would do more damage to him than the moment of temporary happiness she'd manufacture right now was worth.

"I'm really hungry," she finally said. "Will you go into the doughnut shop with me so that I can get a snack?"

Kevin nodded solemnly.

"Okay then," Olivia said. "Let's go."

* * *

On the way back to the house, Olivia called Jamison.

"Good morning," he said.

"Good morning," she returned. "Do you have a moment?"

"For you, I have all the time in the world."

His voice made Olivia smile as she turned the car onto Berkeley Street.

"I have a nearly impossible task that I need your help with," she said. "In fact, it's a cause so important to me that I'm going to be rallying everyone I know. Jamison, we have to find a good family that would be willing to adopt the Kelso boys. Both of them. How do we do that?"

Chapter Eleven

Later that month, Jamison and Olivia attended a re-
ception following the President's State of the Union
address in Washington, D.C. It was their first official
public appearance as a couple since the trial separation, and at functions like this, it was so clear why
they were good together.

Olivia knew how to charm the crowd. Seeing her
in action, he knew that someday, she'd make a
perfect first lady—that the country would fall in love
with her as deeply as he had.

As he stood listening to a junior congressman
who was concerned about the direction of one of the

committees Jamison chaired, he watched his wife across the room.

She wore her brunette hair twisted up off her neck, adding to the elegance of her black dress and pearls.

She'd been working tirelessly trying to find the Kelso boys a home together. In turn, she'd been spending every spare minute that she was at home in Boston with them. If it wasn't that she seemed so happy lately, he might worry that she was getting too attached to them herself.

But then again, that was his wife. Always putting her heart and soul into everything she took on, always looking for the win-win solution. Another case in point of why she'd be a good first lady—she was the ultimate humanitarian.

Tonight, she seemed to glow from within as never before. Their gazes snagged and held for a moment. He could read the "I'm ready to leave whenever you are" look in her dark eyes, even though the message would've been missed by anyone else. Even in a crowd they'd always been able to communicate wordlessly across the room.

Jamison smiled at her and the congressman stopped mid-sentence and turned to see who he was looking at.

"Gorgeous, isn't she?" the congressman said. "I noticed her earlier tonight during the President's address."

Jamison snickered. "Did you?"

The other man nodded.

"That's my wife," Jamison said. "I'm glad you approve."

The young man's eyes widened. "I hope I didn't offend you. It's just that she's stunning. I couldn't help but notice her because she's the spitting image of Audrey Hepburn. You're one lucky man."

"Indeed, I am," Jamison said. He excused himself and made his way over to Olivia, who was just finishing a conversation with a former first lady.

When there was a break in the conversation, Jamison whispered to his wife, "Come on, let's get out of here." He whisked Olivia away, helped her into her coat, and hand in hand they walked outside to the waiting limousine. After they were settled in the car, he said, "Was she giving you pointers for 2016?"

Jamison put his arm around her and pulled her in close.

Olivia smiled up at him and his heart turned over in response. How did he get so lucky to be blessed with her? They may have had their ups and downs, but they always rebounded, stronger every time.

"She was lovely," Olivia said. "Very warm. And so interesting."

He rested his chin on top of her fragrant hair,

loving the feel of her tucked in so close to him. "Of course, you could probably teach her a thing or two."

She laughed, tilting her face up so that he was able to capture her lips with his. She tasted faintly of mint, and a lingering honeyed sweetness that made him thirst for more.

"I don't think there was a head in that room that didn't turn when you walked by." His voice was a hoarse whisper. "I had to get you out of there before someone decided to steal you away."

She shook her head, a seductive smile coaxing up the corners of her mouth.

"Really?" she said. "What on earth would anyone else want with a powerful political gentleman's pregnant wife?"

Jamison blinked, unsure that he'd heard her correctly, but cautiously optimistic. "Are you saying what I think you're saying?"

"I'm pregnant, Jamison. Dr. Demetrios confirmed it this morning. I wasn't going to tell you until we were back at the apartment, but I couldn't wait another minute."

His mouth fell open, but too many emotions were converging for him to say anything.

"Can you believe it?" she said, smiling. "This time, I really believe everything is going to be okay."

He hugged her and kissed her tenderly on the lips.

Feeling like a protective papa bear, he said, "But should you have flown today? Will the air pressure hurt the baby?"

She shook her head. "That's one of the first things I asked the doctor. He said I'd be fine. He said it was important for me to keep doing all the things I normally do. To be careful of adding too many new things, but that I should live life as normally as possible."

He gazed down at her, thinking that in the amber glow of the street she was the most beautiful woman in the world. Not only was she beautiful, but she was giving him the best gift a wife could ever give her husband. She was having his baby. How could he have doubted that he wanted this? It was simply fear of the unknown. Fear that a baby would change them, when in reality Olivia had been right, a baby seemed to be exactly what they needed.

"Liv, I want you to stay with me here in D.C. I don't want us to be apart. I want to take care of you. I want to experience every stage of our baby growing inside of you."

"But, Jamison, my doctor is in Boston. I just don't think it would work."

Of course he wanted what was best for the baby, but he also wanted his wife.

"I need you by my side," he said. "When is your next doctor's appointment?"

"Two weeks."

"How about this? Why don't you stay in D.C. with me until your next appointment and then let's see what Dr. Demetrios says. If he thinks it's safe for you to move down here with me, then maybe he could refer you to a specialist."

The look on her face hinted that she wanted to say yes, but something was troubling her.

"What is it, Liv?"

She sighed. "It's the boys—Danny and Kevin. I can't just abandon them, Jamison."

It was getting easier to forget that the child growing inside her wasn't really hers. Part of it was because she already felt attached to the baby. Another reason was her rationalization that what she'd done couldn't be too terribly wrong since the pregnancy had taken and seemed to be thriving. Even she had to admit that she had a glow about her. She looked and felt good. Better, in fact, than she had in years. Not even a hint of morning sickness.

Curious as to why this pregnancy seemed to be working while the others with her own eggs hadn't, she'd done some research. Apparently, in early onset menopause sometimes the eggs could be damaged or not as high quality as those from a woman whose body was more typically in tune with her chronological age. There was no way she could confirm this with her doctor since he had no idea that the eggs he'd implanted weren't really hers, but it made sense.

And if this pregnancy gave them their child, well, then this was the child—the gift from God—that they were meant to receive.

Jamison seemed so earnest when he asked her to move to D.C. with him. After she thought about it— and received the all clear from her doctor, who had no objections as long as she was able to make it back for her checkups—she couldn't deny her husband. Things were going so well with them, and she wanted that time with him. Though the time apart had made them realize how much they loved each other, it was the time together that was helping to heal and nurture them as a couple and move them forward into this next exciting chapter of their life.

There would've been no question about what she should do, if not for Danny and Kevin. But Jamison had been right when he reminded her that the boys were in good hands with Pam. Still, Olivia felt an overwhelming need to see them and explain to Kevin that even though she'd be away and visiting less frequently, she'd still be there for them.

It was an eight-hour train ride—and even faster by plane, she told herself as she arranged the football and new toy truck she'd gotten them on the backseat of the car. She'd grown so close to the boys since they'd arrived at the Children's Home, and she couldn't help this urge she felt to shower them with love—and gifts—so that they knew that they weren't alone in the world.

Kevin greeted her enthusiastically and helped her buckle Danny, who was clutching his dump truck, into the car seat that had become a permanent fixture in the back of her Jaguar.

"Who does *that* belong to?" he asked, eyeing the football.

Olivia smiled at him. "Oh, goodness, how did that get in my car?" She winked at him. "I don't suppose you know anyone who'd like to have that, would you?"

The boy beamed and hugged the ball to his chest. Danny was less excited about the new truck, clinging to the tried and true dump truck for which he'd traded in his pearl. But that was okay. Kevin's gusto was enough.

Today, she was taking them to Public Gardens. It had become one of their favorite spots—even in the cold of winter. Today she'd packed a thermos of homemade hot chocolate and a batch of freshly baked cookies. Sometimes on weekends, when it wasn't too cold, they'd bring a picnic and find a patch of sunshine where they could spread their blanket and eat their lunch. Other times, they'd seat

Danny in an umbrella stroller and she and Kevin would walk the grounds. This, she'd discovered, was the best way to get the older boy to open up. And he would, sometimes going on for a solid hour about his friends at school, his teacher and the classes he loved most. But never a word about his parents or his feelings about the tragic loss he'd suffered.

Olivia didn't push him. She figured he'd open up in good time—if he wanted to. All that was important now was that he always seemed glad to see her.

When they got to the park, Kevin asked, "Do you know how to throw a football, Olivia?"

"No, I don't. Will you teach me?"

He tried his best. While Danny sat on the blanket bundled up in his winter coat spinning the wheels of his truck, Kevin and Olivia tossed the football. She dropped it more than she caught it, she wasn't able to throw the ball into the distance when he ran long, and she broke two fingernails, but she tried her hardest. Even so, Kevin seemed to tire of her efforts quickly and decided he needed to check on Danny.

They sat down on the blanket and she poured him a cup of hot chocolate.

"Why don't you offer Danny a cookie?" Olivia suggested. "He can eat that while his cocoa cools."

Olivia's heart swelled as she watched the younger boy respond to his older brother and take the cookie.

It was such a beautiful moment. What a shame that she'd have to spoil it with the news that she was leaving, but she needed to tell him while they were sitting here. She dreaded it, but the longer she put it off the harder it would be.

"Sorry I'm not very good at football," Olivia said, buying a little more time.

The boy lifted one shoulder to his ear and let it fall, then stared down at the football in his lap. "It's okay. My mom wasn't very good at it, either. It was something my dad and me used to do together."

Olivia's skin prickled. It was the first time he'd ever mentioned his parents. She wondered whether her telling him that she was leaving would affect his progress. On one hand, his opening up could mean that he was starting to adjust to his new environment. On the other, her leaving might cause him to retreat back into his shell.

I can't leave him now.

The possibility danced through her mind, but she shoved it out as quickly as it appeared. Jamison and the baby were her family. As much as she loved the Kelso boys, her family had to be her first priority.

Still, it didn't erase the sick feeling of dread that washed over her.

She reached out and smoothed his bangs off his forehead, relishing the silky softness of them.

"You miss your parents, don't you?"

He nodded, still not looking at her.

"It's okay, Kevin. You know that Mr. Mallory and I are here for you, don't you?"

He bobbed his head again, just barely this time.

"I wanted to let you know that I'm going away for a couple of weeks, but I'll be back."

Kevin looked up at her, alarm widening his chocolate brown eyes. "That's what my mommy told me and she never came back."

"Oohh…" Olivia choked back a sob. "Come here, sweetheart."

She pulled the boy onto her lap and held him tight for a long moment. He didn't cry, but he held on to her as if she were his lifeline.

"I'll see you again in two weeks. And when we get home, I'll mark the days on a calendar for you so that you can see exactly how quickly I'll be back. Would that make you feel better?"

The boy didn't answer her. He simply tightened his hold on her. Olivia sat there, hugging him back.

"If it would make you feel better, I'll call you every day after school so that you can tell me about your day. Would you like that?"

Still no answer.

"I'll even give you my cell phone number so that you can call me whenever you'd like to talk. Because

I want you to know that Mr. Mallory and I will do anything in the world for you and Danny."

The boy released his grip and looked up at her.

"Anything?" he asked.

Olivia nodded. "Anything. You can call me anytime of the day or night."

"Will you take Danny and me with you? Will you be our new mommy?"

Jamison went with Olivia to her next prenatal appointment, which happened to be on Valentine's Day. The best Valentine she could've ever asked for was to get the news that she'd checked out fine, that the baby was growing and that everything seemed to be textbook perfect. They celebrated with lunch at Salvatore's down on Boston's South Port waterfront.

After ordering lunch—Jamison chose the lobster ravioli and her mouth watered in anticipation of their famous salad with gorgonzola, walnuts and green apples—he presented her with a pearl bracelet from Tiffany's. It had a heart-shaped diamond dangling from the clasp.

"Oh, Jamison, it's gorgeous. Thank you."

He smiled. "I thought it was significant. The diamond represents our baby. Just don't wear it around your little friend with the pearl obsession."

The thought made Olivia smile, too, as she slipped the bracelet on her arm. She missed her little guys. She hadn't seen them in two weeks. Two weeks during which Kevin's question had haunted her—"Will you be our new mommy?"

She'd managed to sidestep the little boy's question by using the excuse that he and Danny couldn't come with her to D.C. because Kevin had to go to school. She told him that she wished it were as easy as agreeing to be his new mommy, but that the situation was…complicated.

He had no idea exactly how complicated it really was.

The excuses hadn't meant anything to him, and Olivia saw him cry for the first time when she marked off the days she'd be gone on his calendar and said goodbye to him and promised him she'd come see him her first day back.

Actually, she didn't know who the farewell was harder on—Kevin…or her.

"How do you tell a little boy like Kevin Kelso that you can't be his mother?" she asked Jamison. "He's only seven years old. He's smart as can be, but it won't make it any easier on him to tell him I would if I could, but I can't. All he'll hear is, 'No' and he'll feel like he's lost someone he cares about all over again."

"Are you going to regret getting involved with the boys?" Jamison asked.

Olivia paused, fork midair and gaped at her husband. "Of course not."

Jamison cut another bite of ravioli. "I didn't think so. So don't be so hard on yourself, Liv. You're giving them a lot right now, when he and Danny need you the most."

He popped the bite into his mouth. Olivia sighed and set down her fork. "What I'm saying is that I don't want to cause him further pain. He doesn't know that we're going to have a baby of our own. He won't give a flip that we need this time for our own family. He'll feel as if we rejected him."

Jamison sipped his iced tea. "I don't know, Liv. He sounds like a pretty resilient little guy to me. I'm sure he'll be okay. Just because we can't adopt him and Danny doesn't mean that you can't continue to see them. Probably even after they're adopted by another family."

"Why can't we adopt them, Jamison?" She startled herself with the question. Where had it come from?

She was just opening her mouth to retract the question, when Jamison said, "One reason I can think of is because I've never even met them. I mean, I feel as if I know them since you talk about them so much, but you know, hey, we've never actually met."

The realization hit Olivia like a bolt. It had been nearly two months that she'd been talking about them, but, no, he *hadn't* met them.

"How about if I come by the Children's Home with you?"

It was a great idea. They had just enough time to do that and then get back to the house so that they could get ready for dinner with their families. Even though she was only about six weeks along, they couldn't wait to share their news—especially after the good checkup earlier that day.

Jamison had left the decision of when to share the good news up to her and she'd felt confident about making the announcement tonight. This time, it just felt different. But first, she had an introduction to make. The three most important men in her life had to meet each other.

Jamison steered Olivia's Jaguar into the parking lot of the Children's Home. She held his hand and led him up the steps.

After they were buzzed in, Olivia immediately set out to look for Pam and the little boys who had so captured her heart.

Jamison stepped into the living room and knew from the description that Olivia had given him that he'd stumbled upon one of them. He'd heard so much about these boys he felt as if he already knew them. He'd bet money that this was Danny, who sat quietly in the corner, spinning the wheel of a toy truck.

Jamison walked over and knelt in front of him.

"Hi there, little guy. What do you have there?"

The boy didn't say anything, and for a long while, Jamison would've sworn that the kid didn't even know he was there. That's why he was surprised when, as he started to get up, the boy held out the truck and let Jamison take it.

The moment after Jamison accepted it he didn't quite know what to do with it. Should he roll it on the ground? Should he make truck noises? He didn't want the boy to start screaming again the way Olivia had said he did when someone tried to take his favorite toy. For lack of a better idea of what to do, Jamison gave the wheels a spin, the same way Danny had been doing when Jamison entered the room.

The boy stared transfixed. Once Jamison saw the boy was okay with sharing his truck, he relaxed and both of them fell into a contented companionship with each other. Though he knew feeling sorry for him was probably the worst thing he could do for the boy, he couldn't help but be moved by the fact that the kid was so young to be without his family.

Despite how Jamison had all the material advantages money could buy, thanks to an absent father and a mother who was an emotional wreck, his childhood had been less than ideal. Even so, he had his *people*. He'd always had his brothers around him.

Sitting here with Danny, recalling everything Olivia had said, he fully understood why it was so important to keep these boys together.

When Olivia, Pam and another boy, who had to be Kevin because he looked like a slightly larger version of Danny, walked in, they stopped in their tracks and gaped at them as if they were afraid that they might startle a wild deer.

"He shared his truck with you?" asked Kevin.

"He shared his truck with you," Olivia said.

"He shared his truck with me." Jamison beamed.

He'd been with the little guy for less than fifteen minutes and he could already see why Olivia was so smitten. If it wasn't that he and his wife already had a baby on the way, he'd definitely entertain the possibility that the boys come live with Olivia and him.

But that was impulse talking. Jamison had just met the boys. He hadn't even spent time with them. Even if did and fell in love with them the same way Olivia had, it wouldn't work. It would simply be too much for Olivia to care for a newborn and two emotionally fragile older boys—especially one with special needs.

Particularly since Jamison would be so busy with work.

His own childhood flashed back at him in one, larger than life mental collage of lies and deception. Six little boys who desperately needed a father. A father who was never there for them. A mother who was so overwhelmed by the fact that her marriage was unraveling that she drank herself into a stupor on a regular basis.

There were so many unanswered questions and the memory sent a steel door slamming down on Jamison's overloaded emotions.

As much as he was sure the boys were wonderful and worthy of love and a good home, he and Olivia simply weren't their new family. It would be too much. Overload. Somehow, he had to make Olivia see that.

Chapter Twelve

"It was a sign that he is going to be a great father," Olivia said to the group of family gathered around the dining room table at their house. "Danny was drawn to Jamison. And in the time I've known him, I've never seen him share with anyone that way."

"Who, Danny or Jamison?" Paul asked, and everyone at the table doubled over in a fit of laughter.

"Danny, of course." Olivia reached for her husband's hand.

"Right, because Jamison hasn't learned to share yet. I think the three-year-old is setting a good example,"

Paul continued, and drew more laughter. Jamison was a good sport and chuckled along with them.

"This evening was not intended to be a roast honoring my husband," Olivia said. "But we do have some very exciting news to share. In fact, if not for this news, we might even consider adopting the Kelso boys, we've come to care for them that much. But one thing at a time."

As the server they'd hired for the evening distributed flutes of champagne—and a glass of sparkling cider for Olivia—she beamed at her husband, who seemed to be in a daze and frowning slightly. When she raised her glass to him he seemed to snap out of his fog. Because he smiled, she decided not to read anything into it.

This is a happy night. Don't borrow trouble.

"Jamison, would you please do the honor and share our good news with our family?"

Olivia's mother, Emily Stanton Armstrong, seemed to anticipate the announcement and gasped. Her hand flew to her mouth as if she were holding in the happy, hopeful question that wanted to pop out.

In turn, Emily's reaction elicited a muffled squeal from Olivia's sister, Lisa. "Oh, I hope you're going to say what I think you're going to say."

Jamison's mother, Helen, sat poker-faced in her seat to the right of her son, who was at the head of the table.

"Oh, for God's sake," she hissed. "Would everyone be quiet so he can talk?"

Jamison cleared his throat, a sign that his mother's brusque manners had embarrassed him.

"Relax, Mother. I'm waiting until everyone has been served champagne."

Helen gave an aloof half-eye roll that might have been a smirk, but it was hard to tell.

"Oh, smile," cajoled Olivia's father, Gerald. "You're actually quite attractive when you do."

Emily and Helen glared at Gerald, who, in his day had quite a reputation for being a womanizer. But Olivia knew he'd changed his ways and truly loved her mother. She knew her father was a good man, even if she'd never been as close to him as to her mother.

Every single member of Olivia's family was present tonight. Derek was a bit subdued, but he'd come. Paul had even brought his fiancée, Ramona.

Olivia was overjoyed they were all there, because nothing made her quite as happy as being surrounded by her family.

Helen, however, was the only member of Jamison's family who could make it tonight. Four of his brothers lived out of town; Payton and Grant had their own Valentine's Day plans, which was understandable, and actually preferable to Olivia. Because invariably, Payton would've found some way to upstage their announcement.

Olivia shook away the ugly thought. She wasn't going to let anything spoil the night. Especially not ugly thoughts aimed at a sister-in-law, whose only faults, really, were being impossibly fertile and well liked by their mother-in-law.

Olivia was neither of those things.

Still, this was her and Jamison's night. A time to enjoy their family and bask in the glow of the happy news they were about to share.

When everybody had flutes of champagne, Jamison sat up straight and said, "Olivia and I are very happy to announce that we are expecting a baby, which will arrive in October."

Shouts and squeals erupted. The family toasted and hugged one another as they congratulated Olivia and Jamison. Olivia even thought she saw evidence of a smile on Helen's face—but it was gone before she could be sure.

When everyone settled down, Helen said, "October? That means you aren't even two months' pregnant, Olivia. Don't you think it's a bit risky to start making announcements this early?"

A hush fell over the dining room and everyone

gaped as Helen's thoughtless remark loomed, almost palpable, in the air.

"The doctor said that everything looks good, Mother." There was a sharp edge to Jamison's voice. "Besides, we're going to be spending a lot of time in D.C. over the coming months. Tonight was the most convenient night to get the family together, seeing that you happened to be in town tonight, too. Perhaps you could think positively and wish us well?"

"Of course," Helen said, then downed the rest of her champagne.

In an awkward moment, all gazes seemed to turn to Olivia. She wasn't sure if the crushing weight she felt was due to the hormones or simply disappointment that even on the night she announced she was finally pregnant, she couldn't seem to please her mother-in-law, who had to spoil the moment by shining the spotlight on Olivia's worst nightmare—that they might possibly lose the baby. Again.

She hated it, but she felt tears burning her eyes. There was no way she was going to let Helen know she'd gotten to her. No way she was going to sit her and cry and validate her mother-in-law's morbid suggestion.

Olivia summoned her most cheerful voice.

"If you'll excuse me, I'll just go into the kitchen and let the staff know that we're ready for dessert."

As the servers bustled around her, Olivia stood in her kitchen struggling to regain her composure. She did it by focusing on the good, replaying the wonderful day she'd had in her head—the good news that they'd received at the doctor's appointment; the wonderful lunch with Jamison and the sentimental bracelet he'd given her; the way Danny and Jamison had taken to each other; and now being able to share the good news with the family.

Despite Helen's sourpuss attitude, for once the world really did seem nearly perfect. Olivia put her hand over her stomach, which was still perfectly flat. She couldn't change her mother-in-law's outlook, but she could refuse to let it bring her down. Because, really, the only way life could be better would be if she were holding her baby in her arms right now.

She turned at the sound of someone behind her. It was Derek.

"Is everything okay?" she asked.

"Everything seems fine, my dear sister. Well, except for Helen. She's quite a piece of work, isn't she? But really, you should be quite pleased with yourself for pulling this off."

He patted his stomach. Something in the tone of his voice sent a chill skittering down Olivia's spine.

"Derek, don't start with me. I've had enough drama tonight. Did you need something? Otherwise,

I was just getting ready to go back out and join the family in the dining room. We don't want the ice cream to melt."

He started to say something but stopped. His expression was making her uncomfortable.

"I just felt compelled to ask—aren't you glad you listened to me? Because I'm quite enjoying this little secret we're sharing."

Racking her brain because she didn't quite know what to say to him, she glanced around to make sure nobody had slipped into the kitchen and heard his remark. When she was sure the coast was clear, she lowered her voice to just above a whisper.

"Please don't ever bring that up again. Not even when we're alone, okay?"

He laughed a dry laugh that seemed almost evil.

"No, Olivia, I think we're going to have to talk about it at least one more time."

His comment made her blood run cold.

"What are you getting at, Derek?" she muttered the words through gritted teeth.

"Now is not the appropriate time or place. But we'll talk soon, little sister. We'll talk."

As the celebration wound down, Jamison asked his mother to step into the office for a private word before she left for her hotel. Despite their large home and numerous offers, she never stayed with Jamison and Olivia when she visited.

"What's the matter, son?" she asked.

He knew her too well to believe she was really oblivious to what he wanted to talk about.

"Why did you act that way tonight?"

She blinked. "What on earth do you mean, dear?" She was acting a little too wide-eyed and innocent to be believable.

"You know exactly what I'm saying. At every turn of good news you had something snide to say. With all that Olivia and I have been through, it was pretty awful of you to suggest that it's too early to share the pregnancy with our family. For God's sake, we're not sending out a press release to the general public. This night was to celebrate. Family is supposed to rally around you and build you up. Not tear you down."

Helen's mouth pursed into a thin, flat line and pure venom seemed to pool in her eyes. In the split second before she could blast him with her poison tongue, Jamison held up his hand.

"Don't say a word. You're going to hear me and you'd better take to heart what I have to say. I am sick and tired of you being disrespectful to my wife. You will treat her with respect or you will not be welcome in our home. Do I need to make my point any clearer?"

She glared at him. A slight coloring bloomed on her face, hard and cold as a stone.

Over the years, Jamison had tried to convince Olivia that she shouldn't take his mother's chilly demeanor personally. Helen had never like *any* of the women he or his brother, Grant, had brought home (girlfriends of their four, unmarried younger brothers weren't even on Helen's radar). In fact, it was only after Payton had given her a grandchild that Helen had softened toward her. That gave Jamison hope that one day his mother would open her arms and invite Olivia in, but tonight, he'd officially quit hoping. He was demanding it.

He'd accepted the fact that even if his mother was revered in her social circles—the kind of reverence only afforded those with power and old money—she wasn't nice.

"Mother, I love you. I know that you're fighting your own demons. But you have to understand, the past is gone. Nothing can change it. I'm sorry that Dad hurt you. I'm sorry that he was a rotten father to me and my brothers, but I will no longer let the past rob me of the happiness I deserve. For a while now, I've been questioning whether I even wanted children because I was so afraid I'd end up being like my father—being a horrible, horrible husband. But just today, it dawned on me that I am nothing like him—"

"You are *a lot* like him," Helen spat. He wasn't sure if that was a compliment. "That's why people love you. They see in you everything they wanted to believe about him."

Their gazes locked and at that moment, Jamison saw the tears in his mother's eyes, glimpsed all the hurt and anguish that was bottled under the surface.

"Mom, we cannot let the past keep tearing us apart. Olivia is my wife. She is your daughter-in-law, not your competition. So please show her the respect she deserves."

Later that night, Olivia lay awake next to her husband long after he'd fallen asleep. Derek's words rang in her ears. No matter how she tossed and turned, she couldn't quiet her restless, worried mind.

If she didn't know better, she might think Derek was intending to blackmail her.

Surely not, she told herself as she flipped over onto her back and stared at the ceiling. Her brother was capable of a lot of diabolical things, but extorting a family member?

Surely not.

Even so, his careless remark had uncorked the guilt she'd managed to suppress during this time of happiness and celebration.

She turned back onto her side, facing her husband.

His handsome face looked so peaceful and relaxed in the sliver of moonlight that shone through the space in the curtain.

Maybe she should tell him the complete truth.

A wave of panic threatened to drown her.

How could she? He was so happy. They were doing so well.

Again, she flopped onto her back, lacing her hands over her stomach.

How could she possibly keep the secret of using donor eggs from Jamison? Especially if there was a chance Derek was going to spill the beans.

But Derek would have to come up to D.C. if he wanted to have the discussion he seemed so dead set on having. Because she'd decided that's where she was going to be spending most of her time until the baby was born. It wasn't what she wanted—especially because it meant leaving Danny and Kevin again—but putting a safe buffer of four hundred and fifty miles between her and her brother seemed like the best survival tactic right now.

If nothing else, it would force Derek to really think about his actions.

Wouldn't it?

Even though Jamison wanted his wife with him in Washington, he knew she was much more at home in Boston. Her family and her volunteer work were there—as were her boys.

That's why he was torn when she asked Chance Demetrios to refer her to a specialist in D.C., claiming that she wanted to live there full-time with Jamison for the rest of the congressional session.

On one hand, he wanted her to be there with him. That's what he'd wanted since they'd reconciled; but on the other, he knew it wasn't realistic. In fact, it would be selfish to ask her to leave behind all the things she loved to be by his side. But in the end, she went back with him, returning to D.C. two days after their family dinner.

Exactly two weeks later, he could tell that Olivia was bored out of her mind. She'd tried to make friends, but the political circles in which they traveled were transient at best, and other times power-hungry and shallow. In a city of grand dames who were often traded in for trophy wives and mistresses who were vying to become trophy wives, a woman as beautiful as Olivia proved a substantial threat to those who were insecure in their station.

After wearing herself out shopping, setting up the kitchen in their Georgetown apartment so that she could cook, and going to see every ballet, museum exhibition and concert offered in the city, Olivia finally confessed to her husband that she missed

Boston. He was in the process of persuading her to go home for a visit when, out of the blue, his mother called him at the office to see when he and Olivia would be back in Boston because she wanted to have lunch with them.

This was a huge gesture on his mother's part. Though Jamison wanted to believe his words on Valentine's Day night had made an impact on her, she was Helen Mallory. Nobody told the Ice Queen how to behave.

So when Helen said, "I realize it's difficult for you to just pop back into town since you're not exactly next door. However, I'd like to get something on the calendar because… Well, Jamison, I simply feel as if Olivia and I need to bond," Jamison was determined to make it work.

"Mom, that sounds wonderful. I'm sure Olivia would be delighted to see you. The only problem is that I don't know when I can get away. You and Olivia should schedule something without me."

He leaned back in his leather chair, stretching his long legs out in front of him as he waited for his mother's reply. The pause seemed to last for years… nearly as long as the tense relations between his mother and his wife.

"I'd really hoped to see both of you together, Jamison. The luncheon date can wait until you're free."

"Mother, take Olivia to lunch and the three of us can schedule something for another time. This is important. Especially since she's carrying your grandchild."

Another stretch of silence loomed.

"Mother, call Olivia. Invite her to lunch."

Helen's sigh was audible even over the telephone line.

"All right. If you insist. I'll call her later this afternoon."

Jamison smiled to himself as he disconnected the call. All peace talks began with a single kind gesture. This was a huge step for his mother. One that made him very hopeful. One, he was certain, Olivia would appreciate.

Even so, he thought it might be a good idea to prepare her for his mother's call. He hit the speed dial key that connected him to Olivia's phone. As it rang, a warm glow of satisfaction coursed through him.

Fate was finally smiling on them.

After Olivia digested the idea of lunching with his mother, she'd see it that way, too.

Olivia hated hiding from Derek. To be completely truthful, that's what she'd been doing—hiding in Washington, D.C., from the implied threat he'd flung the last time she saw him.

At first, she brushed off the need to stay away as

simply wanting to be with her husband, but the wakeup call came—literally—after Helen phoned and invited her to come to Boston for a "girls' getaway" during which they'd go to a spa, take in a special production of *Swan Lake* staged by Olivia's former Harvard Ballet Company, and collaborate on a fundraiser for the Children's Home.

Olivia's first impulse had been *No!* because she couldn't imagine spending several awkward mani-pedi, salad-lunching days with her mother-in-law. Helen's call hadn't caught her off guard since Jamison had prepared her. Though she was only expecting a lunch date offer—not a "girls' getaway."

Though she was touched by Helen's effort to connect with her through a Children's Home fundraiser, Olivia wasn't kidding herself. Helen hadn't suddenly awakened a changed woman, wanting to embrace the daughter-in-law she'd kept at arm's length for years. Olivia understood that Helen's motivation was the baby Olivia was carrying. For a fleeting moment, she wondered what Helen would do if she knew the baby growing inside Olivia wasn't her biological child.

That's what made Olivia apprehensive. Because when she thought about coming home, she heard her brother's malevolent words about how they were due to talk about their "little secret," and the thought of coming face-to-face with her scheming, black-hearted brother was what had Olivia thinking about saying, "thanks, but no thanks," to Helen's generous offer.

While she was cautiously pleased by her mother-in-law's reaching out, the main thing that prevented her from completely burying her head, or even enticing Helen to come down to D.C. for their getaway, was what her avoiding Boston would cost the Children's Home. The support Helen Mallory could generate with a simple nod of approval was amazing. By attaching her name to a fundraiser, the potential was staggering.

So there was no way she could refuse.

There was no way Olivia could fly her down to Washington because that meant she wouldn't be able to give Helen a tour of the Children's Home—the final determining factor in exactly how much support Helen would offer, and Olivia was determined to get the maximum.

And if she followed Helen's rules, there was always the potential that she and her mother-in-law might actually bond. Wishful thinking, but a girl could dream. Olivia knew that nothing would make her husband happier than for Olivia and Helen to have a relationship. That in itself was enough incentive to keep believing.

She just had to figure out a way to keep her brother from ruining everything. Maybe the best defense was a little offense.

Maybe she needed to see her brother while she was there and set things straight once and for all. She had to stop hiding from Derek and go back to Boston. The reality was, if her brother wanted so badly to get this *message* to her, he could call her…or Jamison. He hadn't done so since they'd last spoken on Valentine's Day.

Derek was evil, but would he actually stoop so low as to blackmail his sister? She'd been over and over their conversation and she couldn't figure out what else he might have meant by it. Unless he was messing with her. But Derek didn't have the time or patience for games like that. Not unless he stood to gain from them.

Olivia was more than a little nervous when she met Helen at the Four Seasons Hotel in Boston. Of course, she was nervous about the one-on-one time with her mother-in-law, but she was also afraid of running into Derek.

He was the last person she wanted to see. Especially in the company of Helen.

She'd made up her mind to hope for the best. That's all she could do. It helped a little when

Jamison assured her that his mother was determined to make peace between them. Olivia could see how important it was to him. How could she not try?

It was simply two nights in a hotel suite; one day of spa treatments, which actually proved to be quite relaxing; and finally, on their second day together, the moment that Olivia had been waiting for—her chance to show off the Children's Home.

Though Helen had been a little aloof yesterday in the spa, Olivia reminded herself that just the fact that they were together—just the two of them, doing girly things together—was a milestone. Olivia knew not to expect Helen to make an effort at small talk. So she took the reins. By the time their limo stopped in front of the old Georgian mansion, Olivia had given Helen a rundown of the nonprofit's history and mission statement as well as their current financial needs.

"There are two small boys of whom I've become especially fond. I can't wait for you to meet them."

"Well, I certainly must say, you are quite passionate about this organization, aren't you?"

Olivia nodded. "Yes, I certainly am."

Wanting to give Helen the full experience, she led her up the wide steps to the front door, rather than escorting her around back to the kitchen entrance, where Olivia usually entered when she visited.

Pam was right there to greet them and welcome Helen. Since it was the middle of the day, Kevin was at school, but Danny was sitting in his usual spot with his beloved truck, spinning the wheels, every bit the same as the last time she saw him. It made her a little sad to think of him sitting there alone while his brother was in school. Had Pam talked to Danny's doctor about enrolling him in a program to help him?

She made a mental note to ask her before she left.

Pam led them on an extensive tour, which ended with her presenting Helen with a packet of information, including a sheet that prioritized the home's needs.

"As you can see, this is a worthy organization and we appreciate all the financial help we can get. Even though we're fiscally sound, we do encounter surprises periodically. For example, if you'll look over there, you'll see little Danny Kelso. He and his brother were orphaned on the evening after Christmas. It's a sad, sad story. No relatives. The parents hadn't made any provisions as to who was to get custody of the boys in the event of their death. Because of Danny's special needs, the Department of Children and Family asked us to take them in, even though technically we were at our budget-dictated capacity. We have a reserve fund that we can dip into for special cases such as this, so that we never have to turn away a child in need."

"Well, you can't keep them indefinitely. What will become of them?"

Pam glanced at Olivia and bit her bottom lip, a gesture that betrayed the fact that her friend had something on her mind.

"We're constantly working to place the children in loving families. In fact, just last week I successfully placed a ten-year-old girl. She'll be joining her adoptive family next week. As far as the Kelso boys are concerned, we're working hard to find a family to take them both, but because of Danny's autism, it's proving difficult."

Helen regarded Danny. "Autism, is it? I wondered what was wrong with him."

A mother tiger instinct that Olivia had never experienced before sprang to life inside her. The boy was autistic, but he wasn't deaf. Olivia had no idea if he knew when people were talking about him, but it didn't feel right carrying on as if he weren't in the room. Olivia had to bite her tongue to keep from telling Helen as much, but she held off. Embarrassing Helen Mallory was not the way to endear her to the Children's Home.

Pam's phone rang and she excused herself to answer it.

"I'm waiting for calls about the pending adoption and I see by the number this is one of them. If you'll excuse me, I have to take this."

Olivia took that opportunity to walk over to Danny. She knelt beside him. "Hi, honey. How are you?" Danny didn't look up. "I've missed you, little guy."

Still no response.

"I'm off to have another look around." Helen sounded bored and she left Olivia to her one-sided conversation with the boy.

Olivia missed her work at the Children's Home. She missed seeing the boys. She'd been checking on them often via phone calls to Pam, but it wasn't the same as being in the same room with them. The only thing missing now was Kevin. Olivia's heart ached with how much she wished she could see him.

A moment later, Pam reappeared. "I'm sorry about that—where did Helen go?"

"She's looking around."

"What do you think? Will she take on our cause?"

Frankly, Olivia had no idea. It had been impossible to read her mother-in-law's impassive poker face. Maybe it was a defense mechanism, because Helen had obviously perfected it a long time ago.

Pam glanced around the living room, as if she were making sure the coast was clear. "I have to tell you something. I'm not sure this is the best time to break it to you, but there's news."

Pam nodded in Danny's direction and Olivia's heart flip-flopped.

"You got him enrolled in the special education program?"

Pam grimaced. "Not exactly. Well, not *yet,* anyway." She gestured toward her office with a flick of her head. "Come in here where we can talk privately."

Every muscle in Olivia's body tensed. She had a feeling she knew what Pam was going to say before she said it. Even so, the words, *we've found a family that wants to adopt Danny,* sounded surreal when they bounced off her ears.

"What about Kevin?"

Pam shook her head. "I'm sorry. I'm afraid they can't take both of the boys. They want Danny. They're even willing to pay for private education for him."

Olivia felt as if her heart had been ripped out of her chest. She'd known it was going to be tough to get them into the same household, but it saddened her to think of those sweet boys spending the rest of their childhood in an orphanage. However, it was even sadder to think of them being split up and sent to different homes. Kevin would be devastated, too young to understand that this was a good opportunity for his little brother. She couldn't let him suffer another crushing blow like that.

What in the world was she going to do?

"Pam, please. No—"

But before Olivia could finish her sentence, Helen appeared in Pam's office doorway.

"I've seen enough. I'm ready to go. Thank you for your time, Ms. Wilson."

Pam looked at Olivia. Olivia looked at Helen.

Helen's face was impassive.

"What did you think? Will you help us with a fundraiser?" asked Olivia.

"I don't know yet. I'll have to get back to you. Come, Olivia, let's go."

Despite how much she wanted to stay, needed to stay, to ask Pam how they could rectify the situation and keep the boys together, Olivia tore herself away.

Neither woman said a word until they were tucked safely inside the limo. Olivia's head was too full of the news Pam had just sprung on her. Too full of sadness for Kevin. She barely heard her mother-in-law when she said, "Rule number one about supporting charities, Olivia, never commit yourself right out of the gate. Especially if you have every heartrending, poignant nonprofit in the northeast begging for your help. You can only choose a handful at best. And believe me, they're all worthy causes."

Helen sat and studied Olivia for a moment. Her perusal was so bold, it almost felt as if she were picking her apart piece by piece.

Olivia felt so weighted down, all she wanted to do

was turn away and rest her head on the car window. She had no fight in her right now and if Helen was going to pick her apart like a vulture on carrion, well—

"I mean, of course, I'm going to support your Children's Home, but we need not tell that Pam so right off the bat. Let her worry for a while. Oh, but that's right, you're on the board, aren't you?"

And then the strangest thing happened—Helen smiled. She actually smiled at Olivia.

"Congratulations, dear, I'm quite impressed with your charity. Together, you and I are going to raise a lot of money for it. But let's get you through this pregnancy first. Events of the magnitude that we're going to throw are exhausting." Helen reached out and laid a hand on Olivia's stomach. "I must confess, since you're going to be the mother of my grand-child, I realized that you and I needed some time to get to know each other better."

So Olivia had finally earned her spot next to Helen.

This was the equivalent of Helen patting the couch and beckoning Payton to sit next to her.

Olivia heard herself uttering words of thanks, but it was almost as if it were someone else saying the words. While she was glad the Children's Home would benefit, she was heartsick over the news that the Kelso boys would be split up. And underneath it all, she couldn't help but feel like a fraud.

What would Helen do if she knew the baby Olivia was carrying wasn't really hers? It was Jamison's seed fertilizing some mystery woman's egg. Olivia was just the incubator.

Well, Helen would never find out.

Chapter Thirteen

Olivia was relieved when her visit to Boston passed with no contact from Derek. Actually, it put her worried mind to rest.

Had she misunderstood what he'd said?

Maybe.

Who knew?

But he had been pretty cryptic that night in the kitchen. Why?

Forget *why*. She really didn't want to know.

Still, that didn't keep her from pondering the puzzle and worrying over the pending adoption of Danny Kelso. She told Jamison, hoping that somehow, someway they could find a solution that would allow the boys to stay together. It might be possible because the adoption process was not going smoothly. Pam had even decided to wait until all the paperwork had been approved before breaking the news to Kevin.

With this scant glimmer of hope, Olivia prayed for a miracle that somehow, someway her boys could stay together.

It was a much-needed distraction when the invitation for the State dinner honoring the president of Tunisia and his wife arrived in the mail.

Jamison had been so busy with work, and they'd both been so tired most evenings, that they hadn't gone out as a couple in a while.

It was fun shopping for her dress and planning for their big night out. It was especially exciting when she discovered that she'd gained a dress size.

At this point she wasn't really *showing* as much as she was starting to fill out. Her breasts were fuller—which Jamison loved—and she was starting to lose the definition in her waist.

Since the new silver-beaded gown she bought for the dinner was only one size larger than what she normally wore, she'd easily be able to take it in after she was back to her pre-pregnancy weight.

With all the shopping and preparation of getting

ready for the important dinner, Olivia wasn't surprised that she was exhausted the day of the event.

After she got back from having her hair done, she lay down and rested for a couple of hours, but even that didn't help refresh her.

When it was time to get ready, she was actually feeling a little bit nauseated, but she thought it was just because she was hungry. As she was getting ready, she ate some toast and drank a cup of herbal tea.

That seemed to take the edge off of it, and she was glad, because the event tonight was so important to Jamison.

Influential people would be there. Those whose support it would be necessary to secure if he was to gain the nomination for the 2016 presidential race.

That seemed like lifetimes away. In fact, by then, their baby would be seven years old and would probably have a sibling—just the thought of that gave Olivia a boost of energy.

But as far as the presidential race was concerned, the clock was ticking. Jamison needed to utilize every opportunity that came his way and, as the future first lady, Olivia needed to be by his side.

Especially tonight.

So she donned her silver gown and white gloves. She helped Jamison fix his bow tie, and together they set out to win over the decision makers.

When they arrived at the White House's north portico, the place was alive with honor guards from all branches of the military in full dress uniform. A few minutes later, Jamison and Olivia looked on as the President and First Lady formally greeted the president of Tunisia and his wife.

They were among a scant handful invited to join the pre-dinner cocktail party. As they joined the dignitaries, they paused at the top of the grand staircase to give the media an opportunity to shoot photos before disappearing upstairs for cocktails.

That's when Olivia first started to feel the cramping. At first she wasn't sure. She brushed it off as exhaustion and promised herself that she'd sleep all day tomorrow if her body needed it.

Jamison was in top form tonight and she couldn't hold him back. Especially when the President himself introduced Jamison as "a man to watch."

As they spoke, Olivia greeted the Tunisian first lady and exchanged pleasantries. But she was relieved when the woman was whisked off to meet the next person, because Olivia had to sit down. The cramping was getting worse.

No. This can't be happening. Not tonight. Not any night.

She managed to hold herself together until the entourage descended the grand staircase and paused in the entrance hall to listen to the Marine Corps Band play "Hail to the Chief" and the Tunisian anthem.

Finally, after the other formal festivities, they walked down the Cross Hall to the state dining room, full of tables lavishly set with gold-edged official china that sat atop gold-and-white tablecloths vying for space with riots of white-flowered centerpieces and glowing candelabras.

Olivia knew she was in trouble and had to leave the dining room before the President took the lectern to deliver his speech. She excused herself to the ladies' room.

She leaned in to Jamison and whispered, "I'll be right back."

Jamison asked, "Are you all right?"

"I'm fine." She smiled through a cramp. "I just need to use the ladies' room before the President starts his address."

Jamison and the other men at the table stood as she rose from her seat. She felt a bit light-headed as she traversed the room to the door, where a staff member opened it for her and discreetly directed her to the lavatory.

As soon as she was inside, she felt a sticky dampness between her legs and thought she might fall apart. But she couldn't. She had to stay calm. She had to think logically. She took her BlackBerry from her purse and dialed her doctor's number.

Unfortunately, it went directly to the answering service, where she left an urgent message. She knew she had to get off her feet. With the help of staff she found in Cross Hall, she was able to find her driver, who immediately took her home.

She called Jamison from the limo, but as she expected, the call went to voice mail because he'd silenced his phone.

She purposely steadied her voice and left him a message. "Jamison, it's me. I don't want you to worry, but I wasn't feeling well and I went home to lie down. Please don't worry or rush. I'll be fine."

When Olivia didn't return after fifteen minutes, Jamison excused himself and went to look for her. Out in the hall he paused to check his phone and saw the message.

The moment he heard her voice, he knew she wasn't fine and felt an urgency to be with her. By the time he was ready to go, the driver had returned and confirmed that he had just dropped Mrs. Mallory off at their Georgetown residence.

It momentarily staved off Jamison's worries when the driver told him that she'd appeared tired and was quiet, but nothing alarming had happened on the ride home.

Everything changed when Jamison entered the apartment and found Olivia collapsed on the bathroom floor.

Not only did she lose the baby, but she'd injured herself when she fainted and hit her head on the tile floor.

The attending physician seemed to take pleasure in telling her that she was lucky that she hadn't ended up with a cerebral hematoma, which could have cost her her life.

But Olivia didn't seem to care. All she wanted to do was sleep, because when she was awake all she did was cry over the child they'd lost.

Jamison felt utterly helpless—nothing he tried seemed to help his wife.

Finally, he excused himself to call her family. He had to let them know that Olivia was in the hospital…and that she'd miscarried.

Strangely enough, the only person he was able to reach was Derek.

"Derek, it's Jamison. I'm afraid I have some bad news."

After he'd relayed the news to his brother-in-law,

and established that she was, indeed, going to be all right, he was taken aback when Derek lit into him.

"Are you finally going to ease up on pressuring her to give you a child?"

Tired from having spent a sleepless night at Olivia's bedside, Jamison flinched at Derek's tone.

"Excuse me? What are you talking about?"

"This is your fault, man. You and your overbearing mother. Olivia only underwent those treatments to please you and your demanding family. If anything happens to her, your ass is history."

His harsh words bounced off Jamison's ears like crashing cymbals. He'd never pressured Olivia. In fact, he'd been the reluctant one. But he certainly wasn't going to stand there and argue with Derek when Olivia was lying in a hospital bed.

Still, he couldn't let it go without putting in his two cents. "I don't know where you get off saying that. Olivia wanted a child just as badly as I did, but I'm certainly not obligated to explain anything to you. I just called to let you know that your sister is in the hospital and to ask if you could pass along the message since I've already tried the others and couldn't reach them."

"She confided in me. Told me what a jackass you've been. That your marriage was on the rocks. That's where I get off saying these things. You have no idea the lengths my sister has gone to to please you. You've got to stop pushing her to get pregnant or you're going to kill her."

With that, Derek hung up the phone, leaving Jamison's head spinning as he tried to figure out exactly what had just happened.

Olivia had confided in Derek?

He and Derek had never seen eye-to-eye. There was something about the guy that always seemed a little off—unlike Paul, who was the best brother-in-law a guy could ask for.

He couldn't believe that Olivia would open up to Derek of all people. But obviously she had.

You have no idea the lengths my sister has gone to to please you.

Was he talking about the trial separation? The fertility treatments?

Jamison had hated what she'd gone through. The only reason he'd supported it again this time was because she so desperately wanted a baby.

But it was becoming clear that wasn't going to happen. He couldn't stand by while she continued to put her body through such turmoil. Because it was obvious that she wasn't strong enough and each miscarriage seemed to be more severe.

He didn't like Derek very much, but he did agree with him on one point: enough was enough.

* * *

Two days later, the doctor released Olivia, who was restricted to limited activity. She tried to convince Jamison that she was fine. Still, he insisted on taking the rest of the week off and staying home with her.

There really wasn't anything for him to do other than pick up takeout food and take out the trash, but Olivia couldn't convince him to return to work.

"I'm sure I'm up to throwing away a cardboard carton, Jamison," she said. But he wouldn't hear of it. It seemed as if he simply wanted to be near her. Sometimes she'd look up from the book she was reading or glance over at him while they were watching TV and catch him staring at her.

"What's the matter?" she'd ask.

He'd shake his head and blink as if he were clearing cobwebs from his mind.

Of course, the only thing on Olivia's mind was talking to Chance Demetrios about how long she needed to wait before they could try another in vitro procedure.

The following Sunday, as they sat enjoying bagels and the Sunday paper, she said, "I'm flying back to Boston on Tuesday. I have an appointment with Dr. Demetrios. We're going to discuss when I can start the process again."

Jamison put the paper down and looked at her as

if she was crazy. "Olivia. Please. You can't go through this again."

"Yes, I can."

"Well, *I* can't," he insisted. "Look, I talked to Derek while you were in the hospital."

Derek? Olivia's body went numb with shock. "And what did he say?"

Jamison simply looked at her for a minute and, though she didn't think it possible, the longer he stared, the more frightened she got.

"He told me…" Jamison stopped mid-sentence and shook his head.

Oh, my God.

"He told you what?" she demanded.

He shook his head again. "Let's just not do this again, okay?"

"Jamison, I'm sorry. I wanted to tell you, but I didn't know how you'd take it."

Her husband's face clouded with confusion. "Tell me what?"

Uh-oh. Maybe she'd spoken too soon.

He knew that look. She was keeping something from him. Probably the same thing that Derek was hinting at when he told Jamison he had no idea of *the lengths my sister has gone to to please you.*

"What did Derek tell you?" she insisted.

He knew it wasn't fair, but his instincts were telling him that perhaps his wife hadn't been putting all her cards on the table. So he opted for an old bluff he'd employed when he used to practice law.

"He told me everything."

First, Olivia's face turned white. Then it crumpled. As much as he hated to see his wife in mental pain, especially after what she'd been through physically, he needed to know the whole story.

"How could he do that to me?" Olivia's voice was a shock-induced hoarse whisper.

Every muscle in Jamison's body tensed. "Why don't you start from the beginning and tell me your version of the story?"

And she did. Telling him again about the appointment with Chance Demetrios where she learned that she was not able to have any more children and then about how she'd cried on Derek's shoulder and he'd come up with the plan to switch the eggs.

Jamison's blood started to simmer, and with each detail of how she'd deceived him, how she'd taken matters into her own hands and purposely left him out of the decision-making process about *his* child, his blood began to boil until it finally reached the point where he knew he had to get away from her to process all the lies and deception. Because sitting here, looking at her sad eyes and beautiful face, he was tempted to overlook the fact that she'd lied to him about something so serious.

And in a big way.

Lies and deception. Not exactly the same brand that wrecked his parents' marriage, but stripped down to the bones, a lie was a lie was a lie.

He'd had to trick her into telling him the truth. He didn't know if he could live with a woman he couldn't trust.

He certainly couldn't live a life marred by lies and deception.

He stood.

"Where are you going?" Her voice was panicked.

"I need to go out for a while. I need time to think, time to process things. I need to figure out how you could lie to me about something so important."

She reached out to him.

"Jamison, please don't go. We need to talk this out."

He shook his head and let himself out the front door.

Chapter Fourteen

They decided it would be best if Olivia moved back to Boston while Jamison finished the congressional session. Olivia didn't like it, but he said he needed time to sort things out and she wanted to give him room.

She let him know that she loved him and would be waiting for him…forever, if that's how long it took.

Back in Boston, as she put her things away, she realized that they were back to square one. No, this time it felt like square minus one, and she didn't know if the damage could be fixed.

It was Derek's fault.

She wasn't blaming him for offering her the donor egg or for encouraging her to deceive her husband. She took full responsibility for that. She should've told Jamison.

That way, Derek wouldn't have had anything to use against her. How could he have done it? How could he have gone straight to Jamison and spilled the beans without first giving her the chance to clean up her own mess and tell her husband herself?

First the blackmail innuendos, now this.

As far as she was concerned, her relationship with her brother was over.

But first she intended to give him a piece of her mind.

Olivia drove to the institute and went immediately to Derek's office. She pushed open the closed door and found him talking on the phone.

"Get off the phone, Derek," she said, like a woman possessed. Suddenly, she knew how Danny Kelso must feel when he threw back his head and wailed at the top of his lungs. That's what she wanted to do now.

But since she still possessed a modicum of self-control, she refrained.

She did, however, raise her voice a few decibels when Derek ignored her and kept talking.

"I said get off the phone, Derek. I need to talk to you now!"

This time she got his attention. He ended the conversation.

"What the hell is wrong with you? Can't you see I was on a business call?"

"Yes, I could see that. I just decided to come in here and start messing up your life like you've messed up mine. Oh, but there's one problem—you don't have a life. Is that why you derive such pleasure in messing with other people's?"

He threw his hands up in the air. "Olivia. What are you talking about?"

She wanted to take her hand and swipe it across his desk, knock everything on it to the floor. She wanted to grab him by the shirtsleeves and shake him until his teeth rattled.

"You know what I'm talking about. You know what you told Jamison."

Either he was a good actor or he truly was puzzled. "I talked to Jamison, but I didn't really tell him anything. Except that I thought he needed to call off the dogs when it came to pressuring you into pumping out babies."

"You told him about the donor egg."

"No I did not."

"But he knew."

"Well, he didn't hear it from me."

Derek shrugged, to indicate case dismissed. Brother off the hook.

"There's nobody else he could've heard it from, if not you. What I don't understand is why you would set up your own sister for extortion, Derek. That's about as low as it gets."

His eyes shuttered.

"I have no idea what you're talking about."

A different look from the adamant way he'd denied telling Jamison passed over his face. A completely different demeanor. Suddenly Olivia wanted to back-pedal, because she was sure she'd missed something.

"You know what I'm talking about. The Valentine's Day dinner party at my house when Jamison and I told the family I was pregnant. You followed me into the kitchen and said that we needed to *talk*. What did you want to talk about, Derek? A payment plan so that you'd keep my secret?"

It turned her stomach, but she could tell that's what he'd been setting her up for. That he hadn't contacted her…well, maybe he'd still felt a murmur of a heart or a conscience or a soul and he'd chickened out.

"I just don't understand why you'd feel compelled to tell my husband what you did while I was lying in a hospital bed not even twenty-four hours after my miscarriage? What was in it for you? Could you just not stand to see somebody happy?"

He glanced down at his hands, fisted them, and then flexed them before he answered.

"I didn't intend to blackmail you. What I wanted to talk to you about was the blood type of the donor. After the fact, I realized that your blood types didn't match and that could've caused a snag in your seamless plan."

Olivia studied her brother, trying to determine whether he was telling the truth or not. She wanted to believe him, but she couldn't.

"Show me proof, Derek. Call up the file of this donor and show me what type of blood she has."

He scratched his nose. "I can't. I destroyed the original file."

"You destroyed the file? You expect me to believe that?"

He blinked rapidly. "I couldn't just transfer her eggs to you and leave the file empty. That's called a paper trail. Someone could've followed it."

She wasn't buying it.

"You'd go to great pains to destroy a file to make the scheme, as you called it, seamless. Yet you'd forget all about the red flag of blood type. Doesn't make sense. This is your business. It seems like blood types would be right up there in standard info right next to dark hair and dark eyes."

His mouth flattened into a hard, straight line. "My

background is in business, Livie, not medicine. I had no idea what to look for beyond skin, hair and eye color. I was trying to make sure the baby looked like you. It didn't occur to me to match the donor's blood type with yours until was deleting the original file and saw it."

He scratched his nose again. She'd read that was often a signal that someone was lying. But who knew for sure? Especially with Derek.

"I guess I'll really never know the truth, will I?"

Derek shrugged.

"I many not have solid proof that it really was the blood I was concerned with, but I do have proof that I wasn't the one who told your husband about the donor eggs. If you don't believe me, just ask him."

She left the institute more confused than when she arrived. Strange how her heart wanted to believe that he might be telling the truth, but her head still wasn't buying his story.

She got home and the place seemed so empty. The Valentine's Day dinner, the girl's getaway with Helen and all those nights that she and Jamison had made love until the sun came up seemed like a distant memory.

She sat in her bedroom window seat, gazing out over the Gardens, which were just starting to show the first signs of spring, and held the phone for a long time before she could bring herself to make the call.

When she finally did, she was surprised when he answered on the first ring.

"Hi, it's me. I'm sorry. I'm *so* sorry. I never intended to lie to you. It just seemed like my last chance. Our last chance. And I so desperately wanted to give you a child. Can you ever forgive me?"

As much as Jamison disliked Derek, he had to give the guy credit. Derek might possibly have saved his and Olivia's marriage.

Despite how rough around the edges and unpalatable the guy could be, he was right. Jamison and his family were partially to blame for Olivia's desperation to have a child.

A desperation that drove her to go so far she'd do something that forced her to lie to him.

Maybe it was because she'd never lied before. Or maybe it was because Jamison felt partially responsible. It was definitely because he still loved her, despite what had happened and maybe even because of the lengths she'd gone to for him. But two days after they'd talked, he'd hopped on a Boston-bound plane and found himself wandering through the Public Garden at noon.

Pam had told him he'd find her there. Olivia had taken the Kelso boys on a picnic.

As he rounded a copse of trees that shaded a statue, there she sat on a red plaid picnic blanket with Danny in her lap. The boy held his truck, spinning the wheels, seeming perfectly content sitting there.

She was saying something to Kevin, who was running around the grass in front of the blanket throwing a football up in the air.

But her mouth froze mid-sentence when she saw Jamison. For a moment, he couldn't speak, either. Seeing her sitting there with the boys was a picture.

They looked like a family. The small, dark-haired boys could've easily passed for her children. Not much of him and his Celtic coloring, but then again, anyone knew that dark hair and eyes were usually the dominant gene.

He stood there savoring the picture for a moment as everything important snapped into perfect focus. Suddenly the world seemed to make sense, or at least it seemed as if it could if the four of them became a family.

Then Olivia finally found her voice and said, "I'm so glad you're here. I thought I'd lost you forever."

He shook his head and lowered himself onto the blanket. "What kind of fool would I be if I let you walk out of my life? I'm not saying it was okay to keep those things from me—there is nothing you can't come to me with. But I love you and I'm glad you're my wife."

He leaned in and kissed her tenderly on the lips.

"Truck!"

When he looked up, Danny was offering him the toy truck and Kevin was asking him to toss the football.

As he was throwing the ball with the older boy, he glanced at the love of his life sitting on the blanket like the Madonna with her child. He knew exactly what she was thinking because he was thinking the same thing.

There had been snags in Danny's adoption. He had to believe that had happened because the boys were meant to be their children. Part of their family.

The family they chose.

* * * * *

PRIVATE PARTNERS

BY
GINA WILKINS

All the characters in this book have no existence outside the imagination of the author, and have no relation whatsoever to anyone bearing the same name or names. They are not even distantly inspired by any individual known or unknown to the author, and all the incidents are pure invention.

First published in Great Britain 2011
Harlequin Mills & Boon Limited,
Eton House, 18-24 Paradise Road, Richmond, Surrey TW9 1SR

PRIVATE PARTNERS © Gina Wilkins 2010

ISBN: 978 0 263 88862 1

23-0211

Harlequin Mills & Boon policy is to use papers that are natural, renewable and recyclable products and made from wood grown in sustainable forests. The logging and manufacturing processes conform to the legal environmental regulations of the country of origin.

Printed and bound in Spain
by Litografia Rosés S.A., Barcelona

Dear Reader,

As much as I try to plan every detail of the books I write, often the characters take over the stories and surprise even me. When I started this series about five medical school friends, I knew Anne Easton had a secret, but I wasn't sure what she was keeping from her schoolmates (and from me). I started planning a romance for her — only to discover that she was already secretly married! I had a lot of fun finding out why she was hiding her hunky hubby from her friends and family, and telling the story of how they overcome the obstacles keeping them apart.

The members of the study group are in their second year of medical school in this book and the pressure mounts as they face their first licensure exam. In book three, they'll finally start seeing patients, while still dealing with their own private lives. I'm thoroughly enjoying the *Doctors in Training* series, and I hope you are, too. Visit me anytime at ginawilkins.com for more details about my works in progress and upcoming titles.

Gina Wilkins

Gina Wilkins is a bestselling and award-winning author who has written more than seventy books. She credits her successful career in romance to her long, happy marriage and her three extraordinary children.

A lifelong resident of central Arkansas, M. Wilkins sold her first book in 1987 and has been writing full-time since. She has appeared on the Waldenbooks, B. Dalton and *USA TODAY* bestseller lists. She is a three-time recipient of the Maggie Award for Excellence, sponsored by Georgia Romance Writers, and has won several awards from the reviewers of *Romantic Times*.

Thanks again to Kerry for all your help, and to Justin for patiently listening through a long Q and A session outside the tool stores!

Prologue

"Only one more week."

Anne Easton shook her head in response to Liam McCright's regretful murmur. "Don't say that. It makes me too sad. I can't enjoy our last few days together if you're going to be counting down the minutes."

They stood at a rock wall of the Argyle Battery of Edinburgh Castle, a breathtaking view of northern Edinburgh, Scotland, spread in front of them. Tourists with an intriguing mix of accents mingled around them, examining and exclaiming over the ancient cannons and battlements. Anne and Liam ignored everyone else, concentrating exclusively on each other on this beautiful summer day.

A brisk, warm breeze caught her fine, blond hair and she reached up to brush a lock away from her mouth, but Liam's hand was already there. His fingertips glided across her cheek when he tucked the errant strand behind her ear, then bent his head to press a quick kiss against the lips he'd uncovered.

She smiled up at him, enchanted by the way his thick, dark hair, worn in his trademark long and tousled style, waved around a face so appealing that her throat still tightened when she looked at him. She couldn't see his blue-gray eyes behind his dark glasses, but she knew they were focused on her face as though nothing else around them was of interest to him. That heady attentiveness was one of his more seductive talents.

"I'll miss you," he said, pulling her into the crook of one arm to nestle her against his lean body as they turned to gaze out over the streets of the historic city.

"I'll miss you, too." The simple words weren't enough to express how much she would feel his absence in her life.

They had just spent a blissfully private eight weeks in London, and this jaunt to Scotland was a last celebration of their time together. In only one short week, she would return to Arkansas, where she would begin medical school in August, and Liam would fly to the Galápagos Islands on an assignment for his job as a globe-trotting journalist.

"I don't want our relationship to end this time. Not like the last time."

She bit her lower lip in response to the pain that shot through her. "There were reasons why we broke up three years ago. I'm not sure they've changed all that much."

"Except that you're an adult now, not an inexperienced college freshman. You're twenty-three years old, Annie. Your parents can't tell you how to run your life now. You have the ght to be with me if you want, even if they still hate me."

y don't hate you."

d. "Right. Which is why you haven't even told ogether again for the past two months."

Because she wasn't sure she could win that argument, she said instead, "They weren't the only reason we broke up anyway."

"Maybe. But it's different now. The eight weeks that have passed since we ran into each other in London have been great, haven't they?"

"They've been perfect," she agreed wistfully.

As if on impulse, he turned to face her, using his body to block her from the view of any others around them, giving them a semblance of privacy in their very public surroundings. "Then why does it have to end?"

They both knew the answer to that question, but she shrugged and replied, "Because I'm starting medical school in Arkansas in just over a month and you're contracted to travel the globe for the next year. Longer if your show gets renewed, which I know it will."

He brushed that logical argument aside with characteristic impatience. "We don't have to be joined at the hip to be committed to each other. You can go to medical school and I can pursue my career. We have phones and computers to stay in touch when we aren't physically together, and airplanes to get us both to the same place at the same time whenever we have a few free days."

She sighed, thinking of how unlikely it was that such an arrangement could last the entire four years she would be in medical school. Of course, maybe Liam wasn't thinking that far ahead. Maybe he was just thinking about playing it by ear after they went their own ways next week. He wasn't known for long-term planning.

"I would love to hear from you anytime you want to call," she agreed. "There's certainly no reason we can't stay in touch after we go back to our separate careers."

He shook his head, his expression dissatisfied. "That's not what I meant. I don't want to be computer friends, or whatever the modern equivalent of pen pals might be. I want us to be connected. A real couple."

She laughed somewhat quizzically. "You want to go steady?"

"No." He wasn't smiling when he dropped his hands on her shoulders and gazed somberly down at her. "Marry me, Anne. Now. Before you go back to the States next week."

"M-marry?" Shocked into stuttering, she stared up at him. "Liam—"

He kissed her into silence, then raised his head with a new look of determination on his dashingly stubbled face. "Marry me," he repeated. "Let's make it official. Even if we aren't together all the time, no one can ever really separate us again."

Even as elation swept through her, she tried to keep herself grounded in reality. Liam had obviously lost his mind. He'd had a pint of Guinness at lunch—they both had—but she hadn't thought the ale was strong enough to addle his wits. "We can't just get married."

"Why not?" He grinned suddenly, letting himself get carried away with his reckless plan, as he was so prone to do. It was the trait that had landed him his coveted career. He was becoming increasingly famous as a daring adventurer who was willing to take great risks in pursuit of a marketable angle. "Who's going to stop us?"

"But—"

Glancing around at the new influx of tourists into their area, he took her arm. "Don't answer yet. Let's go have another pint and talk about it."

Shaking her head in bemusement, she allowed him to tow her away from the stone wall, though she promised herself she would not let him sweep her into an impulsive elopement. No matter how charming and persuasive Liam could be. There were entirely too many reasons why she couldn't go along with this crazy, impulsive proposal. Too many strikes against them from the start.

One of them had to be sensible—and that responsibility always seemed to fall on her shoulders.

Chapter One

"Are you sure you had the time to join us for dinner this evening, Anne? I hope we didn't disrupt your study plans."

"I can take off a couple hours for dinner, Mother. I can't study every minute of every day."

Though it felt sometimes as though that was exactly what she did, Anne Easton thought as she sliced into the roasted chicken her mother had served for this Friday evening family meal. Even when she tried to rebel and spend an afternoon resting or reading or watching TV, guilt and anxiety soon had her back at her books, working even harder than usual to make up for the lost time. Just as she would do tonight after returning to her apartment from this evening with her family.

"You've lost weight." Her mother, Deloris Easton, a retired family court judge, studied her intently from across the table. "And you look tired. Are you getting enough sleep?"

Anne couldn't help but laugh a little at that. "No. But don't worry, I'm getting by."

Her father, Dr. Henry Easton, Jr., a prominent and still-practicing Little Rock, Arkansas, neurosurgeon, listened to the exchange from the head of the formal dining room table. His thin silver hair gleamed in the light from the crystal chandelier overhead. Behind the lenses of his silver-framed glasses, his dark blue eyes focused piercingly on his only daughter. "It's all well and good to join the family for dinner occasionally. We enjoy spending the time with you. But don't let yourself get behind. You know what I always say…"

"Yes, Dad. If I fall behind, I'll never catch up," she recited, stabbing a glazed carrot with a bit more force than necessary.

"Back when I was in medical school, I was lucky to have a sandwich and a three-hour nap most days." Seated at the other end of the table, Dr. Henry Easton, Sr., retired thoracic surgeon, dabbed at his silver mustache with the corner of a linen napkin.

Anne's older brother, Stephen, had once suggested that Granddad had grown the mustache when the last of his hair had fallen out years earlier, just to prove he could still grow hair if he wanted to. Both Anne and Stephen had inherited their mother's blond hair and light blue eyes rather than the sandy brown hair and darker blue eyes from their father's side of the family.

Stephen, a third-year surgical resident and almost five years Anne's elder at twenty-nine, exaggerated a shudder. "Remember when I had the flu the second semester of my first year of med school? It was all I could do not to fall behind, even though I was feverish and aching and coughing my lungs up."

Anne focused on her plate, though her rapidly tightening throat made it increasingly difficult to swallow.

"I never missed a day of school due to illness," Granddad boasted. "Not a day of work, either."

Since she doubted he'd never been sick a day in his life, Anne wondered how many germs he had shared with associates and patients. Wisely, she kept that irreverent question to herself.

"You're making time to study for Step 1?" her father asked, referring to the first part of the medical licensing exam. "I know it's only early February, but June will be here before you know it. You'll want to be ready."

"Yes, Dad." She'd actually have three chances to pass the exam, but she knew her family would be appalled if she didn't sail through on the first attempt. Failure was not an option for an Easton, not even the type that would only set her back a few weeks on her long-term schedule. "I've already started going through the prep books. Whenever I'm not studying for a class, I work on the sample Step 1 questions."

"Not much time left for a social life, huh?" her brother teased.

Neither of the older men looked amused by the quip.

"She'll have plenty of time for a social life after she finishes her career training," their dad said firmly.

Their grandfather nodded agreement. "Just be glad you got rid of that McCright boy in college. Can you imagine how much harder this would all be if you had to stayed involved with him?"

"If she'd gotten into medical school at all," her dad muttered.

That McCright boy. It was the way they always referred to Liam, even though he was almost seven years older than Anne. He'd done a hitch in the army before enrolling in the university where they'd met.

They still blamed him for the B she had received in chemistry her freshman year. For an Easton, a B might as well have been an F. Had she not been involved with that McCright boy, she would have been able to focus on her schoolwork, they had proclaimed.

Anne took a sip of her iced tea, pleased her hand was

steady as she lifted the glass to her lips. It was her right hand, and a pretty little diamond and sapphire ring glittered on her finger. She'd worn it home from her year studying abroad after her college graduation, telling everyone she'd bought it as a souvenir in London. She never took it off.

"I saw him on TV the other night when I was flipping channels to find a good movie to watch." Her mother shook her ash-blond head in disapproval. "He was filming in another one of those dangerous, unstable places he's always going to. That long, floppy hair looked like it hadn't been trimmed in months, and he had at least a week's worth of stubble on his face. He looked like a pirate. I don't know how any woman could handle being involved with such a restless adventurer. I believe he's one of those adrenaline addicts I've read about. Never really happy unless he's risking life and limb somewhere."

Reckless, impulsive, footloose. Terms her family had used to describe Liam when she'd dated him that year. He had been all of those things, of course, and more. Had it been despite those traits or because of them that she had fallen so desperately in love with him?

Her dad abruptly changed the subject, as he always did whenever her college romance came up. "How's your car performing, Anne? Is it still giving you problems? Don't know why you won't let me buy you a newer one."

"I like my car, Dad. And it's running fine since you had your mechanic work on it for me. I don't need you to buy me a new one." It was the same car he'd given her for a high school graduation present six and a half years earlier. She had always intended to buy her next car for herself. She had certainly inherited her share of the Easton pride.

"Humph." He looked both annoyed and pleased by her refusal. "You always have been stubborn about letting me help you."

She smiled at him. "You raised me to be independent and self-sufficient, remember?"

His eyes softened. "So I did. What was I thinking?"

"Isn't this nice? I'm so glad we could all be here this evening. It's the first time we've all been together since Christmas."

"Not quite all of us, Mother." Stephen glanced pointedly at the empty chair beside him.

"Oh, I know, and I wish Danielle could have been here, too. Tell her we missed her, will you?"

Danielle Carpenter, another surgical resident, was on call that evening and couldn't leave the hospital. She and Stephen had been engaged for a few months, though they were in no hurry to set a wedding date. They seemed quite content for now to live together in their downtown Little Rock loft and focus all their attention on their jobs. Her family approved heartily of Stephen's choice for a mate. They considered the ambitious, brilliant and attractive Danielle a fine addition to their overachieving clan.

Both Stephen and Danielle had admitted they weren't sure they wanted children, though they weren't ruling out having one child in the future. Of course, they would be extremely busy in their surgical careers, but that was what nannies were for, right?

Having been cared for by several nannies during her own childhood as the daughter of career-obsessed parents, Anne knew it was possible to hire daily child care and still remain active and involved in a child's life. Her mother and dad had certainly kept a close eye on her. Still did, for that matter.

She had no doubt Stephen and Danielle would be just as successful at parenting as they were at everything else.

Anne prepared to leave not long after finishing her dessert. As much as she loved her family, she was ready to get back to her own apartment. She'd thought an evening break would do her good, but she was more stressed now than she'd been when she'd arrived. Her family didn't try to detain her; all she had to do was mention that she needed to study and they practically shoved her out the door.

Leaving the men in the den to discuss Stephen's chances of becoming chief surgical resident—something Anne had no doubt he would achieve—her mother offered to walk her to the door. Anne waited patiently while her mother reached for her aluminum cane, which she used to steady herself as she moved carefully through the large house.

Though only fifty-nine, Deloris Easton had suffered a massive stroke nineteen months earlier. It had happened only a month before Anne started medical school, only a few days after she had returned from abroad. Anne had brought home a secret she hadn't been able to share with her family while her mother lay near death for several days, nor during the long, still ongoing period of recuperation. Her mother had made great strides since her stroke, but it still broke Anne's heart at times to see the formerly robust and fiercely independent woman looking so frail and vulnerable.

"There's something I want to give you before you go, Anne. I found it when I was cleaning out my jewelry armoire earlier, and I thought you'd like to have it. It belonged to my mother." Her voice was only a little slurred, though it had taken a great deal of effort and therapy to achieve that success. Resting one hand lightly on the cane handle, she reached with the other into the pocket of the melon-colored blazer she wore with a matching shell and camel slacks. From that blazer pocket, she withdrew a small, flat jewelry box.

Anne opened the box curiously. She studied the necklace inside with a lump in her throat. Small baguette diamonds surrounded a larger, round-cut diamond that caught the light from the foyer chandelier and reflected it cheerfully back at her. The pendant hung from a deceptively delicate-looking gold chain. "It's lovely, Mother. I think I remember Grandma Henderson wearing this."

"It was one of her favorite pieces. My brother gave it to her not long before he died in Vietnam. I know you'll treasure it."

"Of course I will." Almost unbearably touched, Anne reached up to fasten the chain around her neck. She'd worn her long hair pinned up, so it didn't get in the way as she secured the clasp. The pendant nestled into the neckline of the crisp blue shirt she'd worn with black pants for this family dinner. "Thank you."

"It looks lovely on you." Her mother sighed lightly. "I still miss her, you know. Every day."

"I know you do." Anne's heart clenched at the memory of how close she had come to losing her own mother. "Thank you again for the necklace. I'll take very good care of it."

"I know what a difficult time you're having now. I remember from Stephen's experience that the second semester of the second year is one of the most challenging parts of medical school. Several of his friends suffered severe burnout during that time, and I suspect Stephen was more stressed than he allowed us to see. I just want you to know your father and I are so very proud of you."

Anne was immeasurably affected by her mother's words. Yet, why did she now feel even more pressured than she had before? "Thanks, Mother. I'll try to live up to your expectations."

Her mother laughed and reached up to kiss her cheek. "We'll always be proud of you, no matter what."

Anne left without responding to that sentiment. As sweet and as heartfelt as it had been, she was fully aware she could disappoint her parents all too easily.

Anxious to get back to her studies, she parked her aging compact in front of her West Little Rock apartment and hurried up the stairs. Her small, two-bedroom apartment was on the second floor of the two-story, outward-opening building. She was already thinking about what subject she would study first when she paused in front of the door to insert her key in the lock. She wondered how much her study group had accomplished that evening. Maybe she should have met with them instead of taking the night off to dine with her family.

If she fell behind, she would never catch up.

Liam had always accused her of requiring too much of herself, on top of the expectations of her family. He'd told her she couldn't hope to be perfect, that she didn't have to live up to anyone's expectations but her own—which were set much too high for an ordinary mortal. He'd never quite understood what it was like to be an Easton.

Less than half an hour after arriving at her apartment, she'd let down her hair and changed into comfortable clothes—a T-shirt and yoga pants with fuzzy socks. She booted up her computer in preparation of a few hours of studying before she crashed for the night. It was only 9:00 p.m., so she figured she had three or four solid study hours before her brain shut down.

She had just plopped down in her chair to get started when her doorbell rang.

She wasn't expecting visitors that evening, and certainly not at that hour. Approaching the door warily, she ran through a mental list of possibilities. Maybe it was Haley from her study group, bringing by some notes or study materials, though Haley usually called before dropping in. Could be one of her neighbors, though she didn't know any of them very well, since she was rarely home and usually locked in with her books when she was there. Her brother, maybe? Had she left something behind at her parents' house?

When she looked through the peephole in the door and saw the face on the other side, she realized she never would have guessed correctly. It actually took her a moment to recognize him.

Disengaging the locks, she threw open the door. "Liam!"

"Hello, Annie."

"What on earth are you doing here?" Had she somehow conjured him with her earlier thoughts of him?

Perfectly fitting the description, "tall, dark and handsome," Liam gave her the kind of wickedly charming grin that could make an impressionable young woman do all kinds of crazy and irresponsible things.

"I wanted to see my wife," he said in that beautifully modulated voice that whispered in her dreams so many nights.

Glancing instinctively around the otherwise empty landing to make sure no one else was within hearing, she moved aside. "Don't just stand there. Come in."

He didn't hesitate to accept the invitation. He moved through the open doorway, scooping her into his arms and kicking the door closed behind him.

The kiss seemed to last for a very long time, and Anne would have been perfectly satisfied had it never ended. Only the eventual need for air brought them reluctantly to the surface.

Opening her eyes with a dazed blink, she realized she had practically climbed Liam like a tree. Her legs were wrapped around his lean hips, and his hands supported her beneath her bottom. Her arms had locked strangle-tight around his neck. The metal-framed glasses he rarely wore sat a little crookedly on his nose and there was a smudge on the right lens.

Liam seemed to have no complaints about any of the above. He smiled at her with a flash of white teeth, looking as though he wouldn't mind taking a bite of her as he nuzzled her cheek and nestled her more snugly against his notably aroused body. "Now, that's what I call a welcome."

Her cheeks warming—though not as hot as the temperature burning deep inside the core of her—she disentangled herself and stumbled an inch or so away from him. He let her go, making no effort to hide his reluctance to do so.

Anyone observing their reunion would find it hard to believe they had parted in a quarrel only a few months earlier, she realized with a hard swallow. But then, it had always been that way between them. When they were together, the explosive attraction between them had a way of making them forget the many reasons why they shouldn't be.

She pushed her hands through the fine blond hair that tumbled in loose curls to the middle of her back. "I wasn't expecting to see you tonight. Why didn't you call?"

"I've been trying for the past hour. You didn't answer your phone."

She clapped a hand to her mouth. "Oh. I turned off the ringer earlier. I guess I forgot to turn it back on."

She hadn't wanted to interrupt her family dinner, and she hadn't even thought of her phone since. She hadn't been expecting any calls.

"You cut your hair." She'd noticed immediately that his signature mop of almost shoulder-length dark curls was now tamed into a cut just a little longer than military length, but she'd been too distracted by his kiss to comment at first. He looked so different without all that hair. She'd once teased him that his hair was more famous than his face.

His usual rakish stubble was missing, as well. He was clean shaven, his sideburns trimmed to a conservative length. With his glasses replacing his usual contact lenses, the change was quite dramatic. She studied him curiously, trying to decide how she felt about this new look. She'd never seen Liam with short hair, or looking quite so…well, preppy. He looked good—but then, it would take a lot more than a haircut to mar Liam's good looks.

"Yeah." He shrugged, his smile endearingly sheepish. "I guess this is my attempt at going incognito. You'd be surprised how well it works. I haven't been recognized all day."

"That's not so surprising at all. It really makes you look different."

"In a bad way?"

Amused by his sudden and wholly uncharacteristic moment of insecurity, she shook her head. "You look great. As always."

"Thanks. So do you."

Suddenly a little nervous, she ran a hand self-consciously down her faded T-shirt, rather wishing she still wore the professional, tailored clothing that had given her an air of confidence when she'd faced her family. "I just put on a pot of coffee. It should be ready now. Would you like a cup?"

Liam glanced at his watch. "Coffee at this hour? Is it decaf?"

"No. I was planning to study for a few more hours. I figured it would wear off by the time I turned in."

"Of course," he murmured, just a hint of disapproval on his face. "I should have realized you'd be studying. Am I interrupting?"

He was, of course, but she shook her head. "I hadn't even gotten started yet. I had dinner with my family this evening, and I've only been home for a little while."

"Ah." He followed her into her tiny kitchen, which seemed even smaller when filled with him. "That explains why you looked so tense when you opened the door."

"I happened to have a very nice time with my family tonight," she retorted, feeling the diamond necklace still nestled beneath her T-shirt. "They were on their best behavior."

"Didn't pressure you at all about your grades or your résumé?" He looked skeptical.

"Well…not too much."

He nodded as if she had confirmed his suspicions. "Mmm-hmm. Did my name come up tonight?"

She took two mugs from a cabinet to avoid looking at him. "What makes you think your name would come up during my family dinner?"

"Because it so often does. I'm the dire warning they use to make sure you stay in line. I'm sure they remind you you'd never be doing so well in medical school if I were still around. After all, I caused you to get that B."

He was so precisely on target she almost wondered if he'd somehow bugged her mother's dining table. Pushing that fanciful thought aside, she said lightly, "My mother mentioned she saw you on TV last week. Dad changed the subject quickly enough."

"I'm sure he did."

Following her father's example, she moved quickly to a topic less contentious than her relationship with her family. "Have you eaten?"

"Yeah. I had dinner a couple hours ago."

"Would you like dessert? I have half a chocolate cake hidden in the pantry."

Her wording seemed to amuse him. "What did you do, hide it from yourself?"

"No." She laughed and shook her head. "I hid it from my friend, Ron. He's a fiend for chocolate. I wanted to save some for snacks this weekend, in case I don't find time for a grocery run for a few more days."

"Ron?" His tone was carefully neutral.

"He's in my study group. I've told you about them. There are five of us in all. We get together several times a week to study our lecture notes and slides."

"Oh yes, I remember. So this would be old, ugly, married Ron?"

She lifted an eyebrow. She wasn't asking him who he spent time with when he wasn't around—wasn't even sure she really wanted to know. "No. This would be young, cute, single Ron."

"Humph."

She wasn't quite sure how to interpret that sound, but she had no trouble deciphering the look in his eyes when he moved closer and placed his hands on her hips.

"Actually," he murmured, "I have something besides chocolate cake in mind for dessert."

Suddenly breathless, she rested her hands on his chest, feeling his heart beginning to pound beneath her palms. "Do you?"

"Mmm." He bent his head to give her earlobe a teasing nip. "All of a sudden, I'm ravenous."

As was she. She melted into his arms, parting her lips in invitation as he pressed his mouth to hers. His tongue plunged eagerly, tangling with hers in a dance of desire.

"Annie," he muttered, lifting his mouth a fraction of an inch. "I've missed you. I hated the way we left things between us before Christmas."

"So did I," she admitted, remembering their quarrel with a sharp pang. She'd returned to Arkansas convinced that their unlikely marriage was coming to an end, which had made it very difficult for her to enjoy the holidays. She knew her family had attributed her unseasonable somberness to worries about her studies, but it had been Liam who'd been on her mind when she'd torn the wrappings from her gifts.

They'd talked since, of course. Neither of them had mentioned that painful argument, though she suspected it had been on his mind as much as it had her own.

His hands slipped beneath her top to explore the sensitive skin beneath. Ripples of pleasure seemed to trail from his fingertips as he caressed her throat, her breasts, her stomach— then lower. She moaned when her knees gave way.

Liam held her closer, and there was no mistaking he was as aroused as she. "Can you take just a little more time away from your books?" he asked, his voice hoarse.

At that moment, she would have gladly thrown her books over a cliff. Whatever he was there to tell her, whatever the future held for them, she didn't want to waste one moment of their time together.

Drawing his head to hers again, she murmured against his lips, "I'll start early in the morning."

He swept her into his arms and headed back toward the bedroom.

Anne lay against the pillows, waiting for her heartbeat to return to normal—as if that were possible with Liam sprawled in the bed beside her. He lay on his back and his eyes were closed, letting her see faint lines of weariness on his handsome face. He'd probably had a long day of traveling to get to her, though he hadn't let exhaustion affect his vigor, she thought with a sated smile.

She studied his profile, trying to get used to his new appearance. Trying to convince herself he was really there. Wondering why he had come.

Her smile faded when she remembered the last words they had spoken to each other when they'd parted in December. Telling her friends and family she needed a little time to herself to rest and study, she had slipped away during her winter break to meet Liam in Memphis a week before Christmas. It had been only the third time they had managed to see each other in the past year and a half.

They had spent a long weekend at the famed Peabody Hotel, locking themselves in their suite and hardly coming out except for the occasional meal. It had been glorious, but had ended with an argument that had rapidly escalated into anger.

The emotions between them had always been volatile and very close to the surface.

They had apologized later, but had parted rather stiffly, the words still ringing between them even as they had kissed goodbye. They'd talked only a couple of brief times since when Liam had a chance to call from some distant place. Though they spoke cheerfully each time, she was often in tears after the calls ended. She hoped Liam didn't know that.

His right hand lay limply on his perspiration-sheened chest. Her attention was drawn to his ring finger, on which he sported a simple band of twisted gold and silver. She had presented the ring to him during their wedding ceremony, the same time he'd given her the diamond and sapphire ring she never removed. Every time she'd seen him on TV or in photos since, she'd noticed the band on his right ring finger, making her believe he wore it as faithfully as she did hers.

Tearing her gaze from Liam, she glanced beyond him to the clock on the nightstand. It was almost 11:00 p.m. With a smothered sigh, she slid toward the edge of the bed, trying not to jostle the mattress.

She hadn't realized Liam was awake until he spoke, his voice still huskier than usual. "Where are you going?"

She settled back against him. "I— Nowhere."

She didn't think he'd want to hear she'd been slipping from the bed to return to her studies. She could take another few minutes.

Opening his eyes, he turned on his side to face her, sliding a hand down her bare side from her shoulder to her hip. "You've lost weight."

"And you have a new scar since I saw you before Christmas," she commented, tracing a puckered line just beneath his rib cage on his left side. "Do I want to know how you got this?"

"Probably not."

She looked at his face. He looked utterly relaxed, lazily content. His newly shorn dark hair was mussed into appealing spikes, showing hints of the curls he'd cut off. His clear, gray-blue eyes reflected his easy smile. Faint dimples creased his lean cheeks, bracketing the beautifully shaped mouth she so loved to kiss. She had always thought Liam was the most handsome man she'd ever met. That opinion had not changed with the passing years.

Propped on his elbow, he toyed with the ends of her hair, pushing it away from her face and arranging it around her bare shoulder. "I guess we can agree that we both need to take better care of ourselves."

She conceded with a faint smile. "Probably."

"How's school going?" he asked, fully aware of the primary reason she hadn't been taking the best care of herself lately.

She shrugged. "It's pretty tough right now."

"How many subjects did you say you're taking this semester?"

"Seven. Microbiology, which includes immunology and parasitology. Pharmacology. Pathology. Ethics. Genetics. Behavioral science. And ICM—Introduction to Clinical Medicine 2."

He shook his head in consternation. "How do you keep up with all of that?"

"It's not easy. We have tests every two weeks, covering anywhere from fifty to eighty lectures per exam."

"Damn, Annie."

She could feel her throat tightening again. "I'll be studying all weekend to make up for taking the time off for dinner with my family tonight." Realizing what she'd just said, she blinked. "Um—how long were you planning to stay?"

His smile was just a little crooked. "Don't worry, babe. I won't interfere with your studying."

Wincing guiltily, she reached out to touch his face. "I don't want you to think I'm sorry you're here. It's always good to see you, Liam."

Dragging her hand to his lips, he brushed a kiss across her knuckles. "I've missed you."

"I've missed you, too," she admitted.

She had loved him almost from the moment she'd laid eyes on him more than five years earlier. She hadn't stopped during the years that had passed after they'd broken up so painfully during her freshman year in college. She'd only fallen harder when they'd met up again accidentally in London. Which probably explained how he had charmed her into this impulsive marriage that still seemed to have an unlikely chance of long-term survival—something she didn't want to think about just then.

He tangled one hand in her hair. "You didn't really want to leave just yet, did you?" he asked, his breath warm on her lips as he spoke only an inch or so away from her mouth.

"No. Not just yet." Wrapping a hand around the back of his head, her fingertips sliding into his short hair, she closed the short distance between them.

Studying could wait just a little longer.

Propped on one elbow, Liam watched Anne sleep. The bedroom was almost dark, but just enough light spilled in through the curtains and from the bathroom night-light to illuminate her pale face against the sage-green pillowcase. Her long, wavy, light blond hair tumbled around her in a rather decadent manner, falling across her bare shoulder and the upper curves of breasts visible above the sage sheet that covered the rest of her.

One strand of hair drooped over her left eye. He wanted to reach out and brush it away, but he was afraid of waking her. She needed her sleep. She looked exhausted, and he couldn't claim full credit.

Though he'd tried to hide it, he'd been startled by her appearance when he'd entered the apartment. It had been only six weeks since she'd sneaked away to join him for their weekend in Memphis during her Christmas break. He had commented then that he could see the toll her hectic schedule was taking on her, but the evidence was even more visible now.

She was too thin. Her light blue eyes were shadowed by purplish hollows her careful makeup didn't quite hide. She was still beautiful in his eyes; nothing could change that. But he worried about her.

He knew all too well the pressure her family placed on her. Almost as much as she placed on herself. That was most of the reason this marriage had been kept such a secret. Anne worried about her mother, who had been taken so ill very soon after they married. And she had said she couldn't handle the burden of her family's disapproval and disappointment on top of the stress of medical school. She needed her family's support and encouragement during the long stretches when she and Liam were separated, she had said. Though he tended to believe her family's support came with too many strings, he had agreed.

He'd had reasons of his own for going along with her request to keep their marriage to themselves. Yet he hadn't realized at the time how burdensome this sneaking around would become. Nor quite how much he would miss her when they were apart, even though he had known from the beginning that their time together would be limited.

Seeing how wan and tired she looked, combined with the sad condition of her pantry, had convinced him he'd done the right thing by coming here now. She needed him. She just didn't realize it yet.

He wondered a bit warily what she would say when he told her he had no immediate plans to leave.

Chapter Two

Liam wasn't in the bed when Anne woke Saturday morning. She lay very still for a few moments after glancing at the clock and noting it was just after eight. Her instincts told her she was alone in the apartment.

He wouldn't take off again without telling her goodbye. He'd probably gone out to pick up breakfast, considering there was no food in her kitchen.

She stumbled toward the shower, deliciously sore and loose-jointed after the night's activities. Running the water as hot as she could stand it, she scrubbed her skin until it glowed and washed her hair with a peach-scented shampoo she knew he liked. Rather than take the time to blow-dry the long waves, she pulled her hair back into a loose braid. She applied makeup carefully, accenting her eyes and brushing blusher over her cheeks in an attempt to look less pale and tired.

She'd just finished dressing in a bright green sweater and slim-fitting dark jeans when she heard Liam's key in the door.

He entered with his arms loaded with grocery bags. He hadn't just bought breakfast; it looked as though he had enough food to make a month's worth of meals.

She hurried to help him with the heavy bags. "You didn't have to do this."

"You said you have to study this weekend. When would you have gone for yourself?"

"I'd have managed. Eventually."

"Now you don't have to." Smiling over his shoulder, he moved toward the kitchen.

He wasn't wearing his contacts again this morning. She'd always teased him about looking like Clark Kent when he wore his glasses. Deceptively mild-mannered and average. All it would take was a quick whip of his hand to remove both the glasses and the ordinary persona, turning him back into the daring, reckless superhero who had captured plenty of female hearts from the covers of travel magazines. He'd always laughed, but she could tell the comparison secretly pleased him.

They worked together to unload and put away the groceries he'd purchased. Now her pantry and fridge were better stocked than they had been in almost longer than she could remember. It amused her to think of Liam pushing a cart down the aisles of the grocery store, tossing items haphazardly into the cart. Still, his choices had been good ones, giving her plenty of options for quick, nutritious meals.

While they ate breakfast, he entertained her with stories about his most recent excursion to a politically unstable country in Africa, about some of the people he had met there, some of the adventures he'd had. She knew he didn't tell her everything; he was careful not to worry her about how dangerous his life could be, even though she was all too aware of the risks he took in pursuit of a story.

Liam had become moderately famous as a human interest reporter during the five years since they'd broken up in college. He was even the host of a weekly adventure-travel show on a popular cable channel, journeying all over the world to show settled-in-place couch potatoes what lay beyond their own familiar boundaries. The program had been renewed for another season, but as of the middle of December, he was on a three-month hiatus from filming during which he was concentrating on other work projects.

He was known as a daredevil and an adventurer, one who had the inside scoop on worldwide politics and cultures because he wasn't afraid to immerse himself in those foreign lands. She'd seen him eat fried scorpions in Beijing, ride a camel through the Gobi desert, dance with Aborigines in Australia, tramp through South American rain forests and dive from a cliff in Hawaii. He'd accompanied African game wardens in their never-ending battles against wildlife poachers, interviewed extremists who would have killed him without hesitation if they'd thought they had anything to gain and covered a deadly raid on a Mexican drug cartel.

He'd been named by a popular gossip magazine as one of their most beautiful people, and was considered one of the country's most eligible bachelors. Refusing to answer questions about his personal life had only added to his mystique and popularity.

It had been suggested frequently that Liam led a charmed life. Anne couldn't help dreading the day when his luck ran out—another one of those things she tried not to think about too much. She was getting pretty good at sticking her head in the sand.

"You still haven't told me why you're here," she said as they cleared away the dishes after their meal.

"Yes, I did. I said I missed my wife."

She looked at him over her shoulder. "Now, how about telling me the whole truth?"

He laughed and shook his head. "I never could pull the wool over your eyes."

He leaned against the laminate countertop in the small, white-on-white kitchen, and she saw the glint of excitement in his eyes. Something big was up, she realized, slowly closing the dishwasher door. She braced herself.

"I have a book deal, Annie. That idea I pitched about a book of the stories I've been told by people I've met during my travels? I sold it."

Her eyes went wide. "Liam, that's wonderful!"

She stood and rounded the table to throw her arms around his neck. "Congratulations."

Returning the hug, he grinned. "The publisher is really enthused about the sample chapters I sent in. They like the angle I've given it—the way I interviewed senior members of so many different cultures and societies to get their take on world history as they saw it unfold. They think it's a sure bet to hit the nonfiction bestseller lists, and they think I'm a strong enough pitchman to make the publicity circuits and pitch both the book and my future projects."

She took his face between her hands and planted a kiss on his smiling mouth, her nose bumping his glasses. Laughing, he reached up to adjust them.

"I'm so proud of you. Why didn't you tell me sooner?"

"I had other things on my mind last night," he said, stroking a hand down her back and making her shiver in remembrance.

"This is so exciting. Is the book finished?"

"Mostly. I have to do some revisions. Quite a few, actually. First book mistakes, I guess. There will probably be more revisions to come."

"But still, they liked what they saw enough to buy it."

"Yeah." He looked a little dazed. "They did."

She kissed him again. "It's going to be a blockbuster. I just know it."

He'd already written several well-received magazine articles about his adventures during the past five years, but she knew he had always wanted to publish a book. She was thrilled for him that his dream was coming true. She was glad he'd told her in person rather than over the telephone.

She caught his hand as it sneaked under her top and placed it firmly back on her thigh. "So, what's the plan now? You'll hole up in your apartment in New York and work on your revisions until you start filming your show again?"

"Um." What might have been a nervous expression briefly crossed his face.

Her eyebrows rose as she sensed there was something he was hesitant to tell her. "What?"

"I can't get anything accomplished in my apartment. Everyone knows how to find me there. I thought if I crashed somewhere no one would ever expect, keep my head down for a few weeks, I'd get a lot more done."

"Where did you have in mind?" she asked, growing nervous herself now.

"I thought I could stay here. With you."

Her heart gave a hard thump in her chest.

"Think about it before you answer," he urged quickly, even as she slowly disentangled herself from his arms. "No one would have to know I'm here. You've said your parents never come here to you, that you always go to them when you want to see them. I can make myself scarce when you have your study group over, maybe go to a coffee shop or a library to work."

She laced her fingers together in her lap, her knuckles white from the pressure she exerted on them. "I would love to have you here, of course, but I'm so snowed under with classes and tests…"

"I could help you. Do the shopping, the errands, the housework, the laundry. You wouldn't have to worry about a thing around the house. That would free up even more time for studying, wouldn't it?"

She thought about her study friend Connor Hayes, who had married during the past summer. Connor seemed somewhat less stressed now that he had Mia to share the load around his house, especially when it came to his seven-year-old daughter, Alexis. He was still as inundated with schoolwork as the rest of them, of course, but he'd confessed rather sheepishly that he liked having a wife to keep his household running smoothly. She remembered Haley had groaned and retorted that she wouldn't mind having a hunky guy to do all her chores while she concentrated on nothing but med school.

Now a hunky guy was volunteering to do that very thing for Anne. And she wasn't at all sure it would go as smoothly as he promised.

"I don't know, Liam. This has so much potential to blow up in our faces."

He leaned slightly toward her, sincerity etched on his handsome features. "We could try it for, say, a week or so. It shouldn't take me much longer than that to finish the revisions. If there's any hint during that time that I'm interfering with your studying, I'll clear out. You know I'd never do anything to cause you problems."

"Well—"

"Just consider it," he added with a smile that arrowed straight into her heart. "This could be the perfect time for us to be together. I don't have any other assignments for now, and you need some help around here. It would be the first time since we exchanged vows that we can actually live together like a normal married couple."

"A normal couple who have to keep their marriage a secret," she reminded him nervously, thinking of their quarrel at Christmas. Liam had been annoyed with her then for refusing to go to a popular Memphis nightspot with him. She'd declined for fear he would be recognized and too many questions would be asked, which had led to a heated argument about how committed she really was to their marriage. How much worse would it be if he had to hide in her apartment around the clock?

If he shared her memories, he kept his thoughts well hidden when he nodded cooperatively. "That won't be a problem. I've left word I'm holing up to work and won't be available for a couple of weeks. No one's going to be looking for me, and I certainly won't draw attention to myself here."

The very thought of dealing with her family's shock and outrage if the truth came out, on top of her hectic class-and-tests schedule, made panic rise up from somewhere deep inside her that threatened to choke her. Her reaction must have been visible on her face, because Liam immediately re-assured her again, "No one will know."

Though she felt a bit cowardly, she nodded. "That would be best."

He reached out to take her hands in his, his gaze holding hers captive as he spoke in a low voice. "I think we need this, Anne. You have to admit that we've been drifting apart the past few months. We need to do something about that."

Thinking of the tears she'd shed after their increasingly more uncomfortable phone calls, she swallowed painfully. Would Liam's visit repair the rift between them—or widen it? She was almost afraid to find out. And yet, she couldn't bring herself to ask him to leave. "I guess you're right."

He searched her face. "So I can stay?"

She moistened her dry lips. "We can try it. You said it would just be a couple of weeks?"

"Yeah, sure. Piece of cake to keep my presence quiet for that long, right?"

Uneasy with his too-optimistic attitude, she frowned. "I guess we'll see. But we'll have to be very careful. I just couldn't deal with my family right now if the truth got out. Not to mention the media attention you would probably draw if they found out you've been secretly married for a year and a half."

"I doubt I'm as much a celebrity as you seem to believe. With this haircut and my glasses and a baseball cap pulled low, I wasn't given a second look at the market this morning. But we'll be careful, anyway."

"Okay, then." She drew a deep breath, wondering if she were making an enormous mistake. "You're welcome to clear out a drawer and closet space for your things. You can use the small bedroom for your office. I set it up to serve that purpose for me, but I'm hardly ever in there. I usually spread out here on the kitchen table or on the couch in the living room when I'm not studying somewhere with my group."

"Are you supposed to meet your group today?"

She nodded. "We're meeting at one. We'll probably work five or six hours, but I can get away early if…"

"No," he interrupted firmly. "You won't change one minute of your schedule for my sake. If I see you only ten minutes a day, I'll be content with that. I promise you, Annie, you aren't going to regret agreeing to this plan. In fact, you're going to like it so much you're never going to want me to leave."

Which only gave her something else to worry about, she decided immediately.

"Will your neighbors be a problem? Do I need to try to sneak in and out of your apartment while you're gone?"

She shook her head. "The apartment on the right, the one that shares my landing, has been empty for a few weeks. I think it's being repainted or something. The neighbor on the left works nights and sleeps days, so I almost never see him. He wouldn't notice if a whole family moved in with me, as long as we're relatively quiet while he's sleeping."

"I'll keep that in mind." He moved toward the doorway. "I'm going down to get the rest of my things out of my car. Then I'll find a place for everything so my stuff won't be in your way."

"I can help you."

"Nope. I can handle it. You study or whatever you need to do this morning."

Hoping she would be able to concentrate with him moving around in the background, she nodded. They might as well get started on finding out if this impulsive scheme of his would work.

She wasn't at all sure she wouldn't have to ask him to leave eventually. The thought of doing so filled her with both dread and sadness that she pushed aside as she spread her books and her computer on the kitchen table.

Liam had seen Anne study before. Even on the few long weekends when she'd sneaked away to join him somewhere, she'd brought along her computer and notes. She'd always kept her books open and accessible even when she'd focused on him.

She'd studied at least a couple of hours a day when she was with him, and he had never complained, since he'd usually had responsibilities of his own to tend to. Both of them were much too busy to let an entire two or three days pass without at least part of that time being spent on their careers.

He needn't have worried too much about disturbing her, he thought with a wry smile. Sitting at the table with her computer and her books and notes, she didn't even seem to notice when he moved around in the kitchen at noon making lunches for them both. He set a plate holding a sandwich and a handful of raw baby carrots in front of her, and she blinked as if she'd forgotten he was even there.

"You need to eat before you leave to join your study group. This should hold you for a while."

"You really don't have to wait on me while you're here," she said, though she reached automatically for the sandwich. "I manage to feed myself on my own."

Not as often as she should, he thought with a glance at her slender frame. He decided he'd better keep that comment to himself. "It wasn't any trouble," he assured her. "It's just as easy to make two sandwiches as one."

When she'd eaten enough to satisfy him, she began to gather her books in preparation to leave for her study session with her group. "Did you get your things put away this morning?"

"I did. My clothes are in your closet and I set up my computer on the desk in the office and stashed my files in that empty desk drawer on the right side. Everything fit nicely."

"Good. You'll be able to work in the office?"

"Yeah, it's fine."

He didn't care for the politely formal tone of their conversation. This was one of the reasons he'd chosen to work here, from her apartment, for the next few weeks. If it was possible, he wanted to get back the intimacy they had shared that summer in Britain, before their separate career pursuits and her family had driven a wedge between them again.

"I'd better go," she said, picking up her stuffed backpack. "The gang is expecting me at one."

Even knowing she would be spending the next few hours studying with her friends, he still envied them the time with her. And even though she'd assured him they were only friends, he wasn't too happy that the group included two single men. He knew better than to express that objection, of course.

At least he had the satisfaction of knowing she was his wife, and that she took those vows seriously—even if those other men were unaware of her status. During the past months, he had come to the uncomfortable realization that his impetuous proposal in Scotland had at least in part been based on a streak of masculine possessiveness he hadn't realized had been such a part of him. He hadn't wanted to let Anne out of his sight again without making sure she would be thinking of him when she met all those interesting young doctors-in-training.

It wasn't a motivation he was proud of, and he certainly knew better than to mention that bit of insight to Anne. She would have his ego for dinner.

"How long do your study sessions usually last?" he asked, keeping his tone deliberately casual.

She shrugged. "Depends on what we need to accomplish and whether anyone has other plans. Most weekends, we usually study for three or four hours straight, take a break, then go another two or three hours. Sometimes more, as the tests get closer."

He couldn't help frowning. "Long hours."

"Yes, well, we've already established that. As I've told you, I'm surviving."

Maybe so, but he didn't like the toll it was taking on her. Still, she looked a bit better this afternoon, he decided, studying her surreptitiously. She appeared more rested than she had when he'd arrived. There was a bit more color in her face now, and he liked to think he'd played some part in putting it there.

She tried to deal with too much on her own; that was the problem. Easton pride and self-sufficiency kept her from asking for help, even when she needed it. So he figured he would have to help her without being asked. By the time he finished his revisions, he wanted to make sure she was healthy and relaxed, prepared for anything medical school could throw at her.

Unlike her family, he cared more about her happiness than her accomplishments.

"I hope you get a lot done today."

She nodded. "Thanks. Good luck with your revisions."

He moved out of her way when she walked toward the coat closet to grab a jacket. Despite the extra bedroom, her apartment was more efficiency than roomy. The kitchen was so small that Liam had bumped against her several times while they'd put away the dishes. She'd merely smiled when he'd apologized. He knew she wasn't accustomed to sharing her space, but she didn't seem to mind the close quarters. For now.

He predicted that as her next test approached, she would grow even more tense and distant. He could deal with that, he assured himself. Maybe he could even help her relax occasionally. He had a few tricks up his sleeve for just that purpose.

He smiled in anticipation.

The study group gathered at James Stillman's condo that afternoon, as they so often did. James was single, his condo was spacious and his housekeeper always left plenty of home-baked snacks for their enjoyment, so they liked meeting there. He seemed to enjoy playing host, though Anne often had trouble reading James.

One thing she knew about him, he came from money. Perhaps that was just one child of privilege recognizing a kindred soul. The other three of their study group came from middle-class and blue-collar backgrounds, not that such social distinctions meant much when it came to the grueling demands of medical school. However disparate their backgrounds had been, med school exams had a way of leveling the playing field, so to speak.

James welcomed her in when she rang the bell. Though it was only ten past one, she was the last to arrive.

Tall and slender, with black hair and dark eyes, James always brought the word "elegant" to Anne's mind. She considered him a study in contradictions. He moved with a somehow utterly masculine grace, interacted warmly with their group of friends while still holding a part of himself back and studied as hard as any of them though the material seemed to come to him almost without effort on his part. At twenty-seven, he was the second oldest in the group, Anne being the youngest. James had obtained a PhD in microbiology before entering medical school. He'd explained that he'd decided too late to attain an M.D. to combine the two degrees into one program.

Haley, Ron and Connor gathered around the big table where they always spread their computers, books and papers, holding cups of coffee and helping themselves to chocolate chip cookies from a china plate.

Haley spoke first. "Hi, Anne. We were beginning to wonder where you were. You're never late."

"Ten minutes isn't very late." Anne dropped her heavy computer-and-book bag onto "her" chair and moved toward the coffeemaker.

"For you it is." Haley Wright smiled from the chair where she always sat when they met here. Of medium height, the amber-eyed brunette was slender and long-legged, though somewhat more curvy than Anne. Anne was aware that she, herself, had lost a bit too much weight recently, resulting in a more fragile and waiflike appearance than she would have liked, so she snagged a couple of cookies to go with her coffee.

Sandy-haired, blue-eyed Ron Gibson had a smear of

chocolate on his full lower lip when he grinned at Anne. "How was the family dinner last night?"

She rolled her eyes. "It was very nice—though I endured at least three separate lectures about not falling behind, in addition to maybe half a dozen stories about how much harder medical school was for my grandfather, my dad and my brother."

Always the clown, Ron laughed. "It's like I keep saying. You're sticking much too close to the family tree. You should have joined the circus or something and then you couldn't be constantly compared to the other family physicians."

She didn't have to fake her grimace. "Yeah, that would have gone over real well with the Easton clan. Their daughter, the circus performer. I might as well have driven a stake through their hearts."

Haley looked at Anne over the screen of her laptop computer. "Despite what you say, spending the evening with your family must have been good for you. You look a little more relaxed today than you have lately."

"I guess you're right." Anne busied herself with her own computer to avoid any further reply.

Ron released a gusty sigh as he dragged a thick stack of papers in front of him. "Man, they loaded us up with slides this week. We'll never get through them all."

"Of course we will." Ever the optimist and the group cheer-leader, Haley spoke firmly. "We just have to keep pushing ahead, a few at a time."

Ron retorted with typical facetiousness, "That's all we have to do, huh? Gee, I wish I'd known it would be so easy. I wouldn't have had to worry so much."

Haley started to snap back at him, but James interceded smoothly. "Where should we begin? The pharmacology or pathology slides?"

Even as she participated in the ensuing discussions, it

bothered Anne that Haley and Ron seemed to be quarreling more lately. The stress got to all of them occasionally, but Haley and Ron seemed particularly inclined to take it out on each other.

She still remembered an embarrassing incident last year when she'd broken down in tears in front of her study mates. She'd been overwhelmed with schoolwork, her mother had suffered a setback in her recovery, she hadn't heard from Liam in weeks and she'd been seriously sleep deprived. All of which had contributed to a meltdown that humiliated her even now when she thought about it. Her friends had been very supportive, which made her feel even guiltier at times for not telling them about Liam. Especially Haley.

The five of them had drifted together during their first semester to study as a group, and they had become true friends since. Anne didn't know what she would have done without them. While lying had become a part of her life during the past year and a half, she thought it was even harder to lie to her study friends than it was to her own family. Which seemed so wrong until she reminded herself primly that it was her family's own fault the lies had been necessary.

They had been studying for two hours without a break when Ron groaned and tossed down his pen. "I've got to move around, guys. My neck's killing me."

"How about a quick game?" James motioned toward the large-screen TV in his living room. It was connected to a top-of-the-line gaming system—another reason why the guys liked studying at his place. He theorized that game breaks helped keep the blood flowing to the brain, which increased the efficiency of their study time. Haley and Anne thought that was blatant male rationalization, but they didn't begrudge the breaks and often joined the games.

"I'm not in the mood to play today, but you guys go ahead."

Haley stood and bent sideways to loosen her stiff muscles. "I just need to move around a little, then I want to check my e-mail."

She stretched, lifting her arms high above her head and going up on tiptoes. The movement made her blue knit top rise to show an inch-and-a-half gap of creamy skin above the waistband of her jeans. Anne noticed Ron focusing on that exposed area for a moment.

She had always wondered if there was something more to the sparring between Haley and Ron than either would admit—maybe didn't even realize themselves. Or maybe they really did just get on each other's nerves, she thought, telling herself not to look for hidden romances everywhere just because of her own situation.

She couldn't help laughing when the guys moved eagerly into the living room. "Just like three first grade boys when the recess bell rings," she muttered.

Haley laughed as she punched a couple of keys on her computer. "Exactly. You and I need to do something fun soon. Why don't we take a couple of hours to go shopping next weekend? I'm getting pretty desperate for some decent pants to wear on ICM days, when we're supposed to look professional. I can't imagine why they don't consider our usual class wear of ratty jeans and sweatshirts to be professional enough."

Anne laughed at the joke, then groaned, "You're forgetting Margo."

Margo was another student in their class. Known derogatorily as a "gunner," she was always at the front of the room, making herself very visible to the professors, highly competitive with her classmates, arguing for every extra point on the tests and making sure everyone knew her scores were among the highest every time.

Margo would never be seen in the jeans and sneakers most of her peers wore to lectures. Her hair and makeup were always perfect, her clothing tailored and perfectly pressed. She even wore heels. Every day.

How Margo kept up her appearance and still managed the same grueling study hours as everyone else was anyone's guess; Anne certainly couldn't do it. Most days, she barely managed to throw on casual clothes and slap a little makeup onto her too-pale face. Her hair was usually in a loose braid or ponytail or clipped back with a barrette. She dressed the part of a doctor-in-training for her Introduction to Clinical Medicine days, when she actually saw patients under highly supervised and very limited conditions, but more often she looked like what she was. A harried student.

"Margo." Haley scowled. "The woman isn't human."

Anne chuckled. "You could be right."

"So, what do you say? Shopping? Next Saturday? To celebrate the completion of one more test cycle before we have to start the next?"

Anne considered the suggestion. Liam would still be at her apartment next weekend. But keeping in mind their agreement that she would go about her schedule as if nothing in her life had changed, she nodded. "That sounds like fun."

"Great." Haley laughed wryly. "It's not as if we have anything better to do, since neither of us have a social life. I can't even remember my last date. Can you?"

"Mmm." Leaving that to be interpreted however, Anne shuffled papers to avoid saying more.

"Maybe we should go to a bar and try to pick up a couple of guys. Just for fun."

Anne winced at the suggestion. "I don't think I'd be interested in that right now. I don't have time for myself, much less anyone else."

"I didn't say we should go looking for soul mates." Haley

rolled her eyes teasingly. "Just a couple of Mr. Right Nows to entertain us for a few hours."

"That would require way too much energy. I'd rather just shop and then crash for a lazy evening before starting the next cycle."

"Like you're going to spend a whole evening not studying," Haley accused.

Anne laughed shortly. "You're probably right. But maybe I'll take a couple hours to soak in the tub and then relax in front of the TV or something before I start."

Both preferably with Liam, she thought, looking down at her books to hide any hint of that thought from her friend.

"Did you hear about Kevin Brownlee and his wife? They're getting a divorce. Laura told me yesterday."

"Ouch. That makes like the third divorce in our class this year, doesn't it?"

"We all knew how tough this would be going in," Haley said with a shrug. "How little time would be left to devote to anyone else. The spouses should have known, as well. Maybe it really is best to wait until after med school to even consider marriage. Personally, I can't imagine trying to juggle everything I'm dealing with now in addition to trying to keep a marriage together."

Anne swallowed hard. "I guess it would be easier if the spouse in question had an equally demanding schedule. A busy life of his or her own."

"So they would basically never see each other?" Haley frowned in consideration before shaking her head again. "Don't see how that's much better. Sounds like a setup for disaster to me. Growing apart, infidelity, that sort of thing. That's what happened to Vivien, you know. Her husband found someone to entertain him while she was studying."

Anne couldn't take much more of this conversation. "We're gossiping like a couple of my mom's friends at a day spa," she said with a light laugh. "We shouldn't."

"True. I guess I just have to remind myself sometimes why it's better that I don't have a social life. Why sleeping alone is the best option for the foreseeable future…even if it does get a little lonely sometimes. I can't even get a dog or a cat to keep me company. I'd feel too guilty about how little time I could spend with it."

Thinking about Liam sitting alone in her apartment less than twenty-four hours after he'd arrived to see her, Anne pressed a hand to her clenched stomach. "Um, Haley…"

James returned to the table at that moment, smiling at them both as he played the host. "Is there anything I can get for either of you?"

"We'd better get back to work," Anne said, deciding the interruption had been well-timed. This wasn't the occasion to spill her secrets to her friend. "We still have to go through the pathology slides. And we haven't even started micro."

Returning in time to hear her, Ron groaned and looked over his shoulder. "Better grab another cookie for energy, Connor. Anne's got that slave-driver look on her face again."

With a laugh, Connor slid into his seat and Anne pushed her personal issues aside to concentrate again on her schoolwork.

Afternoon was fading into evening when a quiet beep from Anne's cell phone signaled an incoming text message. Looking away from a mnemonic drawing Connor had created to help them remember several terms they needed to know for pharmacology, she glanced at the phone screen.

Sry 2 interrupt. R U eating out?

No, she typed in response to Liam's query. Almost done.

Connor had just commented that he had to leave in about twenty minutes to join his family for dinner, and James had said he had plans for the evening. He didn't share what those plans were, but then they were used to not knowing exactly what James did when he wasn't with them.

I'll cook. Any pref?

Srprz me, she tapped back.

She could almost see the sexy smile he wore as he replied, Gladly.

She slipped the phone back into her pocket. "Sorry. What were you saying, Ron?"

He looked at her, one sandy brow lifted quizzically. "Making plans with your secret lov-ah?"

"Yes," she replied without missing a beat. "We've just arranged an intimate dinner followed by a night of blazing passion."

Ron grinned in response to what he took as a sarcastic retort. "Okay. Touché."

Haley laughed. "I tried to talk her into going with me to a singles' bar to raise a little hell next weekend after the test, but she said she preferred staying home and studying. How boring is that?"

"I said I preferred a bubble bath and a couple of hours of TV," Anne corrected her, relieved her honesty had been rewarded—by everyone thinking she'd lied. "But I admitted I'd probably end up studying instead."

Ron's attention had turned to Haley, his expression uncharacteristically disapproving. "Were you serious? About taking Anne to a singles' bar?"

"We were teasing. But why not? Surely we should be allowed some fun even in med school. We've got other classmates who make time to party between test cycles. Just because none of us particularly enjoy class keggers doesn't mean we can't let loose some other way every once in a while."

"At a singles' bar?"

Her smile growing tight, Haley shrugged. "It was just a joke, Ron. Let it go."

Connor started gathering his things. "We made a lot of

progress today. I think I'll head on home to spend a little time with Alexis before she has to go to bed."

Giving Ron a now-look-what-you-did frown, Haley reached for her computer bag. "I'll finish looking through this stuff at home. Are we meeting tomorrow?"

"I have other plans for tomorrow." James set his notes aside.

"Maybe we should all study separately tomorrow and then get together after class Monday," Anne suggested.

Perhaps they'd been spending a bit too much time as a group. Even the best of friends needed a break from each other occasionally.

Anne walked into her apartment soon after leaving James's place. "Hi, honey, I'm home," she called out teasingly, assuming Liam was in the kitchen.

He stepped out of the room she used as an office instead. Wearing a gray sweater that brought out the gray in his eyes, a pair of faded jeans and socks without shoes, he looked quite at home in her apartment. He carried a perfect red rose that he presented to her with a flourish.

Touched, she accepted the gift and lifted it to her nose, inhaling the sweet fragrance. "Thank you. Is this my surprise?"

"Oh, no." Snagging one arm around her waist, he drew her toward him, his head already ducking toward hers. "I've got quite a few of those in store yet."

Holding the rose in her right hand, she looped both arms loosely around his neck and brushed her lips against his. "I can't wait to see what they are."

His hands beneath her bottom, he hoisted her into the air. She laughed and locked her legs around his hips. "What about dinner?"

Carrying her as easily as if she weighed nothing at all, he moved toward the open door to the bedroom. "It'll keep another half hour or so. Let's start with something to whet our appetites, shall we?"

"I think that's a brilliant plan," she said, then pressed her lips against his again.

Chapter Three

"So, how did your study session go?" Liam asked when they settled in the living room a couple of hours after she'd returned home.

"Not bad. We got quite a lot accomplished, I think. What about you? Did you get started on your book today?"

He studiously examined his fingernails. "Um, yeah. Sort of."

"Not going so well?"

"I spent today sort of settling in. Setting up my stuff in the office, getting organized. I glanced over the revision letter again, but I thought I'd wait until tomorrow to really dive in."

"That makes sense. Do you have everything you need in the office?"

"Sure. All I really need is a place to set up my computer. The desk in there is fine. Comfy chair."

She smiled wryly. "Dad bought it for me. He said I need a comfortable place to study. I've sat in it maybe half a dozen times. I study a lot better sprawled on the couch or sitting on my feet in a kitchen chair than at a desk."

"Maybe that was the reason I couldn't concentrate in there. I'm not accustomed to being comfortable when I work. I've written most of this book in hole-in-the-wall hotel rooms, and on airplanes and buses, or wherever I could find a quiet spot to set up my laptop or pull out a pen and pad."

Her smiled felt a bit strained. "I guess you'll just have to get used to staying in one spot for more than a few days at a time, and having nothing to do except concentrate on your writing."

"I think I can manage that," he replied, his own smile bright. "Having you here—at least part of the time—is certainly a nice side benefit."

She wrinkled her nose. "I'm not sure how I feel about being called a 'side benefit.'"

He laughed. "No offense intended."

Settling against him on the couch, she leaned her head against his shoulder, enjoying the rare moment of intimacy. "I could probably take another hour off before I have to get back to my books tonight. Want to watch some TV or something?"

He rested his cheek against her hair. "I'd rather just sit here with you."

She liked the sound of that.

They spent that hour snuggling and talking and laughing. She could get used to this, she thought as they chuckled together over another funny story he told her about his travels. Too easily, actually. She had a difficult time returning to her studies when she could be nestled against Liam instead.

It was probably just as well he was only staying for a couple of weeks. She could concentrate exclusively on her work again after he left. Assuming, of course, she didn't miss him too much to focus on anything but his absence, she thought uneasily.

She was up early Sunday morning, anxious to make up for lost time. While Liam had watched television, she had only managed a couple of hours studying last night. She'd assured him the noise wouldn't bother her while she sat at the kitchen table immersed in her books. She could study in noisy coffee shops, on buses and planes, anywhere she could find a place to sit with a book or her computer. She had the ability to tune out everything else except the material in front of her.

Although it wasn't always easy to tune out Liam. Several times last night she'd found herself gazing at him as he'd focused on the flickering screen, admiring the way the flashing light danced over his face, the way his mouth curved upward when he was intrigued or amused, the way he frowned when he disagreed with something spouted by a political "expert" on the news programs he favored. Each time, she'd had to force herself to return to her studies, though what she'd really wanted to do was climb into Liam's lap and taste that so-expressive mouth.

He hadn't said anything about how late she'd worked, though she'd become aware of his looks of concern and disapproval. She'd urged him to go on to bed whenever he got tired, but he'd assured her he was still adjusting to central time and wasn't ready to turn in yet. Finally deciding they both needed rest, she'd shut down her computer and accompanied him to the bedroom, where they'd fallen asleep wrapped in each other's arms.

It would be all too easy to grow accustomed to waking with him lying beside her, she mused as she turned on her computer for a new day of work.

Liam ambled out of the bedroom, his short, dark hair still wet from the shower, his face freshly shaven. His jeans looked old and comfortably worn, and the cuffs of his blue twill shirt were turned back to reveal strong, tanned forearms. He wore his glasses again, but the "mild-mannered reporter" image was negated by the slight swagger in his walk as he crossed the room, knowing she was watching him.

He stopped by the table to brush a kiss over her lips. "Have you had breakfast?"

She motioned toward the cup of coffee next to her computer. "I'm starting with caffeine. I'll work up to food eventually."

Shaking his head, he moved toward the refrigerator. "I'll make breakfast."

"That's not necessary."

"Oh, it definitely is necessary. I'm starving."

A common condition for him, she thought with a smile. Liam had the metabolism of a hummingbird, burning off calories even during the rare times he sat still.

She'd been so wrapped up in her studies that she hadn't even realized Liam had gone out to the newspaper stand in the parking lot until she saw the paper folded beside his plate. Trying to be a little more sociable than she'd been so far that morning, she asked, "Anything interesting in the news today?"

He shrugged. "The usual conflicts overseas, sniping between politicians and celebrity gossip. Lots of ink given to that ugly divorce between Cal Burlington and Michaela Pomfret."

Anne grimaced. She rarely glanced at Hollywood gossip, but even she had heard too many details about that famous acting couple's acrimonious split. It was particularly juicy because they'd made headlines only a few years earlier by leaving their former, equally famous spouses for each other during the making of a film in which they had costarred. Now there was a child involved, along with very public accusations of infidelity, emotional cruelty and substance abuse. "You've met Cal Burlington, haven't you?"

Liam nodded. "He was one of the three celebrities who

appeared on that documentary I was involved with last year—
the one about the crisis of the rain forests in Central America.
The producers thought we'd get more viewers and attention
if some big-name guests tramped through the forests with us
to show the devastation there, though I lobbied for more
screen time to be given to credible experts. Cal and I spent
only a few days together. He seemed like a decent enough guy,
despite the overinflated ego most actors have to develop just
to survive in Hollywood."

"It must be humiliating for them both to have so much attention directed toward their private lives now. The painful breakup
of a family shouldn't be fodder for public entertainment."

"No. But I guess it should be expected when they've spent
the past decade doing everything they could to stay in that
spotlight. They certainly weren't shy about exploiting their
courtship and the birth of their child. Now they want privacy—
and while I understand, and I believe they should have it while
they sort out their personal problems, I can't help wondering
if they're enjoying the attention in some twisted way."

Anne shook her head, suppressing a shudder at the thought
of living in such a fishbowl. Liam wasn't nearly as famous as
Cal and Michaela, of course, but he had been steadily building
his public reputation. His agent and publicists had been busy
during this break preparing for the launch of the new season
of his cable program. The publication of his book would make
him even more of a celebrity.

How long would they really be able to keep their secret?
And how much attention would they attract when they made
their announcement?

She swallowed hard, hoping she would be prepared for that
scrutiny when the time arrived. Sometime in the future, she
assured herself. When they were ready.

Either growing bored or uncomfortable with the topic of

celebrity marriages—or rather, the end of one, Liam changed the subject. "What have you been studying this morning?"

She was just as eager to move to a new topic. "Shigella."

"That's a bacteria, isn't it?"

"Yes. It's a rod-shaped, gram-negative, nonspore-forming bacteria. There are four serogroups of shigella. *S. dysenteriae, S. flexneri, S. boydii* and…um…oh, yeah, *S. sonnei. S. dysenteriae* is usually the cause of epidemics of dysentery in close quarters such as the refugee camps you've visited."

She had recited the facts without looking at her computer screen, tensing when she'd momentarily forgotten the name of the fourth serogroup.

"Wow. That's a lot to remember."

She nodded grimly. "We have to know how many serotypes are in each serogroup, the differences between each group, what diseases are caused by each, the symptoms of those diseases and the medicines used to fight them."

"I don't know how you remember it all."

"That's just one organism. There are four bacteria in this lecture alone. We have to know as much about all of them."

"Is there anything I can do to help? I'd be happy to quiz you."

She glanced at the stacks of papers she had yet to wade through, including several pages of practice test questions. "Don't you have to work on your revisions?"

He shrugged. "I can work when you're in class and with your study group. Really, I'd love to do something to help you. I'll probably stumble over the pronunciations of all that stuff, but I'm willing to give it a shot."

"Well…"

"Okay, then. Let's finish our breakfasts, then I'll clear away the dishes and make a fresh pot of coffee and we'll get at it. The studying, I mean," he added with a wicked smile that made her giggle.

Having him here wasn't going to be a problem at all, she thought, feeling the muscles in her shoulders relax. As long as they continued to avoid drawing attention to themselves, she added silently, with one more little ripple of nerves.

"Okay," Liam said an hour later, "tell me again how many serotypes are in each serogroup of shigella."

"Group A, *S. dysenteriae,* twelve serotypes. Group B, *S. flexneri,* six serotypes. Group C, *S. boydii,* sixteen serotypes. Group D, *S. sonnei,* one serotype."

"Try again on Group C, *S. boydii.* How many serotypes?"

He watched the muscles tighten around her mouth as she sensed that her previous answer had been incorrect. "Sixteen?" she repeated, less confidently this time.

He shook his head. "No, it's eighteen."

"Damn." She brought her fist down on the tabletop in frustration, the thump making her third cup of coffee slosh perilously close to the rim of the large cup. "I always get that wrong. Why can't I remember? Eighteen. It's eighteen serotypes of serogroup C."

"You're getting too tense. Just relax."

"Relax? I've got to remember all of this for next Friday's test." She made a choppy motion toward the thick stack of paper in front of her. "That doesn't even count the four days of lectures this coming week—at least 480 more slides—that will also be covered on the test. Since I have no idea what questions will be asked from each lecture, I have to learn everything, just in case, and I can't even remember how many serotypes are in freaking serogroup C of this one bacteria! How am I supposed to pass the exam when I don't even know that?"

Her voice grew a bit louder and shriller with each word. Liam stood and reached out to take her coffee cup. He set it on the counter out of her reach. "I think it's time to switch to decaf. Or herbal tea. How about a nice cup of chamomile?"

"Don't tell me what to drink." She buried her face in her hands and drew a deep, shuddering breath.

He kept his voice soothing when he returned to the table and glanced at the next practice question. "How can *S. sonnei* be differentiated from the other serogroups?"

Without lifting her face from her hands, she answered in a muffled voice, "By positive b-D-galactosidase and ornithine decarboxylase biochemical reactions."

"That's right. See, you know this material, Annie. One little slip doesn't mean you'll fail the test."

"It isn't just one little slip! It's one of the easiest things I should know. How can I remember everything else if I can't remember that?"

"Annie." His tone was a bit firmer now. "How many serotypes are in serogroup C of shigella?"

"Eighteen."

"Right. And serogroup B?"

"Six."

"You've got it, babe. You'll do fine."

She groaned into her palms.

Liam walked around the table and placed his hands on her shoulders, feeling the knotted tension there. He began to rub slowly against the taut muscles, pressing his thumbs into her skin until she gave another little moan, this one of pleasure. With satisfaction, he felt her shoulders relax beneath his ministrations.

"That feels good," she murmured, arching like a purring cat into his palms.

He pressed a little harder against one stubborn knot, eliciting a sound that was half aah, half ouch. "How often do you panic like that?"

Sighing ruefully, she admitted, "At least once a day."

"That can't be good for you."

"I'm dealing with it."

"I've been doing a little research on stress in medical students."

She looked over her shoulder with a lifted eyebrow. "You have? Since when?"

"I did some computer searches yesterday while you were with your study group. Burnout in the latter part of the second year is very common."

"I'm not burned out," she said immediately, defensively. "It's just difficult to get through all the material."

He didn't respond directly to her denial. "Medical students tend to be overachievers, you know. Most were top of their class in high school and college, and it's a shock for some to be among evenly matched classmates. Students who were accustomed to being ranked among the top ten percent or higher are suddenly faced with being in the middle of their class— or even lower. That's a serious blow to the ego."

"I'm still in the top ten percent of my class." Her defensiveness seemed to be increasing as he spoke.

"That's great. But you know the old joke. What do they call the student who graduates lowest in his medical school class? Doctor."

He could feel her muscles start to tighten again. "I have to stay high in my class rankings to get into the most competitive surgical residencies."

"You haven't even started rotations yet. How do you know surgery is what you want to do?" He'd never thought she'd shown any real enthusiasm for that highly demanding specialty. He suspected her family of surgeons had heavily influenced her decision. "Maybe you'll like pediatrics. Or family practice. Or dermatology or psychiatry. Shouldn't you keep an open mind at this point?"

"I've always intended to be a surgeon. I'm considering neu-rosurgery," she added somewhat defiantly.

Which would add years to her training, he mused grimly. But wouldn't that impress Daddy?

He didn't point out that she said she'd always *intended* to be a surgeon. Not that she had always *wanted* to be. Maybe this wasn't the right time for this particular conversation.

Sensing his massage was no longer effective, Liam returned to his own seat and glanced down at the sheet of sample questions. "What are the two basic clinical presenta-tions of shigellosis?"

Looking relieved the personal conversation was over, she seized on the question, answering with a renewed confidence. He wondered how much of that was feigned. It bothered him that she wouldn't allow herself to talk about her fears and doubts even with him. Her demanding, perfectionist family had really done a number on her, he thought with a slight shake of his head.

He had probably come as close as anyone to breaking through Anne's deeply ingrained Easton reserve. Yet he was aware there was still a part of herself she hadn't allowed even him to see. He wondered if he ever would—and if he would ever be completely satisfied with not having all of her.

Anne had been studying on her own for another three hours, after she'd convinced Liam to stop quizzing her and go concentrate on his own work, when her telephone interrupted her. Recognizing the ring tone she had assigned to her mother, she answered without glancing at the ID screen. "Hi, Mom."

"Hi, sweetie. I hope I'm not interrupting anything."

She pushed away the notebook in which she'd been scrib-bling key words for sequences she needed to remember. "I need a break, anyway. What's going on?"

"Nothing in particular. I just wanted to say hello."

"I'm glad you called. How was church this morning?"

"Very nice. Jenny Patterson was there. She said to tell you hello. Said she hasn't seen you in months."

"I should give her a call sometime. I'm afraid I've lost touch with a lot of my old friends."

"That's understandable. I told her you've been very busy. She said she understood. She's pregnant again. Did you know?"

"Again? Didn't she just have a baby?"

"Their little Anthony is a year old now. He'll be almost two when the next one comes along. Close together, of course, but Jenny said they planned it this way."

Several of her friends from high school were either expecting or already had children now, Anne mused. She couldn't imagine being responsible for a child yet. Nor could she envision a time in the next ten years or so when she would be in a position to become a mother.

"Annie, where do you—"

Holding the phone closer to her ear, she motioned frantically to Liam to be quiet when he entered the room talking. He grimaced when he saw the phone in her hand, and mouthed an apology, freezing rather humorously in midstep.

"Anne? Did I hear someone speak? Is your study group meeting there this afternoon? I'm sorry, I didn't mean to interrupt."

"You didn't interrupt anything, Mom. I told you, I was ready for a break." She didn't specifically lie about her study group, she told herself, though she was aware that choosing not to correct her mother's mistaken assumption was a deception in itself. "I always enjoy hearing from you. You know that."

"I'll let you get back to your studies."

"Okay. I'll talk to you later. Thanks for calling."

"I'm sorry," Liam said as soon as she set her phone aside. "I didn't know you were on the phone."

"It's okay. That was my mom. She thinks you're one of my study group. I didn't bother to correct her."

"I did study with you earlier. So it wasn't entirely a lie."

She made a face at him. "Nice rationalization. Did you need something?"

"Oh. Yeah. Do you have any extra file folders lying around? I'm trying to get organized before I dive into the revisions."

She was beginning to wonder if there was a reason he kept procrastinating about those revisions. "There's a whole box of folders on the top shelf of the office closet. Far right corner. Help yourself."

"Thanks. And sorry again about the call. I'll be more careful in the future."

"Good idea. This situation is tricky enough."

"Don't worry, Annie. I promised I wouldn't blow our secret by staying here, and I'll keep my word."

"I know." She reached for her notes again. "Let me know if you have any trouble finding those folders."

"I will. Thanks."

Left alone with her books again, Anne gazed into the distance for a few moments before returning to work. Liam had seemed genuinely concerned he'd blundered into her chat with her mother. He'd always assured her he was no more anxious than she was to have their marriage discovered, by her family or by anyone else.

He'd admitted being seen as single was advantageous to his career. Producers were less hesitant to send him into potentially risky situations, celebrity magazines found him more intriguing and he didn't have to bother with answering questions about his wife or their unusual living arrangements. She had always secretly worried that he liked being thought of as single for other reasons, but she refused to dwell on those concerns now or at any other time.

They'd had vague plans to announce the marriage once Anne had a chance to prepare her family for the news. A month or two at the most, they'd agreed. They'd been prepared to spend most of their time apart for the first few years, but they hadn't really expected to keep the secret this long. Her mother's stroke had changed those plans. Anne just hadn't had the heart to upset the family even more at that time, and Liam had agreed—maybe a bit too quickly?—there was no need to go public anytime soon.

Just about the time when Anne had thought she couldn't maintain the lie any longer, her mother had suffered a setback. So, here they were, a year and a half into their marriage and still living a lie. It was no way to maintain a marriage, especially when combined with the long periods of separation. Their phone calls had been less frequent, their lives so different, so very separate.

She had tried to brace herself for the time when Liam confessed he had grown tired of the pretense—or worse, that he had met someone else. She had chided herself for not having more faith in him—in them—but the fears had lingered regardless. When she tried to look into the future, it was growing harder and harder to see them settled down together somewhere with the traditional picket fence and retirement plan.

Maybe this time together would reinvigorate their relationship. Or maybe it would show them once and for all they'd made an impetuous mistake on that beautiful summer day in Scotland.

The patient lay on the examination table in front of Anne and the other three medical students in her ICM group Monday morning, his thin body covered by a hospital gown, a tolerant smile on his lined face. He smiled at them all as they finished their lesson about his condition, Crohn's disease.

"Thank you, Mr. Dalrymple." She shook his hand, as did the other students, all thanking him for making himself available to them.

The patients they saw in ICM were volunteers. During the first year, they had seen actors who taught the physical exams; this year, her patients had real ailments, giving the students a chance to see for themselves the physical characteristics of the maladies.

Anne thought she was getting pretty good at taking patient histories and doing a preliminary checkup, but she was still a little shaky with some of the more detailed exams. Second-year students spent so much time in class every day there was little chance for patient interaction. Her only real-world medical experience that year came from shadowing her preceptor, a surgical mentor who'd been assigned to her at the beginning of the school year, and whom she'd followed into the operating room three times since. She didn't actually get to do much during those days, but she was allowed to scrub in and observe closely. Dr. Burkhaven had even let her put in a few sutures the last time, which had been both scary and exciting.

She looked forward to third year. Step 1 would be behind her and she would rotate through several different medical specialties. She knew the hours would be long and her performance would be judged critically by the mentors in each area, but at least she would be seeing real patients, not sitting at a desk listening to seemingly endless lectures.

As they had agreed earlier, she met Haley in the cafeteria at just after noon. Both still wore their short white coats over professional clothing. The pockets of the hip-length student coats bulged with examination tools, note cards and pens.

Sitting at a small table with their salads, they had to raise their voices a bit to be heard over the noise in the large dining room. Employees and visitors milled around the room and sat at other tables, talking and laughing, some almost shouting into cell phones. Trays and silverware clattered on a conveyor belt that ran across the back of the room, moving dirty dishes into the kitchen for washing.

A pregnant woman sat at the table next to Anne and Haley, talking emotionally to an older woman who could be her mother. Anne tried not to eavesdrop, but it was hard not to overhear snippets of their conversation—apparently, the younger woman was experiencing difficulties and had been told she would have to undergo a C-section the following week, a bit earlier in the pregnancy than she or her doctors would have liked.

Anne would have liked to know what those complications were, but she refused to allow herself to blatantly listen in. She concentrated on her friend instead.

Haley had been telling her about the man she had met at a friend's house the evening before. "So, anyway, he seemed really nice and he asked if I'd like to go out for dinner sometime. I told him how crazy my schedule is right now, and he seemed very understanding about it. I said I'd think about it and let him know later today."

"Is he cute?" Anne asked with a grin.

"Very cute. Dark blond hair, blue eyes, a dimple in his chin that made me want to poke it with my pinkie finger."

Anne laughed. "So, have dinner with him. It could be fun."

Pushing a lock of brown hair out of her amber-brown eyes, Haley wrinkled her nose. "I'm tempted. But it's so hard to find any extra time right now."

"You can make time for a dinner with dimple-chin guy, especially this weekend, after the test."

"Maybe I will, then."

"You should. Remember what the counselors in the burnout prevention sessions keep saying. We should take breaks and try to live balanced lives—ha—or we'll suffer the consequences."

"Yeah, it's all I can do not to laugh out loud every time they make that speech. But I'll go to dinner with Dimples, anyway. That's about as balanced as I can manage right now."

"What's his real name?"

"Kris. With a *K*. His last name is Colton. I think. Anyway, I'll ask him if he wants to have dinner Saturday night. And then I'll put in an extra couple of hours studying Sunday to make up for it. Maybe I'll find something to wear when you and I go shopping Saturday morning. We're still on for that, right?"

"Sure. I can shop for a couple of hours. We'll find you something to wear that will knock this guy out of his shoes."

"What about you?" Haley looked across the table with a speculative look. "Want me to ask Kris if he has an available friend?"

Anne swallowed a bit of lettuce and reached for her water glass. "Um, no, that's not necessary."

"Are you sure? Like you said, it could be fun."

"I have plans for Saturday evening, actually."

"Family stuff, huh?"

"Yes." It wasn't a lie, she assured herself. Liam was family.

Haley pointed her fork like a disapproving fingertip in Anne's direction. "You need to do something fun yourself. And I'm not talking about listening to your dad and granddad and brother blow about their successful surgical careers. You need to let your hair down, find a good-looking guy, party a little."

Her thoughts going off in a direction that made her cheeks warm—not to mention other, less visible parts of her—Anne focused on her lunch. "I'll keep your advice in mind."

"You should."

Anne changed the subject. "You're joining us at Connor's house tonight, aren't you?"

"Oh, yeah, I'll be there. We're going to have to meet every night this week to get ready for the test Friday. This one's going to be a killer."

"They're all killers."

Her attention drifted to the next table again. The pregnant woman and her mother were standing, stacking their used dishes on their trays to carry to the conveyor. Anne glanced at the younger woman's bulging stomach, then at her face, automatically looking for clues as to her condition. High blood pressure? Preeclampsia? Complications of diabetes or some other disease? She saw no obvious signs, but then, she wasn't sure she would recognize the signs if they were present.

She looked forward especially to her ob-gyn rotation. Though she didn't plan to specialize in the field, she found it fascinating. The development of human life, the miracle of birth, the whole mechanism of the female reproductive organs had always intrigued her, though her father had always been somewhat dismissive of doctors who practiced in the field.

"Baby-catchers," he called them. Often women, these days. She didn't want to think that had anything to do with his attitude, but she didn't discount the possibility, either.

She was sure she would do well in a surgical career. She had the patience and the determination. She hoped she had the confidence. Surgeons were known for their self-confidence— to the point of arrogance, in many cases. She'd seen the lifestyle firsthand, so she knew what to expect. How little time she would have for a life outside the hospital. She could handle it. It wasn't as if Liam expected her to be a stay-at-home wife, any more than she expected him to be a stay-at-home husband. Assuming their challenged marriage lasted through the next ten years or so of her training, of course.

Because that thought depressed her, she glanced at her watch. "We'd better hurry. Class starts in ten minutes."

Haley heaved a sigh of resignation and gathered the remains of her meal. "Okay. I'm as ready as I'm going to be."

Anne returned home after classes to change into grubbier and more comfortable clothes for her study session. The group had agreed to meet at six-thirty at Connor's place.

Liam greeted her with a kiss. "How long before you have to leave again?"

"Just long enough to change and have a quick sandwich or something."

He nodded, and if he resented that she would be leaving again so soon, he kept it to himself.

He followed her into the bedroom, draping himself on the bed as she rummaged in the closet for jeans and a comfy, loose sweater. "Cold out today, wasn't it? I went out to pick up some supplies and that wind was bitter."

"It was cold. I'm ready for spring." She wondered where Liam would be come spring. In a desert somewhere? A jungle? The Antarctic?

He watched as she shrugged out of her white coat and placed it on a hanger in the closet.

"How was your day?"

"Long. The afternoon lectures were so dull, I nearly fell asleep. Dr. Emerson had ninety slides, with words so tiny we almost need magnifying glasses to see them. And he's the one who writes the nitpickiest questions for the exams."

"Bummer."

She smiled briefly. "That's one way to phrase it. How about you? Did you make much progress on your revisions today?"

He shrugged and made a sound that gave her no answer at all. Something about his expression made her suspect he'd accomplished little. She hoped he hadn't taken time away from his work just to shop and cook for her.

She reached for the top button of her blouse, then looked at him with lifted eyebrows. "Were you planning to watch me change?"

Moving with amazing swiftness, he came off the bed and stood in front of her, his hands covering hers. "Actually, I thought I'd help you."

Her knees weakened as the first button opened, revealing the curves of her breasts to his eager eyes. Liam had that look—the one that always ignited sparks inside her. She cleared her throat when he teased another button from its hole. "I don't have much time."

His grin was wicked. "Then we should make the most of the time you have."

Sliding her arms around his neck, she decided it would be worth missing dinner if it meant enjoying these stolen minutes with Liam.

Chapter Four

They were finishing the quick meal they'd thrown together when someone rang the doorbell just before six. Liam and Anne both froze, staring at each other wide-eyed across the table.

"Are you expecting anyone?" Anne asked in a low voice.

He frowned. "Of course not. No one even knows I'm here."

She scooted her chair back and hurried across the room, checking the peephole in her door. Her face paled.

Panic edged her stage whisper. "It's my father."

Muttering a curse, Liam grabbed his dishes and shoved them out of sight in the kitchen. Casting one quick glance at the table to make sure it looked as though she'd been dining alone, he almost ran into the office and closed the door behind him as the doorbell pealed demandingly again.

"Dad. This is a surprise." Anne's voice was a bit muffled, but still clear through the thin door of the office/bedroom.

Henry Easton, Jr.'s, booming voice was much more distinct. "What took you so long to answer the door?"

"I was, um, on the phone. Come in."

She wasn't a great liar, Liam thought, but her father was too self-absorbed to notice, anyway. He heard the front door close as Anne invited her father inside.

"Smells good. You cooked dinner?"

"I was in the mood for grilled ham and cheese tonight. I hope nothing's wrong at home?"

"No, nothing's wrong. I know you weren't expecting me. I guess I should have called first."

"You're always welcome here, Dad. Sit down. Can I get you anything?"

Liam glanced at his watch, hoping her father's surprise visit wouldn't last long. He could stay quiet, but he wasn't sure he hadn't left some clue to his presence lying around the apartment. The longer her father stayed, the more chance there was that he would notice something different.

"No, I can't stay. Can't even sit down. I've got a meeting to attend tonight. Just wanted to stop by and give you this."

Liam heard a crinkle—a paper bag, perhaps? And then Anne asked, "What is it?"

"It's a new Step 1 study guide. I ordered it for you a few days ago and it arrived today. I've heard good things about it. Wasn't sure you'd think to order it for yourself."

"Gosh, it's thick. Must have been expensive. Let me reimburse you for it."

"Not necessary. You know I want to do whatever I can to help you. Pay close attention to the pharmacology sections. And physiology, of course. A good deal of the Step 1 exam will come from those two sections, though you don't want to neglect any of the others."

"I know, Dad. We've talked about this. Thank you for the book. I'll start working through it the first chance I get."

"Good. Let me know if you have any questions."

"I will. Are you sure I can't get you anything? A cup of coffee?"

"No, I really have to go. Glad to see you're eating well. Your mother worries about your diet."

"She shouldn't. I'm taking care of myself."

"How are your classes going? Ready for the test this Friday?"

"I've been reviewing the material we've gotten so far. My study group is meeting this evening to go over today's lectures. We'll be meeting every evening this week to study the new material as we get it."

"Good. Glad you're keeping up."

"I am." Liam heard the door open. "Thanks again for the study guide, Dad. It was sweet of you to think of me, though you didn't have to order it. I would have done so for myself if you'd mentioned it to me."

"I can give my girl a gift occasionally, can't I?" her father asked with an indulgence that set Liam's teeth on edge.

He waited until he heard the murmured goodbyes and the sound of the door closing before he risked peeking out to make sure Easton was gone. Anne stood in the center of the room, holding a heavy-looking paperback tome in both hands. The stress was back in her face, he saw immediately. The rosy color had faded from her cheeks, leaving her looking wan and drained. It annoyed him to see the results of even that brief of an encounter with her father.

"That," she said on a long exhale, "was close."

"You think we pulled it off? He really believes you were here alone?"

Tucking a strand of hair behind her ear, she nodded in

relief. "Oh, yes. He'd have said something if he'd noticed anything out of the ordinary."

"I thought you said your family never drops by unannounced."

"They don't, usually. That was the first time."

She still looked too tense, despite her confidence that they'd gotten away with their subterfuge. "You should finish your dinner."

She shook her head. "I've had enough. I'd better go join my study group. We have a lot of material to cover tonight."

She set the heavy study guide on the coffee table, looking down at it as if she were wondering how she would ever get through all of those pages in addition to the stacks of books, notes and guides already scattered through the apartment.

"Some gift," he grumbled. "He could have brought flowers or candy, but he brought more work for you to do instead. Real thoughtful of him."

He knew she'd taken the criticism wrong when her chin lifted defensively. "Actually, it *was* a nice gesture. This guide probably cost close to a hundred dollars. And it should be very valuable in helping me study for the Step 1 exam."

"Why do you always make excuses for him, when all he does in return is pressure you into becoming what he wants you to be?" He honestly didn't understand her loyalty to her domineering father. How could she even pretend to appreciate the gesture when the stress of the drop-in visit was still evident in the lines around her mouth?

She looked away. "I'm not making excuses for him."

"Then why don't you tell him to butt out and let you worry about your own study schedule?"

"He only wants what's best for me, Liam."

"So do I," he returned evenly. "But you don't see me piling more work on to you and expecting you to thank me for it."

She sighed. "You just don't understand how it is between me and my family."

"No," he said flatly. "I guess I don't."

Liam's parents had split when Liam was young, and his alcoholic father had returned to his native Ireland not long afterward. Two years after that, Liam's mother died, leaving Liam to be raised by his mother's aging parents, now both gone. He'd been fond of his grandparents and had loosely reconnected with his father in the past five years, but he supposed it was true he'd never known the same kind of strong family ties Anne had with her family. Looking at the stress reflected in her eyes now, he figured he hadn't missed much.

He squeezed the back of his neck with one hand. "I don't want to fight with you about your father."

"I don't want to fight, either." Avoiding his eyes, she turned to clear away the remains of her abruptly interrupted dinner. "I'll just clear this stuff away and then I'd better go. You probably want to get back to your revisions, anyway."

"Yeah," he muttered, doubting he would accomplish much that evening. "I guess you're right."

The study group worked hard that evening, with even less small talk and foolishness than usual. Even Ron was uncharacteristically subdued and focused on the material. Anne had been warned by upper classmen that from February on, she would be inundated with material and tests, in addition to the rapidly approaching Step 1. One of her third-year acquaintances had particularly bemoaned the fate of Valentine's Day in the second year; the romantic holiday was pretty much buried between test cycles, which made taking the whole evening off from studying both perilous and guilt inducing.

Since Valentine's Day was over a week away, she had no idea if Liam would even still be with her by then. Even if he were, she would still have to devote at least part of the evening to her studies, which she was sure he would understand. They'd been half a world apart last Valentine's Day. Yet he'd still sent her a lovely card and a beautiful hand-dyed scarf from India.

But she couldn't think about Liam this evening, she reminded herself for perhaps the dozenth time in the past couple of hours. She had to focus on the physiology, pathology and pharmacology notes.

"The three types of plague are bubonic, septicemic and pneumonic," Haley muttered, hands over her eyes as she committed the types to memory.

"Treatment for plague is antibiotics within the first twenty-four hours, ideally. First-line antibiotics are streptomycin or gentamicin," Ron recited, speaking to himself.

"And chloramphenicol for critically ill patients," Connor added.

James turned another page of his notes, silently internalizing the material. He glanced up to throw out a sample quiz question to the group. "Name two facultative anaerobes."

"Yersinia is a facultative anaerobe," Anne said, beating Haley to the punch. "As are Staphylococcus, E. coli and Listeria."

"Very good," James said with a smile. He licked his forefinger and marked the air, as if awarding points on an imaginary scoreboard.

"Question for Haley," Connor tossed out, following their usual pattern of challenges and prompts. "Of Staphylococcus, E. coli, Corynebacterium and Listeria, which ones are gram positive and which gram negative?"

Haley groaned. "Wait, I know this. Only one is gram negative, right? E. coli?"

"Right. Twenty points to Haley."

Following a recent joking tradition, everyone made a

writing motion in the air with their index fingers. It was the first moment of silliness in the past intense hour of studying. Anne could feel some of the tension among them ease as they sat back in their chairs grouped around Connor's dining table and stretched.

Judging it was a good time to interrupt, Connor's seven-year-old daughter, Alexis, a towheaded cutie with charming dimples and a gap-toothed smile, bounced up to the table. Dressed in pink pajamas decorated with gray kittens, she was obviously ready for bed. She was followed more sedately by her stepmother, Mia, an attractive woman with light brown hair and kind blue eyes.

"I'm going to bed now," Alexis announced to everyone as she paused by her father's chair. "Good night."

A chorus of smiling good-nights from the study group answered her. Connor gave her a hug and a smacking kiss. "Good night, princess. Sleep well."

"I will. Study good, Daddy."

He chuckled. "Yes, I will. Want me to come tuck you in? The group won't mind if we take a little break."

Alexis looked pleased by the offer. "Okay." Taking her father's hand when he stood, she waved again to the others. "Night."

James yawned. "I think I'll step outside for a minute to clear my head. Maybe the cold air will wake me up a little."

"Hang on, I'll come with you," Ron said, reaching for his jacket. "I need to go out to my car, anyway. I need the cord to my laptop. The battery's getting low."

"Alexis gets cuter every time I see her," Anne said to Mia as the three women sat around the table chatting while the men were away. "Is she really as well behaved as she always seems when we're here?"

"Pretty much," Mia replied with a pleased smile. "Connor or I rarely have to reprimand her, though it does happen occasionally. Usually for running in the house. She's always in such a hurry."

"Oh, to have that much energy again," Haley groaned.

"Seriously." Anne sighed wistfully before asking, "How's your school year going, Mia?"

Mia taught advanced English classes on a high school level. "It's been a pretty good year, so far. A few pain-in-the-patootie students, as usual, but that's to be expected."

"Are you still planning to start grad school next fall?"

"Yes. I've already submitted my applications and talked to the admissions office. Connor and I figured we should be able to work around our schedules next year, since he'll have more evenings free from studying to help with Alexis. Connie Porterfield, the mother of Alexis's best friend, McKenzie, has already offered to provide after-school care and chauffeur services when both Connor and I are tied up."

"That was nice of her."

"She needs someone to watch McKenzie on weekends, when Connie works part-time. I figure I can study some while the girls play together on the weekends, and in the evenings after Alexis goes to bed. It will be a busy time for us, with Connor in his third year of med school and me in my first year of grad school and Alexis in the third grade at her school, but we should be able to work it all out."

Anne had watched Connor and Mia together, and they made a great team. Both were organized and goal-oriented, yet both put their family first even with all their other responsibilities. She didn't envision them being defeated by the obstacles that had already ended several of her classmates' relationships.

Whether she and Liam would be able to survive was another story…one she couldn't think about tonight.

Mia looked from Anne to Haley. "Poor Connor's been studying so many hours I can't help but worry about him, but at least he makes time to play with Alexis for a little while every day. That's good for both of them, I think. I hope you're both finding some time to just relax during this cycle."

Haley and Anne exchanged wry looks and shrugs. "We try," Haley murmured for them both.

"Speaking of which." Anne studied Haley over the rim over her coffee cup. "Did you ever call that guy? Kris with the dimple?"

"Kris with the dimple?" Mia repeated, looking intrigued as she studied Haley's suddenly pink cheeks.

"I sent him a text," Haley replied. "We're going out Saturday night."

"You have a date Saturday night?" Mia clapped her hands. "Good for you, Haley. You really deserve a break."

"Haley's got a date?" Connor rejoined them just in time to overhear. "Who's it with, Haley? Anyone we know?"

"It's no one you know. Just a guy."

"Who are we talking about?" James asked, slipping out of his leather jacket as he came back inside, his tanned cheeks a bit red from the cold night air. "What guy?"

Connor answered, "Haley's got a date Saturday."

"No kidding. Who with, Haley?"

Haley's cheeks were bright red now. Anne grimaced apologetically. She shouldn't have brought this subject up when the others could overhear, she realized. They would tease Haley mercilessly, just because they were guys.

Ron, she noted, had an odd edge to his voice when he asked, "Yeah, Haley. Who's the poor sap—I mean, who's the lucky guy?"

Haley shot Ron a scowl, then held up her hands and shook her head. "It's no one any of you know, okay? And I'd like to keep it that way."

"How about you, Anne? Do you have a big date this weekend, too?" James asked, his dark eyes alight with his pleasant smile.

"I offered to fix her up, but she turned me down. Again." Haley shook her head in disapproval.

"I figure that's a good call, Anne," Ron gibed. "No telling what kind of clown Haley would dig up for you."

"Hey!"

Ever the peacemaker, James directed everyone's attention back to their purpose for being there. "We'd better get back to the books. Question for Ron— What's the first-line treatment for *Y. enterocolitica* infections?"

"Ampicillin or tetracycline," Ron shot back, his eyes still looking a bit dark as he slid into his chair.

"Fifty points," James conceded.

Everyone obligingly marked the air, but since their light moods seemed to have evaporated, they went back to work without further foolishness.

It was rather late when Anne returned to her apartment, but Liam was still up. She found him in the office, slumped in the desk chair and glaring darkly at his computer screen. Several crumpled sheets of paper lay on the floor around him. They'd been ripped from the legal pad sitting by his right hand, as though he'd been making notes but had not been happy with what he'd written.

"How are the revisions going?" she asked when he turned in the chair to greet her.

She wasn't surprised when he sighed and answered, "Not well."

"What's the problem?"

He pushed a hand through his dark hair, then looked at that hand as if it still surprised him his hair was so short. Or maybe she was just projecting because it still startled *her* at times. "I'm not sure, exactly. I'm having trouble figuring out how to handle the transitions between anecdotes. My editor said I need to make the segues smoother."

"Maybe I can help. Would you like me to read what you have so far?"

He smiled, shook his head and reached out to turn off his computer. "You've got enough on your plate already. I'll dive into it again tomorrow. I'm sure I'll figure it out. How did your study session go?"

"We got through most of today's material."

Lifting an eyebrow, he glanced at his watch. "It's after ten. It took you that long just to get through one day's material?"

"I said most of it," she returned wryly. "I'm going to spend another hour or two looking over anything we might have missed."

"Don't you have an early class in the morning? You should get some sleep."

"I will. After I've looked over these notes. Feel free to turn in whenever you get tired. I'll try not to disturb you when I come to bed."

"But, Annie, you need—"

She shot him a look that silenced him midsentence. "I need to study. I'll turn in when I'm finished."

Though disapproval was evident in his expression, he held up both hands in a gesture of surrender. "Fine. Do what you want. I'm going to watch some TV, then turn in."

She could tell he was a little annoyed with her for not listening to his advice, just as she was with him for trying to pressure her into doing so.

Arranging her study materials on the dining table, she bit her lip, wondering if she and Liam would even be able to survive a full week of living together. They had already quarreled twice today alone. That certainly didn't bode well for the state of their future marriage.

The noise of the vacuum cleaner Liam pushed across the bedroom carpet drowned out any other sounds in the apartment. He had only a couple of feet left to sweep and he'd be finished cleaning. The scents of lemon furniture polish and antiseptic cleaners filled the air, a fresh aroma that made him think of his grandmother's Saturday-morning cleaning routine.

He'd scrubbed every surface in the kitchen and bathroom, mopped the kitchen and bathroom floors, dusted everything in the apartment and vacuumed every inch of the bland beige apartment-grade carpet in the living room and bedroom. It was almost four, and he'd been cleaning most of the day.

Running the vacuum cleaner over the last square of carpet, he flipped the switch to cut the power. The silence was immediate and quite a relief.

"Looks like you've been busy."

Turning, he saw Anne standing in the open bedroom doorway, her arms crossed over her chest as she leaned against the jamb and watched him.

Pushing his glasses up on his nose, he greeted her with a smile. Though she'd been in classes all day, after little sleep the night before, she still looked fresh and appealing in her crisp white blouse and dark jeans, her hair pulled back in a loose braid. He'd hoped to have time to freshen up before she came home. The gray T-shirt and faded jeans he wore with white socks were rumpled from his day's activities, and there was a smudge of grease on his shirt from when he'd cleaned the stove.

"I got restless sitting in front of the computer," he explained. "I thought a little physical labor would get my mind in gear. Besides, I know you don't have time for this sort of thing right now."

She kept her apartment tidy—mostly, she'd told him, because she didn't like coming home to a mess—but he knew it had been a few weeks since she'd had time to really scrub the place top to bottom. Now she'd been given a reprieve from trying to schedule that chore. It felt good to do something to ease her load at this stressful time.

She pushed away from the doorjamb. "How did you do on your writing today?"

He shrugged as he wrapped the power cord around the hooks on the side of the vacuum cleaner. "I worked some this morning."

He supposed the nonanswer was an answer in itself. She could probably tell from his tone that he hadn't accomplished anything.

He had no idea why he was having so much trouble diving into this project. It wasn't like him to procrastinate when there was a job to be done. It was certainly out of character for him to be so full of doubt about his ability to competently complete the task. Lack of confidence wasn't really a problem for him; so what was this? He'd spent a lot of hours stewing about that today, and he still hadn't come up with an answer—nor accomplished any more on his revisions.

Seeming to sense his concerns, Anne asked, "Are you sure you don't want me to help you in some way? At least let me read the revision letter."

Liam waved a hand dismissively in the air. "I've got it covered. If I'm still having trouble with it in a couple of days, I'll call my editor and ask for some advice."

"But, Liam, I—"

Someone rang her doorbell three times in quick succession. Anne and Liam froze.

"I'll stay in here," he said, waving at her to go answer the door. "I won't make a sound."

Nodding grimly, she turned and closed the door behind her. He hoped he wouldn't be trapped in here for long. He could really use a cold drink.

Silently, he sank to the side of the neatly made bed, making himself as comfortable as possible. This really was getting ridiculous, he thought a bit glumly.

He'd never expected to spend his marriage hiding behind doors.

Anne heard a child crying before she even reached her door. Puzzled, she looked through the peephole, then pulled the door open. She didn't know the young woman standing on her doorstep holding a screaming toddler, but she'd seen them before. The duo had moved into an apartment downstairs only a few weeks earlier. "May I help you with something?"

Speaking over the child's wailing, the woman—who couldn't be much more than twenty—asked a bit frantically, "You're a doctor, aren't you? I've seen you wearing your white coat with the stethoscope in your pocket."

"I'm a second-year medical student. What's wrong?"

Her dark eyes filled with tears, the slightly chubby brunette caught her child's flailing hand and held it toward Anne. "I'm Rose Duggar, and this is my son, Parker. He rubbed his hand over an old chest in my bedroom and he got a splinter under his fingernail. He says it really hurts. Can you look at it?"

"I'm sorry, but I really shouldn't. As I said, I'm not a doctor, just a medical student." For many reasons, primarily liability concerns, medical students were discouraged from practicing medicine without supervision. Anne was particularly reluctant to take that risk with a child she didn't even know. "Do you have a family doctor or clinic you can take him to?"

A fat tear escaped Rose's left eye, trickling pitifully down her pale cheek. "I just started a new job and my insurance coverage isn't effective until next week. I'm a single mom. I can't afford a medical bill."

The young woman looked as though she were going to sit on the step and wail with her child.

Anne sighed. She'd removed a few splinters in her time. Her friends in college had always come to her with their minor injuries because she'd been a premed major, her dad was a surgeon and she had a way of staying calm when others were freaking out. The latter reason had been more valid than the former two; she'd never quite convinced her friends that being a doctor's daughter did not make one qualified to practice medicine. Neither did being a second-year medical student, she thought, but she figured she could offer her assistance as a good neighbor, rather than a doctor.

"I'm Anne Easton," she said. "Please, come in, and we'll see if we can deal with this together. If it's only a splinter, it shouldn't be too serious."

"Thank you," Rose breathed, stepping quickly over the threshold with her son.

Parker screamed even louder when Anne tried to catch his little hand so she could see if there was anything she could do to help him.

She spoke in a soothing voice to him, "I'm just going to look at it, sweetie, okay? Will you let me see your hand?"

Only somewhat lulled by her tone, he drew a shuddering breath, fully prepared to shriek again at a moment's notice. His mother patted his back, her own expression heartened. "Let the doctor see your hand, okay, baby? Just let her look."

"I'm not a doctor," Anne muttered in despair. "I'm just a medical student."

The distinction seemed meaningless to Rose. She continued to gaze hopefully at Anne.

Vowing to herself that she would pay for the medical bill herself if the child needed emergency care, Anne carefully spread the little fingers and searched for the injury. She found it quickly enough. She was relieved to see that his mother had been right. It was just a splinter. It was a good-size sliver, but only partially buried in the tender skin. It would be easy enough to catch hold of the end with tweezers and pull the splinter out.

"Oh, it's not so bad. Why don't I get a pair of tweezers and then I can hold him while you pull it out," she suggested to Rose.

The younger woman's pale face bleached even more, with a slightly green cast to her cheeks. "I couldn't. I'd faint. I always faint with things like this."

"Okay, then you should sit down now." Alarmed by her lack of color, Anne ushered Rose to the couch, almost pushing her down to the cushions. If she was going to raise a little boy on her own, Rose was going to have to grow a thicker skin when it came to bumps and bruises and minor cuts—and splinters.

Making a sudden decision, Anne hurried to the bedroom door. Parker had started to cry again, not as loudly as before, but sounding tired and stressed. Probably he was picking up some of his mother's panic.

Anne opened the door and peeked in. "Could you help me out here, please?"

Looking a little surprised, Liam nodded and stood, moving quickly toward her. "What's the problem?"

She filled him in quickly, then turned to her neighbors. "Rose, this is my friend—"

"Lee," Liam cut in quickly, walking toward the couch. "Just call me Lee. And who is this fine-looking young man?"

"Parker," Rose replied shyly. "I'm sorry, I didn't know Dr. Easton had company."

"I'm not a doctor. I'm a medical student." Anne spoke a bit more forcefully this time, feeling compelled to make sure her neighbor understood that.

Liam knelt in front of Parker. "Hey, sport."

The toddler caught a sobbing breath, looking at Liam with wary interest.

"What's going on?"

"He has a splinter in his finger," his mother explained, her gaze flickering from Anne to Liam. "I'd take it out, myself, but I'm not good with blood. I thought maybe Dr. Easton would help me."

"Is it okay if I look?" Liam asked Parker even as he took the little hand in his own bigger paw. "Oh, that's not so bad. I could pull it out right now if my fingers weren't so big. Anne's not a doctor yet, but I'd bet she's got a pair of tweezers, don't you, Annie?"

"Of course. I'll be right back."

Leaving Liam to entertain the duo, she hurried into her bathroom for tweezers and an antibacterial ointment.

Chapter Five

Anne cleaned the tweezers thoroughly, then dipped them in a povidone-iodine solution to sterilize them. After scrubbing her hands, she carried the tweezers and ointment into the other room.

She was amazed to find both Rose and Parker smiling at some silliness Liam carried on with the child. It never ceased to amaze her how easily Liam could set people at ease, but she'd never seen him interact with a toddler before. He seemed to be pretty good at it.

At least Rose didn't appear to recognize Liam. Maybe it was the difference in his appearance, with the short haircut and the glasses, or maybe she just didn't watch cable travel programming. Whatever the reason, Anne was relieved. She assumed Liam was, too, since he'd been careful to introduce himself with a shortened version of his name.

Parker looked as though he were going to cry again when

Anne knelt in front of him with the tweezers, but Liam quickly distracted him by standing behind her and making funny faces. Rose watched Liam, too, rather than Anne—probably so she wouldn't get light-headed when Anne extracted the splinter.

Anne was pleased when the tiny sliver slid right out from beneath the little fingernail. She waited until Parker was in midlaugh at Liam's antics, and the child barely twitched when she quickly extracted the splinter. She cleaned his fingertip with an alcohol pad, dabbed on a bit of antiseptic ointment, then sat back in satisfaction. "There. All gone. Does that feel better, Parker?"

Parker looked at his finger, then held it up to show Liam. "All gone," he parroted.

"Why, yes, it is. Good job, Almost-Doctor Easton." He patted Anne's shoulder teasingly as she straightened. She gave him a look.

Rose stood, too, balancing her son on one rounded hip. "Thank you so much, Dr.—"

"Please call me Anne."

"Thank you, Anne. I don't know what I would have done if you hadn't been here. An emergency room visit would have been so expensive for such a minor thing, but I didn't want to leave it in there and let it get infected, and besides, it was hurting him."

"It was nothing, really," Anne assured her. "I'm sure you could have handled it yourself."

Rose drew a shaky breath. "I guess I would have tried, if you hadn't been home. I'm working on getting better at that sort of thing. My boyfriend used to take care of stuff like that, but we split up and he left town a couple of months ago. He's real good to send me child support money, so I can pay my rent, but it's still not easy being a single mom, you know? At least I've got real good child care for when I'm working. My aunt watches Parker for free because she's crazy about him."

It was a lot of personal information in one artless outburst. Anne merely blinked and nodded, wondering if Rose was always so forthcoming or if her image of Anne as a doctor made her so confiding. "I don't think Parker's finger will get infected. The splinter was in for such a short time and the whole area looks clean, but you might keep an eye on it for a day or two. Watch for pus or redness or swelling."

That wasn't medical advice, she assured herself—just common sense. It still made her nervous to treat a child without a license, even under these seemingly innocuous circumstances. At least she had Liam to verify that she'd made it very clear—repeatedly—that she was not a doctor.

"I have to go," Rose said, moving toward the door. "Parker and I are having dinner with my friend Vicky and her little boy, Jeremy. He's just six months older than Parker. We're having pizza. Parker loves pizza. I do, too, especially with extra cheese and pepperoni. Can I pay you for what you did for us, D—um, Anne? I can pay a little, just not as much as an emergency room visit would have cost."

"Absolutely not." Anne saw them to the door. "I enjoyed meeting you, Rose. And you, too, Parker," she added, tickling the little boy's chin and making him giggle.

"Thank you again. If there's ever anything I can do for you, please let me know. Nice to meet you, Lee."

"You, too, Rose. Bye-bye, Parker."

Parker waved his now splinter-free hand in Liam's direction. "Bye-bye."

Anne sagged against the door when she closed it behind her downstairs neighbor. "Whew," she said heartily. "That was an experience."

Liam laughed. "I'd say so. I was surprised when you called me out of the bedroom."

"I was afraid Rose was going to faint and the baby was

going to keep screaming," she admitted. "I didn't think I could handle that by myself. Thanks for entertaining them both while I took care of the splinter."

"No problem. And no harm was done, since she hadn't a clue who I am."

He dropped into a chair. "Maybe you should suggest to Rose that she take some first aid classes. I mean, if she freaks out like that over a splinter, what's she going to do when Parker comes in with a busted head or a broken bone? Little boys are prone to that sort of thing, you know."

"So are little girls," Anne answered with a smile, fingering a thin, almost invisible scar beneath her chin. She had fallen off her bicycle when she was nine and then had run into her mother's immaculate house screeching and dripping blood.

Following her motion, he grinned and nodded. "Oh, yes, I remember you telling me about that. Children and accidents just seem to be connected, don't they?"

"I'm afraid so. If I see Rose again, maybe I will suggest first aid classes. It's a good idea for anyone, especially a single mom."

"You'll be a great mom yourself someday," Liam said, his tone ultracasual. "You were very good with Parker. It's easy to tell you like kids. And you'll have your medical training to fall back on if they should get into a scrape."

She swallowed hard. This conversation reminded her of the recent talk with her mother about a pregnant friend and the direction her thoughts had taken afterward. She summarized those conclusions again for Liam. "It will be years yet before I'm in a position to even consider the possibility."

"Oh, I know. It's not like either of us is in a hurry, with you in school and me traveling the globe. But I don't know. Maybe someday?"

Keeping her eyes on her plate, she shrugged. "Sure. Someday. Maybe. Gosh, I'd better hurry. It's almost time to leave for my study session."

Liam let her get away with the change of subject. "I guess I'll work on my revisions this evening while you're gone. Maybe do a couple loads of laundry."

"You don't have to keep doing the housework," she chided.

He shrugged. "Gives me something to do while I'm sitting here, trying to be creative. I'm not used to being in one place for very long."

Which probably translated as he was already getting restless after being here less than a week, Anne thought glumly. She supposed she couldn't blame him. For a man accustomed to a frantic schedule, constant traveling and lots of interaction with other people, sitting alone in her apartment for hours had to be incredibly boring. The high point of his day had probably been making faces at a crying toddler.

Had he anticipated solitary confinement when he'd chosen to stay here?

The study group seemed to enjoy the tale of the splinter later that evening. Anne gave them all the amusing details, though she carefully left out any reference to Liam. All the others confirmed that they, too, had already been consulted for medical advice by friends and family who'd learned that they were medical students.

"They have no idea how little we've actually learned about dealing with patients," Haley groaned, looking at her stack of books and papers. "If they only knew that all we do is sit in class all day and try to memorize massive amounts of information that we'll probably never remember after the tests are over."

"I've been told we'll remember more than we anticipate," Connor commented. "I hope that's true."

"I just hope I can remember it all until the test Friday," Haley muttered.

"Then maybe we should get started," Ron said, opening a book with a thump.

Ron didn't seem to be in the best of moods that evening, Anne mused. His usual grin and bad jokes were notably absent, leaving him uncharacteristically grumpy. She supposed the pressure was even getting to him. Maybe he hadn't done as well on the last test as he'd hoped. Maybe he was worried about Step 1. Or maybe he had personal issues he hadn't shared with them. Whatever his problem, she figured that the best remedy was to dive into their notes and make sure they all did well on Friday.

"Question for James," she said, opening her binder. "What are the differences between granulomatous colitis, Crohn enteritis and Crohn enterocolitis?"

Anne stumbled into the apartment Friday afternoon so drained and exhausted after her test that Liam sent her straight to bed for a nap. He didn't have to twist her arm. She fell facedown on top of the bedspread and was sound asleep when he looked in less than ten minutes later.

He shook his head in disapproval. She'd had less than four hours sleep the night before. He'd talked her into going to bed at around eleven, telling her that she would do better on the test if she rested before taking it, but when he'd awakened at two, he found her side of the bed empty. She'd admitted that she'd woken up and hadn't been able to go back to sleep without studying for another hour or so.

She looked somewhat better when she walked into the office three hours later. Her hair was brushed and her face gleamed rosily as if she'd washed it to help her wake up. She'd changed her top, from the gray medical school sweatshirt she'd worn for the test to a more form-flattering dark red sweater. His heart gave a funny little kick at the sight of her, as it always did. Damn, but she was pretty.

"Are you working?" she asked.

He turned away from the computer. "Just answering some e-mail." He changed the subject before she could offer her assistance again. "Did you have a good nap?"

"I slept like a log," she admitted with a self-conscious smile. "I guess I was more tired than I even realized."

"No wonder. You haven't gotten nearly enough sleep this week. How did the test go?"

"Pretty well, I think. There were a couple of questions I wasn't sure about, but I think I knew enough about the rest to at least make an educated guess at the answers."

"You must be glad it's behind you."

"I am. Of course, two weeks from today we'll have another test. We'll be studying the genitourinary system next. I'll start reading the material this weekend."

"Fun."

She wrinkled her nose. "Oh, yeah."

"No study group tonight?"

"No, we're taking the weekend off. We'll all study through the weekend, but on our own."

"Okay, then. Since you finished your last unit and made it through the test, what do you say we celebrate tonight?"

"Celebrate?" She looked intrigued. "How do you mean?"

"Why don't we go out? Have dinner, see a movie, maybe have drinks afterward. No one's going to recognize me," he assured her, anticipating her reservations. "I'll make sure of that."

She looked tempted. When was the last time she'd been out for an evening of fun?

"Come on, Annie. It'll be great," he urged.

"Okay," she said in a rush. "Why not? As long as we're careful."

Delighted by her acceptance, he grinned. "Are you kidding? Careful is my middle name."

For some reason, she didn't look overly reassured by that quip.

She should have had more faith in Liam, Anne thought several hours later. As he had promised, he hadn't been recognized once during their evening out. They'd dined at a busy, somewhat dimly lighted restaurant, where their harried server didn't have time to study either of their faces. The food was good and they were seated at a comfortably private booth, where they were able to talk easily enough over the noisy background. Liam paid in cash rather than with a credit card imprinted with his name.

After dinner, they'd seen a movie they'd both enjoyed. It had been fun to snuggle in the dark theater, holding hands and laughing like an ordinary couple out on the town with nothing on their minds but each other. Now they sat in a cozy little bar in the popular River Market District, drinks in front of them as they watched the flow of people on the sidewalk outside the window beside their table. The glass wall could be pushed back in the summer, giving the illusion of an outside patio, but it was too cold for that on this winter evening. As much as she enjoyed the view, Anne appreciated being inside in the warmth.

A lot of young people seemed to be out on this chilly Friday evening, she mused. The bar was bustling, as were the other establishments down the street. Rock music played loudly from unseen speakers, combining with the noise of conversation and laughter to make a festive background as she and Liam sipped their drinks in companionable silence. They were both content for the moment to people watch and relax.

Anne couldn't remember having this nice of an evening in quite a long while.

"I'm glad we did this," she said, setting her drink on the table and leaning forward so Liam could hear her over the din. "I've had fun."

He covered her hand with his and lifted it to his mouth, brushing his lips across her knuckles. "So have I."

"I'm surprised not one person has recognized you tonight," she admitted.

He chuckled wryly. "I suppose my ego should be bruised—but I can live with it as long as it allows me to spend an evening like this with you."

A couple of people had looked at him with slight frowns, as if trying to place him, but had shaken their heads and turned away rather quickly, apparently convincing themselves they were mistaken. Much to Anne's relief. "It's the glasses. And the hair. No one would have expected you to cut off all those curls. Have your agent and your producers seen you like this yet?"

"No. I had it cut only a couple hours before I caught the plane to Little Rock."

"Will they be upset with you? After all, your hair was so recognizable. So much a part of your image."

Frowning a little now, he shrugged. "I'd like to think what success I've enjoyed has been due to my work rather than my hair."

"I wasn't implying differently," she assured him quickly, her fingers tightening around his. "Like I said, it was just an image thing. Long, curly hair wouldn't have gotten you this far. Your talent and your personality have made you such a hit with your viewers."

Though his striking looks certainly hadn't hurt, she added silently.

Somewhat appeased, he murmured, "Thanks. The hair will grow back quickly enough, if I decide to let it. I haven't made up my mind yet."

"I like it either way," she assured him. "You'd look good to me if you were bald."

He grinned sheepishly. "I don't think I'll take a razor to it anytime soon. I have to admit, I whimpered like a little girl when the stylist made the first cut with her scissors. I'm getting used to it, but it still feels strange."

She laughed, delighted by his admission of vanity. She'd never made the mistake of thinking Liam was perfect, but the occasional reminder made her feel a little less daunted by the larger-than-life "image" she'd mentioned.

A commotion at a nearby table distracted them from their conversation. Turning her head to look, Anne saw a thirty-something man frantically motioning toward his companion, a young woman sitting at a table with both hands at her throat, her eyes wide and her expression alarmed.

"She's choking!" the man said, looking around the room for help. "She's choking on a pretzel."

Anne started to rise. She sank back into her chair in relief when the woman grabbed a napkin, coughed into it and then coughed again, color returning to her face in a wave of embarrassed crimson. "I'm okay," she said, waving a shaky hand toward everyone who gaped at her. "I'm fine."

Her companion hovered over her, patting her shoulder and still looking a little frazzled, and a solicitous server approached them to offer assistance. The other patrons turned their attention back to their own business and the earlier light-hearted noise resumed.

Anne glanced at Liam. Rather than watching the other couple, he was studying her, a faint smile on his face. "You were ready to run to the rescue, weren't you?"

She made a face. "Knee-jerk reaction, I guess. I haven't learned much about treating actual patients so far in medical school, but I've known the Heimlich maneuver for years. You don't have to be a licensed physician to stop someone from choking."

"You'll be a good doctor, Anne."

She smiled at him. "Thank you."

"Anne?"

Her attention drawn again, she looked around in response to her name. "Oh. Nick. Hi."

Nick Paulsen was another member of her class. He and another man she didn't recognize had paused on their way to the exit when Nick recognized her.

Nick jerked his chin toward the couple that had caused the excitement. "Were you getting ready to run to the rescue?"

She laughed sheepishly. "Yes, I was. You?"

Nick's friend chuckled. "He was on his way. This guy can't wait to be a hero doctor."

"Stuff it, Grant. How'd you do on the test, Anne?"

She shrugged. "Won't know until we get the grades, of course, but I think I did okay. You?"

"Same here. Tough one, wasn't it?"

"Very."

"Okay, well, I'll see you in class Monday." He looked curiously at Liam, but Anne didn't bother with introductions.

"See you Monday, Nick. Enjoy your weekend."

"Yeah. You, too."

Anne looked at Liam again when the two men had moved on. "What?"

"He's got a thing for you."

She shook her head. "We're just friends. He asked me out last year, but I turned him down and we've moved on. He didn't hold a grudge—or a torch."

"You're wrong there. He's still interested. I know the signs."

Flustered, she picked up her drink again. "I think you're mistaken."

Though Liam was smiling faintly, his eyes were somber. "I just wish I could make it clear to him, and everyone else, that you're off the market."

It wasn't like him to sound so territorial. She wasn't sure how she felt about his tone. "I can handle that myself," she said lightly. "Let's talk about the movie. What did you think of the actor who played the big baddie?"

Liam hesitated only a moment before following her conversational lead. Perhaps he'd realized that this was neither the right time nor place to discuss their relationship.

As for herself, she planned to put off that conversation for as long as she could. Mostly because she had no idea what she would say if he ever asked her to choose between him and the vow of secrecy that she'd cravenly hidden behind for the past year and a half.

Chapter Six

In keeping with their agreement that Anne would continue with her schedule as if nothing had changed, she left Liam in the apartment the next morning while she joined Haley for the shopping excursion they had planned the week before. He assured her that he would utilize the time alone to work on his revisions and urged her to take as long as she wanted with her friend. She needed the girls' day out, he said.

Anne might have enjoyed the shopping outing a bit more if Haley hadn't had such a hard time finding anything that pleased her.

"What's the problem with this top?" Anne asked in bewilderment, motioning toward the very cute wrap-style blouse Haley was trying on. "It looks great on you. The color is very flattering."

Haley twisted in front of the mirror with a look of dissatisfaction on her face. "I don't know. It's pretty low-cut."

"No, it's fine. It's not too revealing, it's just flirty enough. You've got a great figure. What's wrong with showing it off a little?"

"I don't know…"

"Haley, this is the tenth top you've tried on, and you haven't been satisfied with any of them. That isn't like you. What's wrong?"

Haley sighed and shrugged. "I guess I'm having second thoughts about this date tonight. Maybe I should cancel."

"Why? I thought you said the guy's really nice."

"He is. I just don't really have time to deal with dating someone new right now. You know how it is."

"I know you need a night out to have fun." Anne thought of her own lovely time with Liam last night. "Trust me, you'll feel so much better after spending an evening away from the books."

"Oh, I know. It's just…well, first dates are so awkward and weird. I just don't know if I've got the energy for that now."

Which wasn't something Anne had had to worry about with Liam. After knowing each other so long, they were comfortable with each other. Most of the time, she mentally amended, thinking of the occasional awkward moment when they both tried to avoid talking about their future. Or her family. Or their unconventional marital arrangement.

Okay, maybe she did understand why Haley was hesitant to get involved with anyone now. Still, she didn't think one date would necessarily lead to the kind of complications she and Liam had gotten themselves into.

"Just go on the date," she urged, pushing her own quandaries aside to concentrate on her friend. "Have a great time. If you don't want to see him again after tonight, don't."

Haley smiled self-consciously. "You're right. I'm making a mountain out of a teacup, aren't I?"

"Confusing mixed metaphors notwithstanding—yes, you are."

It pleased her when Haley laughed before turning back to the mirror. "So, you really think this top looks good?"

"I really do. I'd tell you if I thought otherwise. Didn't I gag when you put on that pukey green one?"

"Yes, you did. I can always count on you to be honest with me, Anne."

Anne winced, but fortunately Haley didn't seem to notice.

Haley laughed and tossed the "pukey green" top over the door. "Hang that up for me, will you? I'm just going to try on this one last dress and then call it a day."

Anne had just hung the top on the rack provided for dressing room discards when the door opened again. She tilted her head with interest when Haley stepped out in a deep coral dress with a plunging scooped neckline and three-quarter-length sleeves. A soft, full skirt swirled beneath the belted waist, making the dress look very feminine, somewhat retro and quite figure flattering. "Oh, I like that."

"Do you?" Haley plucked at the stretched bodice. "I think it's a little too snug for me across the bust."

"Maybe a little. Do you want me to bring you the next size up?"

"No, that would be too big in the shoulders. It is a pretty dress, though. Why don't you try it on? Your boobs aren't as big as mine."

"Oh, gee, thanks."

Haley laughed. "Seriously, try it on. The color would be gorgeous on you."

Anne hesitated, then nodded. "Okay, sure. Not that I have anywhere to wear it, but it wouldn't hurt to try it on."

A few minutes later, Anne opened the dressing room door to model the dress for Haley. "It seems to fit pretty well."

"Are you kidding? It's perfect! See for yourself." Haley motioned toward the three-way mirror at the end of the short, dressing room hallway.

Anne eyed herself in the mirror. The dress did look nice. The cut emphasized her small waist, yet made the most of what few curves she had. The neckline was just low enough to hint at cleavage—not that she had any to show if it had been lower, she thought in self-deprecating humor. And the length of the sleeves made the garment pretty much a year-round style, very practical for someone living on a budget, as she was.

She thought Liam would like it. And that was all the impetus she needed to say impulsively, "I think I'll buy it. After all, it is marked down thirty percent."

"Always frugal," Haley teased. "You should definitely buy it. It has your name written all over it."

"I wouldn't go that far, but I do like it."

She stepped back into the cubicle to change into the clothes she'd worn shopping.

Haley spoke through the door. "You never said what you did last night. Did you crash at home, too, or did you do something interesting?"

Anne froze with one hand on the zipper of her jeans. "Uh— just a sec."

She finished dressing, ran a hand through her hair and picked up her purse and the coral dress before opening the door. "I went out for a little while with a friend last night," she said casually. "We saw that new action film that opened last week. The plot was kind of weak, but it was fun, anyway."

"Oh, yeah, I've heard it's pretty good. Who'd you say you went with?"

Haley's expression resembled that of a dog who'd picked up an interesting scent, Anne thought nervously. Maybe she hadn't sounded quite as nonchalant as she'd hoped when she'd mentioned her "friend."

"An old friend from college," she said, assuring herself it wasn't exactly a lie. "No big deal."

She must have done a better job of masking her emotions that time. When she immediately changed the subject to their class reading for Monday, Haley went along without further questions.

Driving the short distance home not long afterward, Anne entertained herself by making plans for letting Liam see her in her new dress. The next day was Valentine's Day. Most of the medical students had expressed pleasure that the informal holiday fell on a Sunday this year, rather than in the middle of the week when it would be harder for them to take time off from studying.

As for herself, she'd told Liam she wanted to celebrate the occasion with him at home in private, rather than braving the crowds in the local restaurants. After all, they'd just spent an evening out—and there was no need to press their luck on him not being recognized the next time.

She would study in the morning, then take off early to cook him a special Valentine's dinner—complete with candles and flowers and wine and a sinful dessert. It was definitely her turn to cook. She would change into the dress before sitting down at the table with him. A cozy, intimate evening for two, she thought with a smile of anticipation. Maybe she should have bought some sexy new lingerie to wear beneath the dress—not that Liam would notice. Once he had her out of her clothes, he rarely paused to admire whatever she'd worn underneath.

As a warm feeling spread deep inside her at the thought of how nice their private Valentine's Day celebration would be, she slid out of her car in her parking space, the new dress in its plastic covering draped over her arm.

"Hi, Dr.—er, Anne."

She smiled at Rose, who held little Parker's hand as they walked across the parking lot. Rose carried a couple of envelopes in her other hand, as if they'd just returned from a walk to the mailboxes built into a small, covered structure close to the apartment office

"Hello, Rose. Hi, Parker. How are you today?"

The toddler grinned at her. A smudge on his chin and a matching stain on his superhero sweatshirt suggested that he'd eaten chocolate recently. His cheeks were red from the exercise and from the brisk breeze that was beginning to blow stronger, bringing the colder temperatures that had been predicted for the next few days.

"I saw your friend Lee an hour or so ago," Rose commented. "He was just getting out of his car to go back up to your apartment. He's such a nice guy. He picked up Parker and tossed him in the air a few times. Parker loved the attention. He laughed and laughed."

"Lee's just a kid at heart himself," she said, the new nickname sounding odd to her ears. She wondered where Liam had been that morning. He hadn't mentioned plans to leave the apartment; she'd assumed he would be working all day.

"I could tell," Rose replied with a laugh. "He's so funny. Parker really likes him."

Murmuring something noncommittal, Anne made her escape and headed up the stairs to her apartment.

She found Liam sitting in the middle of her living room floor, surrounded by what appeared to be the parts to an assemble-it-yourself wooden bookcase. He frowned at the instruction sheet in his hand, his expression puzzled.

"Oh, hi," he said, glancing up from the paper when she walked in.

"What are you doing?"

"The shelves on the bookcase in your office are so over-loaded they're starting to sag. I went out this morning and found one that will fit on the opposite wall. I think it will look good there—if I can ever translate these instructions into English," he added darkly. "Not sure what language this is, but it sure doesn't make much sense."

"I thought you were going to work on your book today."

He shrugged without looking at her and reached for a shelf. "I'll work on it while you're studying. Just wanted to take care of this first."

Shaking her head, Anne went into the bedroom to hang up her new dress, saying over her shoulder, "You really didn't have to do that. But it's a nice gesture, anyway."

"I'd hate to see your other bookcase collapse," he called after her. "The way you keep adding those thick medical books, it won't hold much more."

She couldn't help wondering if this was yet another excuse for Liam to procrastinate on his writing. Apparently he was having a hard time getting into that task. Granted, she'd never tried writing a book, but she couldn't figure out what was holding him back. It seemed as though it should be relatively simple; he'd already written a lot of it, now all he had to do was make the changes his editor had requested and finish the rest.

A short while later, she helped him carry the newly assembled bookcase into the office. As he'd said, the new case fit well on the opposite wall from her old one, and the style worked nicely with the room. She took a few books from the old case and arranged them on the new one, and she had to admit that it looked better not having her books so crowded together.

"I should probably start studying," she said, then waved a hand toward the desk that was almost buried beneath his notes and papers. "And now that you've taken care of my storage problem, you should start your own work. I don't like thinking that taking care of me is keeping you from the things you need to do."

Liam frowned. "I'm handling it."

She glanced at the overflowing wastebasket beneath the desk, the many scraps of paper on which he'd scribbled an idea, then crumpled and discarded. "Looks like you're having a little trouble. Are you sure there's nothing I can do to help?"

"I'm sure. Go study. I'll start working in here."

Though she wasn't entirely reassured by his tone, she nodded and left the room to make a fresh pot of coffee before diving into her material.

For the next three hours, Anne studied without a break, looking up only to refill her coffee cup. The material was new, and therefore confusing, and it didn't help that Liam couldn't seem to sit still in the other room. She heard him walking around, maybe looking out the window. Twice he came through to the kitchen, muttering an apology for disturbing her. Once he got a cup of coffee, the other time a soda and a handful of grapes.

She didn't think he got any work done. Resting her chin in her hand when a noise distracted her again, she glanced toward the office. He'd left the door open, and she could see him sitting at the desk. He had made a game out of tossing and catching the purple beanbag cat she kept on the corner of her desk. He was probably unaware that she could see him from her chair, and probably had no clue that his restlessness was affecting her studies. It didn't, usually.

A few minutes later, he wandered into the room again. "Can I get you anything? Something to drink? A snack?"

She glanced at her watch. "It will be dinnertime soon." And she'd gotten precious little accomplished.

"Oh, yeah. I guess you're right. I'll start dinner—what would you like?"

"You don't have to cook, Liam. We can order a pizza or something."

"If that's what you'd rather have."

"I'm just thinking about your time. I'm sure it's better used working than cooking."

His brows snapped together. "I know how to make use of my time."

Holding up both hands, she replied with a sigh, "Sorry. Just trying to help."

"Thanks, but it's not necessary."

His tone was still grumpy, which should have been a cue for her to back off. But because it bothered her that he seemed to be having so much trouble with his work, she couldn't resist offering a suggestion. "Maybe if you give yourself goals… you know, revise three pages before getting out of your chair, or try to do ten pages before calling it a day. That's the way I organize my study time."

"And I'm sure that's all very well for you, but it's not the way I work."

"Yes, but—"

"Look, I've got it covered, okay? Now, do you want pizza or should I cook something?"

"I'm not hungry," she said, deliberately opening a textbook.

"You should eat something."

Her response was curt. "I don't need you to tell me when to eat."

Their terse words seemed to hang in the air for a long minute. And then Liam shook his head. "This is no good. You're stressed, I'm stressed—but we shouldn't take it out on each other."

Still stinging from the tone he had taken with her, she wanted to remind him childishly that he had started it—but he was right. Snarling at each other would not help either of them.

She nodded, but couldn't resist adding, "I was just trying to help. The way you've been helping me."

"I know, and I'm sorry. It's just not going very well, you know? I'm having a hell of a time figuring out what to do with this book. I'm beginning to wonder if I'm going to be able to do this, after all."

His uncharacteristic expression of self-doubt dampened her anger even more. "Of course you'll be able to do it, Liam. I have complete faith in you."

He sighed heavily. "Thanks, Annie. I'm sure you're right. I'll figure it out, eventually. It's just been more difficult than I anticipated. I'm really sorry I'm interfering with your studying. Maybe I should just—"

"Order a pizza," she finished for him quickly. "With mushrooms, black olives and green peppers."

Nodding, he turned toward the kitchen, leaving her to return to her studies until the pizza arrived.

Trying to focus on her notes, she chewed her lower lip. She knew what Liam had been about to say when she'd interrupted so hastily. He'd been on the verge of suggesting that he should leave, go back to New York, perhaps. And while it was probably true that she would study more easily without him here, when it came to having him say the words, she'd realized abruptly that she wasn't ready for him to go.

He would leave eventually, she reminded herself. He'd said from the day he'd arrived that he wouldn't be staying long. She had even been privately relieved to hear that at the time.

It was hard to keep his presence secret, hard to concentrate entirely on her studies while he was here and difficult for both of them to handle the stress of their careers without occasionally turning on each other. She supposed that was only normal for two people cooped up in such close quarters under such difficult circumstances.

But she still wasn't ready for him to leave. She wasn't sure she would ever be entirely ready for that, no matter how diligently she tried to prepare herself. And if they reached a point where she *did* want him to go—what would that say about the future of their relationship?

Anne was startled awake at three o'clock Sunday morning by the buzz of a cell phone. Groggy and disoriented, she started to fumble for her phone, then realized that Liam had already answered his own.

He said only a few words, then she heard him end the conversation with, "I'll be there as soon as I can."

She'd been asleep less than three hours, having turned in at just after midnight, when she'd been unable to study any longer. She pushed her hair out of her face to peer at him when he pushed back the covers and swung his legs over the edge of the bed. "Where are you going?"

"Sorry to wake you. That was my aunt Maura."

She frowned. "Your father's sister? The one in Ireland?"

"Yes. Dungarvan."

"Is something wrong with your dad?"

She heard Liam swallow before he said, "He's had a heart attack."

She pushed herself upright. "Oh, Liam—"

He held up a hand that looked reassuringly steady in the shadows. "Maura said they're cautiously optimistic about his recovery at this point, but she thought I would want to know. I think I should go there."

"Of course you should!" Climbing out of the bed, she turned on the lights, squinting a little until her eyes adjusted. She watched as he pulled his bags out of the closet. Thinking of everything she had to do during the next two weeks, she drew a deep breath and asked, "Do you want me to come with you?"

He stilled in the process of taking shirts from hangers. His eyes were soft when he looked at her. "I can't tell you how much it means to me that you offered—but, no. There's no need for that."

"You're sure? Because Haley could take notes for me."

He shook his head firmly, returning to his packing. "You keep up with your classes and I'll take care of my dad. I'll call, of course."

"Yes, please do. I'll be worried."

Forty-five minutes later, showered, shaved and dressed, Liam packed his bags in his car, then returned to make sure he had everything and to kiss Anne goodbye. "I'll call when I get there."

"All right. Have a safe trip."

He held her tightly for a long hug, then reluctantly let her go. "Try to get some more sleep. You need the rest."

With that, he let himself out, closing the door quietly behind him.

Her arms locked across her chest, Anne blinked back tears as she stared blindly at that closed door. She wasn't entirely sure Liam would return to Little Rock once he'd assured himself that his father no longer needed him. Especially after the silly quarrel they'd had before dinner. He would just as likely decide that he should go back to his own apartment in New York, that his little experiment of living with her had not worked out as he'd hoped.

It hadn't escaped her attention that he'd taken everything with him when he departed, leaving an emptiness inside her that felt much larger than the gap in her closet. Maybe he had privately realized he couldn't work here, after all. She was aware of just how little he'd accomplished during the past week, though he hadn't been willing to discuss his progress—or lack thereof.

Maybe he was tired of hiding behind doors whenever her doorbell rang. Or sitting alone in her apartment while she spent hours in classes and with her study group. She certainly couldn't blame him for that.

Wiping her damp cheeks with an impatient hand, she turned away from the door and moved toward the kitchen. She might as well make a pot of coffee. She couldn't sleep now, anyway.

She had just poured her first, fragrant cup when it occurred to her that this was Valentine's Day.

Swearing beneath her breath, she told herself it didn't matter. It was a silly, made-up holiday, anyway, and Liam had much more important things on his mind. They both did.

She carried the cup to the table, set it down with a thump and opened her laptop. She had to study; she didn't have time to stand there and sniffle.

But she really was going to miss him.

The phone rang at just after noon, drawing Anne out of her perusal of a drawing of the male reproductive system. She'd already been studying for almost eight hours, even though she hadn't even had lunch yet. She was getting tired after so little sleep, but she'd figured she might as well study another hour or so, then take a brief nap before diving in again.

She snatched up her phone and checked the ID screen, trying to keep any trace of disappointment out of her voice when she answered, "Haley. How was the date?"

"I had a great time. Kris is really nice. Very funny. There was this really cute thing he said during dinner…"

Pushing her computer aside, Anne sat back in her chair to listen to her friend's step-by-step description of last night's successful first date. She didn't mind the interruption. She and Haley had grown very close during the past couple of years, bonding through the unique stress only another medical student could completely understand, and she treasured their friendship.

Which only made her feel guiltier for not telling Haley about Liam, she thought with an uncomfortable squirm in her chair. As time had passed since they'd started studying together, it had become too awkward to admit she'd been married all along. Maybe she would confide in Haley soon. Haley would certainly keep her secret.

Anne thought it might feel good to unload. Though honestly, today she had no idea what she would say.

Haley was still chatting when the doorbell rang twenty minutes later.

"There's someone at my door, Haley. I'll see you in class tomorrow, okay?"

"Sure. See you, Anne."

Her caller tapped on the door before she could reach it, sounding impatient. "Hello? Delivery."

A delivery? On a Sunday?

She checked the peephole. The young man wore a uniform shirt and carried a huge bouquet of flowers. She opened the door.

The flowers were roses. Red, lush, fragrant, arranged in a crystal vase. The deliveryman thrust them at her, along with a gold-wrapped box. "Happy Valentine's Day."

"Thank you. Wait, I'll—"

But he was already moving away, waving off her words. "Got a bunch of deliveries this afternoon. Have a good day," he called over his shoulder.

Closing the door with her hip, she cradled the vase of flowers in the crook of one arm and carried that and the box to the table. She couldn't resist burying her nose in the blooms for a moment before setting the vase down. She loved the scent of roses. She also loved chocolates, she thought with an appreciative eye at the familiar box. She would ration those for days, savoring them for as long as they lasted. How sweet of Liam to—

Happy Valentine's Day, Anne. Love, Mom and Dad.

The card had been tucked into the roses. She stared at it blankly for a moment.

Well. Wasn't that thoughtful of her parents, to send her such a nice surprise gift? Her mother always made a point of sending her a card or something for Valentine's Day, but this was more elaborate than usual. Remembering her mom's little pep talk at the end of their last dinner together, she supposed her parents thought she needed the pick-me-up at this point in her education.

She would have to call immediately to thank them. She told herself the roses were just as lovely, the candy just as deliciously tempting as they'd been when she'd thought they were from Liam. It was petty and ungrateful to be even a little disappointed by such a nice gesture.

Blinking rapidly, she reached for her phone, a bright smile pasted on her face in the hope that it would be reflected in her voice when she spoke with her all-too-perceptive mother.

She didn't hear from Liam again until seven o'clock Monday morning. She'd just gotten out of the shower and dressed for class in jeans and a sweater and was tying off her braid when her phone rang.

Noting Liam's number in relief, she answered quickly. "Liam? I was getting worried."

"Sorry, I had some flight delays. I didn't get here until the middle of the night, your time, and I didn't want to wake you."

He sounded exhausted and…sad? "How is your father?"

The faintest of exhales sounded through the very long distance between them, preparing her for his reply. "He didn't make it, Annie. He died an hour before I arrived."

And Liam hadn't had the chance to tell him goodbye.

Her eyes filled. "Oh, Liam, I'm so sorry."

Liam's relationship with his father, Duncan McCright, had been complicated, to say the least. He'd barely known the man who'd left the country when Liam was just a child. They had reconnected five years ago—not long after she and Liam had broken up in college and had kept in touch since.

Liam had told her his father had expressed regrets at his actions after the divorce, and for the alcoholism that had separated him from his wife and his son and from everyone else who had cared about him. Duncan had been sober for ten years. He and Liam had seen each other several times during the past five and had healed a lot of old wounds. Their connection hadn't been a close one, exactly, but had been growing more so.

She'd met Duncan herself that summer before medical school when she and Liam had been together in London. Despite his flaws, she had liked Duncan very much, seeing in him many of the same qualities she'd always admired in Liam.

If only there had been more time....

The thought of losing her own dad so abruptly filled her with even greater sadness. "Are you all right? Is there anything I can do for you? Are you sure you don't need me there?"

"No, that's still not necessary. But it still means a lot that you've offered." His voice was husky with a mixture of emotion and weariness.

"You'd do the same for me."

It bothered her that both times she had offered to join him, she had suspected he would turn her down. Had that made it easier for her to volunteer? Would she have dropped everything, risked falling behind in her classes to go with him? She wanted to believe she would.

Did Liam have faith that she would have chosen his needs over her own, if she'd had to make the choice?

Pushing those concerns aside, she asked quietly, "Do you want to talk?"

"I will, later. Right now I just need to crash for a while—and you have to be in class in an hour. After I've had some rest, I'll have to deal with Dad's estate, not that there's much to settle."

"Rest well, then. Call when you have time."

"I will. I love you, Annie."

"I love you, too."

"By the way—look under your bed when you have a minute. I'll talk to you later."

He hung up before she could ask why he wanted her to look under the bed.

Wiping tears from her cheek, and swallowing a sob she hadn't wanted him to hear, she went into her bedroom and knelt to peer under the bed. She found a large white box there.

Liam hadn't forgotten Valentine's Day after all, she realized, opening the box to find a large, pink envelope sitting on top of something wrapped in sheets of white tissue. Her name was written on the envelope. The card depicted a bouquet of roses. A sappy but sweet poem was printed inside. Beneath that, Liam had written his own Valentine's Day greeting, signing it with love.

A lump in her throat, she unfolded the tissue to reveal an exquisitely beautiful nightgown and robe set in the palest pink satin. Delicate lace decorated the bodice. She ran a fingertip along the intricate pattern, admiring the handiwork. It was a beautiful set, so very pretty that she knew she would never wear it unless he was there to admire her in it.

She clutched the delicate garments to her breast and huddled over them, sobbing in earnest now. She cried for Liam, for his loss of the father he'd only just begun to know. And she cried because she was tired and confused, facing a future that seemed to hold only more stress and conflict and uncertainty.

After several moments, she forced herself to stop crying and went into the bathroom to wash her face, leaving the gift on the bed. Despite her emotions, she had to go to class. Had to somehow hide her feelings from her friends and concentrate on her studies. That seemed to be the only productive action she could take just then.

Chapter Seven

Liam stood in a fine mist, making no effort to stay dry as he lingered in the little church cemetery, staring grimly down at the mound of dirt at his feet. A few flowers, already wilting around the edges, were arranged on the grave. The handful of mourners who had attended his father's funeral had departed. Some would gather for a late lunch at the home of his father's only sibling, Maura Magee. Liam had been invited to join them, but he'd asked for a little time alone first.

He didn't know his father's family very well. He'd hardly known his dad. His feelings for the man were still so complicated he could barely understand them himself. Had he loved his father? Maybe, in a vague, obligatory manner. Had he liked him? Yes. More with passing time, as he'd come to better understand the demons that had driven Duncan from his home, from his family. From his son.

Duncan had been reluctant to talk much about his past, but

he'd confessed to Liam a few years ago that he'd grown up with an angry, abusive, alcoholic father, that he'd been tormented by childhood classmates, that he'd escaped his problems by running away. First to another country, and then into the bottom of a bottle—many bottles. When his drinking had destroyed his marriage to the only woman he'd ever loved—Liam's mother—he'd run away again, traveling aimlessly from place to place until he'd ended up back where he'd begun. Only then had he begun to face his past, with the help of his sister and a few old friends who had still cared about him.

It had been too late to make amends with his wife, but he'd still had a chance with his son, he'd told Liam tearfully. Perhaps they could learn to be friends, if not the sort of father-son relationship he would have liked. Liam supposed they had been friends at the end.

He wished he'd had time to bid his father goodbye. To tell him that, though the old pain of abandonment was still raw, Liam had tried to understand and to forgive.

He'd missed that opportunity by one hour, he thought bleakly. One measly hour, damn it.

"Sorry, Da," he murmured, kneeling to lay the white flower in his hand on the freshly turned dirt. "I tried to be here. I hope you knew that."

He felt very much alone when he straightened. Alone in the cemetery. Alone in the world, somehow. Which was ridiculous, of course, considering he'd never had a close relationship with his father. He had more friends and business associates than he could even count. He had a wife.

Yet none of them were with him now. None of them would be there when he walked into his rarely occupied apartment back in New York.

He'd told himself he was the luckiest guy on Earth. That he had the best of both worlds. He was a footloose bachelor with a great wife. He'd had family, but loosely enough that he didn't have to worry about pleasing them or compromising for them. He had a home, but he'd been free to travel the world on a whim. He had a job most people only dreamed of, yet enough free time to pursue other dreams, like his writing. He even had a deal pending for his first book, once he got past whatever block was keeping him from tackling those revisions. What more could he want?

Pushing his hands into his pockets, he turned away from the grave, reminding himself that nothing in his life had really changed all that much. He was still a lucky guy. He could go to New York, call up some friends, spend an evening out on the town. Or he could head back to Little Rock and spend several quiet, private evenings with Anne. The best of both worlds.

He should probably go back to New York. His presence had obviously been a distraction to Anne, though she was too generous to complain. He knew she'd been worried her family would find out about him, which wasn't something he wanted just now, either. And it wasn't as if he'd gotten anything done at her place, anyway. He and Anne could get together later, after she'd finished her classes for the semester, after she'd taken the dreaded Step 1 exam in June. That was only four months away; they would both be fine on their own until they had a chance to snatch a few precious days together.

So, he would go back to New York. To his nice, small, very empty apartment there.

Yet he had the depressing feeling that making that choice would be acknowledging defeat in his marriage.

Pushing a hand through his short, damp hair, he left the cemetery with a heavy void in his chest he didn't want to contemplate too closely. He had to make a decision before he left Ireland, and he didn't have a clue what the best choice would be.

* * *

Anne parked in her apartment lot at almost eleven Thursday night after a long and exhausting study session. The group had all agreed that this cycle's material was particularly evil—so much to learn, so little time to do so. They'd barely gotten started on the information that would be on next week's test, and already she wondered how she would ever remember it all.

She glanced up at her apartment. Only one light burned in the window, the lamp she left on a timer so she didn't have to enter a dark room when she came home late. The bedroom window was dark, as she expected. Most of the apartments around hers were also dark, considering the late hour.

She'd heard from Liam only once since he'd called Monday morning. He'd called Wednesday morning to reassure her that he was fine, and still in the process of taking care of his father's affairs. He wasn't sure when he'd get back to the States, nor had he decided at that time where he would go when he returned. Though she had assured him he was welcome to come back to her apartment to continue working on his revisions, she'd gotten the impression he'd pretty much decided to go to New York. She suspected he thought that choice would be better for her sake—but maybe he believed it was the best decision for himself, as well.

She would eventually grow accustomed to his absence again, she assured herself as she trudged up the stairs. After all, he'd spent only a little over a week with her. Soon it would seem entirely normal to come home to an empty apartment, to go for days or even weeks without hearing Liam's voice. And maybe she would see him in the summer, after her Step 1 exam. Although, her rotations would begin early in July, so there wouldn't be a lot of time to spare.

Vaguely depressed, she unlocked her door and walked inside.

She paused just inside her doorway, her head cocked, her instincts on alert. The apartment was dark and quiet, as she had expected. The light from the one lamp didn't show anything out of place. There was no evidence that anyone had been inside the apartment while she was out—and yet, somehow, she sensed someone had been there.

Slipping out of her shoes, she tiptoed to the open bedroom door. The lights were off in the room, but the night-light in the attached bathroom provided just enough pale illumination for her to see the dark shape on her bed. Still making no sound, she crept closer.

Fully dressed except for his shoes, Liam lay on his side on top of the covers, as though he'd intended to lie down only for a few minutes. She could just see his face in the shadows. Even in sleep, exhaustion carved deep lines into his forehead and around his mouth. His breathing was heavy and even, telling her he slept so soundly that he was unaware of her presence.

Seeing him there, she realized that she hadn't really expected him to come back, despite his indecision on the phone. She'd been prepared for him to call from New York to tell her he'd chosen to finish his work from his apartment there. She'd have been no more surprised had he called from Malaysia or New Zealand.

Yet he was here. In her bed. Only then could she allow herself to admit to herself how very much she had wanted him to come back.

He never stirred when she slipped into the bathroom to wash her face and brush her teeth, nor when she stripped out of her clothes and donned her nightgown. Pulling a blanket from a shelf in the closet, she spread it over him, then climbed beneath it with him.

He roused a little when she settled next to him.

"Annie?" His voice was thick, the syllables slurred.

"Yes, it's me. Go back to sleep."

"Hope you don't mind—I couldn't go back to New York yet. Didn't want to be alone now."

She touched his face, her heart aching for him. "I don't mind at all."

His voice was growing fainter. "Didn't want to leave things like they were. That stupid quarrel we had—"

"Shh." Snuggling her head into his shoulder, she wrapped an arm around him. "Go back to sleep, Liam. We'll talk tomorrow."

"Okay." He pulled her more closely into him. Barely a minute passed before he was deeply asleep again.

Anne lay awake for a while longer, staring at the darkened ceiling and listening to Liam breathe.

Liam was drinking coffee when Anne walked into the kitchen Friday morning. She wore a casual shirt and jeans, and her hair was still damp from her shower. She had applied a little makeup, not that she needed any. Apparently, she would be in classes all day today since she wasn't dressed to see patients.

"Good morning, Annie."

She smiled, though she searched his face as if gauging his well-being. "Good morning."

He bent his head to brush a kiss across her lips, all he would allow himself because he knew she hadn't much spare time. "Sorry I conked out on you last night. I meant to lie down for only a few minutes, but I guess I went unconscious. I barely remember you getting into bed with me. Or I suppose I should say, onto the bed with me. I didn't even turn the covers back when I laid down."

"You must have been exhausted."

"I guess I was."

She reached up to rest her hands on his shoulders, her expression somber now. "I'm so very sorry about your father. Are you okay?"

He gave her a gentle smile. "I'm fine. But thank you."

"If you need to talk about it, I can skip classes this morning. Haley will share her notes with me."

Touched by the offer, he shook his head. "No way. Have your breakfast and then go to class. We can catch up when you have a few spare minutes."

"You're sure? Because—"

"Annie," he cut in, speaking firmly now, "I'm sure."

After hesitating only a moment longer, she poured herself a cup of coffee. "How was your family in Ireland? Your aunt Maura—is she well?"

"Yes, she looked great. The others were all fine, too— what few there are. Not many left of Dad's family."

Leaning against the counter, she took a tentative sip of her hot coffee before asking, "You got all his affairs settled?"

"It didn't take long," he replied with a slight shrug. "Dad didn't have much to settle. I gave most of his things away. I kept the pocket watch that had belonged to his dad, a locket that was his mother's and a few small mementoes of his time with my mother and me—pictures, mostly. Nothing particularly valuable, other than sentiment."

Her tone was sad when she said quietly, "I'm so sorry you didn't get to tell him goodbye. That must have hurt you."

He kept his gaze focused on his own coffee cup. He didn't want to upset her before her classes by letting her see exactly how much that still bothered him. "I wish I could have been there a little earlier. Aunt Maura told him I was on my way, so at least he knew I was trying. He left a message for me through her."

"Did he?"

He could tell she wanted to ask, but didn't want to pry. He

didn't like that slight distance between them, that cautious hesitation that shouldn't exist between a husband and wife. "Yes. He asked her to tell me that he loved me, that he was proud of me and that he was sorry for his paternal shortcomings. She said he seemed to know somehow that he wouldn't be able to tell me those things himself."

Tears glazed her eyes when he glanced up at her from across the table. "Oh, Liam—"

He managed a weak smile for her. "I'm fine," he repeated. "I'm glad Dad and I were able to make our peace before he died, but it isn't as if he was a part of my life even then. I've only seen him a few times since we reconnected."

"I know. But it still hurts, doesn't it?"

He nodded and reached for his coffee, then deliberately changed the subject. "What about you? How's it been going this week? Are the classes any easier than they were for the last unit?"

"No, not really. But I guess I'm keeping up."

Something in her voice made his eyebrows rise. "What's wrong?"

"Nothing."

Nope. She was still holding something back. "Annie."

She sighed. "It's just—well, something seems a little off with my study group. It's bothering me a little."

"Off? In what way?"

"I can't describe it, exactly. It just feels as though something is changing. We don't seem to be as comfortable together as we have in the past. I don't know if it's the stress getting to everyone, or what, but there's a tension that hasn't been there before. Like I said, it bothers me."

"Maybe you've all been spending a little too much time together," he suggested. "Maybe you should all take a break."

"Maybe," she agreed reluctantly. "But there's so much

studying to do. And it's easier to study together than alone most of the time. Someone always has an answer when the others are stuck, or an explanation for something that's confusing someone else. One of us catches something the others miss, or has a clever method of remembering something that helps the rest of us remember, too. I don't know how I would have gotten through these past semesters without them."

"I'm sure it will pass. You've all gotten too close to let it fall apart now. Like you said, it's probably just the stress."

"I'm sure you're right." But she didn't look entirely convinced.

"You should all do something fun after the next test. Maybe throw a party or go out for pizza and beer or something. You could have the party here. I could clear out for an evening."

She frowned. "I hate that you have to hide whenever anyone comes to my apartment."

He shrugged. "That was the agreement."

"I know. But still—"

"Don't fret about it. I knew what I was coming back to, and I'm okay with it. I'm going to dive into my writing today. I'm hoping to have it all finished in a couple of weeks. After that, well, I'll clear out and let you get back to your studies without worrying about my presence here. Unless you'd rather I go back to New York to finish? If I'm interfering at all, I want you to tell me now."

"Of course you're not interfering," she said firmly. "You've actually been a great help to me here, cleaning and cooking and doing laundry—all things you don't have to keep doing, by the way. If it's easier for you to concentrate here rather than in New York, then stay."

"Then I'll stay for a little longer," he said, dipping into his oatmeal again, choosing to believe her, despite his suspicions to the contrary. "With all the distractions in New York, it's a lot easier to work here."

He kept his reasoning focused on his work, knowing this wasn't the time for an in-depth discussion of the state of their relationship. Anne didn't have time, and he wasn't sure she was ready for that yet, anyway. Perhaps he wasn't, either.

Maybe he had come to a gradual realization for his primary reason for marrying her—wanting to keep that strong link between them when they were apart so that they wouldn't give up as they had back in college—but it had become increasingly clear to him that he wasn't entirely certain why Anne had agreed. Nor whether she stayed married to him, despite the obstacles they had encountered, because she loved him or because her habitual avoidance of conflict extended to him as well as to her family.

He didn't want to believe the latter. He wasn't her father. He wouldn't bully her if she made a decision he didn't like. Which didn't mean he wouldn't try to change her mind, he thought with a ripple of discomfort. He tried to take comfort in assuring himself that he would be much more tactful about it than her family had ever been.

"That's settled, then," she murmured, setting her coffee cup on the counter. "You'll work here for a while longer.

"Should I make dinner for us tonight or are you eating with your group?" He kept his tone light, as if he were asking only for convenience, but he really hoped she would be free to spend a couple of hours with him that evening. He had missed her quite badly the past few days. More than he was prepared to admit to her just then because he didn't want to put pressure on her to push her studies aside for his sake.

She grimaced, and he knew before she spoke that there would be no intimate dinner for them that evening. "I'm sorry, Liam. Today's my grandfather's eightieth birthday. We're celebrating at his country club, and the family will expect me to be there."

So it was her family coming between them again tonight. It was always either that or her studies—and of the two, it was her family he resented most, rightly or wrongly. Nodding a bit curtly, he tried to keep his tone uninflected. "Of course they want you there. Don't worry, I'll fend for myself. I've got a lot of work to catch up on, anyway. Answering my back-logged e-mail, alone, will take two or three hours."

Despite his encouragement, she still looked vaguely guilty. "I wish you could go with me. I wish everyone already knew about us and the drama was all behind us and we could just walk in together as a couple, you know?"

He reached across the little table to squeeze her hand. "That time will come, Annie. Once you've finished these tough classes and aced that big exam—as I know you will—we'll break the news and damn the consequences."

Her smile was a weak attempt. "Of course we will. After I've got that behind me, I'll be ready for whatever their reactions will be. Maybe they'll surprise us and come around quickly once they know there's nothing they can do about it."

"Maybe they will."

But Liam wondered. Would her family ever really accept him when they had taken such a dislike to him all those years earlier? And would Anne ever really be prepared to choose him over them, if it came to that?

Looking very handsome in a beautifully tailored dark suit, Dr. Stephen Easton stood in front of the popular, local swing band that was providing entertainment for the birthday bash and lifted a flute of champagne. The crowd that had gathered for the celebration paused in their eating and conversations to listen as Stephen cleared his throat to signal the beginning of his toast.

Sitting at a white linen-draped round table between her mother and Stephen's fiancée, Danielle, Anne reached for her own champagne.

"To Granddad," Stephen said in a voice that carried clearly around the room. "Dr. Henry Easton, Sr., a man who has been an invaluable asset to his community, a true leader among his peers and a role model to three generations of medical students, including his own. My father, my sister and I are among those fortunate enough to follow in his noble footsteps. Happy eightieth birthday, Granddad, and may we all be privileged to celebrate many more with you."

The praise was a little over the top, of course, a little too flowery—but Anne couldn't deny that her grandfather loved every word of it. Sitting next to his son, he beamed as everyone in the room raised a glass and sipped in his honor.

After nodding acknowledgement of the applause that followed his toast, Stephen motioned for the musicians to resume and rejoined his family at their big, round table. He shook his grandfather's hand, then his father's before sliding into the seat beside his fiancée and greeting her with a quick kiss.

"Stephen, that was lovely," their mother said in misty approval. "I'm so glad both you and Danielle were able to be with us tonight. And Anne, too, of course," she added quickly.

Anne smiled and nodded. Surreptitiously, she studied her mother's face. Her mom looked tired, but happy, she decided. She had insisted on planning and organizing this birthday celebration herself, the first big party she had put together since her stroke, though she'd certainly arranged plenty of social and charitable events in the years before her illness. Anne worried that her mom had overtaxed herself for this evening, but she figured her dad had kept a close eye on her during the preparations.

Glancing around the nearly filled room of friends, family

and business acquaintances, she couldn't help noticing how many couples were in attendance. Her mom had urged Anne to bring a friend—implying that a date would be welcome—but Anne had replied lightly that there wasn't anyone she particularly wanted to bring. And there wasn't, other than Liam, whose presence would not have made the celebration a pleasant one.

She glanced at her watch, wondering how quickly she could get back home to him. She felt terrible leaving him alone like this when he'd just gotten back from his father's funeral. She could almost feel her spirit being tugged in different directions by her need to be with her Liam, her obligations to her family and her responsibilities to her studies. The result was a dull headache that just never seemed to go away these days.

Though she'd hoped to be discreet, her time-check did not go unnoticed. "Looks like Anne's eager to get back to her books," her father said with more approval than censure.

"Of course she is," Granddad replied jovially. "Don't feel like you have to waste any more time at this shindig, sweetheart. I'm glad you could come, but none of us want to interfere with your schoolwork, do we?"

Her family smiled indulgently at her, nodding their agreement.

How would those expressions change if she were to suddenly blurt out the truth about what was waiting for her at home? She wondered how they would act, what they would say. How long it would take them to forgive her, as she assumed they would, eventually.

Glancing at her mother's slightly pale, still-so-thin face, she forced a smile. "I can stay a few more minutes. At least until after they bring out the cake and we sing 'Happy Birthday.' I wouldn't miss that for anything, Granddad."

Her grandfather smiled contentedly again, basking in the attention. Maybe Stephen looked at her a bit closely, but no one else seemed to notice anything odd about her behavior. Once again, she had managed to fool everyone, she thought, wishing she could feel a little more pleased with herself and less like an ungrateful daughter and a terrible wife. Mostly, she wished she could feel less like a coward.

Still a little tired from his travels, Liam slept in Saturday morning. Anne dressed as quietly as possible, then crept out of the bedroom, closing the door soundlessly behind her. Liam had barely stirred since she'd slipped out of bed.

She was supposed to meet her study group later, but she was thinking of canceling. She could study here today, and that way she would be available if Liam wanted to talk about his dad.

He'd said he'd come back to Little Rock because he hadn't wanted to be alone in New York after his loss, she thought guiltily. And yet she had spent very little time with him since he'd returned. He didn't seem to blame her for that, but she blamed herself for not making the time to be there for him if he needed her. She could make up for that today, even if it was only to keep him company while they both worked on their own pursuits.

When she'd been rushing between classes and frantically trying to make her family celebration last night, it had fleetingly occurred to her that it would have been easier, perhaps, if Liam had gone back to New York. Yet she was still pleased that he hadn't.

Liam had a way of keeping her head spinning with conflicting emotions, she thought with a weary sigh.

She had just set up her computer when she heard the shower running. Maybe she should make something for breakfast, she thought. Liam would probably be hungry.

She gulped when someone tapped on her door. She hoped fervently that it was Rose, the only person for whom no awkward explanations of Liam's presence would be necessary.

But it was Haley who stood on the other side of the door, wearing an expression that was both harried and apologetic. "I'm sorry to drop by like this. I should have called, but I panicked."

"What happened?" Anne asked, instantly alarmed.

"My hard drive crashed. I had another one installed first thing this morning, but I didn't have all those slides from yesterday backed up. Would you let me make copies from your computer, please?" She held up a portable storage device. "It won't take long."

"Of course you can copy my files." Anne stepped out of the way to allow Haley to enter. She'd have been just as upset if it had been her computer that had crashed, she acknowledged, shuddering at the very thought. Especially now, with so much material to be memorized. "I could have e-mailed it to you, though."

"I know. But I just left the computer store, and I thought I'd just drop by. You're sure you don't mind?"

The shower had stopped. Anne hoped Liam would hear her talking with Haley and stay in the room until the coast was clear. "Of course I don't mind," she said, raising her voice just a fraction and hoping Haley wouldn't find that odd. "I just turned on the computer. We can—"

The bedroom door opened and Liam wandered out, his shower-glistened body bare except for the towel wrapped precariously around his waist. "Anne, I forgot to take my jeans out of the dryer last night. I—"

Suddenly realizing that she wasn't alone, he skidded to a halt, making a hasty grab for the loose knot of the towel.

Her eyebrows raised, Haley gave Liam a rather lengthy

once-over while Anne stood there like an idiot, trying to think of something reasonably intelligent to say.

Haley was the first to recover her voice. "Well, hello, there."

Liam shot Anne a grimace of apology. He looked as though he expected her to strangle him on the spot—and she had to admit, that was an option.

She swallowed hard when Haley turned slowly toward her. Haley's eyes danced with mischief and speculation when she murmured in a suspiciously neutral voice, "Apparently I came at a bad time."

Anne sighed in resignation. "Haley, this is—"

"Lee," he supplied helpfully, obviously hoping to get away with the ruse a second time.

"Liam," she finished firmly. She'd had few qualms about keeping the whole truth from the virtual stranger who lived downstairs, but she would not lie to her best friend. "Liam, this is Haley."

Though he gave Anne a quizzical look, Liam spoke to Haley. "Oh, yes. I've heard all about you."

"Wish I could say the same." Haley gave him another look that made his cheeks go even redder as he stood there with only a big, fluffy towel covering him from waist to knees. His dark hair was still damp, he wasn't wearing his glasses and the muscles in his bare chest and arms were beautifully molded, adding up to a delicious and thoroughly masculine image. Which would have made his blush all the more amusing to Anne had the circumstances been different.

"I'll just go get dressed," he muttered, backing into the bedroom. "Please excuse me."

The door closed quickly between them. Anne suspected Liam stood on the other side punching himself in his head for his recklessness.

"Well, well." Haley set her computer bag on the floor and

crossed her arms over her chest, eyeing Anne with exaggerated accusation. "Someone has been holding out."

"I have," Anne admitted, "but it wasn't because I didn't want to tell you. I just didn't quite know how."

"You didn't know how to tell me that you're sleeping with that gorgeous guy from TV? Gee, I can't imagine why."

So, Haley had recognized him—and Anne had confirmed the identification by giving Liam's real name.

"It's even more complicated than that, I'm afraid." She drew a deep breath before blurting, "Liam is my husband."

Chapter Eight

As if her knees had given way, Haley sank onto the nearest chair. "Your…husband?" she repeated, obviously wondering if she'd heard correctly. "You're married?"

"Yes." Anne cleared her throat. "Let me get you a cup of coffee and I'll tell you all about it."

"Coffee. Yeah, I could use coffee. Black."

Anne nodded. "I'll be right back."

As she pulled coffee mugs from a kitchen cabinet, Anne tried to decide how to explain to her friend that she'd been hiding her marriage for almost two years. And then how to convince Haley to behave in front of their other friends as if nothing at all had changed. It wasn't that she thought Haley would reveal her secret deliberately, but there was no doubt that this news changed everything Haley thought she had known about Anne.

If only she'd had time to prepare. To decide whether to

keep Liam's presence secret or to introduce him to Haley less…dramatically.

Haley accepted the mug of coffee, then held it between her hands without tasting it as she watched Anne settle on the couch with her own mug. "I know you weren't expecting me this morning," she said. "If this is a bad time, we can talk later."

Anne shook her head. "I've been wanting to tell you, anyway. I was just waiting for the right time."

"Waiting for me to show up on your doorstep and meet the hubby in all his, um, glory?"

Anne had to laugh at the ironic query. "No, that wasn't exactly the plan."

"Well, I can't say I'm sorry I got that delectable eyeful." Haley made a show of fanning her face with one hand. "The man is seriously hot."

Hearing herself giggle like a schoolgirl, Anne felt her own cheeks warm. She drew another deep breath, telling herself to get a grip.

"So, how long have you been married?"

Anne replied almost apologetically, "A little over a year and a half. July tenth will mark our second anniversary."

They had spent their first anniversary on separate continents, she recalled fleetingly. Liam had been filming in Bangladesh. He'd been able to call, but their conversation had been all too brief and dissatisfying. It had been another month before they'd managed a long weekend together in New York—one of those covert escapes she had pulled off without anyone being the wiser that she'd even left the state. She was still amazed at times that they'd been able to keep their secret this long.

Liam reappeared just then, fully dressed now in a polo shirt and khaki cargo pants, his hair dried and neatly combed, his glasses perched on his nose. He looked at Anne a bit warily, as if wondering if she were mad at him for his lack of caution earlier. "Is there any more of that coffee?"

"Yes, it's still hot."

While Liam fetched his coffee, Anne filled Haley in about the details of her unannounced marriage. Even after he rejoined them to sit on the couch beside Anne, Liam said little, letting Anne choose how much to reveal. She couldn't tell how he felt about her confiding in her friend. His expression was politely neutral during the conversation.

Haley looked a little confused when Anne finished speaking. "So, let me get this straight. The two of you dated in college, but your parents made you break up with him?"

Liam nodded. "Yes."

"No." Anne frowned at Liam. "That wasn't why we broke up in college."

He lifted an eyebrow at her. "Of course it was. They said I was holding you back, distracting you from your studies."

She shook her head. "Liam, we didn't break up because my parents made me. You wanted to drop out and tramp around the world doing your travel reporting. I wanted to get my degree and go to medical school."

"I believed at the time that you didn't really want to go to medical school, that you were just doing what your parents wanted you to do. The year you took to study abroad after college proved me right, you weren't ready to go straight into medical school then."

She shook her head. "That had nothing to do with what happened between us. We simply agreed that we just weren't in the right places in our lives to maintain a relationship."

"That's not quite how I remember it," he murmured.

Perhaps she'd made it sound easier than it had been. Less traumatic. She remembered a few heated discussions, plenty of tears—but she'd always believed the decision, while hard, had been mutual.

Haley studied them both. "Then you ran into each other by accident in London when you were studying abroad, Anne?"

"Yes."

This time it was Liam who replied, "No."

Anne blinked at him. "What?"

"I knew you were there," he said with a shrug. "Heard it through the grapevine, you could say. I made sure we ran into each other."

Thinking back to that seemingly random encounter in a Chelsea fish and chips place, she stared at him in astonishment. "You found me intentionally?"

"Um—yeah."

"And why, exactly, did you not tell me this before?"

He shrugged. "I guess it just never came up."

Haley choked on what might have been a muffled laugh. "Do you two ever actually, you know, talk?"

"We haven't really been together all that much," Liam admitted with a wry look at Anne. "During our entire marriage, we've spent only a total of maybe four weeks together—two of them in this one visit. Most of our conversations have been on the phone or through e-mails."

Haley's smile faded. "That has to be tough. And I understand why you didn't feel like you could spring the news on your family when your mother was so ill, Anne. But she's a lot better now, isn't she?"

"She had a troublesome setback last year, but on the whole, she's doing much better now."

"So, why don't you tell them? Wouldn't that be easier than all this sneaking around?"

Anne and Liam looked at each other quickly, and then away. "It's just not the right time," Anne muttered. "You know how tough school is right now. Not to mention that we're about to have to start studying in earnest for Step 1. My family would be in such an uproar that I couldn't possibly concentrate on my studies."

"And I'll have to leave again in a few weeks, anyway," Liam added, sounding as though he agreed completely with her on this point, at least. "I'm staying here only until I finish writing a book about my travels, then I'm taking off for Haiti in a couple of months to report on the orphaned street kids there. I'd hate to leave Anne to deal with the fallout of our announcement by herself. It would be better to wait until we can live together openly."

It was the first Anne had heard about him going to Haiti. Was this a new development for him, or had he simply neglected to mention it before? Haley was right, she realized abruptly. She and Liam really didn't communicate enough.

Not to mention that he seemed no more eager to break the news about their marriage than she was.

"So you're just going to go on the way you have been?"

Anne and Liam shared quick glances, then nodded in unison.

"For now, anyway," Anne said.

"It seems best," he agreed.

After a moment, Haley shrugged. "Whatever works for you. You can both be assured that no one will hear the truth from me."

Anne smiled at her. "Thank you, Haley. I knew we could trust you. I wish I'd told you sooner. It bothered me to keep it from you when you and I have become such good friends. I hope you can forgive me."

"There's nothing to forgive," Haley replied immediately. "You had your reasons. Nothing at all has changed between us. Except I guess I'll have to stop trying to fix you up with guys," she added with a laugh.

"I'd appreciate that," Liam said wryly.

Propping her chin in her hand, Haley studied Liam openly. "You look really different with the short hair and the glasses. It's no wonder you haven't been recognized around here."

"How did you recognize him?" Anne asked curiously.

This time it was Haley's turn to blush. "I'm a huge fan. I've seen all your TV episodes. I recognized you as soon as you stepped out of the bedroom—even if you weren't wearing your usual safari gear," she added with a little giggle. "As soon as Anne confirmed your name, I knew I was right, as unlikely as it seemed."

He smiled, looking flattered, which made Anne tempted to kick his shin. Just because. She could all too easily imagine that he met plenty of gushing female fans—and Haley was the only one who knew he was unavailable. Anne didn't even like to think about his encounters with the ones who considered him fair game.

"Are you going to grow out your hair again?"

"Probably. As Annie has pointed out, the hair's more famous than I am," Liam said with a laugh.

"Oh, I doubt that. It's your talent that's gotten you where you are. You make all your reports so interesting and so informative. Sometimes I feel almost as if I'd visited those places myself after I've watched one of your shows."

"Thank you. That's what I hope to accomplish."

Haley glanced at Anne. "It must be hard for you to sit here in this apartment studying while Liam's off seeing so many fascinating places."

Anne forced a smile. "I'm doing what I have to do to pursue my own career," she said with a light shrug. "Liam has his dreams and I have mine."

Something about that statement didn't sound right, she thought after she'd said it. Too much "his" and "mine" and not enough "ours," maybe. But since that was the state of their marriage for the time being, there was no use fretting about it.

She stood rather abruptly. "We should start transferring those files you need, Haley. It won't be long before we have to go meet the guys for our study session."

"And I should get to work myself." Liam stood and smiled at Haley. "It was a pleasure meeting you, Haley. Anne, I'll be in the office if you need me for anything."

She nodded, not quite meeting his eyes as he walked away. He closed himself into the other room, leaving her alone with her friend. Fortunately, Haley seemed to sense that Anne needed to concentrate on school concerns for a while, rather than any further discussion of her complicated relationship with Liam.

While there was some relief in having her friend know the truth, Anne was beset by a sudden, uncharacteristically superstitious fear that one accidental discovery could lead to a domino effect of everyone she knew uncovering the secret she'd been trying so hard to hide for more than a year. Though at the moment, discovery seemed to be only one of the perils she and Liam faced.

As Anne had expected, Haley was entirely circumspect in front of their study group about what she had discovered. With the exception of making no more jokes about blind dates or singles' clubs, she treated Anne no differently than she ever had, making it easier for them both to pretend that nothing had changed. And yet, Anne felt that the accidental revelation had deepened their friendship. Perhaps it was because she no longer needed to lie to Haley, even by omission, which gave her the freedom to be completely herself in front of her friend. It was nice to have one person, at least, other than Liam with whom that was possible.

The group met for intensive study sessions both Saturday and

Sunday afternoons. Maybe because they were so focused on their common goals, the tension Anne had been sensing among them lately seemed to ease. Even Haley and Ron stopped sniping at each other and started cooperating more with helping all of them learn as much of the material as possible.

Still, Anne believed something had changed in the past couple of months, and she couldn't quite figure out what it was. Maybe it was her own guilty conscience, she thought with a slight wince, though she didn't know why she should feel at all remorseful about keeping her private life hidden from the guys in the group. It wasn't as if she knew everything about their lives, after all.

She didn't know why Ron had grown slightly less jovial during the past few months. He was still the one who could most easily make everyone else laugh, but he wasn't quite the class clown he'd been when she'd first met him. Maybe it was just that he, too, was having trouble dealing with the pressures of classes and tests.

As for James—well, she doubted that any of them really knew James. They all liked him, they considered him a real friend, an important part of their group—but there were parts of James that he kept hidden from all of them. She and Haley had discussed that a couple of times when they were alone, wondering idly together what made James so obsessively private. They'd decided it was none of their business, really, and they chose to like him, anyway, just as Anne believed he genuinely liked all of them.

If she could respect his boundaries, why should she feel so uncomfortable about having one rather significant secret of her own?

They ended their session at just after five Sunday afternoon, because several of the group had other plans. Anne and Haley paused by Anne's car for a moment before going their own ways.

"I dread Daughtry's lecture tomorrow," Haley confided in a grumble, continuing a conversation they had started inside. "He was so boring last week, it was all I could do to stay awake."

"Not to mention all those snide comments he made about how if we were too stupid to understand all the material he was throwing at us, we'd never pass Step 1 and we'd all wash out of med school."

"I know, right? He was just in an all-round lousy mood that day."

Anne was aware of that, but it hadn't stopped her from being stung by the instructor's grim warnings, even though they had been addressed to the whole class equally, and certainly not to her personally.

"How are things at home?" Haley asked in a furtive voice, changing the subject after looking around to make sure no one else could hear them. It was the first time she'd asked about Liam, even indirectly, since she'd left Anne's apartment Saturday, probably because this was the first time they'd been alone since.

Anne wrinkled her nose. "I haven't been there much to tell. You should know. We spent all day studying with the group yesterday until late last night."

And there came the guilt again, she thought, squirming a little. She should be spending more time with Liam, especially since he had just lost his father. But he had insisted she meet with her group, as she would have had he not been there. He was fine, he kept telling her. Busy with his revisions, which he still seemed reluctant to discuss with her.

"No more unexpected visitors?"

Laughing a little, Anne shook her head. "No. Our secret is still safe."

"Was Liam upset that I barged in that way and saw him there?"

"No, I don't think so. He enjoyed meeting you."

"So he's been here a few weeks and I'm the only one who has recognized him?"

"He wears a ball cap pulled low when he goes out in public. But, yes, as far as I know, you're the only one who's identified him."

"I've seen his photo in a few magazines," Haley confessed. "I've been intrigued by his career since I first discovered his cable program while flipping channels one night a couple years back. Everything about him just seems so…larger-than-life, I guess. On TV, anyway."

Amused, Anne asked, "Not in person?"

"Oh, he's still interesting in person. Still seriously good-looking. He was just, well, more normal than I expected him to be. I mean, married and living in your apartment and doing laundry and working in your office rather than tramping through some exotic location."

Anne bit her lip. Was that part of what Liam had worried about? That being seen as a settled, married man would make him less interesting to his viewers, and as a result, to his sponsors?

"So, when are you going to tell your family the truth?" Haley asked curiously. "Have you decided on a particular occasion?"

"Not really. We keep waiting for the right time, but we haven't actually defined what that time would be. The longer we wait…well, the harder it is, you know?"

"I can imagine. It would be tough enough to announce a new marriage to your disapproving family, but if they find out you've actually been married for more than a year…"

Anne gulped. "You see why it's so complicated."

"I guess. Liam's okay with waiting? He isn't pushing you to tell your family soon?"

"He's in no more of a hurry than I am. He's not looking

forward to the mayhem, either. And he has his career to think of. He's the footloose, bachelor adventurer, remember? He has to consider how this news would affect that image."

"It would make headlines," Haley conceded. "At least in certain venues. Some of the gossip columnists might be intrigued that the adventurer chose a quiet, brainy medical student from Arkansas as a mate. How will you feel about being photographed and interviewed with him, with people wondering about whether you're a suitable match for him?"

Anne shuddered. "Gee, thanks, Haley. Just what I need to give me nightmares tonight."

Haley looked instantly apologetic. "Sorry. I was just speculating. It's not as if Liam's a rock star or anything. You wouldn't be surrounded by paparazzi or anything like that."

But Haley was right that there would be some media attention given to Liam's marriage, Anne reflected glumly. Especially when his book was published to add to his public image. And, being the private type she was, she wasn't looking forward to that scrutiny.

She and Liam hadn't even talked about that part of the future—like so much else that they'd avoided discussing or planning. How had she ever let herself get into this crazy situation? Was it really only because she hadn't wanted to upset her parents during her mother's health crisis? Because of her own stress over the first two difficult years of medical school? Or was there more to their hesitation to go public? Were they holding back because neither of them was really sure the marriage would survive if they tried to make it more authentic? More "normal?"

Haley being who she was—unafraid to broach the more difficult topics—asked carefully, "Um, you don't suppose there's any other reason Liam wants to keep the marriage secret, do you?"

Anne didn't have to ask for clarification. "If you're talking about other women, I trust Liam completely," she said, trying to speak with total assurance.

After a moment, Haley smiled wryly. "That either makes you very confident in your man—or incredibly naive. I'm not sure I could be so trusting."

But then, Haley probably wouldn't have gotten into a situation like this to begin with, Anne thought glumly, making an excuse to be on her way. As she drove the short distance back to her apartment, she told herself that she did trust Liam as far as other women were concerned. But could their marriage survive the other obstacles between them— his antipathy toward her family, and theirs toward him, his constant traveling and her commitment to her career training, the parts of themselves they had never fully revealed to each other? Her answer to that nagging question didn't come as easily to her.

She tried to push her worries aside and put a smile on her face when she entered her apartment. She had an entire evening to spend with Liam. Even if she would use part of that time for studying, there was no reason they couldn't set aside an hour or so for…

She stopped short just inside her apartment door. "Um— what's going on here?"

Liam was on his hands and knees in the middle of the living room floor. A squealing toddler straddled his back, somewhat sticky-looking hands clutching Liam's hair.

Liam grinned ruefully up at her. "Hi, Annie."

"Horsie!" Little Parker kicked his bare feet insistently into Liam's sides, making Liam wince and then rear obligingly up on his knees, pawing the air with his hands and making whinnying noises. Parker shrieked in delight, the shrill sound driving itself into Anne's eardrums like a shard of glass.

She raised her voice a bit to be heard above the tiny cowboy's laughter. "Is Rose here?"

"Rose is at work. Her aunt had to cancel babysitting services at the last minute this evening, so Rose begged me to fill in. She promised it would be just this one time."

The rather breathless explanation was punctuated with whinnies and more squeals, but Anne followed along easily enough. She could picture the scene— Rose had probably been desperate and tearful and Liam couldn't say no. She suspected she might have done the same under the circumstances, despite her better judgment.

She crossed the room to set her books and computer bag on the table, pushing them to the center to make sure they were out of a toddler's reach. "When will she be back?"

"She said she gets off work at nine. So she'll be here shortly after that."

Anne glanced at her watch. Another three and a half hours? Really? What were they supposed to do with the child until then? And how would she ever get anything done with Parker here?

"The horsie needs a rest, Park-o," Liam said, smoothly rolling Parker off his back and onto the floor. He rose a little stiffly, scooping the toddler onto his hip at the same time. "Don't worry, Annie, I'll keep the kid occupied. I'm going to feed him dinner and then take him down to his place for b-e-d. Rose gave me her key. She said he's usually out cold by eight."

"She gave you her key?" Her young neighbor was certainly the trusting sort, to leave both her child and her key with a man she'd met only a couple of times, she thought disapprovingly.

Liam shrugged. "I've talked to her a few times when our paths crossed outside. Played with Parker a bit in the courtyard. I guess she figured she could trust me by now."

She didn't realize he'd gotten quite so friendly with the

duo. She supposed he'd been lonelier than she had realized here by himself so much. "Oh. Well."

"Play, Lee," Parker insisted, tapping Liam's cheek for attention.

"Okay. How about we play with the farm set you brought with you?" Liam carried Parker to the other side of the room, where a thick canvas bag was propped against the wall, next to a brightly colored red plastic barn. Distracted by the sight of Parker, Anne hadn't noticed those things before. She watched as Liam sat cross-legged on the floor and opened the hinged barn, shaking out cartoonish plastic animals, a tractor and trailer, and a big-headed farmer. A moment later, noisy and improbable animal sounds came from that direction as Liam and Parker enthusiastically shuffled the herd into the trailer.

Liam glanced around at her with a smile. "Maybe you should study in the office," he suggested. "If you close the door, the noise won't be so disturbing."

He was making it clear that he didn't expect her to help him with the favor he'd taken on. She appreciated his consideration. Glancing at the office doorway, she thought about taking him up on his suggestion, but then she shook her head. "I'll make dinner while you entertain Parker. What do you think he would like to eat?"

"Hmm. What do you like to eat, Park-o?"

Giggling in response to the nickname, the child answered cheerfully, "'Ghetti."

"Spaghetti?"

He nodded eagerly. "'Ghetti."

Thinking of the mess to come, Anne swallowed hard and turned toward the kitchen. "Okay. Three orders of 'ghetti, coming right up."

Liam laughed.

* * *

Somehow Anne ended up spending almost an hour on the floor with Liam and Parker after their messy, ultracasual meal. They played with the farm animals and with some plastic kitchen utensils and pots and pans from Anne's kitchen. Parker pretended to cook for them, and they made a show of eating the imaginary food, to his delight. Anne was surprised by how much she and Liam laughed during the game; she wouldn't have thought playing with a toddler would have been so entertaining.

When Parker began to yawn, Liam glanced at his watch. "I'll take him down," he said, gathering their "toys." "Rose told me where to find everything."

"You're sure you don't need help?"

"I've got it covered, thanks. I'm sure you're ready to get back to your books."

She wondered what his friends and associates back in New York would think if they heard that a young single mom had asked him to watch her toddler, having no idea who Liam really was. And that Liam had shown no more fear of being responsible for a two-year-old than he did of the wild animals he encountered on his program.

He made her feel like such a coward sometimes, she mused after he'd taken Parker down to bed. It seemed sometimes as if she was overwhelmed by everything, whereas Liam feared nothing. Just one more item to go on the list of differences between them, she thought, her smile fading.

She was buried in her studies again when Liam returned a little over an hour after carrying Parker off to bed. She glanced up and smiled faintly when he entered. Tossing the book he'd taken to read while Parker slept onto a table, he sank onto the couch with a gusty exhale.

"Did you have a hard time getting him to sleep?"

"Not really. He was worn out. I know the feeling. Toddlers are exhausting. I don't know how Rose does it by herself."

"She has her aunt to help her, but you're right, for the most part she's on her own. I know she must have been grateful for your help this evening."

Liam grimaced. "She offered to pay me, can you believe that?"

"I'm sure she didn't know how else to express her appreciation."

"Sorry to have cut into your study time this evening. I didn't know how to tell her no. I guess I could have watched him down in her apartment, but I didn't really want to mess around in her kitchen for dinner."

"It's fine, really. He was on his best behavior. I enjoyed spending time with him."

"Yeah, it was kind of fun, wasn't it? Not that I'd want to do it very often," he added with a crooked grin.

He pushed himself to his feet and moved toward her. "I'll go answer e-mail for a while and let you get back to work. But first…"

He leaned over to place a long, hard kiss on her mouth. "Thanks for cooking the 'ghetti," he murmured when he finally released her.

Turning abruptly, he headed for the office. "Don't study too late," he said over his shoulder. "You need your rest."

Blinking, she shook her head a little to clear her fuzzy mind and made herself look at her computer. The fact that it took her a moment to remember how to read was entirely Liam's fault.

Chapter Nine

Liam was growing concerned about Anne the next evening. She'd told him she should be home around ten, but it was more than an hour past that time when he looked at his watch. It wasn't like her to be out this late when she had ICM the next morning, and she had told him that she did.

He tried to focus on his revisions, but they were still proceeding with painful sluggishness. He still couldn't figure out why he was having so much trouble finishing this project, though he found himself wondering if he was subconsciously stretching out the work as long as possible. After all, once he'd finished the book, he really should go back to New York and to all the projects he'd left hanging there.

While there was some grain of truth in that excuse, he knew it wasn't the only reason for his difficulties. He just couldn't quite identify the other problems.

Giving up on any attempt at working, he began to pace,

trying to convince himself that it was foolish to worry about Anne. Her hours were always erratic, and it wasn't unusual for her study group to lose track of time as they plodded through all their material.

He spent a few minutes wondering how other spouses and significant others of second-year medical students dealt with being pushed to the background so often. When they weren't actually in class or buried in their books, med students seemed to be frequently tense and distracted and moody, from what little Liam had observed. It was no wonder so many relationships broke up during these years.

He didn't want to think that his own marriage might not survive the pressure of their demanding careers.

She spent so much time with her study group. Haley and those three men, two of whom were single. They were probably getting to know each other very well. They had so much in common. He pictured her studying and laughing and teasing with her friends, bonding through pressure with them in a way outsiders would probably have a difficult time understanding. He remembered how fondly she had smiled when she'd talked about having to hide chocolate cake from her buddy, Ron. Were she and Ron sharing a late, sweet snack at that moment?

He pushed a hand through his hair in irritation as a surge of savage jealousy crashed through him. That was uncalled for— and totally unlike him. As much time as he spent away from Anne, they had to trust each other or they might as well give up now. He was just letting his worry about her get out of hand.

But he still didn't like the thought of her being so chummy with those other guys.

His cell phone beeped to signal an incoming text message. Snatching it from its holder on his belt, he read the terse note. Hide. Dad w me.

"Great." Shoving the phone back into its case, he glanced around the living room to make sure there was no evidence of his presence, then moved into the bedroom and closed the door, wondering what Anne's father was doing with her at this hour. How long would he have to cower behind the door this time, holding his breath and hoping he wouldn't be discovered?

Though Anne had assured him that she rarely had visitors, this apartment had been a very busy place during the past few days.

He found it grimly interesting that he was not particularly relieved to find out that Anne was with her father, rather than her single male study buddies. Liam was well aware who was most likely to come between himself and Anne—and it wasn't her chocolate-loving pal.

He'd been in the bedroom less than ten minutes when he heard the door open in the other room.

"Just set that bag down on the floor, Dad," he heard Anne say. "Thanks for bringing it up for me."

"You shouldn't carry so much stuff around in your car," her father replied, his voice clearly audible through the thin bedroom door. "It's not a rolling closet."

Anne laughed ruefully. "I know. I kept meaning to clean it out, but I just never seemed to find the time."

"How are you going to get to class tomorrow? Do you need me to come get you?"

"No, that's not necessary. I'll catch a ride with Ron or James. My apartment is on the way for both of them."

Liam felt his eyebrows lower into a scowl.

"You can't get by without a car," her father scolded. "Nor do you need to be distracted from your studies by trying to deal with this. I suspect that the repairs on your engine will be expensive—more than the car's worth, most likely—not to mention time-consuming. Let me buy you a new car. I'll pick one out tomorrow and have it delivered to you tomorrow afternoon."

"No, Dad, you aren't buying me a new car." Anne's voice was firm. "If I need a new car, and I won't know that for certain until I hear what the mechanic says, I'll take care of it myself. I still have my savings, and I have enough in student loans to cover a modest car payment. I told you when I started medical school that I wouldn't let you support me financially, and I meant it. I'm an adult. I intend to act like one."

"Fine." Her father sounded annoyed. "Consider it a loan, then. When you've finished your surgical residency and you're making a good salary, you can pay me back. With interest, if that makes you feel better."

"As if you'd let me. Please, let me handle this. I really appreciate your help tonight, but I can take it from here. I'll call if I need anything else, I promise."

He argued a few more minutes, but Anne was resolute. She escorted him out with reminders that it was late and that her mother would be worried if her dad didn't get home soon.

Liam waited until he heard the door close, then another couple of minutes just to be sure Easton was gone.

"Liam?" Anne opened the bedroom door, both looking and sounding weary. "I'm sorry about that. I barely had time to get a text message to you without alerting Dad what I was doing."

"No problem. I heard most of what you said. What happened to your car?"

"It died," she answered simply, spreading her hands. "Just sputtered and quit at a traffic light. I couldn't get it restarted. Dad thinks it's serious. He had it towed to his mechanic, who will look at it tomorrow and give me an estimate."

"You called your dad?" Liam tried to keep his tone neutral.

"Yeah. Like I said, I was stranded at an intersection. I'm just glad there weren't many other cars there at that hour. The ones that passed by were able to go around me. A couple of people stopped as if to help, but I waved them on. Fortunately, Dad arrived quickly, so I didn't have to sit there long."

"It never occurred to you to call me?"

A small frown creased her brow. "I'm sorry. Were you worried because I was so late?"

"I didn't mean you should have called me to tell me you'd been delayed," he answered impatiently. "I was asking why you didn't call me to come get you. To help you with the car problem."

He could tell by the rather blank look on her face that the idea had never even occurred to her. "I guess I just thought automatically about my dad because he had his mechanic look at the car a couple of months ago when I had some problems with it. He arranged tonight for a tow truck to take the car back to the same mechanic to find out how extensive the damage is this time."

"I see."

Anne looked at him with confusion in her eyes. "Liam, are you actually annoyed that I called my father instead of you?"

"Your daddy instead of your husband, you mean?"

Maybe that came out a little snippy. Anne planted her hands on her hips and tipped her head, her eyes narrowing. "And just what was that supposed to mean?"

He shrugged. "I'm just saying. It seems a little odd that you'd call him, especially knowing you'd be lectured the whole time you were with him. And even though by having him bring you home, you were taking a risk that he might notice something that would make him suspicious about us."

"I knew you would stay out of sight when I sent you the message. I wasn't too worried about Dad seeing anything."

She seemed to be worrying less and less about her family discovering their secret. Was she getting overconfident—or was there a part of her that almost hoped they would be found out? "I still think you should be more careful. I'd have come for you, and I'd have helped you get the car towed. Your family wouldn't have had to even know about it until you got around to telling them."

"I know you would have been happy to help. It's just that Dad has always helped me when I had car problems, so I guess it was simply out of habit that I called him tonight."

"It's that sort of habit that keeps you under your family's thumbs," Liam muttered. Even he didn't quite understand why it stung him so much that Anne hadn't even thought to turn to him when she'd had a problem. Maybe he had more male ego than he'd realized, especially when it came to his wife.

And if he didn't shut up, he was going to end up sleeping on the couch tonight like the stereotypical husband in the doghouse, he thought with a wince as Anne's face flushed with anger. Judging by the glint in her eyes, he'd be lucky if he didn't end up sleeping on the sidewalk.

"I am not under my family's thumbs," she said, very slowly and deliberately. "I live on my savings and my student loans. I pay my own bills and make my own way. Perhaps I ask my family for advice or minor assistance occasionally, but that doesn't mean I am dependent on them. I could have arranged my own tow tonight, if necessary, and found my own way home, but I knew Dad wouldn't mind helping out."

"Damn it, Anne, you should be letting *me* help you. Let me pay for the repairs or buy you a new car. We're married. My money is your money."

"I don't see it that way," she replied defensively. "Especially since no one even knows about our marriage. I don't need my family to take care of me—and I don't need you to do so, either. Considering how rarely you're even in the same country, I'd say it's a good thing I *can* take care of myself."

That little barb hit its target. Liam shoved a hand through the hair he'd chopped so he could spend time with her. "You knew when we married that my job would involve this much travel. You said you didn't mind, that you would be too busy with medical school to spend much time with me, anyway."

"And that's still true," she said, though her tone was rather flat. "So don't blame me for not being in the habit of calling you for assistance with the kind of minor issues that occur in my regular routines here."

"I'm not blaming you," he muttered, conflicted emotions tangling inside him. "I just don't understand why you complain about your family's interference in your life and then you choose to turn to them when you have a problem. Every time you're around them, you come home looking even more pressured, but you still go back to them whenever they summon you."

"They're my family. I love them. And they love me." She shook her head in apparent exasperation as she snapped her response. "Just because you weren't close to your parents doesn't mean I should become estranged from mine."

Maybe something showed in his face that he didn't intend to let her see.

"I'm sorry," she said after a brief, taut pause. She took a step toward him and laid a hand on his arm. "I'm sorry. That was a terrible thing to say to you, especially now."

He didn't like seeing the tears gathering in her eyes, and knowing he was responsible for them. "It's okay," he said gruffly. "You're right. I wasn't particularly close to my parents."

"Not through any fault of your own. You were only a child when your father left and your mother died. It was unforgivable of me to use that against you. I'm sorry."

"I'm the one who should ask for forgiveness." His stomach tied in hard knots, he reached out to brush a tear from her cheek with the pad of his thumb. "You're exhausted. It's been a very long day and you're trying to get ready for the test Friday. I promised you I wouldn't add to your stress while I'm here, and what did I do? I snarled at you because your car broke down and you took care of it without my help. I'm sorry."

She sniffled and shook her head. "I still shouldn't have spoken to you that way."

He forced a smile. "We could stand here apologizing to each other all night. Let's agree to put it behind us, shall we? Why don't you go freshen up and I'll make you some chamomile tea to help you relax before bed."

She nodded and drew a shaky breath, looking as relieved as he was that the quarrel was over—at least for now.

Fortunately, the car repairs were not extensive as Anne's father had feared. Relieved that she wouldn't have to deal with buying a new one until summer, at least, Anne drove a loaner car arranged by the mechanic until she got her own back Wednesday afternoon. Though he offered, she refused to allow her dad to pay for the repairs. She was still stinging over Liam's words Monday evening, even though they had been almost formally polite to each other ever since.

It seemed to be the week for conflict. As Friday's test drew closer, the tension in the study group mounted. They argued about the best ways to study for the tests, they disagreed on some of the slide interpretations, they even quarreled once about where they should meet to study. Saying he was tired of sitting in various kitchens, Ron suggested a coffee shop or the library, while the others asserted there were fewer distractions in someone's home than in a public place.

Attempting to analyze was what going on with the group, Anne decided that burnout was taking its toll on them all. They hadn't had a break since Christmas. The weeks had passed in a blur of classes, lectures, clinical lessons, study sessions and exams. The instructors were beginning to harp more and more on the looming Step 1 exam, which merely added to the dread already gripping the class. The students were all dazed and sleep deprived. It was no surprise they were so tense and snappy. Nor any wonder that so many relationships had suffered—marriages, romances, friendships, even study groups.

She tried not to blame her group's problems solely on Ron and Haley—after all, they had all snarled occasionally—but she had to admit that Ron and Haley, in particular, were taking out their anxiety on each other. She still didn't quite understand their relationship—was there an attraction, did they just rub each other the wrong way or did they simply not like each other? Whatever the issue, she wished they could set their differences aside long enough to get through the rest of the semester. She depended so much on the encouragement and support of this group; it already made her sad to think they'd be splitting up next year and going into separate rotations.

Thursday evening, the night before the test, was particularly distressing. None of them—with the possible exception of James—felt completely ready for the exam and they had several differences of opinion about what facts they should be focusing on in their studies that evening. Each had a different idea of what topics would be covered most heavily on the exam. They ended up splitting up early for the evening, each going to their individual homes to study on their own.

Sensing that Anne was upset, Liam was particularly supportive that evening. He kept fresh tea in her cup, saw that she had fruit to munch on for quick energy, even quizzed her on some practice questions. He didn't even nag her—much—to get some sleep when he finally turned in after midnight, leaving her still awake, promising him she just wanted to look over "a few more things" before she joined him. It was after one when she finally gave up and succumbed to sleep.

As was her custom after an exam, she returned to her apartment drained and bone-tired, heading straight for her bed for a nap.

She woke to the scent of roses. Before she even opened her eyes, she inhaled deeply, letting the soothing fragrance waft through her. When she finally blinked and pushed herself upright, she was greeted with the sight of a dozen gorgeous orange roses in a crystal vase on the nightstand.

Delighted, she buried her nose in the cheery bouquet and inhaled deeply. Only then did she see the new dress she hadn't yet had a chance to wear draped over the chair in the corner of the bedroom. A note lay on top of the draped skirt. *A fancy night out or a casual night at home? Your choice.*

She had to smile at his wording. He'd obviously made plans for the evening, but he wasn't entirely sure she would be in the mood to go out. She picked up the dress and slipped into the bathroom.

Fifteen minutes later, she had freshened her makeup, pinned up her hair and donned the dress, accessorizing it with her grandmother's diamond necklace. She wondered what Liam had in mind for the evening.

He waited for her in the living room. Dressed in a dark suit with a crisp white shirt and a deep red tie, he held a white rose in his hand. Her heart nearly stopped at the sight of him looking so very handsome.

He presented the rose with a little bow that made her come very close to a girlish giggle. "You're wearing the dress. Does that mean you're in the mood to go out?"

"I would love to get out," she assured him. She assumed he would take the usual precautions about not being recognized. She thought the short hair, glasses and conservative suit would go a long way toward that end. He hardly resembled the wild-haired adventurer who was most often seen tramping through jungles and wading through muck.

She couldn't decide at the moment which side of Liam she preferred.

He had made reservations at an exclusive and expensive Little Rock restaurant. They dined in a secluded, romantically dim corner lit only by the table's candles and one ruby-shaded sconce light. Soft music filled the room, underscoring the suitably restrained conversations around them, making the dining experience even more intimate. This, he told her when she expressed her pleasure at this nice surprise, was the dinner he had planned to share with her on Valentine's Day. She felt as though that holiday had been held over just for the two of them this year; she couldn't imagine a more perfect way to celebrate.

Liam advised her not to order dessert at the restaurant, giving her a hint that there was more in store for her. Rather than taking her straight home after dinner, he drove across the Arkansas River into the city of North Little Rock, where he parked in the lot of a traditional Irish pub she had always wanted to visit, but had never found the time.

Stepping into the pub, which had been built in Scotland and imported to Arkansas, was like going back in time to their summer abroad. The gleaming woods, the amber pendant lights, the smells of stout and stew. The sound of Celtic music being played by a quartet in one corner, and of darts hitting boards in a back room. The conversation here was louder, more raucous than at the restaurant. The accents were more Southern than Gaelic, but Anne could still pretend they were back in Scotland.

She felt herself going rather misty and she blinked rapidly a couple of times before turning to Liam with a smile. "Let me guess. You want a Guinness."

He grinned. "Of course."

They jostled through a rather tipsy group to find a table near the window where they could watch pedestrians, cars and trolley cars pass outside. Liam ordered a pint of Guinness and chocolate mousse cake; Anne requested half a pint and bread pudding. They lingered over their desserts, laughing and talking and reminiscing, never once mentioning her classes or her squabbling friends or her family or their own uncertainties. Anne thought she knew now why she'd always found an excuse not to visit this particularly local establishment. She couldn't imagine being there without Liam.

Their desserts were down to crumbs in the bottom of the serving dishes when she excused herself to visit the ladies' room. She wasn't gone long, but by the time she returned, some other woman had already invaded her territory.

Pausing across the room, she watched with narrowed eyes as an attractive young blonde with well-displayed assets flirted with Liam. Did the woman recognize him? Or was she simply making a move on a strikingly handsome male sitting alone in a booth—and not wearing a wedding ring on his left hand?

She slid into her seat with a brilliant smile for Liam. "Did you want coffee before we go?"

The blonde drifted off with a sigh of resignation. Liam chuckled and tossed some cash on the table. "No, I'm ready to leave if you are."

Anne glanced sideways. "A fan?"

"No. Just a friendly local."

"Mmm." A little too friendly in Anne's opinion, but since Liam was already grinning at her, she said no more about the incident.

By the time they finally arrived home, she was pleasantly tired and utterly relaxed. "That was such a beautiful evening out," she said to Liam when he closed and locked the front door behind them. "How did you know it was exactly what I needed tonight?"

He smiled and walked across the room to turn on the MP3 player she kept in a speaker dock. Even that move had been planned, apparently. The music that drifted from the speakers wasn't from her usual playlists; Liam must have loaded some romantic instrumental numbers just for tonight.

He took her into his arms in the middle of the living room, swinging her into a slow, sensual dance. Wrapping her arms around his neck, she followed easily, her hips moving with his. "Why, Mr. McCright—I do believe you're trying to seduce me."

His teeth flashed in a smile. "Is it working?"

Pressing her breasts against his chest, she almost purred against his throat, "I believe it is."

She loosened and removed his tie as they danced. He let down her hair. Still swaying to the music, she slid his jacket from his shoulders and tossed it aside. He unzipped her dress.

The music seemed to follow them as they drifted toward the bedroom, leaving a trail of clothing behind them. Liam didn't bother turning on the light. Falling onto the bed with him, Anne wished very hard that she could make this perfect night last for a very long time, keeping all the problems of daylight far away from them.

Anne was already at her books when Liam came out of the shower late the next morning. Rather than sitting at the table, she had spread out on the couch this time, her computer in her lap, her bare feet propped on the table in front of her.

He leaned over the back of the couch to brush a kiss against her cheek. "You look exceptionally beautiful today. Just as you do every day."

Tilting her clean-scrubbed face toward him, she motioned

toward her ultracasual T-shirt and jeans. "You must have spent too much time in the Irish pub last night. You're full of blarney this morning."

He laughed and circled the couch to sit on one arm to chat with her for a minute before he tried to get back to his own work. "I don't think I asked before—are you meeting with your group today?"

"No, we're taking the weekend off. We're all studying on our own this weekend. We need the break from each other."

"I can see why you would. Do you get a spring break this semester?"

She made a face. "Yes, in mid-March. And we have an exam the day we return, followed immediately by a practice Step 1 exam that we have to do well on or be forced to sign up for a review class this summer. Then in April, we start 'shelf exams'—end of the semester tests for each subject. So, basically, we spend all of spring break cramming for regular exams and shelf exams and trying to find time to prepare for the Step 1 exam. It isn't exactly a vacation."

So much for his vague plan to whisk her away somewhere, just the two of them, for the week off from classes. "And when do you start your third-year rotations?"

"The beginning of July. I'll have maybe two weeks off after Step 1."

"July." He nodded, making a mental note to clear his calendar for those two weeks. "Okay, maybe we can plan something for then. Think you can slip away to join me somewhere exotic and romantic—and private? You could tell everyone you need a vacation, and surely they will understand that. They wouldn't have to know you won't be spending that vacation alone."

"I'll see what I can do." After a moment, she set her computer aside and turned on the couch to face him more fully. "You know, I've been thinking."

Something about her tone warned him that he might not be quite comfortable with what she was going to say. "Thinking about what?"

She moistened her lips and twisted her hands in her lap. "I think maybe we should start thinking about ending this silly charade of ours."

His first, instinctive reaction was that she was suggesting they end their marriage, and that was like a hard punch to his stomach. She had told him how perfect last night had been, and she had certainly shown her appreciation—twice—afterward. Why would she want to end things now?

Which left only one explanation. "Um—charade?" he asked nervously.

"You know what I mean," she said, her expression impatient now. "All this sneaking around. Hiding behind doors and under the brim of baseball caps, jumping every time the doorbell chimes. We never intended to keep our marriage a secret for this long. I think we should start discussing how and when we should make the announcement."

"You're ready to tell your family the truth?" he asked, startled.

He could see the nerves in her darkened eyes, in the lines around her mouth, in the taut set of her shoulders, but she gave a little nod. "I'm getting there. Not immediately, of course. I still think it would be best to wait until after Step 1. But maybe before that July vacation together. What do you think?"

His stomach clenched again and his skin felt clammy. His physical reaction was a bit stronger than he might have expected, but he tried to keep his expression composed when he asked, "I'll be filming then, but I can probably take a little time to join you here if you think the time is right to break the news to your parents. But are you really sure you'll be ready for that right before you begin your third-year rotations?"

Though she looked nervous at the prospect, she gave a

little shrug. "I could deal with it. Probably. I'd just tell my parents that I don't have time for family drama. If I tell them they're interfering with my studies, I'm sure they'd back off. Their biggest fear is that I'll wash out of medical school, so they wouldn't do anything to upset me overly much. Probably."

Which all sounded well and good, but he knew it wouldn't be that easy. Besides, she wasn't the only one who would have to deal with her family once their marriage was no longer a private one.

"I'm pleased that you want everyone to know about us," he assured her, though a tiny, accusing voice inside him whispered that he lied, making him feel like a jerk. "But we shouldn't make any rash decisions. We need to think this through before we do anything we can't take back. You know, make sure it's the right time, and that we're both ready to go public."

Her eyes darkened. "I'm tired of the lies, Liam. It just gets so frustrating."

"I know, babe. But the main problem is, you're just tired. You're running on fumes, and this is totally the wrong time to set yourself up for more problems. Let's just wait until summer, okay? It's not that much longer."

She studied his face with narrowed eyes. "You make it sound as if you aren't in any hurry at all to tell anyone. Is it because of your career? Or are you actually content to go on the way we have been?"

Good questions, he acknowledged. And he had no real answers for her. Because he hadn't been expecting her to suddenly suggest they announce their marriage, he hadn't really thought about when they would get around to making their announcement. "I just think it's a bad time for you, Annie. Focus on your studying for now, and we'll deal with everything else when you're got the worst part behind you."

She shrugged. "Fine. If that's what you prefer."

She picked up her computer again and settled it in her lap. "I guess I should get back to my studies."

"Anything I can do to help? Want me to quiz you?"

"No, thanks. I have a lot of reading to do today."

He nodded and pushed himself off the arm of the couch.

He hadn't handled that very well, he thought as he moved slowly toward the office. It seemed to him as though a light had gone out in Anne's eyes that had been there when they'd awakened this morning. Maybe it was just the reminder of all she had to do within the next few months.

Or maybe, he thought with a hard knot in his chest to match the one in his stomach, she had been hoping for something from him that he hadn't quite known how to offer her.

"I never had a chance to ask—how was your weekend?" Haley asked when she and Anne finally had a chance to speak in private Monday. It had been a very busy morning filled with classes and other obligations and neither of them had even had time for a lunch break. Anne had offered Haley a lift home because Haley had taken the bus to the campus that morning. Haley had eagerly agreed, giving them an opportunity for a brief chat session during the short drive to Haley's apartment.

"It was fine," Anne replied, keeping her eyes on the traffic ahead of her. "I got a lot of reading done for this week's classes. How was yours?"

"Not bad. Kris and I went out Saturday night. We saw a movie, had a few drinks. It was fun."

Anne glanced sideways toward her passenger. "You really do like him, don't you?"

Haley shrugged. "Like I said, he's a nice guy and he makes me laugh. If you're asking if I've started falling for him yet, the answer is no, not really. If he never called again, I wouldn't stew about it. As busy as we stay, I'm not sure I'd notice for a few weeks."

Anne wondered if Kris was as casual about the relationship as Haley. He seemed to be awfully patient and persistent for a man who was only an occasional companion.

"What about you?" Haley asked. "Did you and Liam do anything interesting?"

Anne thought she should probably be amused by the exaggerated stealth of Haley's tone—as if anyone else could hear them in her car. Yet, she found little to laugh about in the situation. "We went out Friday night, after the exam. We had a very nice dinner, then went to that Irish pub in North Little Rock for drinks and dessert afterward."

"Sounds like fun."

"Yes, it was."

"You needed that. Just like I needed to go out Saturday night."

Anne nodded. "I wore my new dress. The one I bought when you and I went shopping."

"Oh, the coral one. It looked great on you. Did Liam like it?"

"I believe he did." Even though he had been eager to peel her out of it once they'd returned home, she thought with a ripple of remembered heat. She didn't bother mentioning that part to her friend.

"I bet he enjoyed going out with you. He's been spending a lot of time cooped up alone in your apartment."

"Yes, he has." Which had been his own choice, Anne reminded herself when guilt threatened to nibble at her. "And he did seem to have a good time."

"How's he doing with his writing? He's been here—what? Three weeks?"

"Well, he arrived three weeks ago, but he spent almost a week in Ireland when his father died."

Haley nodded somberly, having been filled in on that sad detail. "Is he doing okay with that?"

"He doesn't talk about it." It was one of several topics Liam seemed to be avoiding. Like his writing. And their future.

She braked for a red light, then glanced toward Haley. "I, um, suggested to Liam that we tell my parents the truth as soon as I've taken the Step 1 exam," she said, feeling a need to confide in her closest female friend. "I think maybe the time will be right by then."

Haley's eyes went wide. "Wow. You're really ready to tell everyone?"

Anne nodded rather glumly. "Almost. We had such a beautiful night Friday, and I woke Saturday morning not wanting that feeling to end. I guess I just wanted everyone to know that Liam and I are together."

Especially pretty blondes in random bars, she thought grimly, then winced. She really hoped there was more to her wish to finally take that big step than simple jealousy. It wasn't as if she wanted to take an ad out in the next day's paper; she just thought it was time she and Liam began to discuss going public.

"Did you and Liam decide how you're going to make the announcement? Are you going to tell your family on your own, or will he join you?"

"We didn't get that far in our discussion." She cleared her throat, then admitted, "Liam didn't think it was a good time to talk about it. I could tell the suggestion caught him off guard. And not necessarily in a good way."

"What do you mean?"

"He said it was a bad time for me to make any decisions, with all the other stress I'm under. Classes and tests and everything."

"He has a point there." Haley looked suddenly weary as she rubbed the back of her neck with one hand. "I can hardly find time to eat and sleep, much less make any important decisions not connected with the next exam. Let's face it, we're all stretched pretty tightly."

Anne nodded. "I know. It was just—"

Haley studied her perceptively. "Just what?"

The light turned green and Anne turned her attention toward the road ahead as she mentally groped for words. "Liam didn't seem all that impatient to announce our marriage," she murmured finally. "I got the impression that he wanted to put that off as long as possible."

"I see." Haley hesitated a moment before asking, "Why do you think that is?"

Anne smiled wryly. "You aren't a shrink yet, Haley, but you're already talking like one."

Haley shrugged a bit sheepishly. "I still haven't decided for sure that I want to go into psychiatry. But the question remains. Why do you think Liam doesn't want to make the announcement?"

"I don't know." She'd given that question a great deal of thought in the past couple of days. She hadn't liked many of the possibilities that had occurred to her.

"I can think of one significant reason he'd want everyone to think he's single."

Anne shook her head in response to Haley's gentle suggestion. "It has nothing to do with him wanting to see other women," she insisted. She was completely confident about that. Well, maybe ninety-nine percent confident, she thought with a slight frown.

"Is it his job? Does he think he's a more interesting celebrity as a bachelor?"

"Maybe—even though he always refuses to talk about his personal life in interviews. He wants to keep the conversation on his travels and his experiences, not on his broken home or his father abandoning him when he was a kid—or his marital status."

"Makes sense. But it sounds to me as though he's mostly worried about you. I'm sure once the semester is behind us, he'll be very proud to tell everyone the two of you are together."

Anne supposed Haley was right. It wouldn't be much longer until summer, she reminded herself. Which, of course, meant that it wouldn't be long until the Step 1 exam.

"What time are we meeting to study tonight?" she asked, deliberately moving her attention to the more immediate concern.

Anne and Liam met for an early dinner at a popular Chinese fast-food place not far from the campus Wednesday. They had hardly seen each other that week, and Liam had been cooped up in the apartment for days, so they both needed the break.

The place was crowded, as always, and Anne couldn't help worrying a little that she would run into one of her classmates, but Liam was dressed very incognito again. His preppy polo shirt and jeans were far from his usual safari gear, his hair was freshly trimmed and he wore the ball cap again, which he didn't bother to remove for the casual surroundings. He wasn't the only one wearing a cap while eating. They had agreed that if she did see someone she knew, and if introductions seemed called for, she could simply refer to him as her friend Lee.

Conversation was made somewhat difficult by the noise level of the dining room, but they managed to make small talk as they wound pad Thai noodles on to disposable chopsticks. Liam looked rather happy with the amount of work he'd accomplished that day.

"It's going better, I take it?" she asked, pleased that he seemed satisfied with his results.

He nodded. "I think I've finally figured out my strategy for easing from one story into the next. It seems to be flowing well now. I should be able to wrap up a rough draft by the end of next week. I'll send that to my editor for input before I spend much more time on it."

"The end of next week," she repeated, hoping the background noise concealed the hollowness of her voice. "Wow. That would be great progress."

He nodded. "After all the delays, I really have to put the pressure on now. I've got a couple of meetings scheduled in New York the week after that, and it would be a lot better if I get this project out of the way first. At least, this part of it."

So. She had a timetable now. Liam would be leaving in approximately a week and a half. Still longer than he'd planned to stay when he'd arrived almost a month earlier, but it still seemed so soon for him to be off again.

"I'm glad it's going well for you," she said, stabbing her chopsticks into the bowl of noodles. "I was beginning to get worried, for your sake."

"You should have known better," he chided good-humoredly. "I always work things out eventually."

"That's true."

"Guess you'll be glad to have your place back. Your friends are probably wondering why you haven't invited them over to study lately."

She tried to smile. "Maybe a little. Haley keeps jumping in to volunteer her apartment whenever we're not meeting at one of the others. She's really been covering for me."

"I'm glad you have such a good friend in her. I like her."

"Yes, so do I, obviously." She watched as Liam pushed his bowl aside after eating less than half the dish. "Is that all you're having?"

"I'm not very hungry. My stomach's been a little queasy today. Maybe a stomach bug or something."

"There's a nasty stomach virus making the rounds. Maybe you should see a doctor."

His grin was mischievous—and more than a little suggestive. "I've been seeing a doctor quite regularly. And enjoying every bit of what I've seen."

Her cheeks warmed. "I meant a real doctor—one who's already taken and passed all these stupid tests."

"I'll be fine. Don't worry about it."

"If it's not better by tomorrow, I'm going to start nagging," she warned him.

He laughed. "I read somewhere that married men tend to live longer because their wives nag them into seeing doctors. If it makes you feel better, I'll check with a doctor if my stomach is still bothering me by Friday."

She agreed to the compromise with a nod. It probably was just a virus, in which case there wasn't much a doctor could do. Antibiotics were useless—even counterproductive for viruses, which tended to resolve themselves within a week or so. She was probably just being overly concerned, a typical med student's reaction when family fell ill.

She glanced at her watch and grimaced. "I'm sorry to have to run, but I'm supposed to meet the group at Ron's in twenty minutes."

"Of course. I don't want to make you late. I'll walk you to your car."

They stood and moved together toward the door. Halfway there, a rowdy toddler darted out in front of them, almost tangling in Anne's feet. Liam steadied her with an arm around her shoulder while the child's father captured the runaway with a murmured apology.

Anne smiled up at Liam, and he tightened his arm around her as they shared a laugh at the near collision. And then they looked toward the door again.

This time Anne almost fell over her own feet when she stumbled to a shocked halt, causing Liam to bump into her.

"Now what?" he asked with a chuckle.

His smile died when his gaze followed hers.

Anne's parents and grandfather had just walked into the restaurant.

Chapter Ten

An hour after leaving the Chinese restaurant, Anne still felt a little shaky whenever she thought about how very close to disaster she and Liam had come. She could hardly believe they'd managed to blend into a crowd of college-age students leaving the restaurant just as her family had entered. She and Liam had both ducked their heads, and Liam had instinctively sheltered her by keeping himself between her and her parents. Somehow they had gotten out without a painful and public confrontation.

"That was entirely too close," Liam had said as they stood beside her car.

"You're telling me." She'd swallowed the hard lump that had formed in her throat when she'd seen her father. "I knew Dad liked eating lunch here occasionally, but I had no idea they were coming here for dinner this evening."

"Let's get out of here before they spot us," he'd suggested, opening her door for her. "I'll see you back at your apartment later. Have a good study session."

He hadn't even kissed her as he'd all but shoved her into her car. The near miss had seemed to scare Liam even more than it had her.

As a result of that close call, she was a bit on edge when she met with her friends that evening. And she wasn't the only one. Even though the next test was a week and a half away and they'd all had a few days' break from each other, the tension remained within her group when they gathered at Ron's downtown loft apartment. And this time she placed the blame directly where it belonged—on Ron and Haley.

"All right, guys, stop it," she insisted after Haley snapped at Ron for the second or third time that evening and Ron sniped back. "This is really getting out of hand between you two."

"Seriously," Connor agreed, looking relieved that someone had brought up the subject. "I haven't seen this sort of juvenile squabbling since I quit teaching high school. What's going on with the two of you?"

Haley scowled. "I just get tired of him turning everything into a silly joke. This is serious. Maybe it doesn't matter to you if we all pass the next test, Ron, but it matters very much to us. We have to focus."

"I'm just trying to lighten everyone up a little," Ron argued. "All we do is study and drill. It doesn't hurt to laugh every once in a while."

"And I just happen to be the most convenient butt of most of your jokes?" she retorted. "Gee, thanks. That really makes our study sessions more entertaining for me."

"Maybe if you wouldn't be quite so sensitive…"

"I'm not being sensitive! I'm just tired of you always picking at me. Making fun of my quirks, belittling anyone I happen to date, teasing me when I miss a question…"

"Oh, yeah, like that ever happens. When's the last time you were less than perfect on anything, Ms. Genius?"

James cleared his throat, the quiet noise sounding oddly loud in the sudden silence. "That's hardly fair, Ron."

Ron turned on James, then, his usually smiling eyes dark and grim. "I can see why you'd think so. You're at the damned top of the whole class. It all comes so easily to you. I don't know why you even bother to study with us."

"As it happens, I enjoy the companionship," James replied evenly, his tone a bit too patient, as if he were keeping his own temper under control with an effort. "And, yes, I need to study as much as the rest of you."

Ron snorted.

Growing more uncomfortable by the moment with the direction their conversation had taken, Anne noticed that Connor was eyeing Ron intently.

"Ron," Connor asked quietly, "are you under the impression that you are any less valuable to this study group than the rest of us?"

Ron flushed. "Let's face it, guys, you've all been carrying me for almost two years. All of you are so smart and so damned prepared for this career. I don't even know how I got into medical school, and it's all I've been able to do just to keep up so far. I'm not at the top of the class—I have to struggle just to stay somewhere in the middle. It's going to take a freaking miracle for me to pass Step 1 and move on to third year. I don't even know what I want to do when—or if—I get this degree."

He held up his hands when everyone started to speak at once, his expression both embarrassed and chagrined, as if he'd been provoked into revealing much more than he had intended. "Don't start throwing reassuring platitudes at me. I don't need to be patted on the head. I'm just saying that if I act like none of this really matters to me, it's because I just want to be prepared in case I screw up and have to find some other career. If you all agree with Haley that I'm more of a liability than an asset to the group, then I'll start studying on my own. I'll understand."

Haley appeared to be near tears. "I never said you were a liability."

Ron glanced at her with patent skepticism. "You made it clear enough."

Anne drew a deep breath and stood. The others still sat around Ron's round table, and they all looked at her in surprise when she rested her hands on the table and leaned forward, looking from one to the other of the faces turned her way.

"Every single one of us contributes to this group," she said firmly, focusing now on Ron. "We *need* you to make us laugh, Ron. We need Haley to keep us motivated, and Connor to use his teaching skills to make some of the material easier to understand, and James to keep us calm and centered. We're all exhausted. God knows none of us has had a full eight hours sleep in longer than we can remember. We're all worried about next Friday's test, not to mention the shelf exams and the Step 1. I suspect even James worries about that, though he doesn't let us see it."

James nodded shortly. "I'd be a fool not to worry about passing that exam. None of us is guaranteed to sail through it without a hitch."

"Exactly. Which is why we have to stick together," she continued, fierce determination coloring her voice now. "I need you guys. All of you. I would not have been able to get through these past two years without you. I can't imagine preparing for these exams during the next four months without you all. But we're going to have to stick together. Haley, stop taking everything so personally. And Ron, if you don't feel like you're prepared for the next test, then for God's sake, stop fretting about it and say so! That's what we're all here for."

Haley bit her lip, looking somewhat abashed by Anne's uncharacteristic lecture. And then she peeked at Ron from beneath her lashes. "I'm sorry, Ron. I had no idea you feel like you've been struggling. It just didn't seem to matter that much to you."

"It matters," he muttered. "And I'm sorry if you feel like I've been picking on you. I was kidding around—like I do with everyone. I'll stop, I promise."

Haley nodded, but Anne noticed she didn't look particularly happy about Ron's offer.

"Maybe we should get back to work," Connor suggested. "We'll all feel better when we've gotten through the last of today's lecture slides."

Anne took her seat again, even as Ron sprang up from his own. "I'll make fresh coffee. Who, besides me, needs a cup?"

"I'll help you," Haley offered quickly, a bit too courteously. Without actually looking at Haley, Ron nodded to accept her assistance.

Anne supposed it was a start.

Gathering her things, Haley spoke to Ron, "I'll see you tomorrow?"

He nodded. "Yeah. Tomorrow."

Hesitating only a moment, Haley pivoted and moved toward the door. "Are you coming, Anne?"

"Yes. I'll be right behind you."

Anne waited until Haley stepped out before speaking quietly to Ron. "I hope I wasn't out of line earlier. I didn't mean to come down on you like a disapproving mother."

Ron grimaced. "I guess I deserved it. I was acting like a whiny kid."

"No. You were acting like a scared and stressed-out medical student. Trust me, I know all about that."

He pushed a hand through his sandy hair that was in need of a trim, his gaze focused uncertainly on her face. "You really worry about passing the tests? As well as you've done so far?"

"I'm scared every single time," she replied simply. "I come from a whole family of surgeons, remember? If I fail, I'll never hear the end of it."

His smile was crooked. "Yeah, well, I come from a family of ne'er-do-wells, and I'd never hear the end of it, either. They've all been predicting from the start that I would never make it all the way through medical school."

Indignant on his behalf, she said firmly, "They're wrong."

He reached out to give her a hug, and because the gesture was both natural and unmistakably brotherly, she hugged him in return. "Thanks," he said, looking a little sheepish when he drew away.

"Just don't forget that our group needs you," she told him a little mistily. "Good night, Ron."

"We need you, too. Every group of rowdy kids needs a mom." Tugging her braid, he smiled more naturally. "Good night, Annie."

His teasing use of the nickname startled her a little, though she tried not to show it as she let herself out. No one except Liam called her that, and it felt odd hearing it on someone else's lips. She had a feeling Liam would not be pleased to hear Ron speaking to her so familiarly, though she could assure him in all candor that she felt nothing for Ron except affection.

Liam was the only man who would ever hold her heart.

The lights were burning in her apartment when she parked in her space and climbed out of the car, drawing her coat more snugly around her as a cold breeze slithered down her collar.

A hint of impending rain hung in the air, which already felt damp against her cheeks.

Shivering, she gathered her books and computer bag and headed for the stairs, toward those welcoming lights.

Having heard her key in the door, Liam stood in the open bedroom doorway to greet her when she walked in. She wondered if he was still battling that stomach bug. He looked a little pale, and his voice sounded rather strained when he spoke. "You're home early."

She nodded and set down her things. "Long night. We got through today's slides, though. And I think we had a break-through, in a way, in the group. We sort of cleared the air and passed around apologies. I think we'll all get along better now."

"I'm glad to hear that. I know it was bothering you. You need the support of your friends now."

"That's what I told them." She pulled the band off the end of her braid and loosened her hair. "Are you still feeling sick, Liam? Your color doesn't look quite right."

He shrugged. "I've had some nausea since dinner, but I think it's passing now. Still fighting that bug, I guess. I hope you don't get it. You certainly don't have time to be sick right now."

She laughed wearily, though she made a mental vow to get him to a doctor the next day if he wasn't feeling better by then. "Tell me about it. I've been obsessive about washing my hands. Maybe I'll get by without catching it."

"I hope so."

"I'm going to wash my face and put on some pajamas and spend a couple of hours going over my notes before bedtime," she said, moving toward the bedroom doorway where he still stood. He moved aside to allow her past him. "Maybe we could have some soothing tea or something before—"

She came to a sudden stop when she saw the bags sitting

beside the bed. She turned slowly to face Liam, her heart beginning to thud in dread. "Are you going somewhere?"

He stood very still, his face grim, one hand pressed against his stomach. "I'm going back to New York. My flight leaves at five-forty in the morning. I hate to disturb you that early, so I'll bunk on the couch for a few hours, then head out at about three-thirty in the morning or so."

She tried to process what he was saying. "Is there some sort of problem there? Are you coming back after you've taken care of it?"

"There's not a problem in New York," he said, his voice very gentle. "The problem is here. I think it's time for me to go."

She reached out blindly, groping for support. Her hand fell on the top of the dresser, which she gripped tightly. "I don't understand."

What might have been impatience flashed through his eyes. "I don't see how you can say that after what happened at the restaurant tonight."

"Nothing happened. My family didn't see us."

"No. But it was pretty much a miracle that they didn't. Do you know how bad that would have been if we'd come face-to-face with them there? Maybe no one else in the place gave a damn who I was, but do you think your dad would fail to recognize me?"

She swallowed hard. "No. Dad would have known you right away."

"Damn straight he would. And he'd have blown a gasket right there in front of everyone."

"He wouldn't have caused a public scene." Anne wished she could be a bit more certain of that statement. "He wouldn't have wanted to embarrass my mother that way."

The mention of her mother made Liam's face tighten even more. "That was the first time I've seen your mom since her stroke, you know. It's no wonder you've been so protective of her. She seemed very…fragile."

Anne moistened her lips. "She's stronger than she appears. She always has been."

"That may well be, but I'm not going to be the cause of her having a setback. I'm clearing out before the inevitable happens. It was foolish of me to think I could live here with you and not have anyone find out. We've just been lucky so far. Especially lucky tonight."

"So, we'll tell them. We'll tell everyone," she said rashly. "I told you I was almost ready."

He shook his head. "You don't really mean that. The timing is still all wrong."

Shock began to morph into anger. Letting go of the dresser, she planted her hands on her hips. "I'm beginning to think you're the one who is so anxious to keep our marriage a secret. Why is that?"

He frowned. "We've gone over the reasons a hundred times. Your family. Your studies…"

"Yes, those were our reasons originally. But I can't help thinking you're using my excuses to camouflage your own. Why do you *really* want to keep this secret, Liam? Is it your career? Are you afraid being married will negatively affect your fame in some way?"

"I don't worry about fame," he muttered, both arms crossed over his stomach now.

"Of course you do. That's the career you've chosen. While it might not be something I seek, I do understand that publicity is an important part of your job. But other TV hosts and travel writers are married, and it doesn't seem to hold them back."

"I'm not concerned about that," he repeated stubbornly.

"Maybe you have more personal reasons for wanting to be seen as an eligible bachelor."

Temper darkened his narrowed eyes to charcoal in response to that pointed suggestion. "Are you implying that you don't trust me, despite the promises I've made to you?"

"The promises you've made in secret," she shot back at him.

"Damn it, that has nothing to do with it. I don't break my word."

"Is that it? Are you feeling trapped by those promises? Is that the real reason you don't want to tell anyone? Because you don't want to go through a public breakup like your buddy Cal Burlington?"

"He's not my buddy, and he's got nothing to do with us! You're the one who asked me to keep this marriage a secret less than a month after we exchanged vows. I've lived up to my part of the bargain. You knew when I arrived that I wouldn't be staying long. I've already been here longer than either of us expected when I arrived. Why are you acting so surprised that I've decided it's time for me to go?"

She drew a deep breath, trying to calm herself. She supposed Liam asked a reasonable question. They had agreed from the beginning that he wouldn't stay long. And yet…

And yet she hadn't expected him to leave so abruptly. To spend his last night there dozing on the couch so he could leave before dawn the next morning.

Before she could form a reply, her phone rang. Glancing at the clock, she saw that it was just after nine when she pulled the phone from its holder. She grimaced when she saw the number displayed on the screen. "It's my father."

"Of course it is," Liam muttered, and turned away.

She didn't take the time to ask him what he meant by that. "Hi, Dad."

"Are you at home? Am I interrupting a study session?"

She pushed her hair out of her face. "No, I just walked in a few minutes ago. What's up?"

"Actually, I'm calling because of a talk I just had with your mother. I could tell something has been on her mind tonight. When I asked, she said she was sure she'd seen you at the restaurant where we had dinner tonight. She thought you were there looking very cozy with a man, but when she turned to make sure it was you, whoever it was had already gone."

"I, um—"

"I might not have thought much about it, but I ran into Mike Haverty at the club earlier this week and he said he saw you out with some man at what appeared to be a romantic dinner for two last Friday night. Are you dating someone you haven't told us about?"

Several possible answers whirled through her mind. The truth. A carefully worded prevarication. The very valid response that her personal life was none of her father's business at this stage.

She'd thought she'd set that sort of boundary when she'd moved out on her own, insisted on handling her own finances and other business affairs. Yet here he was calling her and grilling her about who she was seeing, just as he had when she was in high school. And in college, she recalled with a scowl, thinking of all the heated arguments they'd had about Liam then.

She chose to respond with a combination of all of the above. "I do go out occasionally, Dad. I'm an adult, remember?"

As if her words had given him a clue to the reason for the phone call, Liam paused in the act of moving away and turned back toward her with a searching look. She shook her head to indicate that it was okay, she was handling this. He didn't leave.

"I know you're an adult, but I'm also well aware of what your schedule is like right now. With your classes and pending exams, I find it hard to believe you have many free evenings for socializing. You'll have plenty of time for that sort of thing after you pass your licensing exams.

"Although, of course, you'll be quite busy with rotations for the next two years, and the first year of your residency will be very demanding. A surgeon's schedule makes it a challenge to maintain relationships, as you know from my own example, but you're still very young. You'll have plenty of opportunities later to find someone who will understand the demands on your time. Someone like your brother found. Perhaps another surgeon."

He was planning her entire future for her, she thought with an exasperated shake of her head. Scheduling a romance for her—preferably with another surgeon—some five or six years in the future. "Perhaps you'd like to find someone for me, when you think the time is right, of course? Maybe you'll even let me meet him sometime before the conveniently timed wedding you arrange for me."

"Now, Anne, there's no need to take that tone." Her father sounded rather startled by her atypical sarcasm. "I'm simply trying to give you advice, as a caring parent. I've been through surgical training, and I know exactly how demanding it is, and how hard it is to sustain outside relationships while going through that hard schedule. I'm just trying to spare you some of the mistakes I've made in life."

"I appreciate your concern, but I'm going to have to make my own decisions. My own mistakes. I will always value your advice, but it's still my choice whether to follow it."

She drew a deep breath, then blurted, "I haven't even decided for certain that I want to be a surgeon. Maybe during my rotations I'll find another field of medicine I'll want to pursue instead."

It was the first time she'd admitted that she was considering other options. To her father—even to herself. The closer she got to having to decide what sort of doctor she wanted to become, the less certain she was that surgery was the answer.

"Of course you want to pursue surgery." He seemed

stunned that she would even consider any other path. "You have a real gift for it, inherited, I'm sure, from your grandfather and me. Sam Burkhaven told me he was very impressed with you so far."

She supposed she should have been surprised her father had sought out her preceptor, but she wasn't really. He'd have taken the position himself had he been allowed to do so with his own daughter. If it were up to her dad, he would be supervising every step of her education to make sure it met his expectations.

"I'm not ruling it out. I'm just saying that the final decision is mine. And when I make that decision—when I make *any* decisions regarding my personal life—I'll expect you to acknowledge my right to do so, and to support me in whatever choices I make. I think that's a fair request."

"Of course I will always support you, Anne. Just as I always have," he added stiffly.

It was amazing how blind people could be about their own behavior, she mused with a faint sigh. She looked at Liam as the thought crossed her mind.

"Just keep in mind the things I've said to you tonight," her father couldn't resist saying. "If you are dating someone, I hope you've made it clear to him that your career has to come first now. This guy isn't the reason you're suddenly having doubts about surgery, is he?"

"No, Dad. I'm the only one making the decisions about my career."

"Good. Because boyfriends come and go, so you should always be in control of your own life. I've raised you to be an independent, self-sufficient woman who doesn't need a man to take care of her."

"Yes, you have." She almost added that she didn't need him to do so, either, but there was no need to hurt his feelings when he was only acting out of concern for her best interests.

Maybe she'd drawn her boundaries a little more clearly during this conversation; more likely, she would have to do so many more times before he finally got the message. Especially when she finally informed him that she was a married woman, and had been for quite some time—if that day ever came, she thought glumly.

"I need to go," she said, trying not to sound too abrupt. "I have some more studying to do tonight. I'll talk to you later. Tell Mom not to worry about me. I'm fine."

"Maybe you should come for dinner this weekend. I think we should talk some more about all of this."

"We'll see. Good night, Dad." She disconnected before he could say anything else.

"Did they see us?" Liam asked as soon as she set her phone aside.

"Not exactly. Mom thought she caught a glimpse of me. And one of Dad's friends saw us at the restaurant Friday night."

Perhaps they *had* been naive to think no one would ever see them. Except for her time away for college and the months she'd spent in Europe, Anne had lived in this area all her life, and her parents were prominent members of society. It was no surprise that she would run into someone she knew almost anywhere she went.

"What did your father say?"

She shrugged. "Just the usual paternal warnings about keeping my focus on my studies and not letting myself get distracted by romance."

Liam made a sound that was half snort, half growl. "Does he really think you're so helpless that you need him to supervise everything you do? This is exactly why I said you should have called me rather than him when your car broke down. He sees every request for assistance as an invitation for him to make all your decisions for you."

She looked pointedly at the packed suitcases sitting by her bed. "As opposed to you?"

Liam flushed, the angry color standing out against his pale, somewhat clammy-looking cheeks. "Don't compare me to your father."

"Why not? You're both so certain you know what's best for me. When I need to study, when I need to go out, when I need to eat or sleep, even when I should be married—at least openly married. All for my best interests, of course. Now tell me again that you aren't like my father."

"I can't believe you said that. I have never tried to control you the way he does."

"Not deliberately, perhaps."

"Not at all," he insisted.

She shrugged, seeing no end to that particular back-and-forth argument, especially since she was growing increasingly convinced she was right.

"Do you really dislike my father so much?" she asked instead, wondering if that was the reason he was so annoyed at being compared to the other man.

"Why should I feel any other way about him?" Liam asked in seething frustration. "He hated me the minute he first laid eyes on me. He's blamed me for everything that ever went wrong in your life. If he knew I was still around, he'd blame me for the way you just stood up to him, and for any doubts you might have about following the path your father laid out for you practically at your birth. He would do everything he could to convince you to dump me now—for your own sake, of course."

She crossed her arms over her chest, where her heart ached. Liam still had his locked arms pressed to his middle, as if their conversation was causing him as much pain as it was her. "And after we tell them the truth? That you *are* still a part of my life? How will you deal with him then?"

The question seemed to surprise him a little, as if he hadn't given much thought to that eventuality. "I don't suppose I'll have to deal with him at all," he said after a moment.

"You think he's going to throw me out of the family, perhaps? That he'll never want to see either of us again?"

"Well, no. I don't think he'll go that far. Probably. I'm sure he'll want to see you again, once he gets over his pouting that you dared to make a major decision without his guidance. But I'll still be gone a lot during the rest of your medical school experience and when I'm with you, we can do what we want, on our own terms."

"So you don't see yourself attending Christmas dinners with my parents, or birthday parties for my granddad or family cookouts in the summers or weddings and funerals and other family events?"

His eyebrows rose. "I hardly think I would be welcome to attend those events."

"Then you'll have to take steps to make sure that you are welcome, won't you? Because once you and I are openly married, my family will also be your family."

The way he almost physically recoiled from that statement made a light flash in her head. "That's the real reason you don't want to tell them, isn't it? Because having my family know about us means they'll become a part of your life, too. You're doing everything you can to prevent that."

"I didn't marry your family. I married you."

She shook her head. "That's the most naive thing you've said yet. My family is a part of me."

"Looks to me like your family causes you more pain than pleasure," he muttered. "They put so much pressure on you that you're always on edge after spending time with them. They criticize your choices. You couldn't even tell anyone about us because you didn't want to deal with their reactions."

"I still think it would have been the wrong time to tell them while Mother was in the initial stages of recovery from her stroke, but I should have told them since. I suppose I was being a coward."

She surged on before he could respond. "My parents aren't perfect, Liam. They make mistakes. But they are my family and I love them."

He cleared his throat. "I can understand that. Hell, I was fond of my dad, and he was no one's idea of a great father."

Sadness made her heart feel even heavier. Did Liam really think she would ever be content to have the same sort of distant, coolly civil relationship with her parents that he'd had with his father? "I thought you understood from the beginning that I would always be close to my family."

He pressed a hand to his stomach, as if this argument escalated the discomfort he'd mentioned earlier. "You said when you married me that you were making a choice. That you chose me over their expectations for you."

"And I did. But that doesn't mean I chose to cut them from my life. Despite dreading the initial confrontations, I always assumed they would come around eventually. That they would concede my choice of a mate and accept you into the family. But that's not what you had in mind at all, is it?"

"I guess I just didn't think that far ahead," he muttered. "You and I get along pretty well on our own. We don't need their interference."

"So you really do see it as a competition," she whispered. "You always have, haven't you? You want me to choose between you and my family."

He met her eyes from across the room without saying anything. His silence, she supposed, was an answer in itself.

She shook her head slowly. "You know what, Liam? I always believed I was the cowardly one, always worrying about failing or disappointing someone or not living up to my potential. I thought you were fearless. Nothing seemed too risky or impossible for you. You wanted something and you went after it, simple as that. I always admired you for that courage—but it worried me, too. I was afraid you would get tired of dealing with my fears. That you deserved someone as reckless and self-confident as you are."

She held up a hand when he started to speak, her heart pounding as she faced him in anger and pain. "I've come to realize lately that you aren't nearly as brave as I always thought you were. All those times you took off on your world travels? Were you really chasing adventures—or were you really running away from potential problems? My family, your own past, a real commitment to this marriage you rushed us into. Why *did* you marry me, Liam? And why do you stay married to me when you don't want to deal with everything that comes with me?"

He started to answer, then fell silent, his face pale and grim as he continued to knead his taut stomach. "This really isn't the time to get into all of that," he said after a tense pause. "We're both tired, and we're likely to say things we don't mean. I'll head back to New York so you can concentrate on your studies for now, and we'll deal with all of this after your Step 1 exam."

She wondered if it were possible to hurt any worse than she did at that moment.

"You want me to study? Fine. I'll study. That should make both you and my father happy!"

Leaving him wincing, she stormed into the office and slammed the door behind her.

Chapter Eleven

The Little Rock airport was nearly deserted at 4:00 a.m. Thursday. Most of the other early arrivals wandered through the glass doors looking sleepy and a little grumpy. The recorded messages were entirely too cheery that early in the morning, earning more than a couple of scowls in the general direction of the speakers. The glare of fluorescent lights was harsh against the predawn darkness outside.

Liam sat on a padded bench, trying to get up the energy to check his bags. There were no lines yet at the security checkpoints, so it wouldn't take long to pass through and find his departure gate. He assumed he could get a cup of coffee somewhere on the way.

His aching stomach rebelled at the very thought.

He wasn't sure what hurt the most. His stomach or his chest. And he wasn't sure he couldn't blame both pains on the way he had left Anne.

She hadn't gotten up when he'd slipped out after a sleepless few hours on her couch. He didn't know if she'd awakened with his movements or not, but if so, she hadn't said anything. He doubted that she'd had an easy time falling asleep last night; he hoped she'd manage to rest enough to get her through her classes that day.

Heaving a sigh, he reached for the handle of his suitcase, then sat back again when nausea roiled deep inside him. Damn it, he didn't need this now. He felt bad enough about the quarrel he'd had with Anne. Did he really need this stomach virus or whatever it was to make him feel even worse?

He pulled a handkerchief from his pocket and wiped his face with it. He wasn't overheated, but he felt a little sweaty. Guilty?

He scowled when the word popped into his mind. Why should he feel guilty? Despite Anne's accusations, he had made the decision to leave based on what was best for her, not for himself. He was trying to reduce her stress level, not add to it. He still shuddered whenever he thought of how close they had come to walking straight into her parents at dinner yesterday. She could deny it all she wanted, but he knew she'd have been horrified had her family found out about them that way.

He wanted to blame the pressure she was under for their quarrel the night before. Apparently, her study group had dealt with some sort of crisis last night and she'd still been stinging when she'd returned home, which perhaps explained her overreaction when she had seen his bags by the bed. Having her father call in the middle of the conversation certainly hadn't helped anything. No matter what Anne said, talking to her father always left her edgy and tense.

Which made it all the harder to understand why she wasn't eager to put some distance between herself and her overinvolved family.

Because she loved them. He scowled as the memory of her impassioned voice whispered through his mind.

His stomach jerked and he pressed a hand against it, almost doubling over from the pain. Damn. Maybe Anne had been right. Maybe he should see a doctor. As soon as he got home, he would…

Home.

He pictured the empty apartment waiting for him in New York. Was that home? Was it a home if no one was there to welcome him back? If he went to bed alone every night and woke alone every morning?

He felt more at home in a tent in some desert somewhere than he did at that apartment.

So why was he going back?

He inhaled sharply, losing patience with his own dithering. He'd made his decision. He was going back to New York. He'd made his choice.

"You want me to choose between you and my family."

Anne had looked almost horrified when she had whispered that accusation. As if the very thought was almost more than she could bear.

He didn't like knowing he had been the one to put that expression on her pretty face.

His stomach twisted again. Guilt could be damned painful, he thought with a scowl.

Anne wasn't in the mood to meet with her study group Thursday evening. She made a flimsy excuse to Haley and decided she would study at home alone that night. Not that she expected to get much done, even though she would have the place to herself. No one there to interrupt or distract her.

How could she concentrate on slides and figures when her heart was breaking?

Was her marriage over? Had it ever really had a chance? What had made them believe they could make a marriage work under those ridiculous circumstances?

She couldn't choose between Liam and her family. It was unconscionable of him to put her in that situation. If he really knew her, if he truly understood her, he would know she couldn't—wouldn't—be backed into that corner.

She wished she could be angry with him. Instead, she was almost numb with pain. And somehow, she had to put that aside and concentrate on her studies. It was going to take a superhuman effort.

"Hi, Dr. Easton!"

Anne stifled a sigh as she nodded in response to Rose's cheery greeting. "Hello, Rose. Hi, Parker."

The little boy grinned and waved a dirty hand at her in recognition.

"We've been to the playground," Rose said by way of explaining her son's grubby appearance. "I'm taking him in for a bath now."

"He looks like he had a great time."

"He did. I haven't seen Lee around lately. Parker always looks for him when we come out to the lot."

Anne just didn't have the energy to explain that Liam wouldn't be around again for a while. If ever.

"Excuse me," she said, hoping she didn't sound rude. "I have to make a phone call."

Rose didn't take offense easily. "Sure. We'll see you around, Doc."

Sticking her key into the lock without enthusiasm, Anne shuffled into her apartment—and then stopped cold just inside the door.

Liam was lying on her couch.

She blinked to make sure she was seeing correctly. "Liam?"

He lifted his head from the cushions. "I couldn't leave it like that."

He looked terrible. His skin was colorless, there were hollows beneath his eyes and a fine sheen of perspiration glistened on his cheeks and forehead. She dropped her things and moved quickly toward him. "You're sick."

"Yeah. But that's not the point. I didn't want to leave with you mad at me. I love you."

"I love you, too, Liam." She pressed a hand to his forehead and caught her breath. He was burning with fever.

He was curled on his left side, his knees bent and slightly drawn up. "I never meant to add to your stress. I just wanted to help."

"I know. Can you lie on your back, Liam?"

"Hurts."

"I know. Just try for a minute, okay?"

He shifted, groaning with the effort. Anne lifted the hem of his shirt to reveal his lean abdomen, muttering to herself, "McBurney's point is two-thirds of the distances from the umbilicus to the anterior superior iliac spine."

Finding what she hoped was that point, she pressed her fingers into his right side. "Does that hurt?"

"Not too—" He gasped sharply when she released the pressure. "Yeah. Yeah, it hurts. Damn."

Rebound pain. Even a second-year medical student knew that sign. "Liam, we need to get you to the hospital. I'm pretty sure you have appendicitis."

And he'd probably been battling it for several days, she thought with a surge of guilt that the possibility had never even occurred to her before this. She'd been so caught up in her own problems and issues that she'd been all too quick to dismiss Liam's illness as a minor stomach virus. The fact that he hadn't really complained, even though he must have been suffering more than he'd let on, was no excuse.

"Stomach bug," he said with a shake of his head. "I'll be okay. We really need to talk."

"We will," she promised. "After you've seen a doctor. Can you sit up?"

He started to rise, then sank back down with a moan. "Going to be sick."

"I'll be right back." She dashed to the kitchen for a plastic bowl, then hurried back to the couch.

Liam was curled up again, his arm over his eyes. "I think it's passing," he muttered.

"I'll call for an ambulance." She already had her phone in her hand and was dialing 911.

"Don't need ambulance. You can drive me."

"Liam, you can't even stand up. I can't carry you down to the car." She only hoped the ambulance arrived before his appendix ruptured.

Anne sat perched on the edge of the waiting room chair, her arms wrapped around her middle, her heart in her throat as she waited for news. Liam had been rushed into surgery only fifteen minutes earlier, and it was apparent from the haste with which the staff had acted that his condition was serious.

Peritonitis, she thought with a catch in her breathing. If it had gone septic, Liam could very well be in critical condition.

And she'd waved it off as a "bug."

She buried her face in her hands, a low groan escaping her as hot tears filled her eyes.

"Anne? I got here as soon as I could. What's wrong?"

Lifting her damp face, she stood and threw herself into her father's arms. "Daddy. Thank you for coming."

He hugged her tightly, obviously concerned by the tremors

that ran through her. "Of course I came. You called and said you needed me here. I'll always come when you call me. What's wrong, sugar? You said you aren't hurt. That was the truth, wasn't it? I did what you asked, I told your mother that you just needed my help with something and that she shouldn't be concerned, but I can tell by looking at you that something is very wrong."

"No, I'm not hurt."

"Is it one of your friends?"

She bit her lip before saying, "You're going to be angry with me, Dad, and that's okay. You have every right to be. Just don't yell at me right now, okay? I need your help."

Looking thoroughly confused, he drew back enough to search her face. "Why on earth would I be angry with you?"

"You asked yesterday if I've been seeing someone?" When he nodded, she blurted, "I have been seeing someone, Dad. It's Liam."

He stiffened. "Liam— You mean that McCright boy?"

Clinging to his shirt, she nodded. "Yes. Liam and I got back together when I was in London, and we've been together ever since. He's been here visiting me for the last few weeks. He was going to leave this morning, but he got sick. He's having an emergency appendectomy now, and I think he's already developed peritonitis."

Her father sank heavily onto the nearest chair, as if his knees simply wouldn't hold up to this shock.

She drew a ragged breath, figuring that was about as much as he could handle hearing just yet. "I was going to tell you all that he and I were together again, but then Mother had the stroke and she was so sick, and then the demands of med school were so overwhelming and I…well, I just couldn't find the courage. It was stupid, I know, and there are more things I need to tell you, but…"

Her breath caught on a sob. "I've made such a mess of everything. And now Liam's in surgery and I don't know how he's doing. He looked so very sick when I brought him in. I'm really scared, Dad."

Her father looked torn between shock, anger and dismay. "I don't know what to say, Anne. That you've actually been seeing him all this time, and you've never said a word about it… It's just…"

"I know. And I still haven't told you everything—but I will. I've wanted to tell you so many times. I just didn't know how," she finished miserably. "You were so adamantly against Liam—against me being involved with anyone, actually. You were so sure I couldn't handle both a relationship and medical school. And it hasn't been easy, but it's been working—for the most part. He's been nothing but supportive of me, so careful not to interfere with my studies. He and I had a quarrel last night about that very thing."

"Last night? After I called you?"

She nodded miserably. "He thought he should leave before you and Mom found out about us. I was ready to tell you the truth, but he thought it was too stressful a time for me and he wanted to wait until after Step 1. I told him he was just like you—always trying to make my decisions for me, for my own good, and we both got mad. And he was sick the whole time, but I was so wrapped up in my own pride and temper and worry about tests and classes and family issues that I hardly even noticed. What kind of doctor will I be if I'm so self-absorbed that I can't see someone is suffering right in front of me?"

She was crying now, racked with fear and guilt. Her father hesitated a moment, still dealing with his myriad reactions to everything she had just thrown at him. And then he put his own emotions aside and wrapped an arm around her. "You'll be a very good doctor, Anne. No one expects you to be ready to practice during your second year of medical school. And maybe he didn't tell you everything he was feeling?"

"No," she said with a sniffle. "He hardly complained at all. He said his stomach hurt and that he was a little queasy, but that's pretty much all he told me. I thought he just had that stomach virus that's been going around so much lately."

"Which is exactly what my first reaction would have been if that was all I was told. Was he running a fever? Did he complain of pain in his right side?"

"No. When I got home from class today, he was lying on his side with his knees drawn up. He was running a high fever then, and complaining of nausea and pain. I finally considered what he might have and I did the McBurney pressure test. He had severe rebound pain, which is when I finally realized that he was seriously ill."

"You can't blame yourself. Liam isn't the usual age for appendicitis, and it sounds as if his symptoms did not present in a typical fashion. That's something you'll learn with practice—*typical* is a very relative term when you're dealing with individual patients. They don't all fit on to a neat checklist of symptoms and signs."

"He's been back there for a long time," she said anxiously, twisting her hands in her lap. "What if the appendix ruptured? What if he's developed sepsis?"

Sepsis was an infrequent, but very serious complication from appendicitis. With sepsis, bacteria entered the bloodstream, traveling throughout the body. It could be life threatening.

Her dad covered her hands with his own big, skilled hand. "Then he'll be treated with IV antibiotics. You can probably tell me which ones."

"I don't want to be quizzed right now, Dad," she said with a groan. "I just want to know that Liam's going to be all right."

He nodded and stood. "Wait here. I'll go see what I can find out."

This, she thought, her breath catching on a last sob, was why she had called him. There was no surgeon, no physician she trusted more than her father. Now that he was here, Liam would be all right.

She had to believe that.

She knew there would be much more to be revealed to her family. More explanations, more apologies, more guilt-inducing recriminations from both her parents and probably her grandfather, too. But they would come around, just as she had always known deep inside that they would.

Now if only she would have the chance to bring Liam around, to make him understand how important her family was to her. To convince him that loving them in no way detracted from how much she loved him. That being a part of her family, difficult though they could be, wasn't such a terrible thing.

The question was—did Liam love her enough to accept the whole package? Her family, her career, her strengths and her flaws? Or would it turn out that their whole marriage had been based on a youthful, passion-driven, fantasy-inspired impulse that could not stand up to the day-to-day challenges of the real world?

Praying that she would have the chance to find out, she drew a deep breath and huddled more deeply into the chair to wait for news.

Liam was so disoriented when he opened his eyes that it took him a little while to figure out where he was. His mind was clouded, probably by the drugs being pumped into his veins through an IV tube, making it hard for him to think coherently.

He remembered bits and pieces—being in the ambulance,

bright lights in his eyes, concerned faces leaning over him. He remembered Anne, looking afraid. He remembered her voice, her tone reassuring even though he'd had a hard time focusing on the words. He sort of remembered waking up in recovery, then drifting out again. Had he dreamed that Anne's father had hovered above him at one point? And then Anne, again. Looking increasingly tired and strained.

He had wanted to tell her to get some rest, but he simply hadn't had the energy. He'd slept, waking only in brief, fuzzy snatches, and she had always been there. How much time had passed? Had she slept? Was she missing classes or exams because of him? He didn't want that.

He should have gone back to New York, he thought, closing his eyes on a wave of self-recrimination. He shouldn't have caused even more trouble for Anne. Even though he knew it was unreasonable, he felt almost foolish for having gotten ill at such an inconvenient time. He was oddly chagrined at being so weak and vulnerable at a time when he needed to be strong for Anne.

He forced his eyelids open again, blinking a couple of times to bring the room into focus. He sensed suddenly that he wasn't alone, and he turned his head, expecting to find Anne sitting watch over him.

When he saw who sat there, he wondered for a moment if the meds were making him hallucinate.

"So you're awake," Henry Easton, Jr., said unnecessarily.

"I— Yeah." His voice sounded rusty, as if it had been days rather than hours since he'd last used it. "Why are you here?"

"Anne wouldn't agree to get any rest until someone agreed to sit with you. Since she was almost asleep on her feet, I told her I'd take babysitting duty for a few hours."

"She, uh—told you?"

"That you're my son-in-law? Yes, she told me. Eventually."

Liam tried to read Easton's expression, finding it very difficult to do so. "You're okay with that?"

"Let's just say you and I have some talking to do yet. But I'll wait until you aren't lying flat on your back."

Liam shifted on the bed, then grimaced when his body rebelled. "I'd appreciate that."

"How are you feeling?"

Liam's succinct response made the older man chuckle. "Has anyone talked to you about your condition?"

"I think so. It's sort of fuzzy. They took out my appendix, right?"

Easton nodded. "You've been out of surgery for about fourteen hours. You developed peritonitis. Almost waited too late to get treatment. You were pretty sick. The antibiotics seem to be working, though, so you'll be back on your feet in a few days. Be a few weeks before you're completely back to normal, though. Hope you weren't scheduled to climb any mountains or wrestle any crocodiles during the next couple of weeks."

"I don't wrestle crocodiles," Liam murmured, wondering if the man had ever actually seen his show.

"Mmm. Bet right now you feel like you took one on, huh?"

"And lost," Liam agreed with a sigh.

"Go back to sleep, if you want. I wouldn't harm a defenseless man."

Maybe that quip was supposed to be reassuring. Liam gave his father-in-law one wary look before letting his heavy lids fall.

"I love her, you know," he muttered as the drugs and pain drew him toward unconsciousness.

"So do I. Why else would I be sitting here now?"

He would think about that later, Liam decided, letting the darkness take him.

* * *

His head felt a little clearer when he woke again. He still hurt, still felt as though he'd been bulldozed, but he knew immediately where he was and why when he opened his eyes.

A male nurse smiled at him as he made notes of the numbers displayed on the vital-signs monitor beside the bed. "Hi, there. I'm Steve. How do you feel?"

"I've been better."

"Are you in pain? On a scale of one to ten, how would you rate your pain level?"

Liam wasn't sure how one went about rating pain, but he made an attempt. "Four. Maybe five," he added with a wince when he tried cautiously to shift into a more comfortable position.

"Okay. I'm putting something in your IV that should make you more comfortable. Let someone know if that isn't enough, all right? We don't want you lying here in pain."

"Thanks, Steve." When the nurse left to tend his other patients, Liam turned his head to look at the chair across the room, wondering if he would find Henry Easton still sitting there, hoping he would see Anne instead.

The chair was empty.

He was okay with that, he assured himself. Easton probably had to work. Anne had classes. He didn't really know anyone else in the area. He didn't need someone sitting with him every minute, anyway. He'd only had major, life-threatening surgery. If he needed anything, all he had to do was push a button and someone on the hospital staff would rush to his side. Probably.

His bout of self-pity was short-lived. Anne entered the room, carrying a lidded, disposable cup that might have held coffee. She smiled when she saw him looking at her, her gaze intently searching his face. "You're awake."

Why did everyone seem to feel the need to announce that to him? "Yes."

"How do you feel?"

He kept his reply rather generic for Anne. "I'm okay."

He glanced at the clock on the wall facing him. Two o'clock—and if he had his days straight, it was Friday afternoon. "Shouldn't you be in class?"

"I skipped classes today. Haley's taking notes for me. I've been sitting in here for the past few hours, since I relieved Dad. He said you'd been awake for a little while this morning."

"Yeah. I was…surprised to see him here."

Setting her coffee on the nightstand beside the bed, Anne stood gazing down at him, her expression hard to read. "I'm sure you were. I didn't think you'd wake up while I was resting, but I wanted someone to be here if you did. Just to reassure you that you'd be okay."

And she'd thought her father would be the one to offer that reassurance? Okay.

"Did you get any sleep?" he asked.

She shrugged, the purplish hollows beneath her eyes giving the real answer before she prevaricated, "Some. I napped in one of the recliners in the waiting room."

So she'd sat with him all night after his surgery. He shook his head against the pillow. "You should have gone home to bed. And you shouldn't have missed classes for me. I'm getting good care here. You should go on now and find your study group. You have to prepare for the next test. Maybe you can stop back in for a little while this evening. I'll be fine until then."

Her eyes narrowed. "I'm the one who decides what I 'should' and 'shouldn't' do, Liam. It's taken me a while to get to that point, but from now on, I don't need anyone making decisions for me. That includes my dad—and you."

He was a bit taken aback by her irritated response. "Uh—sure. Sorry."

Her eyebrows rose in response to his aggrieved tone. "Were you expecting me to cut you some slack because you're lying in a hospital bed?"

"Of course not," he lied. "I was only trying to—"

"Trying to look out for me," she cut in to finish for him. "Just like my family has always done. 'Don't get involved with anyone too early, Anne.' 'Don't let anyone interfere with your studies, Anne.' 'Don't let yourself get distracted from your education, Anne.' 'Don't miss your classes or get behind in your work or fail to do your best on a test or take your eyes from the ultimate goal of surgery, Anne.'"

She leaned over the bed, her hands clenched on the metal railing, her gaze locked with his. "Well, let me tell you, Liam—just as I've already told my dad. All that advice and helpful guidance hasn't been working so well. Because I've tried to please everyone and do everything everyone told me 'for my own good,' I broke up with the man I loved in college. I've worried myself sick through medical school for fear of letting my family down. I made the mistake of secretly getting married and then going to great lengths to keep that secret. And I let myself get so wrapped up in the pressure everyone was putting on me that I didn't even see that my own husband was getting very ill right in front of my miserable and self-absorbed eyes!"

"You couldn't have known—"

"I should have known," she insisted. "I was more concerned about test scores and class ranking than I was about your illness. What kind of doctor does that make me?"

"You're going to be a great doctor. You just have to get through the training, which is so damned hard that no one could possibly blame you for being overwhelmed by it."

She didn't look at all convinced, but he moved on, addressing something else she had said that was bothering him. "You said you 'made the mistake' of secretly marrying."

She lifted her chin a little. "Yes. That's what I said."

He wondered grimly how he would rate the pain he felt now. There wasn't a scale that went high enough to describe the ache in his heart after hearing Anne declare their marriage a mistake. "Does that mean you want a divorce?"

Anne gave a long, deep sigh. "You are such an idiot, Liam McCright."

That was certainly not an answer to the question he had asked. But he felt himself relax somewhat in response to the gentle insult.

She could call him anything she wanted, as long as she didn't change her mind about being married to him, he thought wistfully.

Watching as Liam seemed to draw back into the bed, his face almost as white as the crisp hospital sheets, Anne felt a moment of regret that she hadn't waited to have this conversation later, when he'd had a little more time for recovery. But she was still so angry with herself—and maybe with him, as well—that he had almost died because of their lack of communication, she couldn't wait any longer.

Concerned with his pallor, she placed a gentle hand on his shoulder. "Do you need anything? Are you in pain?"

"I'm already having trouble thinking clearly. I'm okay for now."

"Maybe we should talk about this later," she said, but he shook his head.

"Now you're the one saying what *I* should do for my own good," he muttered.

She had to smile a little at that. "I guess I am. Sorry."

His eyes were dark as they searched her face. "You, uh, you said our marriage was a mistake. Maybe you could elaborate on that a little?"

"I said the way we married was a mistake," she corrected him. "The secret elopement. We— I should have had the courage to take those vows openly, whether anyone else approved or not. I should have told my parents from the beginning that I was seeing you, and that I would continue to do so without their permission. And, we should have spent more time talking and less time playing before we took the step of getting married. We were so intoxicated with the freedom and privacy that we had in London that we let ourselves forget about the real-world issues that would confront us later. Like our busy schedules. And my family."

"I never meant to try to take you away from your family."

"I think you did see it as a choice between you and them," she replied quietly. "Maybe not consciously. But maybe— well, maybe you needed to believe that I would always put you first. I haven't studied much psychiatry yet, but it isn't hard to imagine you'd have abandonment issues, considering your childhood. The way your father left you, and then your mother died when you were still so young."

He flinched, but she continued without letting him respond, "I understood why your own family background would make it hard for you to understand why I remained close to mine, despite my efforts to be independent from them. I just didn't fully realize you would need to be reassured occasionally that I would never let them keep me away from you. Until we talked with Haley last week, I didn't even realize you blamed them solely for our breakup in college, despite the quarrels you and I had back then that had little to do with them."

A hint of color touched his pale cheeks now. He looked

almost sheepish when he muttered, "I'm not a child. I don't need constant reassurance that you aren't going to leave me."

She supposed his stinging male ego made him say that, but she knew it wasn't entirely true. Maybe he didn't need constant reassurance—but he needed to hear it occasionally. Just as she needed to hear from him that their marriage meant more to him than his career or his celebrity or his resistance to becoming part of her family.

His eyelids were beginning to grow heavy, as if he were fighting to stay alert for this ill-timed conversation. "Annie?"

She leaned closer. "Yes?"

"You were right, you know. I'm not all that brave. I've been afraid of a lot of things. I was afraid your parents—or someone else—would take you away from me. I was afraid of trying to fit into your overachieving and overinvolved family. I was afraid of finishing the book and having no other excuse to stay with you—and afraid it will bomb once it's published. And I was so damned afraid that if I left this time, we'd have used up all our chances to make this work out between us."

She didn't know how much of that confession had been fueled by the meds dripping through his IV tube, but there was no mistaking the sincerity of his words.

She laid her hand against his face, speaking very clearly. "I love you, Liam. I always have. I always will."

He reached out to take her hand, and though his grip was still weak enough to melt her heart, his voice was steady. "I love you, too. And I don't care if the whole world knows it."

"That's good," she said, blinking back a mist of tears. "I was told a reporter called the hospital this morning to find out if you're really a patient here. I don't know how the news got out, but it seems that it has. The hospital staff will keep your case confidential, but some tidbits will probably leak out, anyway."

He looked unfazed by that revelation. "I'll call my agent and my publicist later. They'll handle it."

"Whatever you think best."

"Annie—" His words were beginning to slur a little, and his eyelids looked heavier.

"Get some rest, Liam. We can talk more later. We have plenty of time." They would make the time, she promised herself. Whatever it took.

He closed his eyes, then pushed them open again to ask, "Annie—if we weren't already married, and I asked you again now…?"

She smiled, knowing the medications were making him a little loopy, but answering the fanciful question, anyway. "I would say yes, Liam. Always. Forever."

It seemed to satisfy him. Still holding her hand, he closed his eyes. "Me, too. Love you."

She leaned over to brush a tender kiss across his forehead. "I love you, too, Liam."

From this point on, she didn't care if the whole world knew.

Epilogue

Even though the sun was beginning to set, it was still quite warm on this early July Arkansas evening. A sizable crowd had gathered on the sprawling back lawn of Henry and Deloris Easton's home for their long-established Independence Day barbecue. Because of Deloris's health, they'd had to cancel the event for the past two years, but she'd felt well enough this year to insist on reviving the tradition.

Reassuring herself occasionally that her mother was holding up well to the demands of hostessing, Anne mingled with the guests and quietly handled most of the supervision of the catering and festivities. The lawn was attractively crowded with red, white and blue decorated tables and party lights. Discreetly placed fans kept air circulating among the guests, who were heartily enjoying the abundant food offerings. A Dixieland band played on a small, portable stage in one corner, adding to the festive atmosphere, but not so loud to interfere with conversation. All in all, she deemed the event a great success.

She glanced at a table where her study group friends sat eating and laughing. Her mother had insisted Anne invite those friends who had been so supportive in helping Anne survive the past two years of school, and they had all accepted. Connor was accompanied by his wife, Mia, and their daughter, Alexis. Haley had brought her friend Kris. James and Ron had come stag. Ron was actually being civil to Haley's date, though Anne still had her suspicions about Ron's feelings for Haley.

Things would change with the coming school year, Anne thought a bit sadly. After spending four semesters in the same classes, the group would be split up for rotations. Now that they had all taken Step 1, they wouldn't need to study as a group. They hadn't received their test results yet, but they were all cautiously optimistic that they had passed. The upcoming demands on their time would make it hard for them to get together very often on a social basis, though they had all promised solemnly that they would not let their friendship end with the change in their schedules. She hoped very much that it would prove to be true.

"Your friends seem to be having a good time," Anne's mother commented when their paths crossed at the drinks table. "Go join them. Everything's going smoothly here."

"I will," Anne agreed. "I was just getting a glass of lemonade."

Leaning only lightly on her cane, her mom smiled at her. "Thank you so much for all your help today, sweetheart. I don't know how I would have gotten everything done without you. I'm so glad we decided to have the party. I'm having a wonderful time."

Anne leaned over to brush a quick kiss against her mom's soft cheek. "It's a great party, Mother."

Looking over Anne's shoulder, her mom smiled more brightly. "I think it's about to get better for you. Look who's joined us."

Turning, Anne caught her breath in surprised pleasure. "Liam!" she called out, waving to get her husband's attention as he entered the gate to the back lawn.

He greeted her with a hug that brought her feet off the ground, and a kiss that promised much more to come when they were alone. Grinning, he set her back down.

She laughed happily and rested a hand on his chest. "I thought you were going to be tied up until next week in meetings in New York."

"We wrapped up early. I didn't want to miss watching the fireworks with you."

Hugging him again, she said, "I'm so glad you're here."

"So am I." He moved away from her only far enough to greet her mother with a peck on the cheek. Anne noted that he was getting less awkward with her mother as they'd had time to adjust to each other. He and her brother got along quite well, too.

As for her father and grandfather—well, they were coming around, she thought with a wry smile. The fireworks she had expected in response to her marriage announcement had come after everyone was certain that Liam would recover fully from his emergency appendectomy. There had been recriminations and hurt feelings all around, but her family was too tightly knit to allow their disapproval to split them apart. They'd made certain that Anne was able to finish her second year and take her big exam with the support of her family to bolster her.

Her father and grandfather still took great pleasure in referring to her husband as "that McCright boy," and she couldn't say they were exactly enthusiastic yet about her springing a surprise marriage on them, but they were all polite enough when the family gathered. Liam had already charmed his way into his mother-in-law's good graces, and he was making headway with the men. He made the effort for Anne's sake, and she would always be thankful to him for that, especially knowing that he would have been content to avoid her family altogether.

Liam seemed to have accepted in resignation that Anne's family was now a permanent and prominent part of his life, too. She hoped there would come a day when he'd be grateful for that, but maybe that was asking a little too much.

He had been spending as much time as he could with Anne since he'd been released from the hospital three days after his surgery. His job would always demand a great deal of travel, but his home base would be with her from now on. They were both content with that arrangement for the present. Perhaps in the future, they had agreed, he would concentrate more on writing and producing so he wouldn't have to be gone quite so much, but they would concentrate on that later.

Because he loved her, he was making the best of the situation.

"You're looking well, Deloris," he said, using Anne's mother's first name, as Deloris had requested. "Looks like a great party, too."

"It's going very well," she agreed, "thanks to Anne's help."

It had taken her mom a bit to recover from the shock of learning about Anne's marriage, and from the disappointment that there hadn't been a big, elaborate wedding to plan. She made no secret that she didn't entirely approve of the risks Liam sometimes took in pursuit of a story, but she seemed impressed that he would soon be a published author.

"Alice," she called out, motioning toward a woman passing nearby. "You haven't had a chance to meet my son-in-law yet, have you? This is Liam McCright. He's on TV, you know."

Anne and Liam exchanged a laughing glance before he

courteously greeted her mother's friend. Anne stood nearby while he heaped a plate with barbecue and side dishes. Then they joined her study group, who greeted Liam warmly among them, all of them having met him prior to this gathering.

Surrounded by her family and close friends, Anne realized that she had never been happier. She still had a long way to go in her medical training, lots more hard work, grueling exams and exhausting pressure, but she felt more ready now to face those challenges. She would have a fulfilling career, and she would be married to the man she'd loved from the moment she'd met him.

She couldn't ask for anything more.

* * * * *

EXPECTING ROYAL TWINS! *by Melissa McClone*

Mechanic Izzy was shocked when a tall handsome prince strode into her
workshop and declared he was her husband! Now she's about to face an
even bigger surprise...

TO DANCE WITH A PRINCE *by Cara Colter*

Royal playboy Kiernan's been nicknamed Prince Heartbreaker. Meredith
knows, in her head, that he's the last man she needs, yet her heart
thinks otherwise!

HONEYMOON WITH THE RANCHER *by Donna Alward*

After Tomas' fiancée's death, he sought peace on his Argentine ranch.
Until socialite Sophia arrived for her honeymoon...*alone.* Can they heal
each other's hearts?

NANNY NEXT DOOR *by Michelle Celmer*

Sydney's ex left her with nothing, but she needs to provide for her
daughter. Sheriff Daniel's her new neighbour who could give Sydney the
perfect opportunity.

A BRIDE FOR JERICHO BRAVO *by Christine Rimmer*

After being jilted by her long-time boyfriend, Marnie's given up on love.
Until meeting sexy rebel Jericho has her believing in second chances...

Cherish

2 FREE BOOKS
AND A SURPRISE GIFT

We would like to take this opportunity to thank you for reading this Mills & Boon® book by offering you the chance to take TWO more specially selected books from the Cherish™ series absolutely FREE! We're also making this offer to introduce you to the benefits of the Mills & Boon® Book Club™—

- **FREE home delivery**
- **FREE gifts and competitions**
- **FREE monthly Newsletter**
- **Exclusive Mills & Boon Book Club offers**
- **Books available before they're in the shops**

Accepting these FREE books and gift places you under no obligation to buy, you may cancel at any time, even after receiving your free books. Simply complete your details below and return the entire page to the address below. You don't even need a stamp!

YES Please send me 2 free Cherish books and a surprise gift. I understand that unless you hear from me, I will receive 5 superb new stories every month, including two 2-in-1 books priced at £5.30 each, and a single book priced at £3.30, postage and packing free. I am under no obligation to purchase any books and may cancel my subscription at any time. The free books and gift will be mine to keep in any case.

Ms/Mrs/Miss/Mr _____ Initials _____

Surname _____

Address _____

_____

_____ Postcode _____

E-mail _____

Send this whole page to: Mills & Boon Book Club, Free Book Offer, FREEPOST NAT 10298, Richmond, TW9 1BR